DESTINED TO BE HIS

"I love you," she murmured, unable to keep the words secret.

It was a moment before he responded. "Love me?" Releasing his hands from her waist, he raised his arms and caught her face between his hands. Strong, callused hands cherished her gently, as if she were a fragile jewel. "Do you understand what you have just said, madam?"

"Yes. I love you."

"Lawren the warlock?"

"Yes."

He threaded his fingers into her hair. Closing her eyes, Beth luxuriated in the sensations he aroused.

"No matter what happens to me," she confessed, "whether I stay in your century, go to another one, or return to my own, I shall never love another man but you."

"Sometimes it's difficult to tell passion from love."

"I know the difference." Tears sparkled in Beth's eyes, glinted on the tip of her lashes. "Although we are not destined to be together, I shall love only you."

Beth raked her hands through his midnight hair and clutched at the thick length of it at the base of his neck. She was heady, but had long ago discarded caution and had no intention of trying to retrieve it now. If danger had a taste, Lawren was it and she was going to drink her fill.

Because this might have to last her an entire lifetime. . . .

Night Lace

Emma Merritt

ZEBRA BOOKS
KENSINGTON PUBLISHING CORP.

ZEBRA BOOKS are published by

Kensington Publishing Corp.
850 Third Avenue
New York, NY 10022

First Printing: February, 1996
10 9 8 7 6 5 4 3 2 1

Printed in the United States of America

One

The Scottish keep, defying the ravages of time and weather, rose majestically out of the ruins scattered across the small isle. Its turrets and spires sliced into the evening sky and claimed for its banners and standards the ribbons of color that furled from the setting sun. Built nine centuries before, the castle still projected an image of strength and invincibility, of timelessness. Only the keep remained intact, but even this dwarfed Isle Gleann nan Duir. Castle Galloway ruled its ancient Highland domain with firm and quiet dignity.

A natural moat, Loch Duir encircled the isle. It was as protective of the Galloway bastion today as it had been in times past. As if daring invaders to step into its currents, the deep water rushed beneath the centuries-old stone bridge. Bridge Galloway was the only way on or off the Isle of Gleann nan Duir.

Spellbound by the scene before her, Beth parked the rental car in the middle of the bridge and stared. The castle was all that she had imagined it to be. Grand. Imposing. Intimidating. Ageless.

It was more. It was the home of the magical Highland flower, the nightlace. And home of the ancient warlock, Lawren mac Galloway!

In the distance an unfamiliar squall caught Beth's attention. She looked around but didn't see a sign of a living being—not a human, not even an animal. To the right a waterfall, a cascade of sparkling crystal, rushed down the side of the mountain to spill into the loch. To the left, heather gently swayed in the breeze. The meadow, covered in wildflowers, was a banner of brilliant colors. Red, yellow, lavender, and orange, all heralded the arrival of spring.

She was alone, and while she felt her solitude, she didn't feel lonely. Considering the tales she had heard about Castle Galloway and its ancient warlock—an evil man who had cursed his clan with a plague—she thought she would have been apprehensive to be here at this time of day, but she wasn't.

Castle Galloway looked exactly as Minerva Graham, the caretaker, had described it when Beth had talked to her over the telephone. Even had the woman not described it, Beth would have recognized it. The thought startled her. She had never been here before, had not even known this place existed until a few months ago. Yet she felt as if she belonged here. How could this be? Why did she find this ancient castle so familiar?

Because you've done your homework, she answered herself. *You've done a good job on your research of the Gleann nan Duir Galloways. You've read and reread the ancient Galloway manuscript until you feel that you know the family and their home personally, as if you've visited in their home before.*

Beth put the car into gear and slowly accelerated, moving forward. Across the bridge. Over the loch. Up the gravel road. The closer she drove, the bigger the castle loomed, the more imposing, the more ominous. Spires and turrets jutted even higher into the evening sky. The walls appeared straighter, the angles sharper and more austere.

The nearer she came to the old fortress, the more she felt she had been here before, and she didn't think this strong feeling of déjà vu could be altogether attributed to her research. Trying to shake off the queerish sensation, she stopped the car, opened the door, and stepped out. With an artist's eyes for color and texture, she gazed about, soaking in the beauty that was Castle Galloway.

A mist, so delicate as to seem unreal, settled over the keep. The surrounding mountains grasped for the slowly ebbing sun.

Each, a prism, turned the rays into a profusion of colored splendor. Beth imagined the mist, touched by the setting sunbeams, to be a delicate golden veil concealing a magical land of yesteryear.

The prisms of light reminded her of the flags that had flown over the castle in bygone days, of the tournament pavilions that housed jousting knights. In her mind's eye, she saw the castle and its people come to life. She heard the clang of metal as knights rode into the castle courtyard, the clip-clop of horses' hooves over the flagstones. She saw the rush of villagers as they thronged the challengers, as they filled the air with cheers and waved victory boughs.

All of this and more was here, Beth knew, hidden by the magical veil of time. And as surely as she stood here, she knew that one day she would paint Castle Galloway.

The sun sank lower, and shadows turned into dusk, but the magic of the castle did not disappear in the darkness. It merely changed clothing. Where it had been golden, now it was silver. Serenaded by the nocturnal sounds of the Highlands, Beth stood, savoring this mystical moment that was Castle Galloway. Strangely she felt as if she were coming home. But her home was California and had been all twenty-six years of her life.

The evening breeze, gaining momentum, nipped at her cheeks and strands of hair that had come loose from the thick braid that hung down her back. She brushed the curls from her face and started to walk up the solitary path that wound through the gardens. Gravel crunched beneath her feet as she walked.

A disarray of thick, natural gardens surrounded the castle. Wild and rugged, an extension of the Highlands around them, they were filled with bold shades of green, red, yellow, and orange. Vines clung to the gray spiking walls to give them new vitality, strength, and beauty.

When Beth reached the wrought-iron gate, she closed her hand around the handle and leaned her head against the cool metal rods. For a moment she was Alice peering through the looking glass into a wonderland. Excitement rushed through her.

She felt for the first time in her life that she was meeting her destiny head-on. Regardless of the consequences, she was going to part the misty veil and enter into this mysterious land. She swung the gate open and walked into the inner courtyard.

This, too, had been converted into a garden through which the solitary pathway continued to wind. It stopped at the bottom of a flight of narrow and steep stairs that were connected to and built parallel against the castle wall. Constructed of the same stone as the castle itself, they were designed as a defensive mechanism to keep attackers at bay. This was the castle entrance, the caretaker had said. How formidable! Enough to make a person want to turn back. Not Beth!

Again feeling as if she had been summoned by fate, she opened the gate and walked through. Her hand brushed against a flower, the touch of the soft petals a gentle plea to stop and to savor the beauty around her. The inner-courtyard gardens, well-tended and cared for, were set out in a deliberate casualness that lent itself to the natural ambience of the isle. Their soft colors gentled the castle.

As the bold and brilliant gardens outside the wall reflected the daring wild and rugged beauty of the Highlands, these softer ones mirrored its ageless and indomitable spirit.

Beth started walking again, not stopping until she reached the stairs. She stood at the bottom and looked up, straight up. Thirty! she counted. They were steeper and more narrow than she had first thought and loomed even higher.

Carefully, Beth held onto the railings that had been added in recent years, one to the outside of the stairs and one to the wall side of the stairwell, and began her ascent into the world of the past, into the world of the Gleann nan Duir Galloways. When she reached the landing, a small square of flat rock in front of a huge wooden door, she was breathing heavily.

Although she wasn't that high off the ground, the stairs were so steep, the landing so small, Beth had a dizzy sensation. With a trembling hand, she caught the wrought-iron knocker and rapped it against the door. Inside she heard the faint gong of the bell. The wind blew. She swayed. She yelped and pushed closer to the door.

The wind ripped around the building. Shivering, Beth was glad that she had worn heavy slacks, a long-sleeved blouse, and a sweater. She pulled the sweater closer about herself and huddled in the dark. She knocked again, then waited. She heard the dull click of a lock and the grate of metal as a bolt slid out of place. The door creaked open.

Beth raised her head and looked into a weathered and kind face framed by white hair. An ethereal face that seemed to be as ageless as the castle itself.

"Mrs. Graham?"

"Aye?" The woman spoke softly with a thick brogue.

"I'm Beth Balfour."

"I've been expecting you." The woman opened the door wider and waved her hand, motioning Beth inside. "I thought you might be giving a call to tell me you were lost."

"No, your directions were great." Beth stepped into a large anteroom that was lighted by electrified candles, positioned intermittently on wrought-iron corbels on the wall. The soft glow illuminated the floor-to-ceiling bookcases and cabinets that lined the room. She was enthralled by the rustic beauty. Before she had only imagined she had stepped back in time. Now she had.

"We're a long way from the beaten path," Mrs. Graham said.

"Well worth the trouble it took to get here. My father was in the navy, and we've traveled a lot during my life. I've seen many glorious sights, but none of them equal the grandeur of Castle Galloway. It's beautiful."

"We think so." Mrs. Graham closed the door and slid the ancient bolt into place. Metal grinding against metal echoed through the room. "You're a research physician from the United States, studying Scottish herbs, your letter said."

"Yes," Beth replied, "I'm a medical doctor, doing my internship at Nature's Way Foundation. In particular I'm looking for some information on the Highland nightlace."

"Well, then, lass, you've come to the right place. According to legend, Castle Galloway was once the home of the Highland nightlace."

"And the warlock," Beth said.

Mrs. Graham chuckled softly. "Aye, and our warlock. Nowadays most people are more interested in him than in the herb."

"If they've read the manuscript, I can imagine why," Beth said. "Although the author tries to paint him with an evil brush, the warlock stands out as a fascinating character."

"And a very sensuous one," Minerva added mischievously.

Beth grinned. During her research she had become as intrigued with the warlock as she had determined to find the Highland nightlace.

"But it's more than fascination and sensuality," the caretaker said pensively. "Our young people have many questions, and the older generations no longer have the answers or the means of finding the answers. We're living in a time of transition, when people's roles in society are not clearly defined. This has taken away our sense of identity and security and has given way to confusion. The new generation, in its quest to find truth, to find self and a purpose for living, is returning to the old gods and the old ways, to the eternal magic of the land."

"But warlocks are of the devil," Beth said, then added, "aren't they?"

"We've given them that connotation," Minnie answered. "And perhaps some of them do worship Satan, but throughout history the majority of witches and warlocks have been herbalists, people who worshiped their gods, loved and protected nature, and performed good. Of course, as with all people, there are those who use their talents for evil, hence the reputation that all witches and warlocks are servants of the devil."

"But the manuscript says that Lawren the Warlock was in league with the devil."

"Aye," Minnie replied, "that's what the manuscript says. It's sad that we have only one person's word for that." She turned and began to walk toward a low, narrow doorway on the opposite side of the room.

Beth followed. "Do you have a lot of people coming here?"

"Nay, we're much too remote. Scotland and the rest of the Highlands have much more to offer the tourist, than does the Isle of Gleann nan Duir."

Surprised Beth said, "But you have the painting of the eleventh-century Galloway chief. I saw a photograph of it at the Edinburgh Historical Museum."

"Aye, we do, but once it was declared a forgery, it was no longer newsworthy," she replied.

Beth remembered what she had learned about the painting. An enigma, the fresco had stumped authorities for years, had raised questions that had never been and may never be satisfactorily answered. While experts could date the fresco at the close of the eleventh century, the painting itself was too modern for that period. The technique, detail, and depth perception marked it as contemporary. Finally they had branded it a superb forgery.

"Will you show it to me?" Beth asked.

"Aye, we Galloways are quite proud of the painting and of our ancestry. We only listen to authorities if they are supporting one of our pet theories. Otherwise, we ignore them, as in this instance."

"When I spoke to Mrs. Forbes," Beth said, referring to a foremost Scottish folklorist, "she said authorities consider the Highland nightlace to be nothing more than a myth. Do you agree with this?"

"Please call me Minnie." Short of the door, the caretaker stopped walking and turned to Beth. "No, I don't agree with Agnes Forbes," she snapped. " 'Twas a flower that once grew in abundance around this castle. 'Tis the flower of the Galloways."

Glad that she had met Minnie Graham and feeling that she had found a sympathetic source, Beth asked, "Are you a Galloway?"

"Aye, the present laird's father was my brother," Minnie replied. "But let's not stand here talking. It's too drafty. We'll move into the study."

As they started to walk again, Minnie asked, "Have you been to a castle before?"

"Several, but none of them were like this one."

"There is no other like Castle Galloway." Minnie caught the handle of the door and tugged it open. "This was the waiting room. Directly below us is the basement and below that is the dungeon." She pointed up. "Above is an opened balcony leading off the second floor of the castle."

The doorway was so low, Beth hunched as she stepped through it and into the round tower. She looked up to see another set of stairs that were as narrow as, but steeper than, the entrance set. And these were angled and spiraled!

"As was everything in the castle," Minnie explained, "these were designed and built for defense. An attacker climbing up would find it difficult to use his sword."

"I just find it difficult to climb up," Beth grumbled good-naturedly, "much less wield weapons. I'm surprised you haven't had elevators installed."

Again the soft richness of Minnie's laughter enveloped Beth. "Are you a lazy one, Dr. Balfour?"

"Practical," Beth returned. "If I were a Galloway enemy, I'd be easily vanquished. By the time I climbed to the top, I would be dead or so close to it, they could kill me off with little resistance. I'm on my sixth step now, and I'm already winded."

"Aye, they can be a chore at times," Minnie agreed, but Beth noticed that she wasn't breathless and hadn't slowed down in her ascent. "Perhaps one of these days we'll have the money to do more modernization without ruining the effect of the castle. Until such time, we'll have to do with what we've got."

By the time Beth reached the landing, Minnie had opened the door and was waiting for her in a large, comfortable room on the second floor. A living area, it was furnished with a mixture of modern and antique furniture, the upholstery and accessories a blend of blues and browns. A sofa and two occasional chairs were grouped before a gaslit fireplace.

"Although this isn't the original master's suite, I had it renovated so that Callum, the present laird, could use it. It's close to my bedroom and makes it easier on me to take care of him," Minnie said. "I want to introduce you to him, but first—"

"Mrs. Forbes told me," Beth said gently, wanting to spare the elderly woman the pain of discussing the present laird's debilitating illness, contracted while he was serving in Desert Storm.

"He—he returned from the Middle East like this. He's barely here in body, and certainly not in spirit." Minnie paused. "Callum's my nephew, but he seems more like my son. My husband and I never had any children of our own, but Callum made up for our loss. We've had him since he was five. His parents, my brother and his wife, died in a train derailment thirty years ago, and we became his legal guardians. Now we're his nurse and Micheil's guardians."

"Micheil?"

"Callum's fifteen-year-old son," Minnie replied, her countenance brightening. "You'll probably be seeing him before you leave. He's around here somewhere. In fact, he might be in his father's room reading to him. He generally does that every night before Callum goes to sleep."

"It's nice of you to have him do that," Beth said.

"It wasn't my doing," Minnie replied. "It was Micheil's. He remembers how much he enjoyed having his father read to him when he was a child. Now he—he wants to give that same kind of pleasure to his father. And always there's the hope that—that—"

Blinking her eyes rapidly and breaking off her sentence, Minnie turned and moved briskly across the room. Beth understood her highly emotional state where the laird was concerned. Rather than being offended or embarrassed that Minnie had confided in her, Beth had felt honored. Naturally Beth was curious about the boy, about his mother, and why Minnie rather than the wife was hostess at the castle, but Beth respected Minnie's privacy and wouldn't pry.

Following her into the bedroom, Beth remained by the door while Minnie conversed in low tones with the nurse who was going off duty. As they talked, Beth glanced across the room and saw a man slumped in a wheelchair in front of an opened window. After the nurse left, Minnie walked over to him.

"Callum," she said softly.

He never moved.

"It's time for you to go to bed." She placed her arm around his frail shoulder, and he looked up at her. "But first, I want you to meet our visitor." She turned the chair so Callum could see Beth.

According to Minnie, Callum Galloway was only thirty-five, but he was so emaciated and feeble, he looked as if he were closer to one hundred. He was nothing but skin draped over bones.

"This is Dr. Beth Balfour, Callum," Minnie said.

Beth smiled at him. "Hello, Mr. Galloway."

Slowly he turned his head so that he was looking in Beth's direction.

"She's from the United States, Callum, but she's a Balfour, and that's about as Scottish as one can get." Minnie laughed softly. "Just look at that beautiful auburn hair and those green eyes."

All the time that Minnie talked with her nephew, Beth stared at him. Lackluster eyes, sunk into a gaunt, expressionless face, stared at her, but Beth had seen this look enough to know that Callum Galloway wasn't seeing her or anyone else in the physical world.

He mumbled something. Minnie leaned over, putting her ear close to his mouth.

"What, dear?" She listened, then said, "Autumn?"

"Autumn," he murmured, his voice louder and clearer this time. Even Beth understood him.

"No, dear," Minnie said softly, "it's spring, not autumn."

"Autumn," he repeated.

Beth thought she saw a stirring in his eyes.

"Russet." For a moment, the blankness left his eyes. He was seeing something in the physical world. The corners of his mouth quivered as if he were going to smile.

Giving him a maternal pat, Minnie said, "She's here doing research, dear, I'll bring her back to talk to you another day."

As quickly as it had appeared, the sparkle of life . . . of awareness was gone from Callum's face and eyes. He looked at Beth longer, then lowered his head.

The intercom buzzed, and Minnie answered. To the caller she said, "Yes, Micheil, you'll have time to finish your show before you come read. Jane and Hugo haven't gotten him in bed yet." Minnie listened, chuckled softly, then hung up. "That was Micheil," she said to Beth. "He's watching one of his favorite television shows. He'll be up shortly."

Seeming to be oblivious to all that was going on around him, Callum picked at the blanket laying over his legs. Still holding the receiver, Minnie tapped in a number.

"Jane, it's time for Callum to be put to bed. I'll give him his medicine, and you and Hugo can settle him in for the night. Then Micheil can read to him. I'll be in the master suite entertaining our guest if you have further need of me."

Beth watched as Minnie gave Callum his medicines and listened as she quietly talked to him about the day's events and made plans for tomorrow. When the two servants entered the room, Minnie and Beth left.

The doctors have done all for Callum that they can," Minnie said. "They've sent him home to die."

"I'm sorry. I wish there was something I could do."

"Aye," Minnie said, "so do I." With a heavy sigh, she added, "It might not have been so bad if Lucia had been here when he returned from the war. His wife. She was a beautiful, little thing. We loved her dearly, and she loved us. But it wasn't enough. She couldn't settle into life here at the keep. Just before

Callum left for Desert Storm, the two of them agreed to a divorce." Regret tinged Minnie's voice.

Standing in front of a long hall table, she began to rearrange flowers that didn't need rearranging. "She was a good woman and a good mother. We've really missed her."

In turn Minnie fiddled with everything else displayed, the inkwell, the picture frames, the small crystal compote.

"Lucia took Micheil with her when she left, but she never tried to turn him against us. She let him visit with us often. After she decided to remarry, Micheil asked if he could come live with us. Lucia was disappointed, but she allowed him to make the choice. I'm glad he was here when his father came home. It was so—so—"

The compote slipped through her hands and shattered on the stone floor.

"Oh, my goodness!" Beth exclaimed, horrified that the caretaker had broken a priceless antique. She bent down to pick up the broken pieces.

Minnie caught her by the shoulder. "Don't worry about it, dear. It was a new one and can be easily replaced. Jane can clean it up later."

Beth straightened.

Her cheeks flushed, Minnie pressed her hands to her cheeks. "I'm so sorry. I've never rattled on to a stranger like this before. If I'm not embarrassing you, I'm boring you, perhaps both. I apologize."

"It's all right," Beth said. "I really don't feel much like a stranger."

The women gazed at each other.

"I don't feel as if you're one either," Minnie confessed, "but still I shouldn't have imposed on your friendliness" She smiled brightly. "Let's get on with our tour of the castle and to the purpose of your visit, else you'll believe the Irishmen's claim that we Scots are a dour people."

Again she began to walk briskly. Beth followed.

Leading the way into another room on the same floor, Minnie

said, "This is the study." She walked toward the early twentieth-century furniture, hunter green leather chairs and sofa grouped in front of a huge fireplace.

Beth gazed in awe at the stone chimneypiece that flared out and over the hearth. The bottom of it was higher than Beth was tall, but the way the light fell across it, its exquisite stonework and engravings were clearly visible. On either side of the chimneypiece were two short mantel boards. Next to the fireplace was an arched bay window, the shutters flung open. On either side of the window alcove were benches, covered with multicolored cushions. Two large foot cushions rested on the elevated floor of the private sitting area.

Beth recalled some of her research on ancient castles. For security reasons the windows near the bottom of the walls and towers were very narrow, whereas those at the top were quite wide. They were generally beautifully designed and crafted as were these. Because they were the only source of natural light, the recesses behind them were the size of small rooms and contained built-in window seats. The windows were protected by an ornate iron grille and wooden shutters, which were now closed. Colorful afghans and throw pillows brought a cozy glow to the area.

"When the keep was first built, this was called the master's solar," Minnie said. "Now it's the master's study."

Beth scanned the room for the fresco.

"Some things haven't changed during the last nine hundred years," Minnie continued.

Disappointed, Beth pulled her gaze from the room and looked into the caretaker's twinkling blue eyes. Minnie waved her hand to the chair closest to the fireplace.

"Sit down, Dr. Balfour—"

"Beth, please."

Minnie gazed at her for a moment, then smiled and nodded her head. "Yes," she said. "You're a Beth. Have you had dinner?"

"A sandwich earlier." Beth's stomach growled.

"Then rest a minute and look around," Minnie said. "I'll fix you a tray, and you can eat while we talk."

Beth pushed back into the thick lushness of the chair and gazed around the room. Oddly for the castle to have been almost a century-old, the room was warm and friendly. Although the carpet on the floor was not wall to wall, it was thick and soft, woven in a tartan plaid. Probably the clan colors, Beth thought. She slipped off her shoes and tucked her feet under her.

Glancing over to the wide, opened doorway, she saw light flickering dimly from the other room. As if someone beckoned, she rose and walked across the study into the room. Like the rest of the castle, this room, a bedroom, was illuminated by electrified candles. On the far wall were two arched and re-cessed windows with stained-glass panes.

The master's suite? Beth wondered as she moved deeper into the room. Was the warlock the master and was this his suite? She shivered at the thought.

In a quick visual sweep of the room, she saw the bed, the wall tapestries that framed the head-posts, the two chests on either side of the bed that served for storage as well as for night tables.

The burgundy velvet canopy caught Beth's eye, drawing her attention to the bed itself. By today's standards it was an ordi-nary bed, but thoughts of the warlock having slept on it lent it a sensuality that Beth found exciting. She walked over and touched the canopy, then the bed linens.

The golden warmth of the fire drew Beth's attention to the fireplace that was reminiscent of the one in the study. She gazed for a long time at the red and orange flames as they danced through the air, up into the chimney. The blaze sputtered and embers erupted through the room. One, larger than the rest, shot up high, glowing brighter and brighter. It suddenly exploded into brilliant fire; as suddenly it flickered out. Disappointed, Beth turned her head, catching sight of the fresco portrait. Be-tween the bed and the fireplace, it was cloaked in shadows. She stepped closer and stared at it; the colors were as bright as the day it was painted.

Portraits being her favorite kind of painting, Beth studied this one carefully. She understood why it was such an enigma. Artists in the early Middle Ages did not create realistic paintings; they showed no depth perception in their works. This one was realistic to the point of looking modern; everything about it showed signs of its having been painted during the twentieth century.

As she had been ever since she arrived in Loch Gleann nan Duir, Beth had been overwhelmed with desire to capture the nuances of Castle Galloway on canvas . . . and someone had, and a portrait at that. Disappointed, she moved closer to the fireplace. Here she was inundated with a feeling of déjà vu. Shadowed memories haunted her, present but never coming to the forefront of her mind.

Although she had never seen the fresco before, she seemed to recognize the painting. It was as if she herself had painted it. The strokes, the colors, the texture. All were reminiscent of her techniques.

But she had never seen the painting!

She leaned over and searched for the artist's signature. She finally found a small E just beneath the blossom at the toe of his boot. A lone, cursive E. Beth's heart skipped a beat, and she staggered back. This was the way she had always signed her portraits.

She pondered this irony as she ran her gaze from the boots of the Highlander up to his face, to those piercing blue eyes, encircled in rings of midnight. Tall and powerfully built, he had shoulder-length black hair that framed a darkly handsome face. Beth forgot everything as she lost herself in the magnetism that was this Highlander. She swore he was alive, that she knew him. She felt his presence as greatly as if he were in the room with her. Her hands shook, and she realized that she had been holding her breath. She gasped, filling her lungs with much needed air.

"It can't be a forgery," Beth whispered.

"It's not," Minnie said, from behind her. "It's Lawren mac Galloway."

Intuitively Beth knew it was he. "You have proof?" she asked.

"Not as the world claims proof, but we of Clan Galloway know. What we can't prove tangibly but feel within our hearts, we call heart-proof."

"The chieftain or the warlock?"

"We don't know."

Odd the Galloways didn't know. Beth did. *Heart-proof*, as Minnie called it, assured her that it was the warlock.

Two

The two women stood silently, studiously in front of the fresco.

"In your letter you stated that you had read the Galloway manuscript," Minnie said.

"Yes. I've studied a modern translation of which I have a copy. When I arrived here in Scotland, I saw the original at the Edinburgh Historical Museum. Later, Agnes Forbes showed me her reproduction of it in Gaelic."

"It's a shame that most of the manuscript is gone," Minnie said. "We know so little about the early Galloways, and most of what we know comes through oral tradition." After a pause, she added, "I would imagine that these stories are based in truth, but through years of retelling there has been a blending of fact and fiction until now we can't distinguish one from the other."

"Mrs. Forbes told me that she was compiling a book on Highland folklore," Beth said.

"She came to interview me about it," Minnie said. "Being a descendant of the Adairs, she was most interested in the story about the blood feud between the Galloways and Adairs."

"Blood feud," Beth murmured.

"One of our legends claims that the Adairs hated the Galloways and wanted to wipe our name out of the annals of Scottish history."

"What happened?"

Minnie shrugged. "If there is any basis of truth to the story, the Adairs did not succeed. They are no longer counted a clan, but the Galloways are. Our descendants starred in many colorful scenes of Highland history."

"The most colorful name being that of Lawren," Beth murmured.

"Aye."

Beth moved nearer to the fresco, sweeping her gaze from the top of it to the bottom, to the small cursive E.

"There were two Lawrens," Minnie said, "and they were half-brothers."

"One was a chieftain, the other branded a warlock," Beth murmured.

"Or perhaps the chieftain and the warlock were one and the same," Minnie suggested. "Either way, legend says that each struggled for control of the Galloway clan."

"There wouldn't be all this confusion if both of them had not been named Lawren."

"It was not uncommon for that time. Each mother had intentions of her son inheriting his father's title as evidently did each of the sons."

"One did."

"Aye," Minnie softly agreed. "One did, but we'll never know which one, the elder or the younger, the legitimate heir or the bastard."

The last entry in the manuscript leaped to Beth's mind. *Lawren mac Galloway died, and the plague was stayed. His brother, Lawren mac Galloway, took his place as chief of the Gleann nan Duir Galloways. He and his lady-wife ruled happily.*

"The one became chief," Minnie said, "the other died either during or soon after the plague. Burned at the stake most likely."

"Agnes Forbes said that according to oral tradition the bastard son killed his half-brother so he could become clan chieftain."

"The presumption of the woman!" Minnie huffed. "How dare she speak for the Galloways."

"Is she wrong?"

" 'Tis a tale that historians seem to enjoy telling, but we Galloways haven't accepted it. We have always believed it was a lie told by a rival clansman, probably the Adairs, to discredit our Lawrens." She stepped closer to the portrait. "If only we knew for sure who this was, the legitimate Lawren or the bastard."

The room grew quiet as the two women continued to contemplate the fresco. Beth's gaze rested on the Highlander's tartan, on the delicate, silver-white flowers in his badge. Her heart skipped a beat, and she drew a deep breath. "What kind of flowers are those?"

"We believe it's the Highland nightlace."

The Highland nightlace! Beth shivered with excitement. At last she was seeing the flower she had only read about.

"According to legend, the plants bloomed only at night. Seen in the moonlight, the tiny white flowers looked like lace spread across the glen."

"Surely it can't be mythological," Beth whispered, caught up in the awe of discovery.

"That's what Gleann nan Duir Galloways have always claimed," Minnie said, "but since no one in modern times has seen a flower like the one painted in this fresco, botanists are skeptical." After a moment of silence, she added, "Let's return to the study where we can be comfortable. I have your dinner in there. We'll talk while you eat."

Beth heard Minnie's steps echoing through the huge castle room as she moved away, but Beth didn't want to leave the painting. Food meant nothing at the moment. Her life, her destiny, her entire purpose in being in Scotland seemed to be centered here in this spot, in this painting . . . in this Highlander.

"Would you like to see a photograph of Callum as he looked before he left for the war?" Minnie asked from across the room.

Far more interested in the portrait of the ancient laird than a photograph of the present one, Beth reluctantly backed up several steps. Minnie called again. Beth turned and walked to the long table that set against the wall on the far side of the room. Minnie ran her hand around the picture frame.

"As you can see, Callum looks very much like the ancient chieftain."

Surprised, Beth gazed at the photograph. A vital, healthy man stared at her, one who bore a striking resemblance to the ancient laird. Like Lawren mac Galloway, Callum's eyes were blue, encircled with a ring of midnight. Eyes of the night. Eyes of a warlock!

"He's handsome."

"Aye, that he is. Always turned the ladies' heads, he did. When Callum Galloway walked into a room, everyone knew it. He had a presence about him that caused people to take notice."

She picked up the frame with both hands and gazed at the photograph. Without Minnie's saying another word, Beth could almost read her thoughts. She felt her grief.

Minnie set the frame on the table and turned to Beth. Her eyes were bright with unshed tears, and her voice a little husky when she said, "I'm sure you're quite famished by now."

"A little." Beth smiled at the older woman.

"Come with me," Minnie said, and returned to the study.

Before Beth followed, she stole another look at the fresco. Then she looked at the portrait of Callum on the long table, at the startling blue eyes. The two men were so much alike . . . too much alike.

Disconcerted, Beth moved out of the master's suite into the study. Sitting on the couch, she looked at the ladened tray and realized she was indeed famished. It was all she could do not to wolf down the food. While she ate, Minnie sat across from her, sipping on a cup of herbal tea and tracing the history of Clan Galloway through fact and legend.

After Beth finished her meal, Minnie refilled their cups with tea. "Tell me something about your work."

"As I said before, I'm a research physician. While I strongly believe in traditional medical therapy, I also believe in holistic healing. I've dedicated my life to finding alternative choices for the prevention and cure of disease." Her hunger assuaged, relaxed by the room's warmth and Minnie's friendliness, Beth leaned back on the sofa.

"This foundation you work for is located in California?" Minnie asked.

Beth nodded. "Out of San Diego. We have a fully staffed hospital and clinic. We also publish a magazine called *Nature's Way,* a medical journal dedicated to herbal research and alternative medicine. Recently we've had an outbreak of an unusual illness in a rural town close to the clinic."

Taking several swallows of her tea, Beth thought about the Alcina family: the five-year-old twins, Jenny and Jerry, their sixteen-year-old brother, Greg. All were stricken with the illness. A sense of inadequacy as well as urgency pressed in on her.

"The people aren't sick in the conventional sense of the word. Their first symptoms are acute tiredness, followed by fever and delirium. After a severe rash covers their body, they lapse into unconsciousness and never awaken. We haven't isolated the cause of the illness and can't find a cure." She finished off her tea. "During our research at the clinic, we came across a translation of the Galloway manuscript."

"And you read about our ancient plague."

Nodding, Beth set the cup down and leaned forward on the chair. "It described a similar illness that swept through the Highlands during the eleventh century. One that sounds just like what the people are suffering in California."

"But according to the manuscript," Minnie pointed out, "none of the herbs healed the people."

"That's where the manuscript is a little hazy," Beth said. "It seems that from the way the entry was recorded one of the herbs was effective. But with the missing pages, it's hard to tell."

After a moment of thoughtful silence, Minnie said, "That's why you came here. You think the nightlace is the herb that stopped the epidemic."

"It had to be," Beth replied. "In regards to the present illness, several doctors and I have experimented with all but one of the listed herbs with no success. Now we have to try the nightlace."

"According to our oral tradition," Minnie said, "the plague was not stayed until the warlock died and all his potions and herbs were totally destroyed, wiped from the face of the earth forever."

"Including the nightlace," Beth added.

"Especially the nightlace, since it was his symbol."

"Has anyone done a comprehensive search for it through the Highlands?"

On soft laughter, Minnie countered, "Does anyone ever dive into the ocean off Florida looking for sunken treasure ships?"

Beth grinned. "No one has ever found one?"

"Nothing that could ever resemble it. But I suppose you're going to want to find out for yourself?"

Beth nodded. "We've caught this illness in the beginning stages, but if we don't find something to cure it, we could have an out-and-out epidemic. The last time I visited the clinic, I saw an entire family who was stricken. Five-year-old twins and their older brother. God knows how many more will succumb. I can't live with myself if I don't do all I can to find a cure."

Nodding, Minnie said, "You'll be needing someone to guide you. It's too easy to get lost in these Highlands for you to strike off by yourself."

"Do you know of someone?"

"Aye." Minnie smiled. "My husband, Clyde Graham himself. He's the best around. Knows this part of the Highlands better than most folk know the back of their own hands." Minnie set her cup down but made no effort to restack the dishes. Leaning back in her chair, she studied Beth. "Talking with you is easy, Beth. I'm glad you came. We're so remote that we don't often have guests, and because of Callum I don't leave the castle much."

"I suppose it can get lonely," Beth said.

"I had never noticed the solitude until Callum came home,"

Minnie said. "Now at times, it presses in on me. Thank God, Lucia was kind and wise enough to let Micheil choose whom he would live with. If I didn't have his future to think about, I'd probably go insane."

"I don't think so." Beth leaned forward and laid her hand over Minnie's. "I've only met you today, but from what I've seen and heard, I believe you're a strong woman."

"But even the strong grow weary." Minnie's eyes grew pensive. As quickly the shadow of vulnerability was gone, and she straightened. Beth removed her hand.

Somewhere in the castle a clock chimed the hour, and Beth lifted the locket-watch she wore around her neck. "Oh, my goodness! I had no idea it was this late." She pushed to her feet. "I need to be going, so you can get your rest."

"You don't have to worry about me," Minnie said. "I'm not far from my bed. You're the one I'm concerned about. Where are you staying?"

"At the Gleann nan Duir Inn in the village."

"That's a long drive on a narrow, two-laned highway. It's especially difficult for someone who doesn't know the Highlands." Minnie stacked the dishes on the tray. "How would you like to stay here, Beth?"

Beth was so pleased she was speechless.

"Of course, you might have someone waiting for you," Minnie quickly said. "Your husband?"

Beth shook her head.

"A boyfriend?"

"No one," Beth replied.

And there would be no one! For a moment she thought of Sam—Samuel J. Anderson, M.D., her ex-fiancé. He had been working at the institute when Beth began her internship. From the minute they met, they had become good friends. The friendship slowly developed into romance, and by the end of the first year they were dating seriously. While Beth didn't feel passionately about him, she was comfortable with him and wanted to marry him. She thought Sam felt the same way about her.

She soon learned differently. When it came to a commitment, Sam was unwilling to make one. But he hadn't had the decency to tell her. He had jilted her at the altar a year ago, leaving her heartbroken and humiliated. Her only consolation was that he had also resigned from the institute and she no longer had to work with him. Believing she would not love again, determined not to be heartbroken again, she had sworn off men.

"Then stay with us," Minnie insisted. "I know my invitation comes as a surprise, but I've enjoyed your being here. You've brought a ray of sunshine into my life. While I inundate you with legends of the Galloways, you can tell me all about the outside world."

"I'd love to! I never dreamed you would invite me."

Minnie laughed as she rose and moved to the telephone on the table behind the sofa. Picking up the receiver, she tapped one of the buttons. "This is also our intercom system," she explained. "Clyde and I are not the most technological people in the world, so Callum had a simple system installed. Micheil—" she addressed the person whom she had dialed. "We're going to have a guest at the Keep. I'd like for you to get her luggage from the car." Minnie said to Beth, "Is your car locked?"

Beth shook her head. "I have two suitcases in the trunk. He can open it by pressing a button on the lower part of the driver's door."

After relaying the information to Michiel, Minnie hung up. "He's truly a dear. He helps us out all he can. While we're waiting for him, let me show you around the suite." Again Beth followed the caretaker who walked briskly into the master's bedroom. "You have your own bathroom. We incorporated the original garderobe—"

"Garderobe?"

"The ancient toilet," Minnie explained as she stepped to the side of the fireplace and opened a door. Along one wall ran a huge rock shelf bench above which was a small arched window of stained glass.

"This was one of the many lavatories built into the castle, the long rock seat having a hole cut in it. The forerunner of indoor lavatories." She grinned. "Since we long ago discontinued its original use, we've covered and decorated it with cushions."

The bathroom was beautiful, Beth thought, as she gazed at the turn-of-the-century fixtures, the commode, and the bathtub and shower. All were contemporary in style, but designed to fit into the eleventh-century castle. The room's most outstanding feature was the stained-glass door and enclosure around the entire bathing area.

"It looks so modern yet so in place with the castle."

"The bathtub and shower were installed during the latter half of last century," Minnie replied. "But the lairds have insisted that all renovation remain in style with the original castle."

Pointing to the window, Minnie said, "Glass was used on many of the windows of early castles, but the original panes were replaced many hundreds of years ago with the stained ones. Each scene tells something of the legend of the Gleann nan Duir Galloways."

As Beth moved closer, she could see light from the corbels reflecting against the colored glass. "This one," she said, "it's—"

"Aye, it's the nightlace."

Beth whirled around and gazed again at the shower doors. "The same design was used for them also."

"Aye."

"Auntie M," a young voice shouted, "here's the suitcases."

"That's Micheil," Minnie said unnecessarily, her face beaming with maternal pride. She moved into the master's bedroom. "Bring them in here."

Beth liked Micheil Graham the minute she saw him. He was a tall, slender youth, with straight black hair and vivid blue eyes—just like his great-aunt, perhaps like his father's had once been. Micheil's ready smile and deep chuckle were also reminiscent of Minnie Graham.

After his great-aunt explained Beth's purpose in coming to

the castle, Micheil said, "Any time you want me to go exploring with you, just tell me. I know a lot of swell places where we can go." He swiped an errant strand of hair from his face. "Do you ride horses?"

Beth nodded.

"Great! We'll go horseback riding while you're here."

Minnie laughed. "Get the tray, Micheil, and let's go down so we can greet your uncle when he returns. Good night, my dear," Minnie said to Beth. "We'll leave you now. Clyde will be getting home soon and will want his dinner. If you need either one of us during the night, you'll find the intercom integrated into each phone."

Beth followed as Minnie explained the system. By the time she had finished, Micheil had scurried out with the tray.

"Can I bring you anything else?" Minnie asked.

"No." Beth smiled. "I'm going to take a bath and go to bed." When Minnie was at the door, she said, "May I use the telephone to make calls home? I have my calling card."

"Of course."

As soon as the door closed behind Minnie, Beth picked up her suitcases and unpacked her clothes. Grabbing her pajamas, she headed for the bathroom. For a long time she relaxed in a tub of hot water. Afterward feeling refreshed and revitalized, she put on her pajamas and called Cheryl Faircloth, her best friend and fellow researcher at the clinic. The receptionist answered.

"Hello, Diana," Beth said. "I made it. I'm at Galloway Castle. In fact, I'm staying here while I do my research."

They chatted for a few minutes before Beth asked for Cheryl.

"She's not in."

"Not in!" Beth exclaimed. "That's not like Cheryl. Where is she?"

"Just a minute," Diana said, an odd inflection to her voice. "I'll connect you with Peter."

"Diana—"

A click was followed by soft music. Her hand clammy, Beth

gripped the receiver. She didn't need to talk with the director of the foundation to know why Cheryl wasn't in.

She had contracted the disease she had been studying!

A researcher's worst fear. And Cheryl had been working round the clock on the death-sleep.

It could be something else, Beth thought . . . she hoped. She prayed. A cold! The flu!

She heard another click. The music stopped. Peter spoke.

"Beth—"

"Cheryl has the death-sleep," she blurted out.

Silence.

"No, Peter," Beth cried softly. "She can't have it."

"She has." Peter sighed, and Beth could see him leaning back in his chair and running his fingers through his thinning hair. "I didn't approve your taking your elective time to chase down that Scottish herb, but I'm glad you did. That plant is all we've got so far."

"We don't even have it," Beth said softly.

"What do you mean?"

"There is no nightlace."

"None?" came his stunned reply.

"No one has ever found anything that closely resembles it."

"Dear God!" Peter breathed. "How soon can you get home?"

"I'm staying," Beth told him.

"We're working shorthanded as it is, Beth," Peter said. "Now with Cheryl's illness—"

"I'm not leaving," Beth interrupted. "Not until I've searched for the flower, until I know for sure that it's not here."

"I don't like this," Peter said.

"Please," Beth begged. "This is my time, and I have the right to select what I do with it."

He sighed. "All right. But don't be late returning. Not one day, one hour, or one minute. *Comprende?*"

"Yes," she replied. How well she comprehended.

Three

Long after Beth hung up the phone, she thought about Cheryl, about the Alcina family, Jenny, Jerry, and Greg, about all the people who were suffering from the strange illness, all who would be suffering if something weren't done to cure it. Again a sense of inadequacy and helplessness settled on her shoulders. So far her trip to Scotland had brought her to a dead end. So much for her first headlong encounter with destiny.

She glanced at the table beside the sofa and saw the bottle of Scottish whiskey. Minnie must have brought it in while she was bathing. She slid off the bed, crossed the room, and poured herself a glass. Easing into the chair, she stared at the fresco, marveling at the realism the artist had captured through fine detail and depth perception. The fresco was more than the portrait of a man; it was his soul.

Beth again had the eerie feeing that the man in the portrait was alive, that he was looking at her, willing her to come closer. She tried to look away from him, but couldn't. He held her entranced. She rose and walked to the painting. Slowly her gaze moved over it until she was staring at the toe of his boot. At the nightlace. A delicate, ethereal flower.

"Lawren mac Galloway," she muttered. "You may have fooled the rest of the world, but you don't fool me."

She took a large swallow of whiskey, fire trailing down her throat.

" 'The legitimate son or the bastard? The king or the warlock?' they ask. But I know."

She set the glass on one of the mantel boards, and with her fingertip touched the nightlace that was painted at the bottom of the portrait. The plaster was cool to her touch.

"I wish you would perform some witchcraft and help me."

The words were hardly spoken before the fresco grew warm beneath her fingers and began to radiate a silvery-white glow that embraced Beth. She had the sensation that she was floating. She should have been frightened, but she wasn't. She felt safe and protected.

Abruptly her euphoria ended. The floating ceased. She felt as if she were being jerked apart, as if her body and her spirit were separate entities, each spinning in a different direction. Higher and higher she went. Abruptly the upward spiraling stopped. For a moment she hung suspended in space. Then she began to fall . . . down . . . down . . . down. Faster and faster until she crumbled to the floor.

After the dizziness subsided, she lay there for a moment, her eyes closed. She didn't hurt anywhere. At first, she worried about her blood pressure, about the medical reason why she had almost fainted. She opened her eyes and gazed around the room.

It was the same, but it was different.

She pushed into a sitting position. Candles—real candles— were burning in the wrought-iron corbels. A huge pedestal candleholder with an equally large candle burned in the center of the room. Rugs covered the floor, but beneath them was . . . was straw? Bracken? Heather?

She looked around. Medieval furniture replaced the modern. Two high-backed wooden armchairs with storage space beneath their hinged seats grouped around a short, two-person settle, complete with colorful cushions, embroidered furniture linens, and a decorated footboard. A narrow table, covered with a richly embroidered cloth, sat against a far wall; against another was a large chest topped with cushions.

In the center of the room, beneath the wrought-iron chandelier, stood a round table. On it was a vase of flowers, a cloth-bound book, and a huge candlestick. Close to the table were two folding stools. At the far side of the room, a door led to the small garderobe. The large modern bath had disappeared. Clothing hung from wooden wall pegs.

The study, still an adjoining room, had reverted to the master solar. Through the opened door, Beth saw the desk and trestle stood sitting in the middle of the room. Shelves climbed from ceiling to floor, and books were chained to them.

Beth closed her eyes. The fall had hurt her more than she realized. Something terrible—certainly unexplainable—had happened to her. Counting to ten, she breathed deeply and opened her eyes again. Nothing had changed. Her anxiety turned into fear.

The door to the bedroom opened, and a man walked in. Transfixed, she looked into a face that was dominated by dark blue eyes and framed with raven black hair, the face of the man in the portrait. Quickly Beth's gaze swung over to the space between the bed and chimneypiece. The fresco was gone. In its place hung a tapestry and a shield with two crossed swords.

She returned her attention to the man who moved to the table in the center of the room. Damp from the Highland mist, his dark plaid tartan swayed about his body. He set a lamp on one of the tables near the door and shucked off his gloves. Tossing them beside the lamp, he unfastened the cloak and swirled it off.

Looped around his shoulder was a long black whip, the ivory-colored handle carved out of a hard, glistening material—bone perhaps. Slivers of metal glinted gold and silver in the braided thong as it brushed against his black leather vest. Beth shivered. Like the man, the whip was beautiful but dangerous, deadly. He unhooked the whip and set it on the table beside his gloves.

He wore a gray shirt, opened at the neck, and tight black leather breeches. Sword and dirk were strapped about his waist. Clothing she had seen only in books and in the movies.

When he started to walk to the other side of the room, he saw her. He stopped short and stared. "I didn't expect you so soon."

He was expecting her! Her heart beat so fast she could hardly breathe.

"Charles is not only a resourceful steward, but a wise one," the man said. "He has chosen well for me. You'll help ease the long, dark hours of the night. I'll make sure I reward him amply."

Unable to speak, Beth stared into the man's dark and brooding countenance. He headed toward her. He couldn't be real. She had to be dreaming or hallucinating. Still he came closer. She heard the thud of his boots on the carpet, the creak of leather as he clasped the hilt of his sword. Fearfully she cringed away from him. He caught her by the arms and lifted her up.

Her anxiety over Cheryl, mixed with the potent whiskey, was causing her to hallucinate. This couldn't be happening to her. It couldn't. But it was. Frightened, dumbfounded, she stared at him.

As if he understood her feelings, he said, "Don't be frightened. I won't hurt you."

She had prayed for the warlock to perform some of his witchcraft and to help her, but she had not imagined in her wildest fancies that he really would. Although she shook with fear, she had to keep her wits . . . even if she was having a nightmare.

"Who—who are you?" she murmured.

Surprised, he said, "You came to these chambers without knowing whom you were servicing? Let me introduce myself, lass. I'm Lawren."

Lawren! That didn't tell her much. She started to ask *Are you the warlock?* As quickly she decided not to. He was so fearsome looking that courage abandoned her.

"For a verity, I have lived in the mountains so long that I don't recognize you either." A slow smile, radiating from the depths of his startling eyes, curled his lips. A promise-of-pleasure smile that was somehow amiable and sweet in addition to its obvious sensual allure.

Tiny flutters of heat stirred her senses, and she gave him a tentative smile in return.

"Tell me your name," he said.

His clasp on her upper arm loosened, and he slid his hand down to her wrist. Beth felt the bite of metal and looked down. So did he. In the glow of candlelight she saw the glint of a gold bracelet. Surprised, she stared at it. Other than the locket-watch, she wore no jewelry.

He raised her hand and looked at the piece of jewelry, brushing his fingers over the design. Finally he lifted his head and gazed into her eyes, murmuring, "Little Elspeth."

"You—know me?"

"Aye."

"I—I don't know you."

"You do, but you probably don't remember. You were a wee lass of sixteen when last I saw you ten years ago. Why are you here now?"

"To see you."

Poignant silence wrapped around both of them.

"Many are the times that I have wanted to see you again, lass."

Mesmerized, Beth stared into the stranger's eyes . . . blue eyes circled in midnight. Her fears forgotten, her curiosity piqued, she murmured, "Eyes of the warlock."

As if surprised but pleased by her remark, his expression softened. "You do remember?"

Beth felt giddy, light-headed.

"That's what you told me many years ago when you met me for the first time," he said. Softly he added, "We were younger then. Both of us. Much younger and innocent." His deep resonant voice captivated her. "You made that day so special, lass, I'll never forget it. We were standing at the bottom of the waterfall in a spill of summer sunshine. Brilliant flowers carpeted the mountain sides and glens. The forest sparkled in its spring finery."

He paused as if willing her to recall. "But none of its beauty compared to you."

The warlock's seductive voice worked its magic on Beth. His

memories overwhelmed her senses and touched her heart and soul. She felt a oneness with Elspeth and a sorrow that these were not her memories. Oddly Beth saw the waterfall he described, felt the warmth of spring sunshine, and smelled the fragrance of the flowers.

Lawren continued to reminisce. "It was the day your brother brought you to the mountains so my mother could treat the rash that had broken out on your face."

Beth touched her cheek.

"Do you remember what I told you?" he asked.

She shook her head.

"If my eyes were those of a warlock, yours were those of an enchantress. That one day you would be one of the most beautiful women in all of the Highlands." He gazed softly at her. "And you are."

Her cheeks burned with pleasure, and his smile deepened.

"Your eyes were a beautiful shade of green when you were a child," he said. "Now that you are mature they are even more beautiful. Deeper, richer. The color of Highland magic."

He continued to spin a sensual web around Beth, assuaging her fears and confusion, tugging her closer. His memories were so soft and wonderful she gladly embraced them, gave herself to them.

"Most of all, I loved your spirit, your sense of independence. When Bearnard voiced his fear that you would be scarred for life and that no man would have you, you scoffed and replied that men were such greedy lots they would gladly have you if your dowry were sufficient. If your face were scarred, you went on, he would have to give you more dowry."

Lawren laughed; Beth smiled. Elspeth sounded very much like her kind of person.

"Some claim I have too much spirit." She remembered a recurring argument she and Sam had had about her sense of independence.

"Mayhap your husband thought so," Lawren said.

Husband! She—Elspeth—had a husband!

"Rumor has it the Alastair didn't trust you. That's why he took you with him on his travels around the world."

Beth certainly didn't know any of the details of Elspeth's marriage, but Lawren's arrogant presumptions irritated her. "Perhaps love, not mistrust, motivated his actions. Is it possible to conceive that he loved his wife and wanted her to be with him because he enjoyed her company?"

"An instance where a marriage of convenience between a man who had seen more than his three-score-and-ten years and a maiden of ten-and-nine years brought happiness to the bride and groom as well as to the brother who arranged it." Lawren laughed softly, mockingly. "I've heard that since Alastair died no man will have you for wife even though you inherited a handsome sum. 'Tis also said that you have chosen to stay at the cloister during your period of mourning. That you plan to take the vows of sisterhood and give your wealth to the church."

A convent! While Beth was a practicing Christian, she had never, absolutely never, entertained the idea of entering a convent. She admired those people who did go into the ministry, but a sequestered and celibate life was not for her!

"If I enter a convent," she replied, "it will be because I choose no man for husband."

"Aye, lady, I believe you." So softly he spoke, she wasn't sure she heard him. His eyes twinkled.

She lost herself in their mystical beauty.

"If I marry," she murmured, "it shall be only for love."

"Then you will be most fortunate, lady. Most never know love."

"I could have," she murmured.

"With Alastair?"

"No, with another."

Her head ached dully, and she closed her eyes. Vague memories of Sam flitted through her mind. As quickly as they had come, they vanished. It was as if he had never existed, never been a part of her life. She remembered only the Highlander. She opened her eyes and saw only him.

"I would have married him," she said, "but he did not return my love. He was unwilling to make a commitment of marriage."

An indefinable emotion flickered in Lawren's eyes. Sadness? Regret? Beth couldn't be sure, but the only thing about which she was really sure was her confusion, her aching head.

"Mayhap he was willing but unable, lass."

"Perhaps," she mumbled, then asked, "Do you have a special—er—woman in your life?"

The color of his eyes darkened. "Nay, only in my dreams. I am haunted by a lass with green eyes."

Without moving, he drew her to him, embraced her with his presence. Beth had always scoffed at the idea of falling in love at first sight. Now she was a believer. She could easily love this dark stranger. But the idea of her loving him was preposterous. He was a man of the past, a man who had been dead for centuries. Paradoxically he was alive, very much alive, and she was attracted to him.

"Why is she not a part of your life?"

"She is an Adair and a chieftain's daughter. I am a Galloway and a bastard, and many accuse me of being a warlock."

The man in the portrait *was* the bastard. The warlock and the bastard were the same. Was he also the chieftain? Beth glanced at the space between the fireplace and the bed, the place where the fresco would be painted someday. As she thought about the signature E, a shiver ran up her spine.

"You have taken a great risk in coming here," he said. "Where the Adairs are concerned, the Galloways are out for blood. And they won't care that it's yours, not Bearnard's."

Beth's headache subsided, and with it went the strange sense of familiarity, of intimacy that Lawren had initiated when he described his and Elspeth's first meeting. Unable to understand what was happening, fearing that soon she would no longer be Beth Balfour, that she would indeed have to assume the identity of Elspeth, Beth brushed her hand over her forehead.

She could not allow herself to be consumed with thoughts like these. If she were to find the nightlace and return to the

present, she had to keep a clear head, had to consciously seek
a way back.

"The risk is great," she agreed, "but I *had* to see you."

The words settled quietly, seductively over them as they stood
alone in the center of the room. He was silent for a long time,
and Beth savored the rare beauty of their closeness and knew
in her heart of hearts that she had been searching for this man
all her life . . . for many lifetimes. He was looking directly into
her eyes, and she felt as if he were flowing into her soul, searching out her secrets, filling her with his essence.

"Why? After all these years?" he asked.

A century!

"Are you haunted by a man with eyes like a warlock?"

Yes, she wanted to whisper, *I am,* but she couldn't give herself
to such fancies. She was not of this world. She struggled to
retain her identity, not to be caught up in this magical web of
time-travel, in the sensual web the stranger wove about her.

"I—I wanted to see you about the nightlace."

His smile slowly vanished. His eyes hardened and narrowed,
his lips thinned. "The nightlace," he muttered. Physically he
didn't move, but mentally he withdrew from Beth.

"You're the only one who can help me," she said.

"I had heard that you were devious like your brother, but I
had refused to believe it. Your having taken refuge at the cloister
after Alastair died made me think you wanted to be separated
from Bearnard." Disappointment dulled his voice. "Through
the years I clung to the image of the lass who wanted to help
people." He paused. "What has Bearnard ordered you to do?
Spy and report back to him? Get the nightlace we may have?
Kill Lowrie and me?"

"Kill you?" she sputtered.

He caught her chin in his hand, his fingers digging into the
tender flesh. His blue eyes pierced her. "I have always cared
about you, lass, and probably always shall, but I'll not let you
take advantage of me. Your brother is responsible for my father's
death. If he hadn't raided Galloway castle, Angus mac Galloway

would be alive today. For a verity, none of you will harm Lowrie." His tone was deadly. "I'll kill you first."

The gentle man was gone. In his place was a harsh barbarian intent on murder. Shaken, Beth stared into the dark visage, into the hard metallic eyes and knew the Highlander was not lying. "There's some mistake."

"Aye, and you made it when you thought to make a fool of me."

"I'm not Elspeth."

She tried to pull his hand from her face, but his fingers dug deeper into her flesh. His gaze fastened on the bracelet she wore.

"If you're not, why do you look—and act like her? Why are you wearing her jewelry?"

"I don't know," Beth whispered. "I wish I did."

"If the steward did not bring you to me," Lawren said, "how did you slip past the guards and get into the castle?"

"I'm—not sure."

Four

As abruptly as Lawren had caught Beth's chin, he released it. She staggered back, her feet tangling in her skirt. *In her skirt?* She jerked to a halt. She wasn't wearing a skirt. For the first time since she had entered into this . . . this place, she was aware of clothing, heavy and stifling. She looked down at the green material that swirled about her legs. Most definitely not her lightweight cotton pajamas! Unbelievingly, she raised her head and saw her reflection in the mirror across the room.

"No!" she gasped, automatically bringing her hand to her face—the only part of her that was visible and recognizable. "This can't be happening to me. It can't."

Bell-shaped sleeves billowed through the air—more material than Beth could imagine being in one garment and being on her. She had always despised restrictive clothing. She touched the wimple and veil, made of a soft white fabric, that covered her head and draped over her shoulders.

She slid her hand over her face and neck, over her collarbone to her breasts. Feeling the cool brush of metal against her palm, she glanced down to see her gold watch-locket. As if it were a lifeline and she were drowning, Beth clutched the piece of jewelry, a gift from her mother last Christmas. It was her only link to reality, to her world.

"I don't know what game you're playing, Elspeth," Lawren snapped, frightening her, "but I'm not amused. How did you get into the castle undetected and what do you want."

"Would you believe me if I said, I walked in?" Beth exclaimed, self-preservation coming to her rescue. "With a cloak and hood over her head, one woman looks very much like another. Muffle the voice and they sound alike. And surely guards who had been alerted that a wench was coming to serve you would assume I was that woman. They would relax their vigil."

"Aye," Lawren drawled, "no one would have noticed another wench walking through the great hall." He threw back his head and laughed, the sound nerve-racking and devoid of humor. "How stupid the kindred are going to feel when they learn that an Adair wench slipped past them undetected! By the time I have finished with the guards who allowed Elspeth nea Adair to pass through, they shall be wishing for death. They'll never be so irresponsible again."

"I'm not this—this Elspeth."

"Oh?" His calmness directly contrasted with her agitation.

"I'm Beth. Elizabeth Balfour."

"There is no one by that name up here."

"You can't know everyone."

"Nay, but I know most, and Balfour is not counted among the Galloways or the Adairs. For a verity, there would be no woman named Beth."

"Why not?"

" 'Tis a man's name." He caught the material of her tunic and rubbed it between his fingers. "Fine material, madam. Fit for the wealthiest of ladies. Colors worn only by the richest."

Beth glanced down at the fabric, then back up into his face.

"If you are not Elspeth, I must assume that you have stolen her clothing and jewelry, mayhap harmed her. Why would you do this?"

"No," Beth exclaimed. A trap was quickly closing around her. "I don't know her. I haven't hurt her. I'm not one of you."

"For a verity, you are. You speak without an accent."

Speak without an accent! Startled, Beth stared slack-jawed at him. Finally she closed her mouth. She not only spoke without an accent, but she understood and spoke the stranger's language. She was speaking eleventh-century Scottish Gaelic. *She could*

do this only if she were Elspeth! But she was not. No matter what
he might say, no matter that he claimed she looked or talked like
the other woman.

Beth's heartbeat accelerated, and the room spun around her.
No, she thought, her hand once again tightening around her
locket-watch, she couldn't be someone else, certainly not a
woman from the distant past. The watch was her proof. She *was*
Elizabeth Balfour, here to find the medicine that would save
the lives of her friends, of all whom were afflicted with the
illness.

Someone knocked on the door.

The Highlander crossed the room. Glad for the respite, glad
for a moment to collect her thoughts, Beth moved in the opposite direction from him, the material of her skirt wisping across
the floor. *This isn't really happening to me,* she told herself. *I
want the nightlace so desperately I'm dreaming . . . or hallucinating.*

Metal grated through the room when he unbolted the door
and flung it open. A draft rustled around Beth and the candles
flickered. An elderly woman stood in the hallway. Although she
was clad in long tunic, wimple and veils, she was a tall, brawny
woman. All angles and lines and sinewy flesh. She reminded
Beth of a modern bodybuilder, one in the heavyweight class.

The woman wore a chain-link belt around her waist. Dangling
on a big ring at the end of it were keys and tools—scissors,
tweezers, and a small knife, the best Beth could see. She could
more easily visualize the woman holding a mace in one hand,
a sword in the other.

"Good evening, Annie," Lawren said. "I didn't see you when
I walked through the great hall."

"I just came in myself," she replied. "Sloane said the two of
you had arrived home safe and sound, but I wanted to see for
myself." She moved closer and scrutinized his face. "Your journey to the northern isles went well? Nothing amiss happened
to you?"

He laughed gently. "Aye, Annie, Sloane told the truth. But both of us are tired and hungry."

"Sloane isn't hungry. He's in the kitchen eating his fill." She clamped her hands on her hips and rolled her eyes. "I fear that red-haired oaf isn't going to leave enough for the evening meal. At least, he plaited his beard so that his face isn't one mass of whiskers."

Annie's smile took the rancor out of her voice, and she and Lawren laughed. The tender scene touched Beth and revealed a side of the man she would not have believed possible had she not witnessed it herself.

"I wish the evening meal was my only concern," the old woman lamented. "Since you and Sloane have been gone, rumors are spreading through the Highlands as quickly as the illness. Bearnard has openly accused you of being a warlock."

"If he's coming out in the open with his accusations," Lawren said, "he is gaining support among the clans."

"He says you have cursed us with the death-sleep because you are angry that your father appointed Lowrie his successor rather than you," Annie said, "and he's trying to convince the Highlanders that Lowrie's life is in danger as long as you are alive. He's urging the other chiefs to bring you to trial for heresy."

"So I can be burned at the stake."

"The dog!" Annie cursed. "He's like his Saxon mother. She was obsessed with the idea of creating a separate kingdom out of the Highlands, and so is he. I don't think a drop of Scottish blood flows through him. He wants to create a haven for all his Saxon kinsmen who are fleeing from the Normans."

"Only Lowrie and I stand in Bearnard's way now," Lawren said. "Since the church will probably take care of me, Bearnard's worry is Lowrie."

"He'll want to see Lowrie dead before his birth date and before he becomes clan chief," Annie said.

"Aye, 'twill be easier if he does."

"If we can stop this illness," Annie said, "we can stop the rumors."

"Can we?" he murmured.

No Beth thought, remembering the manuscript, *they won't be stopped until you're dead and the nightlace is destroyed.*

"Sloane said you found no nightlace?" Annie said.

"None. Go fetch Lowrie for me. I want to speak to him."

"He's . . . er . . . he's not here."

Lawren looked incredulous and muttered, "Not here?"

She nodded and brushed her big hands down the white tunic she wore. Nervously she picked at the key ring. "He and two of the lads left this morning to ride into the mountains."

"A pleasure ride?" Lawren scoffed.

"Some of the nightlace has been spotted in Mountain Cat Canyon," Annie continued. "At first, only Rob and Jamie were going to get it. Unbeknownst to anyone in the castle, Lowrie slipped out with them."

"The damn little fool!" Lawren plowed his hand through his hair and paced back and forth in front of the door.

The anger in his voice startled Beth.

"Who told him there was nightlace at Mountain Cat?"

"Rob. He found it when he was searching for stray cattle."

"That's not nightlace," Lawren shouted. "Even if it was, I told Lowrie not to leave. The castle was filled with the kindred. Surely one of them saw him and could have stopped him from leaving."

"No one," Annie insisted. " 'Twas much later that I learned it. But even had I known, I couldn't have stopped him. Once Lowrie makes up his mind to do something, he'll do it. Both of you inherited that streak of stubbornness from your father."

"Where was Evan?" Lawren stopped and whirled around, glaring at her. "He was headman in charge. Why wasn't he watching Lowrie?"

"He was called away. Some of the cattle were ill, among them your prize bull. While Evan and the lads were taking care of them, Lowrie slipped out."

Without an explanation, Beth understood the importance of their tending to their cattle, their primary source of food and clothing during the long, cold winters. Without cattle they could not survive.

"William?" Lawren demanded. "Where was he? Surely one of my headmen was here watching after his future chief?"

Looking miserably uncomfortable, Annie cleared her throat. "We had a new outbreak of illness in the village. Taking what nightlace we could find, William escorted several of the women directly there so they could start taking care of the ill. I traveled into the mountains to tell your mother and to see if she had any more of the plants."

"Neither you nor the two headmen were here when Lowrie left?" Lawren said quietly. "The three of you were gone!"

"He had given his word, and we thought we could trust him," Annie said. "With you being gone, Lawren, we also had other responsibilities to think about."

"When you return to the kitchen, tell Sloane I want every gate and every door to the castle guarded. No one is to pass without being questioned. *No one!*"

Annie's eyes grew sharp. "Are we in danger?"

"If people can slip in and out of the castle as easily as Lowrie did." He cut Beth a glance. "I'll say we're in danger. No telling who may be walking down our corridors, planning our down-fall."

"Lowrie slipped out in disguise," Annie said. "I doubt that the guards would let anyone in that easily."

Lawren looked at Beth, but asked, "Did my mother have any of the nightlace?"

"A few. She sent me back to the castle and took them to the village herself."

"Any news about the illness?"

"Nay, William hasn't returned."

Lawren started pacing again. "How are the cattle?"

"I was gone when Evan arrived, but the kitchen staff reported that he got to them before any damage was done."

"Can I presume he has gone after Lowrie?"

She nodded. "He learned about Lowrie's being gone when he returned from examining the cattle. He and the lads left immediately."

"Let me know as soon as you hear from the village. When Evan and Lowrie return, send them to me straightway. I shall have a reckoning with the lad. I strictly forbade his leaving without either William or Evan."

Perhaps the stories about the hatred and jealousy between the brothers was true, Beth thought.

Annie laid an arthritic hand on Lawren's arm. "Don't worry unduly. The lads are deep within Galloway territory. The Adairs have never ventured as far as Mountain Cat Canyon."

"There's always a first time," Lawren snapped.

"If there is, your father and I taught Lowrie well." She paused. "Angus always insisted that you boys be trained with a live dummy. Until the lads were old enough to be dummies among themselves, I was their dummy. Then Angus himself. Lowrie is quite accomplished with his weapons."

"But he is untried in battle, and his wits are those of a lad of ten-and-five. His irresponsibility in leaving the castle is proof of that," Lawren said. "A seasoned warrior will have no difficulty in cutting him down." He stopped pacing and shook his head. "Jamie. Rob. Lowrie. All of them babes, hardly out of swaddling."

"Babes! Pooh!" She scoffed. "They are warriors. What are we coming to?" she lamented. "We're growing much too soft."

Beth only now realized that it was not anger she had heard in Lawren's voice earlier but anxiety and concern. He seemed to care about the boy and wanted to save him. She stirred, and her hand accidentally hit one of the chairs causing it to grate against the floor.

Annie stared beyond Lawren to Beth. Her mouth went slack; her eyes widened. She stepped across the threshold. "Elspeth nea Adair," she murmured.

No, Beth wanted to scream, *I'm not.* But she didn't. Holding tight rein to her emotions, tapping down her hysteria, she remembered all she had studied about dreams. She decided that she had unconsciously discovered through her research where the nightlace grew, and her subconscious was trying to reveal it to her. She was not going to waste time trying to convince these people of her true identity. She must find the nightlace, get some of the plants from him, then worry about waking up . . . or getting back to the future . . . or the present.

"Our prisoner?"

"Aye."

"Sloane didn't mention her."

"He wouldn't have," Lawren said. "I'm not ready for the kindred to know that I have her. I shall tell them later when we gather in the great hall."

"At last we shall have our revenge," Annie said. Hatred gleamed in her eyes and hardened her countenance. "We shall repay Bearnard in kind for killing our kinsmen. An eye for an eye, a tooth for a tooth." She paused. "A life for a life."

Beth had no illusions about the barbarism of the Middle Ages, but nothing had prepared her for the harsh reality of their culture. Primitive and uncivilized were the gentler descriptions she could think of. The more apt were brutal, cruel, ruthless. Life was far worse than she had imagined.

"I know how you feel about the Adairs, Annie. Killing her would be sweet revenge."

"Aye. I can taste it now."

"But," he added softly, "it wouldn't be the *ultimate* revenge."

Thoughtfully she stared at him. "What would be?"

"Bearnard would rather Elspeth was dead than alive. That way he can get her inheritance. He would be eternally grateful to us if we killed her." He paused. "Keeping her alive is our revenge."

Annie's eyes gleamed with skepticism.

"Believe me, Annie," he said.

"You're right." The woman sighed. "But I would love to see

the Adairs punished for what they have done to me, to all of us Galloways."

"They shall be," Lawren promised. "Sometimes, Annie, there are punishments far worse than death. This is one of those instances."

"This will be a night of celebration," she declared. "Dancing and singing and revelling. I'll be getting back to the kitchen. We're going to need more food and ale." Stretching out a gnarled hand, she moved toward Beth. "Where shall I put her? In the dungeon?"

Beth cringed away from the woman.

"Nay, leave her here with me."

Surprised, Annie glanced at him.

"I wanted a lass to service me. Now I have one."

Annie cackled. "This is an even better revenge than death, sire, and 'twould be all the sweeter if she were a virgin." She paused; her brow furrowed; then she laughed again. "Mayhap she is a virgin. Alastair was old."

"Old doesn't necessarily mean impotent," Lawren said.

"I'll wager he was," Annie said.

"You bastards!" Beth swore, shocked at her vehemence, at her vocabulary. She didn't know any of these people, but she felt a burning need to protect the dead man against these two. In a way it was her own defense. "You sons-of-bitches! It's easy to talk ill of the dead when he's not here to defend himself!"

Annie gasped, and her face turned white.

"You're not punishing Bearnard if you rape me. You're punishing me by violating my body."

"Violating your body!" Annie exclaimed. "Whatever do you mean? A woman's body is made to accommodate a man."

"Only if she allows him to," Beth said.

Annie looked from Lawren to Beth and back to Lawren.

His eyes narrowed to silver slits. "Leave, Annie."

"Let me punish her." Straightening her back, the woman pulled to her full height. She was almost as tall as Lawren and at the moment looked more fearsome than he did. The material of her tunic pulled tightly across her shoulders, accenting their width and muscularity. "I shall teach her to respect her superiors. I'll subdue the wench."

Beth didn't for a minute doubt Annie's words.

Lawren shook his head. Casting pouty glances over her shoulder, Annie strode out of the chamber. Lawren closed and locked the door; then he returned to where Beth stood.

"You have behaved foolishly, madam."

"If protecting myself is foolish behavior, then I shall be guilty of doing it again." She straightened her back. "And again. I won't let any of you take advantage of me."

"Insulting me is not protecting yourself."

"I suppose you're going to punish me?" Beth spoke with more daring than she felt. "As Annie said, *subdue* me."

"Aye."

She stared directly into his eyes, so scared her entire body trembled. "No matter what you do to me, you'll never subdue me. You might as well forget the eye and tooth and take the body. As long as I have any breath in me, I'll fight you."

" 'Twould serve you well not to. I'm the only one here who will protect you."

"I don't want your protection."

"Aye, lady, that's the one thing you do want. The Galloways hate the Adairs and are greedy for revenge."

He reached for the whip, uncoiling and drawing it through his hand. Beth fought back panic.

"Save me or beat me?" she asked.

"If I were any other Galloway, I would beat you."

He drew his arm back, and the whip, a black snake, coiled through the air, hissing toward the wall opposite Beth. Although it came nowhere near her, couldn't have touched her, she tensed, cringed. When it slapped the wall, she jumped. Her imagination was so great she could imagine the whip tearing into her flesh.

"Ten or twenty lashes across your back," he said. "Lashes that would tear through your clothing and cut into your flesh." His voice grew sharper, slicing into her sensitivities as adroitly as the whip would have lashed her body. "Wounds that sometimes leave disfiguring scars, that also leave you alive and in great pain. Suffering, not death, is the object of a beating. A spectator best appreciates torture when it is drawn out."

"If you're trying to frighten me, you've succeeded. You don't have to beat me." She sneered. "But you probably will as a show of your authority, as proof of your manhood."

"I don't need to prove my manhood. If I did, it would not be with the beating of a woman."

His visage darkened, and he stepped nearer to her. She saw the rise and fall of his chest, heard his breathing, felt the warmth and power that emanated from him. At the same time that he unsettled her, he also intrigued her. His physicality enticed and drew her to him.

"You have lived a privileged life, madam, protected first by your brother, then by your husband, but now you no longer have either to protect you. You are our prisoner, and your fate lies in our hands."

"I'm not really your prisoner," Beth said. "You didn't capture me. You don't know for sure how I came to be in your chambers. You have to take my word for it. I came here on my own, seeking your help."

"I don't care how you got here or why," Lawren said. "You'll soon discover that it was much easier for you to get into this castle than it's going to be for you to get out. Rest assured, madam, you are my captive and will remain so as long as I deem necessary."

His eyes pierced her. Slowly he lowered his arm, looped the whip, and slipped it over his shoulder. Moving much closer to her, he said, "Be cautious, Elspeth. I am telling the truth when I say I'm the only person in this castle who will protect you."

Closer he stepped until the odor of worked leather filled her nostril, and the tip of the whip grazed her cheek. All she could see was the broad expanse of his shoulders covered in the soft leather vest.

"Anyone else would have laid the strap to you or done worse.

Another instance where you insult me before the kindred, they shall demand by clan custom that I turn you over to them for punishment." He strode to the door, unbolted, and opened it. "Come, Annie."

The servant tottered into the room, and Beth knew she had been crouched against the door, listening. From the thickness of the walls and the doors, Beth figured she had heard little. Straightening, the old woman looked approvingly at the whip on his shoulder, then glanced at Beth.

"I gave her a gentle beating," he explained, confirming Beth's suspicions about how little Annie had heard. "We do not want to mar her beautiful body until we've gotten our full use of her."

Until *you've* gotten your full use of me! Beth thought.

"Hasten to the kitchen, Annie, and see to the serving of the meal. Also tell Charles I no longer need a wench. Tell Sloane to double the guards."

After Annie departed, Lawren again shut the door but did not shove the bolt into place. He turned to face Beth.

"All of this is for naught," Beth said quietly. "I'm sure I must strongly resemble this woman of whom you and your servant speak, but I am not she."

Leaning a shoulder against the wall, he crossed his arms over his chest and cocked a brow.

"But let's assume for argument's sake—"

"For truth's sake."

She glared at him. "—that I am this Elspeth."

His soft laughter mocked her.

"I have committed no crime. I am here because my friends are dying, and I need some of the nightlace."

Dark anger whisked away his smile; it replaced his mockery. He strode across the room and grabbed her by the upper arms, his fingers biting through the material into her tender flesh.

"I'm sure you do, as do the rest of us," he snarled, his breath warm against her face. "Are you only now aware that the illness may be turning into a plague? Of the dying?" He paused, then added thoughtfully, "Perhaps so. I forget that you and Alastair spent most of your married life abroad and that you have sequestered yourself at the convent since you returned after his death. Mayhap you have not received news of the severity of the illness."

She tried to pull away from him, but he held onto her.

"Or perhaps you're still caught up in your game of pretend." He shoved her away. "Whichever, I don't have a supply of nightlace. Goaded on by your brother, people are destroying the nightlace. He has them believing that it's the flower of hell. If Bearnard has his way, the church will soon join his crusade, and if any plants are still growing, they, too, will be destroyed."

"Nay!" Beth shook her head, her veil wisping around her face.

"Aye, Elspeth, not just the flowers, but the plants along with their roots and seeds."

"But it's the herb that cures the illness," Beth cried.

"It heals some people, not others," Lawren corrected. As if weary, he shrugged, and the whip slid off his shoulder and down his arm. Negligently he tossed it onto the table. "I haven't learned what property in the plant cures them." He laughed shortly, bitterly. "And now I probably shall not. I don't have enough nightlaces to experiment with."

"Could you give me one or two?" she asked. "Not for myself but for those who are dying."

Silence hung between them.

Finally he said, "Almost you persuade me, Elspeth. If I did not know the Adairs for their deceit, I would believe you."

"Push your hatred for the Adairs, for me, aside for the time being," she begged, "and think of the people who need the nightlace, of those who are dying without it."

"You should be talking to Bearnard about this. He's the one who is destroying the plants." Lawren shoved the whip farther onto the table and brushed the tips of his fingers over his gloves.

"Bearnard could not do it by himself," Beth said. "The Highlands must be filled with gullible people ready to do his bidding."

"Frightened people," Lawren said. "They're not as sure as you are that the nightlace is the cure. As I said, some of the people have lived after taking the nightlace. Others have died. My mother and I have not had enough time to separate the curative property in the plant. Also, Bearnard is using their religious convictions to drive them into frenzied hysteria. He exhorts louder than the priests. He claims that once the devil is driven from the land, the illness will leave on its own."

Some things would never change, Beth thought, as she paced back and forth. A few would use whatever means was necessary, especially religious convictions, to manipulate and to control the masses. Her feet caught in the heavy fabric swinging about her ankles, and she stumbled. Irritably she swiped the material up and bunched it over one arm. She started pacing again.

"I have no doubt that Bearnard has some of the plants stashed away," Lawren mused. "He's not a fool. He knows their healing power."

"Yes," Beth murmured, "I'm sure he does."

"Once he has killed Lowrie and me and has broken the powerful Galloway clan, he will replant them. 'Twould be an easy thing to get the church to purge them of their evil properties and to bless them."

Beth was curious about the political machinations of Adairs and Galloways, about the legend of the blood feud between them, and wanted to latch onto every word that revealed the plot, but her primary goal was to get the nightlace. Racing to the door, she grabbed the bolt and slid it open.

Long strides carried Lawren across the room. "Nay, Elspeth." His arms slipped around her, his lean, hard body imprisoning hers. He locked the bolt in place. "You'll not be leaving."

She turned in his arms, her back flattened against the door. The bolt bit into her flesh, and he pressed against her breasts and stomach.

"Not until I've finished with you."

He shifted his weight against her, his broad shoulders blocking out the rest of the room, making her acutely aware of him, of his body heat, of the clean odor of herbs that clung to him. His warm breath fanned against her face, and his eyes softened. But she was frightened of him. His warning, *until I've finished with you,* rang ominously in her ears. Her lips went dry, and she licked them.

"I've always had a tenderness for you." His voice was deep and soft and very near.

She prayed that he still had a tenderness for her.

He pushed the veil from her hair and let it slide down her back. His fingers lingered on her neck. "I find you desirable."

Reaching behind her neck, he picked up the thick braid and held it in his hand, rubbing the shiny strands between his fingers. Flutters went through her, both fear and excitement. Then he laid it across her shoulder. Again his hand lingered.

"Russet. Like the leaves in autumn."

His voice reminded her so much of Callum Galloway that she temporary forgot her fright. She remembered an earlier conversation that seemed so long ago, one that happened in another time and place and with another Galloway laird. Had he, too, been traveling in time?

"Auburn. Also magical color of the Highlands."

"Aye."

She wanted to close her eyes, to break the mesmeric bonding, but she couldn't. Before he had only held her prisoner; now he held her captive. His eyes pierced her soul, prying out her secrets, searching for her heart of hearts, for herself. At the moment he was gentle and seductive, persuasive. But she couldn't forget that he was also the savage who held her prisoner, who had threatened her with a whip and with seduction. She looked around for a means of escape, for a weapon. She saw the whip. She didn't know how to use it; she must find something else.

"Let me leave," she begged.

"Nay." His expression remained soft, and his voice sounded

regretful. "If I did, the kindred would surely turn on me, and they would have reason to. They would accuse me of being a traitor, of conspiring with you and Bearnard, which is probably true. I don't mind for myself, but I have Lowrie to think about."

"You can sneak me out." She was desperate. "They will never know I've been here."

"I can." His warm breath fanned her cheeks. Thick lashes hooded sultry, suggestive eyes. "But I won't."

If this was a dream, and she prayed it was, she wanted to wake up. If this were indeed another world, one of the past, and she prayed that it wasn't, she was frightened and wanted to escape. She must. She was a prisoner to this warlock, to his thoughts . . . worse, to his desire.

He laid his palm across her breasts, and her heartbeat accelerated, her breath quickened. This shouldn't be happening to her, Beth thought. She was a doctor. She understood the biological makeup of the human body, its hormones, its drives. Despite this knowledge, she was attracted to him.

She was overwhelmed by contradictory emotions. He frightened her; he excited her. He was a man of the Middle Ages, one who did not respect women, her in particular. She was a liberated woman of the twentieth century. He represented all that she despised in men. Yet she wanted him. She was drawn to him, to his primitiveness.

Quaking from desire, from anger that she allowed him to unsettle her so easily, she brought her hands up and pushed against his chest, but she couldn't budge him. He leaned closer against her, more fully imprisoning her with his body.

"Bearnard won't tolerate your taking advantage of me." She grasped for any defense she could find. Again she peered over his shoulders as she schemed her freedom, thought of something to divert his attention.

"For a verity. He wants you dead not ravished. He would especially welcome your death at the hands of the warlock." He paused. "Perhaps that's the reason why he sent you. Rather than wanting you to get information for him, he wants us Galloways to kill you. And if the warlock did it himself, how much quicker Bearnard would get the church involved. The sooner I would be declared a heretic and executed."

"He didn't send me!" Beth clipped out the words.

"And he would be grievously humiliated if I should mate with you."

"He would be *grievously humiliated!*" She spat the words. "I don't care what he thinks, and neither should you. I'm the one who would be *grievously violated* and *grievously angered* if you should mate with me."

Lawren threw back his head and laughed. Finally he said, "Madam, do you jest with me? Have you forgotten that I am the man you begged to defrock you when you were ten-and-six?"

Beth felt the blood drain from her face.

"I am the man to whom you wrote when your brother betrothed you to Alastair. Again you begged me to mate with you."

"No," she exclaimed. "The letter? What did you do with it?"

"I destroyed it. No matter what happens to you, your brother can do nothing about it. He has no authority over Castle Galloway."

Lawren moved slightly, and she saw the pedestal holder. The candle flickered; hope glimmered. She would create a diversion by turning it over. She stopped fighting him.

"You're right," she said.

Lawren drew back and looked at her in surprise. She eased closer to the candle.

"I begged Bearnard not to make me do it"—she forced her voice to tremble—"but he is lord of the castle, my brother and the man whom I must obey."

He cocked a brow. "You were at the cloister."

"He came to get me," Beth replied, forcing herself to remember all he had said. "He had a plan and needed my help."

"Aye, now we get to the truth of the matter."

Again she scooted forward, stretching out her leg, her toe almost touching the pedestal.

"As you have guessed, Bearnard wonders how much of the nightlace you have."

She moved the few inches further. She drew in her breath, knowing that she would have the advantage of one kick only. She hoped she was close enough. She threw out her leg, cursed the skirt that bound her, and whacked the candle base. It thudded to the floor. Lawren spun around. The holder rolled in one direction, the candle in the other. Flames shot up, quickly licking up the straw that stuck out from beneath the rug.

"You fool!" he shouted.

He jumped away from her, striding to the far side of the room. The flames leaped higher. The fire frightened Beth. She hadn't realized how quickly it would spread; still, she couldn't think about it now. She must escape, but he was between her and the door. She had to knock him unconscious; she looked around for a weapon. She brushed against the folding table, almost knocking it over. She reached out and caught the toppling candlestick. It was heavy; she grasped it with both hands as he swooped up the basin. His back to her, he tossed the water on the floor, dousing the flame, stamping out the last embers. This was her opportunity . . . possibly her only one. She rushed toward him.

" 'Tis out!" he muttered. "In the future, madam, be more—"

He turned and Beth collided into his chest.

"—careful," he muttered. Dropping the basin, he fastened his hand around her wrist.

Pain shot up her arm; she released the candlestick and it fell to the floor.

"So you came here only to help the ill and the dying!" he charged. "Your purpose was not to kill me!"

"I only want to escape." She scratched his face, the trickle of blood quickly evident on his cheek. He growled, and she brought up her knee.

"Nay!" He clamped both of his legs around hers. Pinning her to the wall with his body, he caught both her wrists and held her hands above her head. "You're foolish if you think you'll get the best of me."

"And you're foolish if you think I'm going to give in to your abuse without a fight."

"Ten years ago you wouldn't have called my advances abuse." He jeered. "I should have taken you then, when you begged me to."

Beth knew he was speaking to Elspeth, about Elspeth, yet something made her say, "I've never begged a man to make love to me."

"We're not speaking of love, but of lust. And you were a lusty young woman of ten-and-six. You flung yourself at me, begging me to mate with you. I had a difficult time keeping my hands off you. There was no keeping your hands off me. You were ripe for the plucking."

Heat suffused Beth's face. She was glad she had no memories of that moment.

His lips curled in a bitter smile. "But I, the bastard, the man with no name or honor, did the honorable thing. I left you alone then and ignored the letter later. Fool I was."

Beth twisted and turned; she kicked his shins. "I slipped undetected into your castle, and I shall escape the same way." She grunted. "You'll not keep me here against my will."

Imprisoning her with his weight, still holding both her wrists above her head, Lawren lowered one arm. "You'll stay."

"Over my dead body." She squirmed and struggled, but only succeeded in insinuating herself more closely against him.

"Nay, madam, over your naked body." He slipped his free hand beneath the laces of her bodice and tugged.

Beth grabbed his hands. "No!"

"Aye, nudity is a simple way of humbling an arrogant spirit and revealing an Adair spy among us."

Courage flowed into Beth; she straightened her back, squared her shoulders. "Strip them off," she said. "You won't humble or stop me."

He chuckled. "Perhaps not, lady, but as chilly as the nights are, you will be hesitant to stray very far from the fire. And you surely wouldn't want a Galloway to find a beautiful, nude Adair woman running loose in the castle, especially not Elspeth nea Adair. No telling what he would do to you."

"You're vile!" Beth accused. "Wretched!"

"Aye, lady, I am all that and more. Be warned, I shall do whatever is necessary to keep you here."

Breathing deeply, she glared at him.

"But I also promise that as long as you behave, I shall protect you."

"Don't you mean do what you tell me to do?"

"Aye. Otherwise, you'll have to fend for yourself."

He moved his arm. As he raised it again, his hand grazed her stomach and abdomen. In the pale play of candle and firelight she saw the glint of his dagger blade. She was so frightened, her breath caught in her chest. He rested the blade at the circle of her neckline, the tip barely touching her skin.

His words, *until I've finished with you,* continued to pound in her head. Before they had angered her; now they frightened her. Dear God, he could be a pervert! A fine sheen of perspiration broke out all over her body; she brushed her palms down her skirt.

"What are you going to do to me?" she whispered.

"Keep you from leaving."

"How?" Her voice was a croak.

"Cut your clothing off."

Relief rushed through her, and if he had not been holding her up, she would have slid to the floor. Although she preferred to be dressed, she could part a lot easier with her clothing than with her life.

"Your heart is beating heavy," he murmured.

"You frighten me."

"I arouse you." His eyes were dark and impassioned.

She refused to be beguiled. "You frighten me."

He lowered his head, his gaze slowly sweeping down her neck and lingering on her breasts. Although she wore several layers of clothing, she felt as if he had undressed her. Beneath his heated gaze, she again trembled, and this time her trembling was from excitement, not fear.

"As you arouse me." When she said nothing, he added, "I've often wondered how changed our lives would be if I had made love to you ten years ago."

He raised his head.

"You'll never know, will you?" she said.

"Nay."

In the far recesses of his eyes Beth saw the stirring of another emotion, one she could not quite make out. A sadness? A gentleness? Whatever it was, it touched Beth. It melted the barriers of time and cultures. She and he were a man and a woman attracted to each other.

Unable to stare into his eyes any longer, knowing her vulnerability was revealed for him to see, Beth lowered her head. Firelight played on the blade he held between them. He tapped her chin with the tip and brought her face back up.

"As long as you do as I tell you, you have nothing to fear. I didn't take advantage of you before. I won't now." He dropped the dagger to her bodice. "But I'm not going to let you take advantage of me either."

Five

Lightly he slid the dagger beneath the bodice and cut the laces.

"You're taking advantage of me now," she said.

"I'm protecting my household."

The green tunic fell aside, the sleeves slipping down Beth's arms, revealing the soft white fabric of her undergarment . . . revealing the full upper swell of her breasts. The blade clinked against the chain of her locket. Her watch! A modern invention! A product of the twentieth century! She had forgotten about it until now.

He lifted the chain with the dagger and let the locket dangle in the air. "What is this? Your talisman?"

"My watch," she replied, taking heart.

He hiked a brow.

"A timepiece."

He looked more closely at it. "It works without the sun or water?"

She nodded and wiggled free of his clasp. "The little hand denotes the hour of the day or night. The large one the minutes. You have no such timepieces, do you?" Not waiting for an answer, she rushed on. "No, you don't. This proves I'm not Elspeth nea Adair."

His gaze riveted to hers. "It could be a witching device."

"It's an invention of the world from which I come."

He studied the locket, then removed the blade, letting it fall to her breast.

"Please, sit down and let me explain," she said.

He still held the knife between them.

"I beg of you," Beth said softly, "listen to me. Hear my story. Then judge who and what I am, the reason for my being here, whether or not I need to be naked."

Nodding curtly, he stepped away from her, returning his dagger to the scabbard. As he passed the round table in the center of the room, he stopped, idly running his hand over the book.

The book! The manuscript, Beth thought. Was this the manuscript?

"Make haste, madam," Lawren said, "and let me hear your tale. I must decide how you can best suit my purposes."

She wondered if this still included his wanting to sleep with her. Groping at the material of her dress, she pulled it over her shoulders and knotted the laces so that it would stay in place. The Highlander crossed the room, moving to the long, narrow trestle table that set in front of the opened window. Picking up one of the flagons, he filled two glasses with wine as Beth moved toward the settle.

Again she noted the colorful cushions and richly embroidered furniture linens that covered it. Only when she was about to sit down and the Highlander stood in front of her with the wine did she realize how large he was, how small the couch was, how close she would be to him if both of them sat on it. Spinning around, she chose one of the chairs instead. She was much too vulnerable and confused to be thrown into close proximity with this upsetting man.

"The settle is more comfortable, my lady." Amusement underscored Lawren's words.

" 'Tis a little too close to the fire for me." Beth hated that she sounded so prim. "I should be far too warm."

"I should imagine," he remarked as he handed her a glass of wine.

Again his voice was richly laced with amusement, and Beth glanced up at him. His face was devoid of expression, but his eyes glinted devilishly. Beth lowered her head and squirmed in the wooden, straight-backed chair, trying to find a more comfortable position.

"May I get you a cushion or two?" he asked.

Immediately Beth stilled. "No, thank you. I'm quite comfortable."

He smiled mockingly at her, then walked over to the fireplace. "I know how comfortable those chairs are, having spent many an hour on them myself."

Staring at the flames, rather than the dark stranger, Beth sipped her drink. Finally she said, "My story is so peculiar, you shall probably not believe it." She sighed. "I'm not even sure that I believe it myself."

He quaffed his wine, returned to the side table, and refilled his glass. He emptied this one as quickly and set his glass down. Then he gazed out the window. Silence stretched tautly through the room.

"Even with the telling you're likely to think of me as a witch." She looked beseechingly at him, at his back, and wished she knew what he was thinking. Was he listening or ignoring her? "But perhaps you'll believe that I'm not your enemy, that I'm not Elspeth nea Adair."

"The day is far spent, madam. I have recently returned from a long journey, and I'm exhausted. I have no desire to listen to silly prattle like this. Tell your story before I lose my patience." He raked his hand through his hair. Still he did not turn around to face her.

"As I've already told you, I'm Elizabeth Balfour," she said. "Like you, I'm an herbalist. A healer."

"How did you get Elspeth's bracelet?"

"I don't know. I'm not sure how I got here."

Turning, he walked to the hearth where he stood to one side of the chimneypiece in a pose that was reminiscent of the one he had assumed for the fresco . . . that he *would* assume for the fresco someday.

"Perhaps you are a witch," he softly taunted.

"No, I'm not from the Highlands . . . or from your time."

He folded his arms over his chest. "What is your time?"

She heard the skepticism in his voice, but couldn't stop. She must convince him. "The future. The closing years of the twentieth century."

"And you have come back to the closing years of the eleventh century!" A sardonic smile curling his lips, he leaned against the tapestry next to the mantel. "Do you often travel about in time?" He mocked.

"Nay, 'tis my first journey." Beth took a large gulp of wine. And if it were so, if she were indeed not dreaming or hallucinating, she hoped this would be her last time.

Lowering the glass, she said, "One minute I was staring at your portrait."

He hiked his brows. "My portrait?"

Nodding, she pointed at the wall between the bed and fireplace. "A fresco was painted there."

Glancing over his shoulder, he said, "As you can see, I have no portrait, over there or elsewhere."

"You will, lord," she muttered, then added, "The next I was spinning through space and landed here."

"Your tale is farfetched, madam."

Aye, Beth thought, it was, even to her. "I'm from the States."

"The States?"

"The United States of America. In the New World on the continent of North America."

"New world, old world!" He took menacing steps toward her. "I am a seasoned traveler, madam, and know there is only our world. What kind of fool do you take me for?"

"Right now, my lord, the New World has not been discovered and won't be discovered for three or four more hundred years. It will be even longer before it is settled by Europeans."

"Europeans or Englishmen?" he countered.

"Actually, my lord, the Irish claim that some of their monks were probably the first to reach America. But that claim can't be substantiated. We do have proof that Vikings set foot in America in the late 900's, but 'twas the Spaniards who claim having discovered it. That was—I mean, this will happen in 1492."

"If you are descended from Vikings and Spaniards, how do you come by the name of Balfour?"

Beth laughed. "Vikings and Spaniards were the first explorers to the New World, lord, but they were quickly followed by the English and French. The United States was settled primarily by the English."

"I might have known that the English were involved in the settling and probably in the displacing of the original inhabitants of your world."

"They were," Beth replied. "But if we go back far enough into the history of any country, we find that the present races have displaced earlier ones. If I remember my history correctly, the Scots were originally Irish raiders who sailed to Scotland and displaced the Picts."

"Nay, lady, you do not remember correctly. We Scots did not displace the Picts. We intermarried, our cultures becoming one."

Beth grinned. "Becoming Scottish."

His glower turned into a reluctant smile. "Mayhap."

Lawren strode to the settle, bunched the cushions, then sat down. Stretching his legs toward the fire, he crossed them at the ankles. Beth quietly told her story, starting with her internship at the institute and with the illness. As she talked, Lawren closed his eyes and she hoped he was listening, that he would believe her. She dismissed entirely the possibility that he was asleep or ignoring her.

She told him about the Galloway manuscript. The Highland nightlace. Minnie and Clyde Graham. Callum Galloway. The fresco. Her tumble into the past.

Lawren was quiet for a long time after she finished. Resting his chin on bridged hands, he asked, "If what you say is true, you are here in Elspeth's place. Where is she?"

The question startled Beth. Her entire presence in this century centered on Elspeth nea Adair. Yet Beth had been so concerned about her own plight, she had given no thought to what might have happened to the Scottish woman. She burned with shame to think she had been so selfish.

"Can she be in the twentieth century," he continued thoughtfully, "where she may have taken your place?"

Taken Beth's place! For the first time, the possibility, the probability, slapped Beth in the face. They could have exchanged places in time with each other. In traveling backward Beth had the definite advantage. She had a general knowledge of the world into which she had stepped. Not so Elspeth. If Beth were confused and frustrated being here in the past, she could only imagine what Elspeth must be enduring in the present. Knowing nothing about the people or customs, she would be pitched headlong into a fast-paced, high-tech world with a career she wasn't educated for, with morals and morays so different from hers. The thought that Elspeth might be her, might be a medical doctor, sent Beth reeling.

"Maybe we didn't change places," Beth murmured, her anxiety growing as another possibility, a far more dangerous one, formulated. She rose and paced in front of the fireplace. "Perhaps both of us are here."

Lawren shrugged. "With her being sequestered at the convent, it may be a while before we know."

Beth spun around, yanking at the material of her skirt, wishing she had a pair of jeans to wear. "Send someone to find out," she demanded, wondering which would be worse, Elspeth being in the future or here. "Then we'll know for sure."

"There's no rush."

"There is." Beth resumed her pacing, stopping every now and then to kick skirt material away from her feet. "Can you imagine what will happen if she is here and people find out that there are two Elspeths?"

"It should prove to be interesting."

"This isn't a joking matter!" She flounced to a stop. "Send one of your warriors, and—"

"I said we'll wait, madam, and wait we will."

He gave her a stony gaze that brooked no argument.

"Sit down," he ordered. "You're making me nervous."

Unceremoniously she flopped down on the settle.

"If your story is true," Lawren said, "it sounds as if Bearnard succeeds in destroying the nightlace and unleashes the plague on the world. What happens to me?"

Beth didn't know if Lawren were serious or not. One minute he seemed not to believe her, the next he did. "The manuscript isn't complete," she replied evasively. "I'm not really sure what happened." She looked at the cloth-bound book on the folding table.

Lawren followed the invisible line of her gaze. " 'Tis a Book of Prayer, not the manuscript you described. There is none like it among the Galloways. So few of us read and write, I would know about it."

"But there is some nightlace."

He turned his head, their gazes catching.

"You would not have let Bearnard destroy all of it," she insisted.

"I saved all that I could," he said, "but my supply is small. I pray there is more, that Bearnard has not destroyed all of it."

"My lord," Annie called, "your supper."

Rising, Lawren crossed the room, unbolted and opened the door. "Any word from the village or from Evan or Lowrie?"

"None."

Annie, followed by two boys and a girl, entered the room. The lads bore laden trays, the tantalizing aroma of food filling the room. The girl, carrying a basin of water, had several cloths draped over her shoulders.

"Annie's charges," Lawren explained. "Lundy, the oldest."

A teenage boy stared solemn-faced at Beth.

"Fenella."

A young girl about twelve years of age smiled.

"And Rae."

The youngest of the trio gave her a snaggle-toothed grin.

"Their parents died from the sickness," Lawren went on. "Fenella caught it and recovered without medication. The boys would have died, but Annie and I found them in time that we could tend to them. They have been with her ever since they recovered. They are as loyal to her as she is to me." His eyes twinkled. "Or as I am to her."

Annie grinned. "I like the flattery. It still works magic." She pointed to the round table. "Place the trays yonder, lads."

"Nay," Lawren said. "The evening has a chill. We will sit here before the fire." He glanced at Beth and smiled. "On the settle."

Beth curled her hand into a fist. He had gotten nowhere with his bullying, so he had evidently switched tactics. Before her eyes he metamorphosed from the crude and callous warrior to a suave man of the gentry, a lover. During her lifetime, Beth had witnessed this unconscionable changing of roles by people who wanted to manipulate, and she was accustomed to it. If she were in the twentieth century, she was confident that she could handle the situation with Lawren, but she wasn't there. She was here with him, and her womanly instincts alerted her that he fully planned to seduce her into giving him the information he sought, that he thought she knew. He had meant it when he said *until I've finished with you.*

"Make haste, lads," Annie said, "set the trays on the folding table. Then move the trestle table over here."

As soon as the words were out of the old woman's mouth, she saw the wrought-iron candleholder laying on the floor in front of the fireplace. Never raising her head, Annie looked around. At the toppled pedestal holder. The candle that had rolled across the room. The burned and water-soaked carpet. The empty basin.

"As you can see," Lawren said, "we had an accident."

Annie finally raised her head and fixed her gaze on his face.

Beth looked over at him also, at the tiny red line running from his temple down his cheek.

"Shall I clean up now?" Annie asked.

"Tomorrow will do just fine."

Annie looked up to see Lundy and Rae, standing to one side of her with the table. She stepped aside. When they had situated it in front of the settle, she straightened the linen that hung to the floor at both ends. Fenella ran over, her arms extended and Annie pulled off one of the cloths, a thick one, and spread it over the embroidered one. She stretched along the table's edge a long bolster of linen of several layers. Another snap of Annie's fingers, and the lads began to lay out the feast.

"Had I known you were returning home today, I would have cooked your favorite meal," Annie said. "Still, I think you will find the fare pleasing. Roasted duck. Onion and beef stew."

As the old woman talked, Beth gazed at the assortment of vegetables and the huge platter of roasted fowl. The heavy aroma of spices filled the room. Although she had recently eaten—or had she?—she found that she was ravenous. Annie set out two silver bowls.

When she laid a thick slice of brown bread in it, Lawren said, "One trencher is enough, good woman. Lady Elspeth and I shall share."

Removing one of the silver dishes, Annie asked, "And will you be sharing knife and spoon also?"

"Aye." He looked at Beth through hooded eyes. "I would be foolish to let an Adair have a knife of her own."

Annie pointedly looked at the mess in the room. "Aye, what with accidents like this happening."

Lawren caught Beth's hand; she twisted it, but his clasp tightened. He led her to the table . . . and the only place for her to sit was the settle.

She paused, not wanting to be any nearer to him than she could help. She disliked him and detested the way he regarded women, her or Elspeth in particular. With a firm hand to her shoulder he shoved her onto the seat. Then he unfastened his sword and dirk, draping the belts over the arm of the settle. When he sat down, Beth pushed as far into her corner as possible. Still he seemed to loom over her.

"Perhaps we should get another chair," she ventured.

"No one else is dining but us," he replied.

He scooted closer, and she felt the heat of his body as it brushed against hers.

"We're much too crowded on this," she said, wishing there was space between them, needing it to think, "I'm sure you will be much more comfortable if one of us is in a separate chair."

"Not I. I find this quite suitable." The girl held out the basin and Lawren washed his hands first. "The settle was built to be cozy."

The children snickered, and heat suffused Beth's cheeks. Was there nothing private in this place? While he dried his hands on the roll of linen, Beth washed hers. When she was finished, Annie removed the drying bolster from the table.

"Shall I stay and serve?" she asked.

"Nay, good woman."

Annie reached for the basin, lifting it carefully, but water splashed over the side onto Beth's lap. Beth and Lawren looked down at the same time. She reached for the cloth, but he was quicker. Beth caught his hand before he could touch her.

"Nay."

"Let me." He drew his hands out of hers. "We don't want your beautiful dress stained."

"Water doesn't generally stain," Beth murmured.

His eyes mesmerized her; his voice seduced. "We can't take that chance."

Gently, he wiped the water spot, rubbing his hand down her thigh. Beth closed her eyes and drew in her breath. She could reason all she wanted to, but her body totally disregarded the conclusions she drew. Even through the thickness of her clothes she felt a wash of heat, an awareness of the Highlander that she had felt for no other man, not even Sam.

The intensity of her emotions concerned Beth; her lunge through space had affected her far more seriously than she had suspected. She was beginning to think like them . . . and enjoying it.

"Tonight I long for quiet and intimacy." He smiled at Beth. "Elspeth shall have the honor of being my server."

Annie snorted. "Watch her sharply, lad, else she may do the *dishonor* of poisoning you rather than serving you. You may have an eternity of quietness."

Lawren laughed as he picked up the duck with both hands and ripped it apart. Grease splattered onto the table. He placed half the meat on his plate, half on Beth's. She grimaced as he wiped his hands on the top cloth.

Lawren took a bite of the fowl and chewed. A greedy gulp of wine washed it down. "Ah, Annie, my love, you've done yourself proud." He turned to Beth. "Are you not eating, my lady?"

Annie laughed softly. "Mayhap she's outraged because the meat has no carver. I hear tell the Adairs have manners like Saxons."

"Then, good woman," Lawren said, "we should not let Elspeth go lacking because she is dining with a savage Scot. Bring me the carving knives. I shall do the honor for her myself."

Annie handed him a wooden case, bound in leather; he opened it and withdrew two large knives.

"I am not a blade master for naught," he said.

Fascinated Beth watched as he sliced the meat from the bones, as he quickly and proficiently cut it into bite-size portions. A shiver slid down her spine. At the moment his dagger was an eating utensil, but only moments ago it had been his weapon, one she imagined he wielded proficiently. The moment the carving knives hit the table, Annie retrieved them. Lawren picked up his eating knife and speared a piece of the duck. He waved the morsel before Beth's nose, then rubbed it over her lips.

"Does it meet with your favor?" he asked.

She touched her tongue to her lips and savored the taste.

Staring and making Beth feel self-conscious, Annie and the children fanned around the table.

"Aye," she murmured.

"Open your mouth," he ordered softly, "and I shall feed you."

The soft tone wrapped her in a sensual web, drawing her ever closer to him, ever closer to intimacy. She parted her lips.

"Mayhap she's not an Adair," Lundy said. "She's far too docile."

Lawren smiled; the others giggled. The spell broken, Beth retreated to her corner away from Lawren and looked at the four gaping faces. Her cheeks burned with embarrassment. How easily she had complied with the barbarian.

"Come, lady," Lawren said. "Your food will get cold."

She shook her head. "I'm—not hungry."

He took the bite himself. As he slowly chewed, he studied her, then glanced at the servants. After swallowing, he said, "Mayhap you're shy, lady. I'll send the kindred away."

"Not on my account." While Beth didn't want to be entertainment for the servants, she also didn't wish to be alone with the Highlander, to be entertainment for him.

"Take the lads and lass and be gone, Annie," he ordered. "If I need you, I shall send for you."

Annie waved the children out of the room, and she followed them as far as the door. She turned. "Do you still want me to send Lowrie up here when he and Evan return?"

Lawren glanced down at Beth. "Nay. I'll talk with him later."

Annie frowned.

"Don't worry," Lawren said. "He will be glad to escape my wrath. Once he learns that I have a wench with me, he'll be hoping that I'll be in much happier spirits on the morrow."

"I pray so," Annie murmured.

She bent down and set upright the candle pedestal. She walked over to the fireplace, her feet squashing in the water-soaked carpet, where she picked up the candle and replaced it on the pedestal. Getting a piece of starter-wood from the fire, she lit the candle. The tiny flame spit and sputtered before it blazed to life. Tossing the kindling into the fire, Annie marched to the door. She turned and looked at Lawren.

"Beware of her. Like her brother, she is a collector of souls. And she wants yours."

Six

The foreboding words ringing through the room, Annie stepped out the door and disappeared.

"She truly hates me," Beth whispered, shocked by such overt hatred and cruelty.

"She hates all Adairs." Lawren laid the knife on the side of the trencher. "They killed her family. Husband. Three sons. Two daughters."

"She hates me in particular," Beth said.

" 'Tis easier to vent your hatred on one or two people than on many. As the figureheads of Clan Adair, you and Bearnard are the ones the Galloways hate the most."

Beth clasped her watch in her fist and squeezed. It had become her talisman, her only tangible evidence of the twentieth century. The hatred and hostility of these people were suffocating her. She had always thought of herself as a strong person, but she wasn't sure now. She didn't know how much more she could endure. Their casual disregard for human life astounded and frightened her. So easily they accused and threatened; as quickly they followed through their threat.

Lawren caught her hand and stopped her worried movement. "For now, Elspeth, there is nothing we can do. Let's put these matters aside and enjoy our meal."

Beth nearly choked on hysteria. He spoke as if it were a matter of insignificance, as if it were a piece of trash that could easily be disposed of and forgotten. Irritated by the power he wielded, the way he manipulated people and situations for his own purposes, she pulled her fist from beneath his hand.

"I may have no choice about many things while I'm here, but I won't accept that I am Elspeth." Her voice was sharp, her words clipped. "I refuse to answer to her name. Call me Beth. I know you said it's a man's name, but it's also mine. It's short for Elizabeth."

"It suits you," Lawren said.

She arched a brow.

"It means lively, and you are." He smiled. "You may call me Lawren."

"Why do you and your brother have the same name?"

After a moment Lawren said, "Are we to pretend that you are from the future and know nothing about the Adairs and the Galloways?"

The firelight flickered over his face, gilding his features, softening their austerity.

"Yes."

A ghost of a smile touched his lips. "So be it."

His smile widened, radiating from deep within his eyes. Once more Beth was amazed at how effortlessly he changed roles and cast a spell of sensuality around her, how quickly a gentle man . . . nay a seducer . . . replaced the barbarian.

He brushed a curl from her face, his fingers lingering on her temple. Without so much as a flicker of conscience, Beth allowed the dark stranger to seduce her. Willingly she became embroiled in his dangerous game.

"Beth from-the-future, 'tis not an unusual occurrence for brothers to carry the name of the same common ancestor. The first Lawren was my grandfather and a distant cousin to my brother. You do not do this in the twentieth century?"

Beth opened her mouth to say no, then she remembered an article she had read recently in a magazine about a set of quintuplets. All of them shared the common middle name of Mary.

"It happens sometimes," she admitted.

"So we may not be as different as you would like to believe."

Picking up a piece of duck with his fingers, he brought it to his mouth. Droplets of sauce glistened on his lips. Beth watched as he devoured even these with the tip of his tongue. He chewed slowly, thoroughly, and swallowed. Then he licked his fingers.

"This is delicious, lady." He tore another tender piece of meat from the bird and held it out to Beth.

Acutely aware of him, she opened her mouth and received the succulent morsel. She closed her lips. His fingers lightly brushed them as he released the food. Although it was an inadvertent caress, his touch sent sparks of pleasure throughout her body. The feeling intensified when he raised his hand to his lips and licked the sauce from fingers that so recently had been in her mouth. Unable to look away from him, Beth chewed the duck, feeling as if she were trapped in a sweet web of magic. He had called her a sorceress, an enchantress; yet he held her entranced.

"How does it taste?" he asked. "As good as the food from your world?"

"Better," she murmured.

His smile widened. "Mayhap we do many things better." He leaned closer to her. Using his thumb and index finger he touched the corners of her mouth. "A spot of grease."

The touch was so intimate Beth trembled.

He watched her eat the meat. She swallowed, and he lifted his beaker of wine and held it out to her. When she went to take it from him, he shook his head and laid the rim gently against her mouth.

"Drink slowly," he advised. " 'Tis a special wine to go with meals. It's hot with fire and spices."

She sipped the pungent drink.

When he removed the glass from her lips, he brought it to his. Riveting his gaze to hers, he placed his mouth over the spot where hers had been and took a swallow. Catching her breath, Beth felt as if he had kissed her.

He lowered the glass. "Hot and spicy. As I like it."

Beth could not have been more aware of him if he *had* kissed her.

He set the glass on the table, but kept his gaze on Beth's mouth. With a fingertip he traced in the fullness of her bottom lip. They quivered beneath his touch. "I am jealous, Beth of the future. I want your beautiful lips caressing me, not a beaker."

Her gaze slid down his neck to the untied laces and the parted material that revealed a wedge of crisp black hair. She wanted to caress him. The intensity of her desire surprised Beth. Since Sam had walked out on her, she had been numb, had not wanted to feel again for fear of being hurt. She had erected a protective barrier around her heart, her emotions, but had been surprised when she learned that it wasn't necessary. She had not even desired a man.

Now she wanted this Highland barbarian and wanted him with a fervor she had never experienced with Sam. Not understanding her motives, wondering why she was allowing her emotions free reign with this man, she moved her head away from his tantalizing touch and reached for the duck and tore off a piece.

He smiled. "I thought you were not hungry."

"I was embarrassed," she confessed. "Your kindred were laughing and making me feel self-conscious." Never giving manners a thought, she crammed the duck into her mouth, chewed, and swallowed. "I find now that I've had a taste, I'm ravenous." She took another bite.

"Aye," he murmured, a mischievous glint in his eyes, "I feel the same way, lady. But my hunger is no longer for roasted duck, and I believe yours isn't either."

Beth nearly choked. She wiped her hands on the cloth as she had seen Lawren do. His face still softened with amusement, he settled back against the cushions and sipped the wine. Through dark, smoldering eyes, he watched her. She took another bite of duck. He leaned forward, his hand moving toward her face. Before he could touch her again, could disconcert her more, Beth swiped the back of her hand across her mouth. He chuckled.

"You missed it."

He brushed the tips of his fingers around her mouth, lightly, provocatively, over and under her chin. Desire, hot and thick, flowed through her veins, taking residence in her lower stomach. She marshaled her willpower and drew away from him. She didn't want to, but she must. She had to protect herself.

Only moments ago she had tried to convince herself that this time displacement would not change her beliefs. But it already had. Within minutes, hundreds of years of education, of advancement, of sophistication were stripped away as if they were no more than a thin strip of veneer. Left exposed was a vulnerable woman.

She could so easily give herself to his charm, his sensuality. So easily she could forget who she was and her reason for being here. But she mustn't. She was the only hope her world had. Cheryl and the Alcinas—how many more?—were depending on her.

She grabbed the beaker. Having forgotten how strong the wine was, she took several large gulps to wash down her food. It burned her throat. Her eyes watered, and she coughed. He gently tapped her back. Draping his arm over her shoulder, he tugged her closer to him. Lifting the hem of the upper cloth, he wiped wine droplets from her mouth. He released the cloth. With callused hands that were gently abrasive to her skin, to her heart, he wiped the tears from her eyes and cheeks.

The Highlander was an enigma to Beth. One moment he was a barbarian; the next he was kind and gentle. Yet both facets of the man intrigued her. As a doctor, a researcher, she told herself, she wanted to find out more about him, about his complexities. If she had more time and didn't need to hunt the plant, she would dedicate herself to studying him, to discovering him layer by layer.

"Thank you," she whispered.

"I wish you were not an Adair."

Earlier it was he asking that they put these matters aside. Now it was her desire. "We agreed that I am Beth."

"Nay, my lady, I agreed to call you Beth for the night. In the morning you will be Elspeth," he said regretfully.

"Yes." How quickly the facade of pretense disintegrated. If she were here in the morning she would, in a sense, no longer be Elizabeth Balfour. She would be Elspeth, sister to Bearnard and enemy to the Galloways. Beth would have lost her family, her beloved parents, her two sisters, her niece and nephew, her brother-in-law. Tears threatened, but Beth blinked them back.

The thought of losing her identity frightened Beth. This was not her world or her people. She didn't belong here; she didn't want to have to assume another woman's thoughts, or body, or life. She wanted her own, and to have it she must return to the twentieth century. She couldn't allow herself to care for the Highlander, nor would she give in to this physical attraction they felt for each other. She must keep him at a distance, must search for a way back to her home . . . must search for the nightlace.

"And in the morning," she said, the only other sound in the room the crackle of the fire, "what will you be?"

"Dead, if Bearnard has his way. If not, alive and protector of a clan that grows more distrustful of me with each passing day."

Lawren withdrew his arm, shoved the settle back, and rose. "I don't suppose I can blame them. All their lives they have heard that my mother and I are servants of the devil."

"Your mother is alive?" Beth asked.

"Aye, she's in the mountains." He walked to the hearth. Holding the bottom of the chimneypiece with his hands, he stared into the fire. "My mother is a Highlander and a Christian, but she is also steeped in the tradition of the ancient ones. Angus, my father, loved her and would have married her, but the church forbade him to unless she renounced the old ways. She refused and was excommunicated from the church. Because of this, many have called her a witch. Still, she and Angus lived together and were happy."

"Is it because of her that you are called a warlock?"

"Aye." He kicked an ember into the hearth. "Finally the day came when the church forced my father into a political marriage. When I was ten-and-three years old, my mother and I left the Galloway stronghold for good and returned to her childhood home in the mountains. The church felt that my going with her was a recanting of my Christian faith. I never understood their argument, but I remained with her. There she taught me the ancient ways."

"Why are you here now?"

"Angus was fatally wounded a month ago during a cattle raid by the Adairs. The clan had need of a champion and a protector of the young chief who is only fifteen years of age, who will celebrate his sixteenth birth date in two weeks. My father sent his headmen, Evan and William, for me."

Beth recalled his mentioning these two men before and referring to them as headmen, but she didn't know what their titles meant. Lawren explained. A clan was made up mostly of *native men,* those related to the chief and to one another by blood ties. Also among a clan's members were *broken men.* These are individuals or groups from other clans who sought and obtained protection of the clan. Each group had its spokesman or headman over them.

Lawren lapsed into silence as he gazed at the fire. Finally he said, "I'll never forget the afternoon Evan and William told me about my father. I had thought Angus was invincible and would never die."

"He loved you," Beth said, "and trusted you, or he wouldn't have sent the headmen to get you."

"Aye, Angus cared for me in his way, and he did trust me," Lawren admitted, "but neither trust nor care for me motivated his actions. He was thinking only of the clan. He wanted me because of who I am. Who would be a better protector and champion than the bastard son, the warlock? He is twenty years older than his brother, a seasoned warrior and the one man Bearnard mac Adair truly fears." He added bitterly, "If Lawren the warlock dies, no one of importance is lost."

Lawren's tale touched Beth. Her sadness pushed aside desire, revealing her need to care, to give love and comfort. Feeling that he had need of a champion as much if not more so than his younger half-brother, she fought the impulse to run to him, to hold him in her arms, to protect him. None of the men to whom Beth had been attracted, not even Sam, had aroused her emotions to the intense pitch that this Highlander did.

"What about Lowrie's mother?" Beth asked. "Surely she had some say in matters. She could have been appointed his guardian."

"She died five years ago. Even if she were alive, she could be his guardian only, not his protector."

"You didn't have to come back to this humiliation. You could have stayed in the mountains. Your father rejected you when he married this other woman."

"Nay." Lawren straightened. "Angus wanted me to stay to be heir to the high seat of the Galloways. I chose to go with my mother."

"Still you returned," Beth persisted.

"I am a Highlander. We have our *enech,* our face or our honor, to think of. That night as I tended to my father's wounds, he stressed to me how dangerous a man Bearnard mac Adair was, how he was obsessed with the dream to create a separate kingdom out of the Highlands. One that would be separated from the Scottish Lowlands as well as from England."

Beth recalled the earlier conversation between Annie and Lawren.

"To have this kingdom," Lawren said, "he must first have the support of the Highland clans. The Galloways have always stood in the way of the Adairs and their obsession."

He said thoughtfully, "Angus believed his death would open the way for Bearnard. Lowrie is young and inexperienced. Angus also feared Lowrie would be killed before he reached his

sixteenth birthday and before he became chief." He paused.
"We have two more weeks before that day arrives."

"Why would Bearnard want to kill Lowrie before he became
chief?"

"To make sure that a man sympathetic to his cause is appointed temporary, possibly permanent, chief of the Galloways." Lawren threw several more logs onto the fire. "No
man is chief of a clan until after he has completed the High
Seat Ceremony, and only when he is chief can he appoint his
successor. If Lowrie were to die now, the Galloways high seat
would be vacant. Bearnard and other Highland chiefs would
persuade the bishop to ride into Castle Galloway and appoint
someone to preside over us until the clan has found its next
successor."

"You're an heir," Beth said. "Why can't you be chief?"

"Since our lineage is reckoned through our mothers, I am
the most direct heir," Lawren admitted, "but I am a bastard and
an outcast of the church. I can't ascend the high seat until I
have reestablished relationship with the church and the clan
votes in favor of me."

"If not you," Beth insisted, "surely the clan has already chosen someone else, even if he cannot be appointed yet."

"We have, but Bearnard is playing on the fears of the Highlanders by persuading them that I want to be chief. They fear
the warlock and don't want one in this position of authority.
They will insist that the bishop intercede." Using a fire poker,
he jabbed the logs further back in the fireplace. "He is a Saxon
with ideas like Bearnard. If that happens, Bearnard, in effect,
will have command of both the Adairs and the Galloways. He
will have the beginning of his kingdom."

"What will happen to you?"

"I shall probably be tried for heresy and found guilty."
Lawren returned to the table and picked up the wineglass. After
several swallows, he said, "Angus knew he was dying, that I
had done all for him that I could. He called Evan and William
to bear witness. I swore I would avenge his death and would

protect Lowrie until the lad became chief of the Galloways, until he could appoint his successor."

"The hatred between the Adairs and Galloways is deep-set," Beth said slowly, "too deep-set for it to have begun with an illness that may or may not escalate into a plague."

Lawren stared curiously at her, looking deeply in her eyes as if searching for something. "I wish I knew if you were playing with me or not. At times, I almost believe your time-traveling story."

"I know how difficult it must be for you to believe me," Beth said, "but it's true."

He breathed in deeply, then nodded. "Aye, the hatred goes back many years, culminating with the illness. At one time the glens along Loch Gleann nan Duir belonged to the Adairs. They were small in number then and were attacked by a much stronger clan to the north. Part of the Adairs, those who lived along the loch, appealed to my grandfather two-times-removed, Keith mac Galloway, for protection. He was a hard man and refused to help unless they became part of the clan and gave the glens to the Galloways."

"This group of Adairs became *broken men* in your clan?"

"Aye, Evan is headman to them."

"Can you trust these people? After all, they are Adairs."

"Through the years, they have intermarried with the Galloways," Lawren replied. "They are loyal to us."

"What happened to the Adairs who did not become part of the Galloways?"

"They moved further east and have hated us ever since. They are still a small clan, but they have survived, and Bearnard is their chief."

Lawren ran a finger around the rim of the glass. "There was no way the Adairs could get the Gleann nan Duir until this illness hit us."

Lawren stopped talking, a bleak silence falling over the room. Beth waited. Eventually he set the beaker aside.

"At first the people didn't listen to Bearnard's claim that I had brought a curse on them," he said, "but as more and more of them have died, they are beginning to believe. It won't be long before even the Galloways clamor for a trial. They fear a warlock more than an overzealous Saxon." He gave her a tight smile. "Since you come from the future, Beth, perhaps you know more about this than I do."

"Not much," she murmured. "As I told you before, the manuscript is not intact." She searched his face. "Do you believe my story?"

"Does it matter?"

"Yes."

His eyes shadowed. "I want to."

"Please help me find a way back to my time."

His answer was slow in coming. "Understand this, lady, whether you are an Adair or a traveler from the future, whether you are Elspeth or Beth, it matters not." His eyes were soft, his voice kind, but his words were firm with resolve. "Fate has sent you to me, and I shall do all in my power to keep you."

"You won't help me?"

"A part of me wants to help you," he confessed, "but the greater part of me is selfish and wants to keep you."

"If I stay here as Elspeth," Beth whispered, "you will still have to reckon with Bearnard and the church."

"Either way that is inevitable."

Beth's head began to ache; she was weak and flushed. She would be glad when she returned home . . . or when she acclimated to the eleventh century. Her transport back in time was depleting her energy, making her sluggish, unable to think sharply.

She pushed aside her lethargy. "If you think I am Elspeth, so will Bearnard and the bishop, they . . . won't allow you to keep me."

"My greatest fear is not Bearnard or the bishop." He paused, and the color of his eyes deepened. " 'Tis myself. And my feelings for you."

Surprised, she said, "You are frightened of me?"

"Of my feelings for you. I care about you."

"Lust for me," Beth corrected.

"Sometimes lust," he agreed. "Most times more."

"Is that so wrong?"

She realized she was eagerly anticipating his answer, that she wished he were thinking of her as Beth and not Elspeth.

"Aye, to care so much that I betray my honor."

Her eagerness plummeted.

"That's what your brother is counting on."

"If Bearnard truly believes you will succumb to my wiles," Beth said, "he has misjudged you. And if you truly believe you care about me, you are deluding yourself. It's easy to say you care about someone, but true caring is more than the utterance of a statement. You haven't begun to fathom the meaning of the word, much less to feel the emotion."

"Emotions should be kept private, lady. If you reveal them, your enemy can use them against you. They make the most deadly and effective weapon of all weapons."

He strode to the dining table and picked up the wine beaker, draining it in one gulp. After he was finished, he fastened his weapons about his waist, then arranged his tartan over his shoulder.

As he tucked his gloves beneath his belt, she walked to him. "Are you taking me with you?"

"Nay. I have matters to discuss with the kindred that I don't wish you to overhear."

"But you'll tell them about me?"

He raised his head. "Aye." He smiled slightly and slid his fingers through the strands of hair that escaped her braid. "I would that it could be different, lady, but it can't. Mayhap if we had met in your time, rather than mine."

In her time rather his! His words echoed through her mind, and she mentally saw the emaciated form of Callum Galloway as he sat slump-shouldered in the wheelchair. If she were Elspeth nea Adair here, would he be Callum Galloway in her world?

"Perhaps we would no longer be enemies," Lawren said.

"Perhaps." For the time being she was weary of arguing with him.

"Don't mention anything about being a time-traveler to any of the kindred," Lawren said. "It will only convince them that you're a witch and will make your situation worse. 'Twould be a simple matter for them to believe witch and warlock have joined together."

She nodded.

"I wish I could stay with you," he said, "but I must go."

As he stepped away from her, Beth caught his arm. "Would you have really ravished me?"

He visually caressed her face, his gaze moving from her lips to her eyes. "I was frustrated because you were here perhaps spying for your brother, mayhap for yourself. I was angry because you deliberately tried to set my home on fire. For either crime, I would have felt justified in punishing you." He paused. "But I consider mating a pleasure, not a punishment. When I mate with a woman, lass, 'tis because she sets my blood afire with desire not because she angers me."

The words hung sensuously between them.

Her eyes, framed by long lashes, sparkled. Her face filled with rosy color; her lips parted. Candlelight shone on her long auburn braid. Small, wispy tendrils curled around her face to brush against her flushed cheeks. She was truly the most beautiful, most desirable woman Lawren had ever known.

She had accused him of not caring; she had been wrong. He had been attracted to her from the moment he had first seen her ten years ago. He had dreamed and fantasized about her during the years, but had never thought to touch her, to love her. He had had women through the years, but this woman— Beth or Elspeth?—kindled a new and exciting desire in him, one he had not experienced in a long time.

Now that he had a taste of her, he wanted more . . . whether or not she was a witch or a time-traveler . . . or a liar or deceiver. He wanted to explore the mysteries that made this woman. But his desires would never come to fruition. The same reasons that had prohibited him from making love to her ten years ago did so today. She was still a chief's daughter, still a Christian; he was a bastard, excommunicated from the church, and branded a warlock.

He could take the lass. It would be an easy task. He was more powerful than she. But he also knew he would do nothing to betray her. His integrity—misplaced as many of his acquaintances pointed out—would not allow him to knowingly bring shame on Beth. Also he had to remember his promise to his father. Duty and honor had to be his first priority.

"Promise me that you won't try to escape."

"Or what? You'll strip me of my clothing?" Without waiting for an answer, she said, "Go ahead. Nudity might slow me down, but it won't stop me."

"I've told you that it's not safe for you to be outside my chambers. Once you leave them, I can't guarantee what the kindred will do to you."

"I understand."

He was reluctant to leave her. "If you were of my world, you would. If you are from another one, I'm not sure you do. Our anger and hatred run deep."

She nodded.

He sighed but made no effort to carry through his threat. "Don't try to leave through the windows. 'Twould be a sure death. The walls are precipitous."

She looked at the huge arched windows and the recessed alcoves. "I know."

"High and perilously steep." When she didn't respond, he added, "There is no way in or out, and I shall set guards outside the door."

When he was gone, the door bolted from the outside, Beth paced the room. Contemplating how she could get back to the twentieth century, she meandered to the window, stepping into the alcove. Sitting on one of the benches she propped her elbows on the casement and gazed into the night shadows. Far below she heard the soft gurgle of Loch Gleann nan Duir.

The sound filled her with aching homesickness. It reminded her of the brook that ran behind her parents' country home, about one hundred miles inland from San Diego. She wanted to be there now, wanted to hear her mother's cheerful laughter, her father's booming voice assuring her that all was well. She wanted to be enveloped by their love.

It was possible she would never see them again. Her sisters, she would miss them, already missed them. They were her childhood playmates, at times her closest friends and confidantes, at other times they were recipients of her anger and frustration. But through it all, they loved one another. Julienne, the oldest by three years, married with a four-year-old daughter and a year-old son. Ginger, the youngest, graduating from college, engaged to be engaged.

Beth's homesickness deepened. She wanted to see her friends and colleagues . . . her patients. But she might never be able to return; she might be destined to remain here. Locked in the past! Never to return! The thought whirled through her mind, and panic rose.

The Highland chill wrapped around her, and she drew back from the window, closing the shutters. Once again she aimlessly wandered the room. She finally stopped in front of the tapestry that hung on the wall between the bed and fireplace where Lawren's portrait would be painted in the future.

This is where she had been standing when she was propelled back through time, she thought. What had she been doing? Touching the painting. But there was no fresco . . . if it indeed had been the medium through which she traveled. She moved the tapestry aside and ran her hands over the plastered wall inch by inch. Nothing. She did it again . . . again . . . and again. Nothing happened.

Weary and frightened, she finally returned to the settle and sat down, stretching her legs out to the fire. After hours of pondering the situation, of coming to no solution, Beth rose and walked to the bed. As she had done once before—so long ago, it seemed, in her other lifetime—she touched the canopy that was pulled aside; she brushed her palm over the beautifully woven covers.

She had wondered if this suite belonged to the warlock, if he slept on this bed. Her fantasy that he did had lent it a sensuality Beth found exciting, and her excitement was growing with the knowledge that this was indeed his room, indeed his bed.

She lay down, curling into a ball and bunching one of the soft bolsters beneath her head. She had ceased believing she was dreaming or hallucinating. She accepted that she had not only traveled through time but was locked in the past. And she didn't have a Dorian or a brilliant scientist to help her get back to her own world.

Seven

Startled, not sure what had awakened her, Beth bolted up in the middle of the canopied bed. Her heart beating erratically, she clutched the cover to her chest and looked around the room, a blend of firelight and shadows. As she brushed a strand of hair from her face, she glanced at the chest next to the head of the bed. The round table in the center of the room. The straight-backed chair. The settle.

She sighed, slumped, and bit back her frustration, her tears. She was still in the past. Despair, a lead weight, settled heavily on her heart; she felt sure she would buckle beneath the load. She had gone to sleep, had awakened, and was still here. Imprisoned by the past.

Outside she heard voices and the grate of the bolt. She scooted off the bed and hurried over to the settle. Lawren was returning, and she didn't want him to find her on the bed. Nervously she looked at her watch. Several hours had passed; it was nearly midnight. She straightened her skirt and brushed loose strands of hair from her face.

The door opened. The two guards, seeing her for the first time, peered curiously. As they stepped aside, however, it was Annie, not Lawren, who walked in. Disappointed, Beth stood behind the settle.

"You're wanted in the great hall," the woman said.

"Lawren told me not to leave this room."

"He sent me to fetch you."

"How do I know that?"

The clash of wills was tangible, hostile.

"You have to take my word for it," Annie hissed.

"You could be leading me into a trap."

"Don't think I wouldn't like to. You may be high and mighty in Adair Castle, but you're nothing here. You have no rights or privileges and can question no one, not even the lowliest of servants." The pale blue eyes narrowed. "I don't like you. I want you punished for all the wrongs you Adairs have done to us."

"Don't you think my being imprisoned is punishment enough?" Beth asked.

"Not nearly."

Beth flinched at the blatant hatred reflected on the woman's countenance and in her voice.

Annie stepped closer. Although Beth was five-seven, Annie towered over her and made her feel quite small and powerless. Still she stood her ground, refusing to be intimidated.

"Be grateful that I trust Lawren to do what is right," Annie said. "If I didn't, I'd take your eye. Your tooth. Your life."

Beth didn't doubt Annie for a second. Nothing, absolutely nothing would surprise her anymore. She thanked her lucky star that she had been born centuries later. As the thought passed through her mind, she felt the gurgle of hysterical laughter. What good was having been born in the twentieth century doing her when she was stuck in the antiquated past?

"Come," Annie snapped. "We have no time to spare. Lawren must prove to the kindred that you are his prisoner."

Beth looked down at her wrinkled dress, at the laces knotted on her bodice.

"No need for you to be getting any fancy ideas about changing clothes." Annie grabbed Beth by the arm, her gnarled and powerful fingers biting into the tender flesh. "Now let's go."

Beth jerked away and glared at the servant. "I'll follow, but I won't allow you to drag me."

Anger flashed in Annie's eyes, and her lips thinned. Finally she harumphed and stamped out ahead of Beth. Down the hallway and around winding stairs they moved, the guards dogging Beth's heels.

The closer they came to the great hall, the louder the music grew, the more frightened Beth became. When she and Annie reached a huge arched doorway, Annie swept aside the tapestry covering and led the way into the banquet hall. Beth followed, pausing in the doorway to look around the enormous room. Ablaze with light, it was a flurry of activity.

Trestle tables and benches, filled with Galloways, extended from either end of the dais and lined the wall. The kindred were talking and laughing, drinking wine and offering toasts. Musicians sat in one corner, brightly lit with torches; in front of them dancers frolicked. In the center of the room a young boy juggled.

The fireplace spread across the entire width of the room, its golden red flames leaping into the air. Seven arched doors, covered in richly woven tapestries, opened into the room. Burning torches and candles were suspended from corbels on either side of all entryways. Candle chandeliers, raised and lowered by a rope, hung from the ceiling.

The walls, like those in the master suite, were covered with a thick coat of plaster. Some were washed in various colors; others were decorated with painted cloth hangings and with weapons of all sorts. The various decorations provided splashes of brilliant hues and contrasting textures. Reeds and sweet-smelling herbs covered the floor.

At the far end of the hall Lawren sat at the high table. Light from the torches attached to the wall on either side of the high seat glistened in his black hair and shadowed his face. Gone was the almost-friendly, almost-believing man who had left her earlier. In his place was a Highland chieftain, a warrior, a man of the eleventh century. His hard, craggy face seemed to be chiseled from the Highland mountains he called home. Next to him sat a burly warrior about Lawren's age. His thick red hair hung in a single plait as did his beard. From Annie's description of the man, Beth assumed this was Sloane.

Lawren's demeanor added to Beth's fears. Here in the great hall, surrounded by his clansmen, he seemed bigger, more imposing, formidable. In the master's suite she had thought him different from other Highlanders, separated from them. Now he was one of them.

"Lawren," the juggler shouted. "Look! Five balls."

"That's no challenge," shouted a kinsmen. "I can do that with my eyes closed. Throw a dirk or two with the balls."

The lad turned to look at his heckler, a brawny man with a puffy red scar running diagonally across his face. "If you think you can, William mac Galloway, come have a hand at it."

"I don't think I can, lad," the man called out. "I know I can, but I won't be doing it tonight." He grinned and winked. "Having just returned to the stronghold from my visit to the village, I'm tired."

"And you're a talker, William mac Galloway!" the boy retorted. "You've never juggled with balls much less with daggers."

As the youth spoke, his gaze slid beyond the kinsman to the door . . . to Beth. His eyes rounded; his mouth went slack, and his arms fell to his side. The balls thudded to the rush-carpeted floor. Guffaws of laughter echoed through the room.

The lad pointed and shouted. "Here she is! The Adair wench!"

"Bearnard's sister," the heckler yelled.

Fearfully, Beth froze in the doorway. Across the great hall, spoons dropped to the table; tankards lowered; hands held suspended in midair sopped-bread. All noises subsided until silence heavily enshrouded the room. Hostility, hatred was palpable. It drummed like a heartbeat.

Although the night was chilly, Beth was flushed, her palms clammy. Her heart raced, and her breathing was quick, uneven. The same loathing she had seen in Annie's face was now reflected collectively in theirs.

"Get on with you," Annie ordered.

Beth still couldn't move. Her legs felt as if they were glued

to the floor. She stared into a sea of hostile faces. She looked
at the high table. Lawren had told her he was her only hope,
her only protector. He was. She had to get to him, before the
Galloways got to her. But the walk across the hall was long and
menacing. She remembered his warning about her trying to
escape through the window, about the perilous descent on the
outer wall of the castle. At the moment nothing seemed more
perilous than this walk across the hall. She didn't know if she
had the strength or the endurance to make it.

"I said move." Annie gouged her in the small of the back.

Beth stumbled forward. With each step she took toward
Lawren, the farther away he seemed to be. She was weak and
queasy; her joints ached. She wiped her hand across her moist
brow, then slid it beneath her hair at the nape of her neck. This
time displacement or dream or hallucination—whatever it
was—was having a physical effect on her. This was the second
time she had noticed how bad she felt, almost as if she were
coming down with the flu.

"Let's have some fun with her," the scar-faced heckler
shouted. He rose, pulling his dirk from its scabbard.

"Aye," others chimed in as they also rose.

"Nay, William!" Lawren's voice cut through the clamor.

The man stood his ground. Through hazy eyes Beth looked
from William to Lawren who had risen and stood like a giant
on the dais. Like an avenging angel. Beth didn't care that he
looked angry and forbidding; he was her savior.

"She is my prisoner."

All but William fell back.

"Sloane," Lawren said.

The redheaded warrior rose. William stepped aside.

"Come, Elspeth," Lawren said.

Frightened of Lawren but more frightened of the Galloways
who thronged the hall, Beth scurried toward him. Annie's cackle
chased her across the room. Finally Beth reached the dais, ascended the three steps, and moved to the high seat. Lawren
clasped her hand in his, and she was glad. For the moment she

allowed his strength, his warmth, his confidence to flow into her. He directed her to the seat of honor next to him.

"You'll let an Adair share the high seat with you?" William snarled.

"For a verity," Lawren replied, sitting down beside her. Unperturbed, he said, "As Annie reminded me earlier today, we believe in the teachings of the holy book." He paused, letting the word sink in. "An eye for an eye, a tooth for a tooth."

A chorus of ayes sang out.

"So be it," Lawren declared. "Right now she will share the high seat with me. When the time comes, I shall share the bed with her."

Laughter filled the hall, and Beth tensed. Humiliation and anger replaced her fear and infused her with determination, with courage. Never had she been treated like she was subhuman. Who did these people think they were? She tried to jerk her hand from Lawren's, but his grip tightened.

"Don't fight me," he warned in an undertone. "You can't win." Louder he said, "Make no mistake, lads, Elspeth nea Adair is *my* prisoner. I will not allow anything untoward to happen to her until I no longer have use for her." He raised his tankard. "Let us show an Adair how the Galloways celebrate."

The building resounded with shouts and huzzahs. Tankards were raised. Musicians played a fanfare. The juggler retrieved his balls and began his entertaining.

"To Elspeth nea Adair," Lawren shouted. "May she bring us all—" He smiled at Beth. "Nay, may she bring us more than we wish for."

Another swell of ayes was drowned in tankards of wine. Lawren called for more food.

"Food, aye," William shouted, "but wine also."

Lawren laughed and ordered his fine, imported wine.

After he and Beth sat down, she murmured, "That man with the puffy scar is one of your headmen?"

"Aye, the one who rode to the village," Lawren replied.

"Was it the sleeping-death?"

He shrugged. Beth hoped he would say more, would mention his mother, but he didn't.

After a while she said, "All of this celebration is over one Adair prisoner."

"Not one Adair," he replied, "but one Adair who is Bearnard's sister. For the first time in months we Galloways have something of value with which to bargain with both Bearnard and the church."

He reminded her that she was nothing more than a pawn.

"What if they don't negotiate?"

"They will," Lawren assured her. " 'Tis in the best interest of both. The church will make sure that Bearnard frees you from the clutches of the warlock. One, because they care about you and your soul. Second, because they care about your inheritance. You have given them reason to believe you may enter the sisterhood and donate your widow's inheritance to the church."

He paused, then said, "Bearnard will because he wants to ensure the support of the church in his acquisition of land and power." Lawren pushed back in the chair, propped his elbows on the armrests, and bridged his fingers. "Aye, they will bargain. 'Tis a way of life with us. A very profitable way, I must add."

"For you, not for me," she replied coolly.

"You might as well get accustomed to the idea and accept it, lady. This may or may not have been your world, but it is now. Mayhap you are here to stay! Never to leave!"

His words pierced Beth's heart. She had thought them, had feared they might be true, but she had not verbalized them. That seemed to imbue them with life, with substance. She gripped the arms of the chair tightly.

"Riders," a man shouted from the far end of the hall. "They're too far away for us to identify."

Lawren nodded, glanced over at the musicians and they began to play. Although an air of revelry yet seemed to hang over the room, Beth felt the subtle change in the atmosphere. The kindred were alert and ready for any surprises. Hands were on weapon hilts; eyes glued to the doors. As they waited, time dragged, suspense mounted.

Finally the hall doors were flung open, and a burly man, his silvered hair tousled about his face, strode into the room. His tartan plaid and tunic were dirty and bloodstained.

"Evan," Lawren murmured.

The older man looked directly at the dais, his weathered face breaking into a semblance of a smile when he saw Lawren. His boots thudded against the rush carpet as he marched down the hall.

When he reached the high table, he said, " 'Tis good to see you, laird. I trust you had a safe and profitable journey."

"A safe one," Lawren replied, straining to see over Evan's shoulders. "Lowrie?" he asked. "Did you find him?"

"Aye." Evan paused, swallowed. When he spoke, his voice was thick, his eyes bright. "He and the lads were attacked by Adairs. Jamie and Lowrie are wounded. Rob is dead."

From the depths of the room a woman screamed out. "Nay! He canna be. Rob is only a lad. The only one I have left."

A man embraced the crying woman and pressed her face against his chest.

"At Mountain Cat Canyon?" Disbelief underscored Lawren's words as a murmur of incredulity swept through the great hall.

Evan nodded. "Two of the attackers were riding out of the canyon when we arrived. At the time we didn't know what had happened, but they refused to stop and acknowledge our greeting. I sent some of the kindred after them. I led the others into the canyon. That's when we found the lads. One of my men died also. Damh."

A mature woman pushed up from the table, gazed disbelievingly at Evan. Tears ran down her cheeks as she silently cried. Several other women moved toward her.

"Did you reckon with them as they had done with us?" Lawren demanded as he stood and strode toward his headman. "Any dead? Prisoners?"

"Nay."

"Nay!" Lawren bellowed. "They rode through our lines without our knowing about it, wounded two lads, killed another, and escaped! And we don't even have a prisoner! We don't even know for sure that it was the Adairs."

"How could it happen?" William demanded. "How did they get so deep into our territory without our knowing about it? One of our men should have spotted them. We should have stopped them at the border."

"Should have!" Lawren slammed his fist against a table. "Should have, but did not! Are the Galloways in league with the Adairs?"

"How did they escape, Evan?" William asked. "Where did they go?"

"The lads reported that they seemed to disappear," Evan replied. "They lost all signs of them."

" 'Tis odd the Adairs know our territory so well they can ride off without so much as a skirmish." Lawren exclaimed. "Without leaving so much as a sign of their having been here."

"I thought so, too," Evan replied.

"We are no longer safe within our own territory," someone shouted. More joined the clamor: "Adairs invaded our territory. Rob and Damh are dead. Lowrie and Jamie wounded."

Fear was their pulse; revenge their heartbeat.

"The lads are bringing Lowrie and Jamie up in an ox-wagon," Evan said.

"Both of them?" Lawren asked. "In an ox-wagon?" Perplexed, he stared at his headman. "Are both hurt . . . nigh to death?"

"Only Lowrie. He was hit on the head with a hammer."

"His skull is bashed in," Lawren said.

"Nay," came Evan's reply. "He wore a helmet, but his head is badly bruised. He's barely breathing and is senseless. He doesn't respond to anyone."

"Sure death." The words echoed ominously through the hall.

"I've seen many a warrior die from wounds where the swelling goes inward."

A hammer blow to the head, Beth thought. The possibility of intercranial bleeding! And they were traveling in an ox-wagon. Even she knew this was one of the slowest modes of transportation available. If only they had brought Lowrie home straightway on a horse. If only he were here for her to examine. Perhaps she could save him. She worried that if he were not already dead he would be by the time he arrived at the castle.

An elderly woman shoved through the kinsmen and laid her hand on Evan's arm. "You said Jamie was going to be all right?"

Evan turned to her. "Aye, good mother. Your grandson took an arrow in the shoulder, and he's lost a great deal of blood, but his wound is clean."

Tears tracked down the wrinkled face.

"It will have to be cauterized."

"I shall attend to that," she replied. "I've taken care of many a wounded warrior in my day. Not a Galloway is a better nurse than I am." She gave a shaky laugh. "None can burn a wound as well as I."

"For a verity, Elsa," Evan replied kindly. " 'Twas you, good mother, who tended me. A right nice scar you gave me."

"You earned the scar in battle. 'Twas I who made sure it did not become inflamed." She sniffed and, brushing her sleeve over her eyes and face, backed away.

"Is Jamie conscious?" Lawren asked Evan.

"Aye, 'twas when I left him. He's the one who told us what happened." Evan laid his hand on Lawren's shoulder. "I sent one of the lads to summon Caledonia."

A shock of surprise rippled through the kindred.

"You dinna?" William exclaimed. "All we need now is to have the witch here at the castle."

"Aye." Evan's gaze flickered over to William, back to Lawren. "That is what we need. If anyone can help Lowrie, 'tis Lawren's mother."

"We need a priest, not a witch," William said.

In a tone that was almost an apology, Evan said, "I sent for him."

Lawren nodded. "I suppose we shall be needing one before first light. Whom did you send for?"

"Shawe," Evan replied.

"Aye, he's from the Lowlands, but he's a Scotsman."

"I didn't want the bishop here any sooner than was necessary."

No more had to be said. All understood the serious and far-reaching consequences of Lowrie's premature death. They grew quiet.

"The cattle are all right?" Lawren asked dully.

"They seem to be," Evan replied. "We've separated them and are hand-feeding them, so we can examine their excrement to see if they might have eaten something that poisoned them. The herdsmen are keeping close watch to see if others are sick."

"If they were poisoned," William said, "it was no accident. 'Twas done by an Adair to get us out of the way while they massacred our chief." He stamped to the center of the hall. "How many more times will a priest be journeying to the Galloway stronghold so that we can bury yet another chief?" He swung his fist in the air. "Is this the way we shall honor our holy days? At Easter instead of our celebrating the resurrection of our Lord and Savior, we mourned the death of our chief. At summer solstice shall we be mourning the death of yet another?"

His words inflamed the kindred, and Beth saw a return of spirit, of resolve. As he continued to rant and rave about injustices and revenge, he worked the crowd to a frenzied level. At any moment Beth feared the Galloways would become an out-of-control mob.

"Then we shall fight the Adairs!" William jerked his sword from the sheath.

He stood beneath one of the chandeliers hanging from the beamed ceiling; candlelight cast his scarred face in ominous shadows. Brandished swords encircled him, their silver blades a menacing gleam in the firelight.

"Nay, they want to ride deep within the Galloway country. Let them. Let them ride to us," William suggested. "Let us send them the head of the wench."

Beth felt every eye in the building rivet to her. Shouts of "kill the wench" resounded. "Draw and quarter her!" others demanded. From another corner came "torture her." Several ran toward the platform. His sword drawn, Sloane stepped between her and them.

The barbaric words clamored through Beth's mind; her heart beat to the people's frenzied cries. Inwardly she recoiled, but forced herself to remain in the chair, forced herself to breathe deeply, slowly, to look calm. But she was more frightened than she had ever been in her life. In fact, she had never known fear until now.

She was not born an Adair, but as long as she remained in the eleventh century she was one. As an Adair she was in danger here at Castle Galloway. Animosity, not mere dislike, separated the Adairs and the Galloways and motivated their actions. Death and war were the chosen methods of settling their differences. If the Galloways had their way, her blood—Beth's Balfour's blood—would be mingled with theirs.

Lawren grabbed one of the men by the arm and flung him aside. The others pulled up short. As if they were animals, they snarled at him. He glared at them. He stepped forward; they scattered.

"Killing her won't help Lowrie or Jamie. It won't bring Rob back."

"Nay," William said, "but killing an Adair will bolster our spirits and deflate the Adairs'."

A chorus of exuberant ayes rang out.

"We have to keep our wits about us," Lawren argued. "If we kill the woman, we may be avenging the wrongs done to us, but we'll be giving up our advantage. Actually we'll be giving Bearnard what he wants."

Evan caught Lawren by the shoulder and spun him around. "You have an Adair wench?"

William pointed to the high table. "Not just an Adair wench, headman, but Elspeth herself."

Stupefied, Evan stepped forward and squinted at Beth, his jaw dropping. His head swiveled in Lawren's direction. "How did you get her?"

"Providence," Lawren replied.

His gaze caught Beth's, and she realized he had not mentioned to any of his clansmen how she might have gotten into the castle. She hoped this meant that he believed her.

"This couldn't have happened at a better time." Evan's countenance brightened visibly. "Under other circumstances, Lawren, she is worth more to us alive, but not now. Lowrie is as good as dead. We can't think about how her death will benefit Bearnard, but how it will affect the rest of the Adairs. We must execute her and send her head to Bearnard."

Evan said the words as if the task were as easily accomplished as picking a flower from a bush, Beth thought. Again she was dismayed and frightened by their total disregard for human life.

"We must send a message to the Adairs, to all the clans in the Highlands, letting them know the Galloways are yet the strongest clan among them, not only able to defend their territories but willing. Let us show them that we Galloways will not be misused."

Warriors, slapping their hands on the table, shouted their ayes.

"Kill the lass, Lawren," Evan insisted.

All looked expectantly at Lawren.

Lawren had intervened successfully a moment ago, but Beth doubted that he would be able to dissuade the Galloways this time. He had said earlier that they were greedy for revenge, and they were. She saw it in their eyes, their expressions, the way they moved. She was the prey, they the predators.

"What about it, Lawren?" Evan asked. "Did you mean what you said earlier?"

Looking directly at his headman, Lawren said, "I meant everything I said, including we shall use her to bargain with."

Evan, breathing deeply, drew back and frowned. Finally he said, "If you won't kill her, rally the lads and let's ride. Let us wreak havoc with the Adairs as they have done to us."

"We have work to do here first," Lawren said. "We have a burying and two wounded men to tend to. After we have taken care of them, we shall discuss the best way to avenge our honor."

William planted himself in front of Lawren. "If we wait much longer, we're not going to have any honor to avenge. Let the women bury the dead and take care of the wounded."

Heads nodded; ayes rumbled.

"Bearnard has destroyed all the nightlace, has killed our chief, and now has killed Lowrie," William continued, his eyes narrowed and focused on Lawren. "If none of us should ride against him, *you* should. Your father appointed you clan champion."

"What are you suggesting he do?" Evan snapped before Lawren could speak. "Immediately after Angus died less than a month ago, Lawren demanded that Bearnard subject himself to a trial by ordeal. If he were innocent of killing Angus in the cattle raid, he would live. If he were guilty, he would die. The church refused to sanction it. The bishop declared that Angus had died honorably in battle. According to him, the Galloways had no grievance against Bearnard." Hardly without a pause, he went on. "During that time Lawren has solidified the clan and traveled to the northern isles in search of the nightlace."

Lawren laid a hand on Evan's shoulder. " 'Tis enough said, headman. All here know the circumstances well." He gazed at the kinsmen who crowded around. "I would like to kill Bearnard, and I have thought about it long and hard. But that is not the answer. Neither is killing Elspeth."

Protests rumbled through the kindred. He held up his hands and quieted them.

"As Evan pointed out, Bearnard has received the sanction of

the church. If we kill him, we martyr him. Others will rise up to take his place, and we bind his cause with that of the church. We give him the added strength that he needs to rally other clans to his side. We must stop this fighting among our clans and unite so that we can drive out the Saxons who are pushing north out of the Lowlands, who are running from the Normans."

The villagers listened.

"We have to stop the illness and prove it is not a plague," Lawren continued, "that none of us Galloways has brought a curse on the Highlands."

William drew his index finger over his scarred cheek. Out of the silence, he said, "Mayhap one of us has."

Heads swiveled in William's direction.

"Me?" Lawren asked quietly.

Sloane moved closer to his liege. Beth tensed. Lawren's posture didn't change, but his expression hardened, his eyes grew sharp. She feared for the headman's life.

"You're the one who is called the warlock." Stepping closer, William dropped his hand to the hilt of his sword. "I advised your father not to send for you. Since the day you arrived, the black clouds of grief and shame have hung over Castle Galloway. 'Tis easy to believe you have brought a curse on us."

"I have no control over what you think," Lawren replied.

" 'Tis not my thoughts you should be worried about," William replied. "I have sworn fealty to your father and to you. 'Tis the others."

The headman locked his hands behind his back and slowly walked down the line of tables. "I don't agree with the Adairs on many issues, but I sometimes wonder if both you and your mother should have been burned at the stake years ago. If you had, perhaps we would not be suffering from this plague. Our chief and his son might be alive."

"And perhaps there would be no Galloway clan," Evan thundered.

Lawren curled his hand into a fist. "We weren't"—his voice was deadly quiet—"and now by authority of my father as wit-

nessed by his two headmen, you and Evan, I am protector of
the clan and its chief. Don't forget it."

The two men stared at each other.

"He won't," Evan said, his tone low and controlled. "William," he commanded, "stand down. Let us not turn against
each other."

William grunted and removed his hand from his sword.

"See what is happening," Lawren said. " 'Tis not bad enough
that we are battling the plague without the one plant that cures
it, but clan is fighting clan, and kindred within a clan are fighting each other."

A lad rushed into the building from the courtyard, a fine
sprinkle of rain glistening on his hair and cloak. Beth heard the
faint rumble of wagon wheels.

"They're here," he shouted.

The kindred thronged to the entrance, kindly allowing the
families of the two slain men to exit first. Beth pushed away
from the table and ran toward the entrance, not reaching it before the two men Lawren had appointed her guards caught and
stopped her.

"Let me go." She twisted. "I'm a physician. I can help him."

"We've seen how you and your kind help," one of the men
drawled.

Through the opened door, Beth observed a woman throwing
herself over one of the bodies in the cart. After a moment, a
man pulled her away and the body was removed. The other
woman, the older one, stepped up to the wagon and gazed down.
At the same time Sloane effortless lifted a second body.

With help from one of the warriors, Jamie slid out of the cart
and staggered off with his grandmother. Lowrie was brought
into the great hall.

"Lawren," Beth called, struggling to free herself from the
men. One of them clamped his hand over her mouth to silence
her.

Dazed, Beth stared at Lowrie who lay limply in Sloane's arms.
For a moment she wasn't sure where she was or at whom she

was looking. The resemblance between Micheil Galloway and Lowrie was uncanny. Black hair framed Lowrie's face; lashes the same shade lay on his pale cheeks shadowed with beard growth. And she would swear without seeing his eyes that they were blue. Lowrie looked like a child, much too young and inexperienced to be a clan chieftain.

Lawren was old enough to be Lowrie's father, was his guardian. As she gazed into Lawren's face, she saw love and care reflected there. She was convinced there was no truth to the legend that the brothers hated each other, that one wanted to kill the other in order to be clan chieftain.

Annie shoved through the crowd. She gently touched Lowrie's forehead. "He's been like my son," she murmured. "I brought him into this world and took care of him when he was little."

"Aye," Lawren said.

Tears coursed down her cheeks and dropped onto Lowrie's face.

"I can't believe this has happened. If only he had stayed here as he was ordered. If only he had kept his word."

Beth tried to pushed forward, but the guard blocked her. If she could examine Lowrie; she would know if he were all right, if he had intercranial bleeding. The guard, caught up in all that was going on around him, removed his hand from her mouth and loosened his grip. Taking advantage of his laxity, she broke away and dashed to where Lawren stood. The men were right behind her. One reached out to grab her, but she clutched Lawren's arm. Looking down at her, he waved his man away.

"Let me examine him," she said.

" 'Tis nothing you or any of us can do for him," he murmured in a dull voice.

"Aye," Evan agreed, " 'tis a blow of death."

Beth moved closer to Lowrie, opened first one eye then the other and gazed at his pupils. They were fixed and dilated. She watched the sporadic rise and fall of his chest.

"He's still breathing on his own." She lifted her head and stared at Lawren. "The injury is not yet fatal."

"These kind always are," Evan snarled. "You have been around warriors long enough to know that."

She kept her gaze pinned to Lawren. "I can help him."

Lawren didn't reply.

"His brain is swelling because blood is collecting in his head. If something isn't done, he will die."

His expression closed, Lawren brushed the dark hair from Lowrie's temples, from his forehead, and gazed at the knot.

"The skull is a closed cavity and doesn't allow for swelling," Beth explained, hoping she was reaching him, was convincing him. "It will compress his brain."

"She knows what to do to assure that he dies even more quickly," William growled.

"In my world—in my travels while my husband was still alive"— she spoke as if she were Elspeth—"I saw many operations like this one performed. The procedure is a common one, and people live."

Lawren turned his head to look at her, and she saw a flicker of interest in his eyes.

"Something must be done immediately or the injury to the brain will be irreversible."

She held Lawren's gaze, silently entreating him. Finally he looked down at Lowrie.

"Can you save him?" she softly asked.

"Nay."

"Can your mother?"

Slowly he shook his head.

"So he's going to die. That's why Evan sent for the priest." When Lawren didn't answer, she said, "You believe he is already dead. That's the worst that can happen to him. I can at least give him a fighting chance, an opportunity to live. Please, Lawren, trust me."

"We never trust Adairs." William snorted.

"Think about the clan," Beth argued. "If Lowrie lives, the bishop will have no reason to interfere."

"She wants to make sure she kills Lowrie even quicker," William accused. "There isn't an Adair who is not deceitful."

Lawren straightened; his face became implacable. He shouted, "Take Lowrie to his chamber. Evan, go with him. William, see to the kindred. This is a black day for the Galloways, one that Bearnard mac Adair will rue the rest of his life."

"Aye." William spun around, marching back into the great hall.

Beth clutched at Lawren's arm, her fingers digging into the hard, flexed muscles. "If you love your brother, give him a chance to live."

Emotion flickered through his eyes, across his countenance. "William spoke our sentiments. We don't trust Adairs."

"I'm not—"

Metallic blue eyes speared hers. "For a verity, I don't trust you!"

He pushed past her and Beth fell against the wall. Her two guards rushed in around her as Annie followed Lawren up the stairs.

"What should we do with her?" one of them asked.

Without a sideways glance, Annie said, "If I had my way, we'd put her in a dungeon. Then we'd be sure she was up to no harm, that she could do Lowrie no more harm."

"The dungeon it is," the man replied.

"Nay," Annie said. "You had better ask Lawren what he wants done with her. She's his prisoner."

The man grunted.

"Once you've delivered her to Lawren," Annie ordered over her shoulder, "wait in the courtyard for the priest. Bring him up as soon as he arrives."

"When he learns that both Lawren and Caledonia are here, he won't be coming."

Annie stopped and smiled down at the Highlander. "We'll

make sure that he comes. Send word to Shawe that we hold Elspeth nea Adair prisoner."

"Do you think he'll come?" the man asked.

"He's the only one who will," Annie replied. "Certainly the only one who will be interested in a fellow Scotsman's soul."

Eight

Beth and the guard followed Annie up the stairwell to the second floor, to Lowrie's chambers. As Beth stepped into the doorway, the tapestry curtain hooked to one side, a feeling of déjà vu swept over her. Not so long ago—actually it was a long time ago, many lifetimes ago—she had been led to these same rooms to meet Callum Galloway.

The suite glowed with light. Flames leaped high in the fireplace; torches burned, and candles glimmered brightly on pedestals surrounding the bed. Slipping into the room, Beth saw Lowrie. He lay pale and listlessly. She couldn't tell if he was breathing or not.

Sloane stood in the corridor at the doorway. Lawren, Evan, and Annie hovered over him, talking quietly among themselves as they undressed him. They dropped his soiled clothing in a heap on the floor. Quietly Lowrie's manservant removed them, and Annie began to bathe him. Beth walked over to the bed and gazed down. Again she was amazed at the close resemblance between him and Micheil.

"He's so young," she murmured. "Too young to die."

"Soon to celebrate his coming of age," Lawren said.

"Soon to be chief of the Galloways," she added.

"Not now! Probably never." Lawren turned, looking at her. "What would you do to save him?"

Surprised but pleased, Beth prayed that she had won the battle, that she had convinced him to let her operate. "Drill a hole in his head."

"Sweet Jesus protect us all!" Annie crossed herself. "Hasn't God put enough holes in our bodies without your making another one?"

"It's the only way to relieve the pressure."

Annie and Evan crowded around them.

" 'Tis the talk of the devil," Annie snapped.

"Aye," Evan growled. "Don't let her do it, Lawren. She will be opening up his brain to evil spirits."

"I shall be letting the—the evil spirits out," Beth argued, using their point of reference. "Once they are gone, he will recover."

"Let the lad die in peace," Annie begged.

Lawren sighed and raked his hand through his already tousled hair. He glanced from Beth to Lowrie, back to Beth. He massaged the base of his neck. Finally he said, "This is common surgical practice in your—in the lands where you traveled?"

"Yes."

Blue eyes riveted to her; they plumbed to the depth of her heart, her soul. "You can do it?"

He was asking her if she had ever done it before, and she hadn't. Had never thought of doing it. She was a medical researcher not a surgeon. But this was not the time for such a confession. Thanking God for the judicious use of little white lies, she answered the stated question, not the implied one. "Yes."

Yes, I can!

"For God's sake, Lawren, don't!" Evan warned.

"Nay," Annie pleaded. "She'll kill him sure."

"He's dead for sure if you don't let me," Beth said.

Lawren paced the room, finally halting at the head of the bed. He looked down at his brother and ran a fingertip across the thick eyebrows, over the aquiline nose. "So be it," he murmured.

"Lawren," Evan snarled under his breath, "have you taken leave of your senses? Has this woman bewitched you?"

"Aye," Annie cried out, "and I warned him about her. She won't be satisfied until she has taken his and Lowrie's souls."

Evan rounded on Beth. Grabbing her by the shoulders, he shook her. Her braid flopped back and forth; strands of hair flew wildly about her face. "If he dies, woman, you shall be held accountable."

Lawren prized Evan's hands loose, and Beth stumbled back. Dizzy, breathless, she shoved hair out of her eyes and mouth.

Evan's attack was not stayed. With a shake of his shoulders, he thrust Lawren from him, but did not lunge for Beth again. "No one, not even Lawren, can protect you. We Galloways shall take your life for the one you take."

Beth looked over his shoulder at Lawren. "Is he—jesting?"

Lawren shook his head.

Again the cruel injustice of the Middle Ages struck Beth. She had read about the ancient physicians being held responsible for the survival of their patients, but she had never dreamed that it would happen to her, that she would be an *ancient physician*. Dazed, she slowly turned to the bed, to her patient.

"What do you need?" Lawren asked.

"A drill," she replied automatically, then when all of them looked at her oddly, she said, "I need something to—" She broke off. "A screwdriver." She began to rotate her hand and to think of tools and implements that they might have.

"A carpenter's brace," Evan said. "Or an auger!"

Lawren nodded.

"Bring one—No, bring several so I can choose."

Turning to Lowrie's servant who hovered in the doorway, Lawren sent him to find the tools.

"I want a knife," Beth said. "A sharp one."

At the same time, Lawren and Evan drew out their dirks and handed them to her. She took both and laid them on the chest next to the water basin. She then had Evan move Lowrie so that he was lying sideways across the bed, giving her better access to his skull.

When they had him resettled, she drew an imaginary circle on the top of his head. To Evan she said, "Shave this area."

The headman nodded and strode across the room. Pulling aside a small curtain, he revealed an arched alcove. The forerunner of the modern medicine cabinet, Beth thought fleetingly as he reached for a pair of scissors and a razor.

"A flagon of wine," Beth called out. "We need to clean his head after it has been shaved and before I drill."

"I'll get it," Annie said.

As Evan prepared Lowrie's head, Annie went for the wine. Beth searched through the cloths until she found a long, narrow strip that she could use as a mask, another that would serve as a hair net to bind her hair. As she held the material up, she realized she was shaking.

A doctor's greatest fear was being placed in a situation in which he or she didn't know what to do. That wasn't Beth's dilemma. She knew what to do. She simply had never done it before, had only seen it performed one time.

She was haunted by the thought that she was a medical researcher, not a surgeon. She didn't have the training for surgery, and certainly not one this delicate. She had to penetrate the skull, but if she allowed the auger to pierce too deeply, she would puncture the brain, and would kill Lowrie. A great risk! One she had to take. If anyone had the knowledge and skills to save him, it was she. Without proper medication and surgical instruments, it would be no mean feat.

She could do it, she told herself. Of course, she could. Didn't the adage go *see one, do one, teach one?* She had seen one; now it was time to do one.

"I have them." The servant raced into the room, his booted feet a whisper on the rush carpets. Out of breath, he added, "Master John sent several augers of different sizes. He also sent a hammer and some chisels. He said you might prefer them to the auger."

As he talked, he pulled the tools from a cloth satchel and laid them on the chest beside the basin and the daggers. "Master

John said handle these with care. They are his best carpentry and stoneworking tools, and he doesn't want anything to happen to them."

The tools still had wood shavings and stone dust on them. Beth had never dreamed of performing surgery, and certainly not brain surgery, without proper equipment. Yet here she was about to drill a hole in a man's skull using unsanitary carpentry and stoneworking tools. She picked up the hammer. It was too bulky, and didn't fit well into her hand.

The servant backed out of the room and took up his vigil in the hallway. Beth laid the hammer down and reached for the chisel. She rolled it in her hand before she returned it to the chest. She picked up the brace. It was quite modern with the exception that it had a simple rather than a spiral bit. Like the hammer, this was bulky, but she could use it if she had to. Laying it down, she went to the augers. One by one she studied the instruments, wondering which would be the best for the task, which would give her the control she needed.

Evan said, "It's hard to imagine that you're going to be boring a hole in Lowrie's head as if he were a quarry face or a piece of wood."

The words hung in the air, mocking her, reminding her of her lack of surgical training, her lack of equipment.

Finally she picked up the smallest auger. With its wooden handle and long shank, it reminded her of a corkscrew. She turned it over in her hand, flexing her hand around the grip. This was small enough to fit comfortably in one hand. She ran her thumb over the point; it was so sharp it pricked the skin.

"Will this penetrate the skull?" she asked.

"Aye, 'twould penetrate anything," Evan replied. "It bores holes in wood that has been water-soaked all winter."

"Toughened wood," Lawren explained.

She drew a deep, steadying breath. Clutching the auger firmly in one hand, she touched Lowrie's head with the other. For a moment she experienced doubt; she was frightened.

"You don't have to do this," Lawren said. "My people have already accepted Lowrie's death."

She breathed deeply, slowly. "I haven't."

"If he dies from the hammer blow, they will blame Bearnard."

"He won't die from the blow. I won't let him."

"If he dies"—Lawren pressed on—"after you operate on him, they'll blame you. You will be tortured unmercifully, painfully." He pleaded with her. "I don't wish this to happen to you any more than I want Lowrie to die."

"Thank you for your concern," Beth said, "but I'm going to save Lowrie's life. Will you help me?"

"Aye."

She smiled. "Take off your weapons and let's get started."

She turned to Annie.

"Wash the tools and the daggers. Make sure they are as clean as you can get them. Then put them in one of the cauldrons of boiling water. Leave them there until I ask for them."

Lawren unfastened his belts and hooked them on a wall peg at the head of the bed, close by where he could get to them if it was necessary. Evan did the same.

Beth turned to the chest where she washed and dried her hands. She picked up the strip of cloth and tied it over the bottom half of her face. "Lawren, wash your hands, mask your face like me, and disinfect Lowrie's head with the wine."

She heard a rustle as the door curtain slid open. A tall woman, wearing a long cloak, entered the room. Her face was hidden in the shadows of the hood, and Beth couldn't make out her features.

"Good evening, Lawren," the woman said. " 'Tis good to see you."

"Aye, Caledonia, 'tis good to see you."

"I got here as soon as I could. Were you able to locate any nightlaces in the northern isles?"

"Nay."

Caledonia raised her hands and removed the hood from her

head, revealing a wealth of thick, black hair—the same color as Lawren's. She was a big woman, her features rather plain. Yet there was something compelling about her, something that set her aside from other women. Her eyes were as blue as Lawren's, even more mystical, but they were not as mysterious as his.

She turned fully, seeing Beth for the first time since she entered the room. "What are you doing here, Elspeth?"

"She's our prisoner," Annie replied.

"She's going to drill a hole in Lowrie's head," Evan put in.

The woman's gaze slowly moved from Beth's masked face, to her bound hair, to the auger she held. "With carpentry tools?"

"Aye, and if those fail with stoneworking ones," Evan replied.

"A prisoner who acts like a physician," the woman said. "An Adair who is going to save a Galloway."

"I wish I had time to discuss this with you, my lady," Beth replied, "but I don't, not now. I am both prisoner and physician, and I am going to save a Galloway . . . if all of you will let me."

"Who sent you?" Caledonia looked directly into Beth's face.

Beth was soon lost in the depth of the older woman's eyes. They compelled her to confess, to tell all, even though Lawren had cautioned her not to. Even if she did not confess, she believed the woman could read her heart and soul and know the truth.

"Fate," she replied.

"You look like Elspeth, yet you are not she."

Beth shook her head. "I'm from the future."

"She claims to be a time-traveler," Lawren added.

Startled, Evan and Annie stared openmouthed at Lawren, at Beth, then at Caledonia. Her expression never changing, Caledonia continued to study Beth.

"I don't know if you're a time-traveler from the future or a witch, but I know you're a healer, and I know fate brought you." She nodded and smiled at Evan and Annie. "We shall help her."

Behind the mask, Beth smiled. Most of her nervousness vanished. She had an ally and didn't feel quite so alone. She quickly explained the burr-hole procedure.

When she was finished, she said, "Someone will have to hold Lowrie so he can't move his head. The procedure is delicate enough if he is still. We can't allow one false move."

"We could get him drunk and let him go into a stupor," Evan said. "He would be rendered senseless."

"Nay, this is not painful, and I want him to regain his senses as quickly as possible." Beth turned to Lawren's mother. "Does Lowrie know and trust you?" After Caledonia nodded, Beth said, "During the operation, I want you to assure him that all is going well, that he will be fine. Recount pleasant times in his life. Tell him of things that will make him want to fight for his life."

As Beth gave instructions, Annie, holding the torch, moved to the side of the bed. Firelight gleamed on all their faces. In the shadowed glow, Beth saw skepticism on Annie and Evan's faces, the want-to-believe in Lawren's, and the absolute faith in his mother's. This was the best she was going to get. It would do.

She took her place and watched Lawren clean his brother's head with the wine. When he drew back, she lowered her hands. As the auger touched Lowrie's scalp, confidence chased away fear. The bedroom became a surgery and the physician replaced the woman. Beth made the incision, then pressed the point of the auger against his skull. In a low, soothing voice Caledonia began to talk; Beth began to drill. Evan grimaced; Annie flinched. The torch bobbed slightly. Stone-faced, Lawren caught the servant's arm and steadied it.

Cautiously, Beth continued to drill, the blade of the auger slowly curling through the bone. Shavings dropped to the side of the pillow. Slowly, steadily, she twisted. Her arm grew heavy; her shoulder joint ached. Her fingers stiffened. The torch flame radiated too much heat and not enough light. Each draft of wind caused it to flicker, spewing sparks through the air.

Covered in perspiration, Beth closed her eyes and drew in a

deep breath. She heard the reassuring drone of Caledonia's voice. Then she felt a soft, moist cloth against her forehead. Surprised, she opened her eyes and gazed into Lawren's face. Deeply blue, his eyes were filled with comfort and support.

"You're doing well." His voice was quiet, reassuring. He blotted perspiration from her eyes. "I believe you."

Even behind the mask he wore, Beth knew he smiled. She saw it in his eyes; she heard it in his voice. His tenderness touched her. His faith inspired her.

"How much longer?" Evan asked.

"Not much." Beth hoped she spoke the truth.

After she drew Annie's arm down so that the flame cast a brighter light on Lowrie, Beth lowered her head and began drilling once more. This time her heart was lighter. With each turn of the auger, she brushed the shavings away. She felt, more than saw, that she was almost finished. She turned the tool again and paused. Turned. Stopped. Turned. Annie caught her breath; Evan looked at her expectantly. Lawren blotted her forehead. Beth twisted the auger again. Then she felt the slight give. Her heart thundered. Blood spurted out of Lowrie's head, staining the gown she wore. Crimson droplets soaked into the linens.

"Merciful God!" Annie cried.

"Is he dead?" Evan bellowed.

Lawren tensed; his mother stopped talking. All stared at Beth.

Laughing, crying, she said, "He's going to be all right. We've released the pressure."

"Nay," Caledonia said softly, *"you* released the pressure."

"Sweet Jesus!" Tears running down her cheeks, Annie crossed herself. The gnarled hand brushed his face; a tear splashed on his face. She sniffed. "Blessed Mary, mother of God!"

Evan dropped his head, but not before Beth saw the glimmer of tears. Gruffly he asked, "How soon before we can talk to the lad? A good scolding he'll be getting from me."

Beth smiled. "By tomorrow. Now we need to elevate him."

She lifted Lowrie's head and ordered, "Put several pillows beneath it."

"What's going to happen to the hole?" Annie asked.

"It will always be there," Beth replied, "but skin will grow over it."

"No warrior could carry a prouder battle wound," Evan declared. " 'Tis a badge of honor."

When they had Lowrie settled, the canopy curtains closed, Beth took off the mask she wore. As she washed and dried her hands, Caledonia and Annie quietly straightened the room. Evan unhooked his weapons from the peg and fastened them about his waist.

Moving over to the fire, Beth fished the tools out of the boiling water. After she dried them off, she returned the daggers to Lawren and Evan. Evan slid his into the sheath at his waist; Lawren walked over to the wall peg and sheathed his in the scabbard. Beth replaced the hammer, chisels, and augers in their cloth satchel and held it out to Evan.

"Return these to Master John, and assure him they're unharmed. Cleaner but definitely unharmed." She smiled wearily. "In fact, headman, I would say they are magical now."

"Aye." Evan took the pouch and clutched it tightly. His eyes were bright, his countenance softened with emotion. "Thank you, my lady, for saving Lowrie's life. We owe you a debt of gratitude that we can never repay."

Overwhelmed by his open appreciation, Beth couldn't speak for a moment. Finally she said, "You owe me nothing. I'm a healer. I heal people. All people."

"But you are also an Adair, and Adairs do not help Galloways, especially not in a situation like this one."

"This Adair helped a Galloway, Evan. Do not forget it."

He nodded.

Beth turned, looking from one of them to the other, Evan, Lawren, Annie, Caledonia. "Thank you for helping me. Together we saved your chief."

Shuffling closer, Annie glared at Beth and wagged her finger in Beth's face. "You may have charmed Evan and Lawren, but you haven't me. I'm grateful that you saved Lowrie and that we're not going to be having an official visit from the bishop, but I don't trust you. I never will. I'll be watching you. I'll not let you harm any of the Galloways."

Venom oozed out of the woman, and Beth could imagine she was a deadly snake. Hissing, poised, ready to strike. Beth didn't dignify Annie's outburst with a reply.

Lawren spoke, breaking the heavy silence that blanketed the room. "All of you can go to bed. I'll stay with Lowrie."

"I'll stay," Evan offered.

"Nay, I will," Annie said.

Lawren shook his head. "Neither of you will."

Both started to argue, but he held up his hand.

"Annie, I shall need you to manage the castle. Evan, I want you rested because we have a score to settle with the Adairs. Join William and the kinsmen."

Evan walked to the door, stopped, and turned. His brow was furrowed. He glanced over at Caledonia, then back to Lawren. "You told your mother that Elspeth was a traveler in time. Elspeth said she was from the future. What is the meaning of this?"

"Aye," Annie snapped, edging closer, gawking curiously.

Caledonia stepped forward. Before she could answer, Beth laid her hand on the woman's arm. Earlier she would have argued, would have tried every persuasive gimmick she could think of to convince them that she was a time-traveler. Not now. She realized the futility of arguing. It was impossible for them to accept that she had defied time, had traveled from her present to theirs.

Smiling at the headman, she said, " 'Twas a manner of speech. Since my marriage to Alastair, I have spent much of my time abroad. I have traveled to lands far beyond our shores and have seen many wondrous things. I have met many wise people—healers, advisors, and teachers. This surgery that I did on Lowrie is one of the things I learned from them."

"You're not a witch?" he asked.

"Nay, only a traveler."

" 'Tis good that you are, lady, and that you were here tonight."

"Aye," Beth said.

"Fate," Caledonia murmured.

"Aye," Evan agreed.

As he walked out, Lawren turned to Annie. "Send one of the lads in to make a pallet on the floor for me. Then you get to bed. You'll need to supervise the morning meal for the kindred."

Nodding, she also left.

Her herb basket in her lap, Caledonia sat in a chair near the fireplace.

"How were the villagers when you left?" Lawren asked.

"Sick to their stomach," she replied.

He hiked a brow.

"They had eaten something that didn't agree with them."

"It wasn't the—"

"Nay, but 'tis the plague that has struck fear in the people's heart and made them think they were sick unto death. The more fearful they grow, the less rational they're likely to be."

And the more likely they would believe Lawren was a warlock who had cursed the Highlands; the more likely they would turn against him, Beth thought.

"Don't you have some nightlaces you could plant?" she asked. "Can't you cultivate gardens?"

"Aye, and we are," Caledonia said, "but it will take years. Years we don't have."

"We're not sure that the nightlace is effective in treating the illness," Lawren said.

"I am," Beth replied.

"How can you be so sure?" Caledonia asked softly.

Kneeling on the floor beside Lawren's mother, Beth told her story, leaving out none of the details.

When she was finished, Caledonia said, "You're a physician

from the future, yet you are studying an eleventh-century manuscript."

"Yes," Beth said eagerly. "It's not intact, but enough remains that I'm fairly certain that the nightlace is the plant that cured the plague."

"That's the conclusion I've come to also," Caledonia admitted. "But I can't be sure. Some of my patients take it and die. Others live."

"Describe your method of treatment," Beth said.

Caledonia set her basket on the floor and leaned back in the chair. As she talked, Beth noted that the illness followed the same progression as the one she was fighting in the twentieth century. They discussed the herbs they had used in fighting the disease. One by one they crossed them from the list.

"Have you kept records on your patients?" she asked.

Caledonia nodded. "But I haven't had time to compile them so I can study and compare them. I shall do that one of these days."

Lawren smiled at his mother. "Don't be telling Beth something like that. She's liable to think you're writing this elusive manuscript she's hunting."

Caledonia smiled. "I'm rather exhausted, and I'm sure that both of you are. We'll discuss this another time."

"I—may not have another time," Beth said.

"You will," Caledonia promised. Turning to Lawren, she said, "Tonight I'll stay with Elsa. I'm sure she's taking good care of Jamie, but I may have some herbs she can use."

After mother and son said their good-byes, Lowrie's manservant entered the room and spread a pallet on the floor in front of the fire.

"Lay yours in the hallway," Lawren instructed the youth. "I may have need of you tonight."

"Annie is sleeping there," the boy said.

"Then let her be. You may sleep in the servants' chamber."

Beth returned to the bed, fluffed the pillow, and tucked the covers around Lowrie's shoulders. Lawren joined her.

"You took a great risk when you operated on him."

She shook her head. "You're the one who took the risk. I knew what I was doing. You didn't."

"I'm glad you were here to save him," he said.

"I'm glad I had the knowledge and the skills to save him. I wasn't sure that I could—" She broke off and stared at him. "I knew what to do, but I wasn't sure that I could do it."

"Your first time?" he asked.

She gazed at him. "How did you know?"

He shrugged. "Intuition."

"My first time," she admitted. "When did you suspect?"

"From the beginning."

"Yet you let me."

"Aye, I believed in you."

"Thank you," she murmured, pride glowing in her heart, tears smarting in her eyes.

Nine

Lawren and Beth turned at the same time, moving into an embrace. She held on to him tightly, afraid that if she didn't she would fall from sheer exhaustion. As if he understood, he said nothing; he simply held her. She pressed her cheek to his chest, savoring the feel of his hands as they moved up and down her back.

After a while, he said, "You really impressed my mother, and she's not that easily impressed."

Burrowing closer to him, wanting, needing his comfort, Beth said, "Your mother impressed me, and I'm not that easily impressed. I think she believes me, about my being from the future."

Lawren chuckled and pulled back, still holding her in the circle of his arms. His eyes twinkled. "That's no consolation. She's a witch, and they believe in the supernatural. When you can really feel impressed is when the priest believes you're from the future."

"He hasn't come yet?"

"Nay, and may not."

Sighing, Beth drew out of Lawren's embrace and moved toward the fireplace. She held her palms over the blaze. "He should. He's a servant of God and the church. It's his duty to be here. For all he knows, Lowrie is dying and needs last rites."

"What you're forgetting," he pointed out, "is that he is a man first, these other things secondly."

"Do you know him?"

"Although I had heard of him for many years, I didn't meet him until my father's funeral."

"You like him," she said.

"I respect him."

"But he is frightened of you and your mother?"

"Not of us personally," Lawren replied. "Of the warlock and the witch whom he believes us to be. And until now, the clergy's fear of us has not been all bad. They have left us alone."

Soft knocks caught their attention.

Lawren quickly crossed the room to stand at the head of the bed, close to his weapons still hanging on the wall peg. Beth didn't know if she would ever become accustomed to this constant vigil, this constant fear of danger.

"Enter," he called.

The door swung open, and William stood at the threshold. His slow glance around the room took in the furnishings one by one until he saw the bed, the curtains closed. He looked up at Lawren.

"Evan said Lowrie was going to live, that Elspeth saved him."

"Aye." Lawren pulled back the canopy. "Come. See for yourself."

The Highlander stepped into the room and quietly walked to the bed. Lawren held the torch while Beth removed the bandage. As she described the surgery, William inspected the incision. When she was finished, the headman looked at her. His brow was furrowed, his eyes dark with concern.

"If he's a slobbering idiot, we'll have to kill him anyway."

"He won't be," Beth replied. "He'll regain his full sensibilities."

Satisfied, William stepped back. "It's unclear to me why you saved Lowrie's life, madam, but I'm grateful."

"Thank you."

He ran his hand down his scar. "Don't mistake my gratitude for my liking you. I don't. I don't trust you. I believe you've done this for some ulterior reason."

"I didn't," she said quietly.

"Time will tell." He looked at Lawren. "Now that Lowrie is going to recover are we going to ride against the Adairs tomorrow?"

"We shall exact our revenge," Lawren promised.

" 'Tis an evasive answer." William crossed his arms over his chest and pushed back on his heels. "Have you changed your mind?"

Lawren shook his head. "Nay, but the entire incident puzzles me, headman. Cattle and villagers getting sick. You, Evan, and Annie away from the castle. The lads riding out to Mountain Cat Canyon for nightlace when they know the plant has never grown in that area. The attackers escaping in our territory without leaving a sign. Something is amiss."

"Aye." William rubbed his chin.

"Law of the land and of the clan demands retribution. I shall honor that," Lawren said. "First, I want to talk with Lowrie and Jamie and with the lads who rescued them."

"Good." William nodded his head curtly. "I've reinforced our border guards, and the lads are looking for anything unusual. So far we can account for all the kindred. With the exception of Damh, Rob, Jamie, and Lowrie, none have even been harmed or killed."

Tuning out the conversation between Lawren and William, Beth sat on the pallet. Only then did she realize the extent of her exhaustion. She drew her legs up, circled them with her arms, and rested her chin on her knees. Going into near-sleep, she was soon lost in memories of home. Pictures of her family, her friends, her patients floated in and out. She had to get back to them with the nightlace. Even if she could not get back—the thought was frightening—she had to find a way to get the nightlace to them.

Finally William left, quietly closing the door behind himself. Lawren remained in front of the fireplace, both hands on the chimneypiece. His tunic pulled across his shoulders, emphasizing his broad shoulders, outlining his flexed muscles. Firelight glinted on the golden buckles of his leather belt. Finally he moved to the bed and checked on Lowrie. Satisfied that his brother was resting peacefully, he lay on the pallet next to her.

Cupping his hands beneath his head, he said, "All of this must seem strange to a person from the future."

"Not strange in the sense that I'm unfamiliar with your time," Beth said, "but strange that I'm here being a part of it."

He rolled on his side, propping on an elbow. "You know all about me and my world, but I don't know anything about you or yours."

Her world! The line of delineation between her world and his was getting fuzzier and fuzzier.

Feeling vulnerable, she gave him the old stock answer: "There's not much to know about me."

"I doubt that," he replied. "But however much, or little, there is, I'm interested in knowing it."

"You believe me?"

" 'Tis a large stretch for the imagination, but I'm trying, lass." A pause, then: "I want to believe."

Happiness warmly permeated her entire body. "What do you want to know?"

"All about you, Elizabeth Balfour."

Lying on her back, she stared at the mesmeric dance of the fire as she began to give him a detailed account of her life: her childhood as a naval officer's daughter; about her sisters, Julienne and Ginger; about Julienne's children, her niece and nephew: Julienne's husband, Donald, an attorney and CPA. Beth described her apartment in San Diego, her parents' home, Sunday dinner with the family. Lawren asked questions; she answered. On and on she talked, finally moving from a description of her life in specific to one of twentieth-century America in general.

When she was finished, he said, "You seem to have many wondrous inventions. Hot and cold water that is piped directly into the house. All kinds of contraptions and gadgets." He pushed up on an elbow and gazed out the window. "Flying machines. You've even traveled to the moon," he murmured, then shook his head. "This sounds exciting, but also confusing."

"Many would agree with you," Beth conceded. "Hi-tech living is quite stressful and demanding. Many people wish for simpler times."

A spark sputtered and landed on the hearth. Beth watched its golden red glow recede until it was a blackened smudge.

"What made you decide to become a physician?" Lawren asked.

"When my younger sister was fifteen, she was diagnosed with cancer. The doctors did all they could through traditional medicine, and she seemed to get worse. That's when she turned to natural remedies. At first my family and I were afraid and worried, but she told us it was her life. She had nothing to lose and everything to gain. All of us became involved in her healing program. Slowly she began to regain her strength and vitality. She's in remission now."

He hiked a brow.

"That's a way of saying she's healed. After that I decided to become a doctor and help others through a blending of traditional and natural therapies."

They were quiet for a few minutes, then Lawren spoke. "You said you were staying at Castle Galloway when you were transported back in time?"

"Yes." She rolled her head on the pallet and looked at him. "The only building intact now is the keep, but it's still imposing."

For a long time her soft voice flowed through the room as she described the land and the castle, and his descendants, the Grahams. He grew pensive when she told him about Callum, the present laird, and his debilitating illness. On a lighter note, she talked about the similarities between him and Callum and between Lowrie and Micheil. Lawren asked questions. For her answers, she drew from the material she had studied and had learned through Minnie and Agnes Forbes, the noted Scottish folklorist.

When she paused, he asked, "Did the manuscript say anything about my mother?"

"Not the part that was saved," she replied and wondered if he would again ask about himself. Earlier when Lawren had asked her what happened to him, she had told him the manuscript was inconclusive . . . and it was. But all evidence pointed to his being the one who was burned at the stake.

Across the room, she heard a noise and thought it was Lowrie. She rose and moved over to the bed. Lawren followed her. Pulling back the canopy on one side, she snagged it on the poster. Picking up the candleholder, she held it close to the bed.

"Is he all right?" Lawren asked.

She nodded. "His color is good. So is his breathing. Why don't you return to your chambers and get some rest? If his condition should change, I'll get you."

He shook his head. "I'll stay."

"You still don't trust me?"

"The kindred don't."

"Will they ever?" she said more than asked.

Lawren shrugged. "There's always a possibility. By now Evan and William will have told them about your saving Lowrie's life. And Lowrie will confirm it when he regains consciousness." He glanced at her. "He will have regained his senses by morning, won't he?"

She nodded and walked away from the bed to the fireplace. Reaching up, she brushed her hand beneath her hair and felt the strip of material that held it back. She fumbled with the knot. Then she felt Lawren's hands on hers.

"Let me," he said.

"Thank you," she murmured, reveling in the whisper touch of his fingers on her neck and shoulders.

"Your hair is beautiful," he said. "Do you always braid it?"

"Only when I work."

"Here maidens are the ones who don't coif and veil their hair."

"To let the men know they're available."

He chuckled softly. "Or mayhap husbands want their wives to coif their hair because they don't want them to appeal to other men."

The cloth fell to their feet, but he didn't move, nor did he turn her hair loose.

"It's soft like silk," he murmured. "Russet. Autumn's fire."

It was a replay of his earlier conversation with her, of the only words Callum had spoken aloud to her. Mentally she could see Callum, but he seemed to be one with Lawren. As her two worlds were slowly and surely merging, so were the two men. She was beginning to wonder if she had imagined the twentieth century.

Lawren unbraided her hair.

"You went to the northern isles for nightlace," she said.

"Aye." After a moment he added, "It doesn't grow up there, but I have sent them some of the plants for medicine. I had hoped . . ." His voice faded into silence. Finished with the unbraiding of her hair, he clasped her shoulders, and she leaned back against him.

"You didn't find any?"

"Nay." He sighed and lay his cheek on the top of her head. "It seems that Bearnard is doing an excellent job of destroying them."

"Your mother said that you had planted more of them."

"Aye, but it will be next year before they can be harvested."

"You have a few left that you're using as medicine." She turned in his arms. "Will you show them to me?"

In the firelight his eyes glimmered silver, yet they were not sharp or cutting; they were soft and inviting, the quintessence of the moon.

"Aye, lass, I will."

Liquid pleasure flowed through her. "You and your mother will let me work with you?"

"I don't know about Caledonia, but I will."

Beth threw her arms around him, hugging him close. "Oh, Lawren, you've made me so happy."

"I wish it was always possible for me to bring you pleasure."

He spoke the words with such sincerity, she drew back. He narrowed his eyes, studying her so intently that Beth felt herself flush. Nothing existed but her and Lawren. She was awash, floating in the deep liquid blue of his eyes.

"You're beautiful, Beth, especially when you smile. Your eyes sparkle and your face glows."

A breeze wafted through the room, stirring her hair, wrapping it over his arm. He caught the strands and held them up to the blaze. "Who was this man you loved?" he asked softly. "Did he give you pleasure?"

Startled, Beth realized that Sam hadn't given her much pleasure. She had always been on pins and needles, trying to please him, always feeing as if she failed.

"I—didn't love him," she murmured, surprised that Lawren had remembered, that he was curious. "I said I could have loved him."

But she had been wrong. She would never—could never—have loved him. She loved Lawren the warlock.

"Sam," she said. "Samuel J. Anderson."

"A doctor, like you?"

"A doctor," she replied, "but I want to think we're different."

For the first time since Sam had jilted her, Beth was no longer a prisoner of her past, no longer bound and gagged in humiliation and a deep-seated sense of inadequacy. She was free of Sam, totally free of him. She wanted to talk about him, wanted to tell Lawren. She wanted no misunderstanding between them about her past relationship.

She caught his hand and led him to the pallet. "Come. Let me tell you about him."

After they sat down, she stared into the flames and began to talk in a low voice so as not to disturb Lowrie. This time in the telling she experienced no negative feelings, didn't relive rejection. She realized that what happened had been for the best although Sam could have made a better decision by having told her how he felt sooner than their wedding day. She felt as if a load had been lifted from her shoulders, a dark blot on her past removed—not the memory of the experience itself but the color had been changed. She viewed the incident and herself differently.

"Do you regret not marrying him?" Lawren said.

"I did when it happened," she answered, "but not any longer."

As she and Lawren talked, she realized she had pushed hers and Sam's relationship in the direction she wanted because she wanted marriage, a husband, a home, a family of her own. She and Sam had seemed to be made for each other; she had been so sure that it was right for them, she had never really given Sam a voice in the matter. She hadn't really tried to please Sam or make him happy either. She had assumed that her dream was his and had swept him along in her plans.

"We really weren't suited for each other," she heard herself say, "and in the long run we would have made each other very unhappy."

"If you had married him, you may not be here."

"Probably not."

"I'm glad you're here," he said.

"If I hadn't been, Lowrie wouldn't have lived."

Lawren caught her hand in his and twined their fingers together. He held them up to the fire. "I must confess my thoughts were not entirely selfless."

Beth gazed at their hands. His calloused one was big, warm, and comforting. It dwarfed hers.

"Your fingers are truly those of a physician. Long. Tactile. Strong, yet gentle. As you performed surgery, I studied them."

He brought her hand up and lightly kissed each of her knuckles. Sensation, wonderful sensation, like brilliant shards of sunshine, spiraled through Beth's body, in, around and through her heart. She sucked in her breath. She stared at their hands and marveled at the emotions that swept through her. She knew that he was holding her prisoner, that to him she was nothing more than a pawn in a political game, yet she was attracted to him.

"I was jealous," he said. "I wanted your hands on me."

"Is this part of the revenge?" she asked.

"Revenge?" He looked puzzled.

"You said that Bearnard wouldn't mind your killing me but that he would be quite angry and humiliated if you—"

Her words were lost as he caught her chin and brought her face to his gaze. Firelight found her hair and gilded it. She was the essence of fire itself. Her hair floated around her shoulders like brushed flames; they flickered in the centers of her green eyes. Her soft lips quivered slightly, and the tip of her tongue darted out to moisten them. His heart bucked, and blood thickened in his veins. His groin throbbed from the pleasure she inflicted.

"Nay." He nudged her chin with his finger, drawing her to him with the sheer power of sexuality. "What I am saying is heartfelt, lady. It has nothing to do with revenge."

But it could be construed as such, he thought, feeling a momentary twinge of guilt.

"Don't ride against the Adairs," she said.

"I must."

"You may not come back."

"That's a possibility. None of us has a guarantee of life. Does the idea of my not coming back concern you?"

"I'm scared," she confessed. "I don't know anyone but you. You're the only one who seems to want me alive. Everyone else hates me. The way they look at me!"

"My mother likes you. I can send her to stay with you."

"Yes," she said, "that would be nice."

But having Caledonia with her was not enough. Beth couldn't bear the thought of being separated from Lawren, of never seeing him again. She had been trying to convince herself that she wanted him on a physical level only, but that wasn't true. She loved him and had from the first moment she had seen him. No, from the time she had seen a photograph of his portrait. A force she could not identify, certainly did not understand, compelled her. This may be the last time she saw him alive. Desperation made her want to push for the moment, to take it. But she had never been one to make decisions in the throes of passion. She couldn't begin now. She had to think about tomorrow and the day after.

This world was hard and cruel. She must keep reminding herself that she was a pawn in this political game between Adairs and Galloways. No matter how kind Lawren might be tonight, how supportive, or how much he might profess to care for her, he was the clan champion. His first loyalties were to the Galloways, and she knew beyond any doubt that no sacrifice would be too great for him to make when it came to performing his duties. As she was a product of the twentieth century, he was the epitome of the eleventh.

"How do the Galloways feel about your mother?"

"The older ones trust her," Lawren replied. "I'm not sure about the younger ones. I think they believe the rumors that she's a witch and are frightened of her. She lived here in this castle for many years. She knows all of its little secrets. If something should happen to me, she would be able to sneak you to safety."

He pulled her into his arms and held her loosely. Peace beautifully settled over Beth. She felt as if she had been searching all her life and had finally returned home. Yes, *returned* home. Now she understood the déjà vu she had experienced the day she arrived at Castle Galloway. It had nothing to do with research, nothing to do with her career. She had lived here, loved here . . . possibly died here.

As she relaxed against him, absorbing his warmth, listening to the beat of his heart, she knew she was home. And home was not a place or building or a particular time. It was her and him together. Time was eternal as was love. One moment of love spanned the ages and bound her to Lawren. Her only concern was that he didn't feel this way about her. He had admitted that he cared, but Beth wasn't sure what caring meant in the eleventh century.

"Lawren." The cry was no more than a croak.

"Lowrie!"

Beth and Lawren pulled apart, leaped to their feet, and raced to the bed. At the same time both of them leaned down, staring into Lowrie's opened and blank eyes. He squinted, blinked, and looked at Lawren. Slowly he rotated his head and gazed fixedly at Beth.

He smiled, and her heart went out to him. He looked so young, so vulnerable.

"Where am I?" he asked. "In heaven?"

"Nay," she said.

"I must be." He gave her a crooked smile. "I'm being attended by an angel."

Lawren chuckled. "It sounds as if you're recuperating quite well, little brother."

"Always you come along, Lawren," Lowrie complained good-naturedly, "to burst my fantasies." He tried to push up on his elbows. "Where am I?"

"Home," Lawren replied. "At Galloway Castle."

"The others?" Lowrie grimaced and caught his head.

Clasping him by the shoulders, Beth gently pushed him into the pillows. "No sudden moves. You took a nasty blow to the head."

"Rob is dead," Lawren replied. "Jamie wounded in the shoulder."

Lowrie's face darkened. He clinched his eyes shut and bunched the coverlet in his fist.

"You would have been too," Lawren said, "but Evan and the lads arrived in time to scare the Adairs away."

"Did you kill any of them?" Lowrie asked in a low voice.

"Nay," Lawren replied, "and we took no prisoners."

"Damn them to hell!" Lowrie swore.

"Did you see who tried to kill you, lad?" Lawren asked. "Would you recognize him again?"

Without opening his eyes, Lowrie shook his head. "All I see is a faceless warrior. No features. Nothing that I recognize." He paused thoughtfully. "Tears," he murmured. "I remember tears."

" 'Tis natural your eyes watered," Lawren said gruffly. "You suffered a severe head wound."

"Not me!" Lowrie sputtered indignantly, his eyes opening wide. "The faceless man. He had no eyes, but he cried. I felt his tears on my face."

"Annie," Beth murmured.

"What's Annie got to do with this?" Lawren asked.

"When they brought him home, she cried over him. Her tears fell onto his cheeks. He's remembering part of his experience, but the earlier part is so horrible, he has pushed it out of his mind."

"Will he ever remember?"

"Sometimes people do; sometimes they don't. We must wait."

Lowrie's gaze shifted to her. "Who is she?"

"Elspeth," Lawren said.

Again Beth didn't protest. Explanations were too complicated and unbelievable. To them she was Elspeth, and if she remained here in this time period she would become Elspeth.

"Elspeth nea Adair," Lowrie murmured disbelievingly. Then laughed bitterly, gingerly touching the crown of his head. "An Adair tried to kill me. An Adair saved my life."

"Aye," Lawren replied. "During her travels abroad she learned how to operate on the skull."

Standing at the head of the bed, looking down at her patient, Beth listened as Lawren gave an apt layman's description of the surgery.

When he was through with the explanation, Lowrie gazed curiously at Beth. "I shall repay you generously."

"Saving your life was repayment enough," she told him.

"Nevertheless, you shall be rewarded." Friendliness was gone. The future clan chieftain spoke. "I do not trust you or your brother, and I don't want to be in your debt."

Summarily dismissing her, Lowrie looked at his brother and grinned. "I won't be ten-and-sixteen for two weeks, Lawren, and I have my first battle scar. I shall keep my head shaved until I have gone through the Coming-of-Age ceremony. Maybe always."

"If you had been where you were ordered to be," Lawren said, "you would not have suffered at all."

"And Rob would be alive," Lowrie muttered bitterly.

"And Damh," Lawren added.

"Damh?" Lowrie mumbled.

"Aye, he was riding with Evan when they went in search of you. Evan split the group up, leading one into the canyon and sending the other after the attackers. Damh was killed."

"What a day for the Adairs," Lowrie mumbled. "How they must have celebrated their victory! Laughed and mocked us."

He closed his eyes and compressed his lips together. Turning his face to one side of the pillow, he brushed his hand over his forehead.

Quietly Lawren asked, "What possessed the three of you to ride out like that, Lowrie? You had given your word that you would not leave the castle."

Looking miserable, knowing he had broken his word, had brought dishonor upon himself, Lowrie said, "I wasn't going at first. Rob and Jamie were. But I couldn't stay behind." Doleful eyes rested on his brother; they pleaded for understanding. "I'm to be the future chief of the Galloways, soon to celebrate my coming of age. I had to be there."

Lowrie picked at the covers. "It seems so long ago and so unreal. Rob found some nightlace. We planned to have it at the castle when you returned from your journey. But when we arrived at the canyon, we couldn't find it. We scattered out, each of us going too far away from the other, that I couldn't see either Jamie or Rob. I rode over the incline looking for them. That's when I saw Jamie on the ground, the two Adairs riding toward him."

"How many?" Lawren asked.

"Two. Maybe three. I'm not sure."

"Two or three!" Lawren exclaimed, his brow furrowing.

"With that few men I can't understand their being so deep in our territory. Lowrie, are you sure they were Adairs?"

"They wore their colors. Green and brown plaid." Sighing deeply, Lowrie closed his eyes.

Beth squeezed Lawren's shoulder. "Talk to him in the morning. He needs to rest now."

"Aye," Lowrie mumbled. "I'm tired."

Worried, Lawren looked at her.

"Does your head ache?" she asked.

"Nay."

"Nausea?"

He turned his head from side to side on the pillow.

"You've had a rough time," she said. "And you're going to be feeling the effects of the blow and the operation for several days. But you're going to be fine. You'll have a full recovery."

Lowrie nodded. As soon as he had drifted to sleep, Lawren unhooked the canopy curtains and closed them.

The events of the night caught up with Beth. She was so exhausted, she didn't think she could take another step. Suffering acute jet lag—without the benefit of the jet—all she wanted was a soft, warm bed and sleep. She looked at her watch. Three o'clock. Two and a half hours before sunrise. Only a few hours had passed since she traveled through time, but it seemed longer.

How much time had passed in the future? she wondered. Unable to answer her question, bombarded by many more, as unanswerable, she sighed.

"Tired?" Lawren asked.

She nodded and lay down on the pallet. Although she was fatigued, she didn't immediately go to sleep. She watched the mesmerizing dance of the fire; she looked at Lawren, sitting there, one leg hiked up, the other stretched out. Deep in thought, he gazed into the blaze.

As if aware that she was staring at him, he turned his head, their gazes catching, locking together. Smiling at her, that slow, full smile that caused her insides to flutter, he fluffed her pillow beneath her head and tucked a blanket over her.

Bending over her, he whispered, "Sweet dreams, my lady." He gently kissed her forehead, then her lips.

She smiled, but her eyes refused to stay open. The last thing she remembered was the touch of his lips to each of her closed lids and his words. "I'll be watching over you."

Ten

First light filtered through the opened windows, casting the great hall of Castle Galloway in hazy light. Lawren, having bathed and changed clothes, lounged in a cushioned chair in front of the fireplace. Evan and William stood on the left of him, Sloane on the right.

Rather than Lawren's wearing leather breeches and vest this morning, he wore a short-sleeved red tunic, a kilted tartan, and cuarans, knee-high cowhide boots. In his hand he held an unopened letter from Bearnard mac Adair. He idly rubbed the pad of his thumb over the sealing wax, but didn't open the parchment. He watched the priest who paced in front of the fireplace.

Shawe was a tan, thin man, his features gaunt, almost haunting. For the most part, Lawren trusted him and thought him to be an honest and intelligent man. Shawe was more open-minded than many of his peers and quite courageous, and he was a Scotsman, not a Saxon like the bishop and many of the other priests. Shawe had never denied his fear of warlocks and witches; yet he had come to the place he considered their lair, a vile place, full of wickedness. Under other circumstances, Lawren believed he and Shawe could have been friends.

Shawe gave account of his actions after having received word first of Lowrie's injury, then of Elspeth's possible imprisonment. He had rushed over to the cloister where the prioress reported Elspeth missing; he had then ridden to Adair Castle to see the bishop who was visiting with Bearnard.

As soon as Shawe made his report, the bishop dispatched

him to the Galloway stronghold to administer last rites to
Lowrie and to ascertain that they did hold Elspeth a prisoner.
The bishop also sent word to the Galloways that he personally
would lead the clan in its selection of their new chief.

Shawe went on to say that Bearnard wanted to storm the
castle, but the bishop had interceded. Ranting and raging over
Shawe's entering into the devil's den, Bearnard had finally con-
sented to provide an escort of Adair warriors. Two stood to one
side of the fireplace; others were positioned at the entrance
door. For every Adair warrior in the room, there were two Galloways close by.

Tension was painfully sharp, almost piercing.

"My lord Bearnard mac Adair penned the letter himself,"
Shawe said. "He and the bishop are very solicitous of young
Lowrie's health."

"Aye, Shawe," Lawren mocked, "that is why both of them
are here to pay their respects. That is why no action was taken
until you received word from my second runner that Elspeth
was my prisoner."

Shawe's faced reddened, but his gaze did not waver from
Lawren's. "I was coming. First, I had to attend to my prayers.
Like you, I do not go into battle unarmed."

"You had finished your prayers by the time you heard about
Elspeth?"

Shawe glared at Lawren. "We'll discuss this matter later. Take
me to Lowrie. I'll administer last rites."

"He doesn't need them."

Taken aback, the priest stared at Lawren. "Your man said he
had received a hammer blow to the head, that the swelling was
internal."

"Aye, he did," Lawren admitted. "Elspeth performed surgery
on him last evening. He is quite recuperated this morning."

"Elspeth?" He stared disbelievingly. "Did you say Elspeth
performed surgery on him?"

Lawren nodded.

"This comes as a surprise," Shawe confessed. "I didn't know she possessed such outstanding medical skills."

"She claims to have acquired them during her travels abroad."

Shawe stepped closer and squinted into Lawren's face. "I don't believe Lowrie is alive any more than I believe Elspeth performed surgery on him. No man recovers from a blow like that. Let me see him. Let me know that he is well."

"Nay."

"I am the overseer of his soul. I demand to see him."

Lawren shook his head.

"Your man charged the Adairs with attacking and killing Lowrie, and I believe he is dead." Shawe caught his rosary and ran it through his hands. *"He is dead!* And you don't want people to know. You fear Highlanders will unite and come against you if they learn that Clan Galloway has no chief but the one called warlock."

He continued to study Lawren, peering deeply into his eyes. "Nay," he muttered, " 'tis Bearnard and the bishop whom you fear."

Lawren's hands tightened around the armrests. Although he respected the priest, appreciated his intelligence, it angered him that Shawe saw the truth, recognized and announced publicly Lawren's fears.

"If I feared any"—Lawren refused to give way to his insecurities by so much as word or deed—"it would be Bearnard and the bishop. Both of them are Saxons, and each has a desire to see more Saxons on our land. Each has the power and determination to bring down the Galloways. Lowrie's death would provide both with the opportunity they need to ride in and assume control of the clan, and I do not want a Saxon ruling over the Galloways." Lawren smiled. "But Lowrie is not dead."

"I was told—"

Lawren held up a silencing hand.

"Since he received what we always called a death blow, my

man thought surely he would die. He had no idea that we had anyone here capable of performing surgery to save Lowrie."

"Nor did I," Shaw murmured.

"I'm sure Bearnard is going to be disappointed when you return with news that Lowrie has recovered from his wound and that his sister is the one who saved him."

"You're wrong in your assessment of the man," Shawe replied. "My lord Bearnard sends his assurance that he had nothing to do with the foul deed. Neither he nor any of his clansmen were in Galloway territory, certainly not at Mountain Cat Canyon. He knew nothing of this incident until your man arrived with news."

Lawren lowered his head, ran his nail beneath the lump of wax, and broke the seal. As he opened the letter, parchment crackled through the building. Bearnard, pleading his innocence in the massacre, sent his condolences on Lowrie's accident, on his imminent death. He swore by holy oath given to the bishop that neither he nor any of the Adairs had been in Galloway country. With so few men none of them would have been foolish enough to enter that deep in enemy territory. In light of the recent events, Bearnard penned, he would reconsider. It seemed the Galloways were easy prey for predators. Bearnard, then, demanded that Lawren release Elspeth.

When Lawren had finished reading the letter, he refolded it. Oddly, he believed Bearnard had written the truth. Bearnard would use whatever means were necessary to regain Gleann nan Duir land, but he would not doom his soul to hell by taking a false oath.

If this were the case, Lawren wondered, who was his enemy?

"The bishop wants me to inform you that he is meeting with a delegate of clan chieftains on the morrow to discuss the plague."

"The plague or the warlock?" Lawren asked.

"The way the bishop sees it, they are the same."

"I always knew his vision was faulty."

Shawe gave him a tight smile. "Is yours much better?"

"I think so."

"I have heard many tales of your valor, Lawren. Bards sing of you throughout the land. Return to the fold of the church. You can be a great Highland chief."

"When I was ten-and-three, the bishop claims that I forsook God and the church. He mandated that in order for me to return I would have to purge my sins openly."

Shawe nodded. "A humbling experience but not painful."

"Aye, priest, it would be painful. Publicly I would have to admit that my mother is a witch, a worshiper of the devil. Then I would have to renounce her and the old way of life. I would have to turn my back on everything Caledonia has taught me."

Again Shawe nodded.

"If I were to do that, priest, I would be confessing a lie. I'd be untrue to myself. Caledonia is an herbalist, a woman of the land, not a devil worshiper." He leaned forward in his chair. "You're a Scotsman, Shawe, and you understand *enech*. Without face we are nothing. How can you ask me to do this? You know I can't and won't do that."

"Nay," Shawe murmured, "you cannot."

Religious philosophies separated priest and warrior; mutual respect and common heritage bonded them.

"If the bishop sends me a satchel of nightlace blossoms and some of the seeds and plants themselves," Lawren said, "I shall release Elspeth to him."

"Nightlaces." Shawe shook his head and laughed shortly. "Where are we going to get them? Once they cloaked the land along the Gleann nan Duir Loch. Now they are gone. Destroyed. None left."

"I'll wager Bearnard will find some quick enough if the bishop persuades him."

"We couldn't locate any for the prioress when she asked," Shawe said, then added: "That's why Elspeth left the cloister. There was a new outbreak of the illness. An entire family had come down with it. The father and mother died, leaving a wee laddie and his sister. Elspeth promised the parents she would save their children. She promised the lady prioress she would find some plants."

Perhaps Elspeth had been telling him the truth, Lawren thought, pensively drawing his finger down his cheek along his jawline. She had come to him directly from the cloister rather than from Bearnard. Or perhaps this woman was not Elspeth, but Beth Balfour from the future.

Last night he had not cared which she was. Last night she had carried him to a magical world where she awakened him to all that he felt was dead, to his inner yearnings. He had been happy to bask in the emotions the two of them had shared, the attraction they had felt between them. It had been easy for him to accept that she was indeed a time-traveler, especially after his mother had recognized that she was different. He still wanted to believe, but in the light of day, it seemed silly, inconceivable.

Shawe rubbed his crucifix. "Do you really believe in the healing power of these flowers, Lawren?"

"I would stake my life on them."

Shawe nodded, walked to the fireplace and gazed at the blaze. "How long do we have to get them to you?"

"Seven days."

"Seven days!" Shawe muttered. "That's not enough time. We shall have to scour the countryside to find them, if we can find any."

" 'Tis all the time you're getting."

The priest walked over to the table, picked up Elspeth's bracelet, and held it in the air. It glinted in the firelight. "You are asking Bearnard to ransom his sister—"

"Nay, Shawe," Lawren said, "I am asking the bishop. Where Elspeth is concerned, I put my trust in you first and the bishop second. You care about her and will wish her to come to no harm. As long as Bearnard gets her inheritance, he couldn't care less about her."

Shawe studied Lawren. "I don't know that Elspeth is your prisoner. Anyone could have stolen her jewelry. This means nothing." The bracelet slipped from his fingers, pinged to the floor, and rolled to a stop in front of the fireplace. " 'Tis your decision to keep me from seeing Lowrie, not so Elspeth. If I am to persuade the bishop and Bearnard to heed your demands, I must know for myself that she is unharmed."

"When you ride off, look up and you'll see her in yonder window."

"Bring her down now."

"The window when you leave," Lawren said softly. "That's as close as you'll get to her. And closer than you'll get to Lowrie."

"You can trust me."

"I trust you more than I trust most people, but not enough to let you close to either Lowrie or Elspeth. No one will accuse me of killing her while she is my prisoner."

The priest paced more, his sandals scuffing against the floor.

"What if we can't find the nightlaces to give to you?"

Propping his elbows on the arms of his chair, he bridged his hands and rested them beneath his chin. "I shall keep her."

"Keep her?" Shawe repeated. "You mean to keep her your prisoner indefinitely?"

"I shall marry her, and let her bear me sons. Galloway sons who will have a claim to the high seat of the Adairs."

"You can't," Shawe exclaimed. "You're excommunicated from the church. No priest will bless a union between the two of you."

"I wouldn't ask." Surprising himself, Lawren said, "I shall go back to a custom and law of the land that is older than the church and much more sacred. I shall handfast her."

Shawe studied him through narrowed eyes. "You're only saying this so I'll repeat it to the bishop and Bearnard. You wouldn't do this."

Lawren's gaze never wavered from the priest. "As surely as the bishop will declare me a heretic and order me executed, I will."

"You may keep Elspeth," Shawe conceded, "but I don't believe you'll carry through with your threats. You're an herbalist who saves lives, not takes them."

"I won't be taking hers."

"Not only her life, but those of her children. Bearnard fears you too much to let your and Elspeth's children live." Shawe closed the distance between him and Lawren. "He would not rest until he had killed them. And Elspeth. And you." When Lawren did not answer, he asked, "You would do this to her?"

"Adairs have done far worse to the Galloways," Lawren replied.

"This woman is innocent. Don't bring your evil on her."

Aye, Lawren silently agreed, Elspeth or Beth, whichever she was, was innocent, and he truly regretted that he must use her. He *was* taunting the priest, sending a message back to the bishop and Bearnard, but the idea of his and her having a child pleased him. His feelings for her were not the callous desires he had revealed to the priest. They were much deeper. He wanted to protect her, to have her by his side for the rest of his life. He wanted to share her laughter, her jest for life. Where she was concerned, he could easily lose himself to sentiment.

He wished things could be different, but they could not. Responsibility rested squarely on his shoulders, and he could not allow his personal feelings for Beth to dictate his actions. He was the champion of Clan Galloway and had sworn to his father that he would avenge his death and see Lowrie established on the high seat. So far he had not avenged Angus's death and Lowrie had nearly died. Leadership of the clan almost fell into enemy hands.

If Lowrie did not regain full use of his mental faculties, the bishop—a Saxon and an ally with Bearnard—certainly would step in and take temporary control of the clan. Knowingly or not, he would be assisting in establishing a new order in the Highlands, one in which Saxons would rule Scots. The idea revolted Lawren, and he swore he would save the kindred no matter how great his personal sacrifices. *Enech,* his face and honor, demanded no less of him.

Marshaling his willpower and intent, Lawren pushed soft and tender thoughts aside. He silenced his conscience and hardened his heart. He remembered his vow to his father, his obligation to the clan and Lowrie.

"Mayhap Elspeth is not as innocent as you think, priest. You see me as evil. She sees me as a desirable man, one she would like to mate with."

"Are you telling me that Elspeth nea Adair is in love with you?"

"Hardly," Lawren drawled. "Surely even you understand the difference in lust and love. She is attracted to me and has been since she was sixteen. Then she begged me to mate with her. Prior to her marriage to Alastair, she wrote and again begged me to mate with her. Twice, Shawe, she was willing to fornicate with the warlock."

The stricken look on Shawe's face told Lawren he had scored a point, but his victory was bitter. "Return to Adair Castle, Shawe," he ordered sharply. "State my terms. Tell the bishop I expect Bearnard to bring the nightlaces in person."

A sense of inevitability hanging in the air, Shawe stared at Lawren. Finally he nodded, turned, and began to walk slowly toward the entrance. Adairs filed behind him. At Lawren's wave, the two headmen and Sloane stepped away from the chair and followed. By the time Shawe and the Adairs reached the door, Galloways had encircled all of them.

"Good priest"—Beth's voice rang out—"you wanted to see me to know that I am unharmed."

Lawren, as well as the priest, whirled around.

A commanding presence, Beth stood in an opened inner doorway, morning sunlight illuminating her, casting her in a glowing nimbus. She was pale, her eyes large. She still wore the green tunic, and it was wrinkled and stained, but she had combed her hair. It hung in a long braid over one shoulder.

From her demeanor, from her comment, Lawren would wager she had heard the majority of his conversation with the priest, if not all of it. It nagged at his conscience, and he wished he could have spared her.

"Look at me, Father," Beth ordered. "Know it is me."

William, Evan, and Sloane fell away from the priest. Shawe, never taking his eyes from Beth, returned to the fireplace. "Are you unharmed, lady?"

She nodded.

"Are they treating you well?"

"I'm their prisoner if you consider that good treatment."

Shawe frowned.

"My lady prioress is worried about you, lady," Shawe said. "You were exhausted from tending to the ill, and she feared you may be coming down with the sickness yourself."

"Please tell her I'm doing fine."

"She bids me tell you that the last bit of nightlace you had seems to be working on the laddie and lassie. Our holy mother believes they will recover."

"Good." Although Beth didn't know these children, she thought of the Alcina twins. She understood the ravages of the disease. Tears of thanksgiving washed her eyes.

"How is Lowrie?" Shawe asked. "Is he alive as the warlock claims?"

"He is alive and is making a speedy recovery," Beth replied.

"Lawren said you did surgery on him? That you learned this during your travels abroad?"

She nodded and succinctly described the procedure to the priest.

When she finished, Shawe asked, "Will he be fully recovered, my lady? Both intellectually and physically?"

"Fully," Beth replied.

"Inform the bishop that Lowrie will ascend the high seat of the Galloways on his sixteenth birthday," Lawren said.

Shawe nodded.

Lawren extended his hand to Beth. "Don't hover in the doorway, madam. Come join me."

Her head held high, her back straight, Beth swept into the

room, past him. The deliberate snub irritated Lawren, but his irritation did not override the pride he felt at seeing her in total control of herself, of the situation. Not even the wrinkled, blood-stained dress with knotted laces detracted from her regal entrance.

When she stood beside Lawren, the priest said, "He—hasn't—you—haven't—"

"Haven't what?" Beth demanded, yet she looked defiantly into Lawren's face. "Fornicated? Nay, not yet."

Visibly disconcerted by her outspokenness on such a delicate subject, Shawe cleared his throat. Lawren grinned. He had to admire the woman; she had spirit and audacity.

"Have you a message for your brother, lady?" Shawe asked.

"Please tell Bearnard that his argument is with Lawren mac Galloway, not with innocent clansmen, women, and children who are coming down with the illness and dying without the nightlace. I shall expect him to settle his differences with Lawren mac Galloway and to send a supply of the plant here for treatment. If Lawren mac Galloway mates with me because of Bearnard, tell my brother that I shall seek revenge against him."

"Against your brother?"

She nodded.

"Your brother professes to having no plants," Shawe said, "but we shall find some. I promise. We shall get you out of here as quickly as we can."

"Until then, Shawe," Beth said, "I would like for you to bring me some clean clothing."

He nodded. "I shall return with your belongings shortly, my lady."

He strode out of the great hall, the Galloway headmen and Sloane following him, leaving Lawren and Beth alone. Lawren searched her face, her eyes, but could read nothing. She had lowered an invisible shield over them, was denying him access to her feelings.

"Good morrow, Beth," he said. "I had not expected to see

you up and about so early. After all that happened last night, I thought surely you would sleep until later in the morning."

"Lowrie awakened me," she said. "He's hungry. I would have sent Annie for some food, but she and her pallet were already gone from the hallway, and Lowrie's manservant had not yet arrived."

She slowly raked her gaze over Lawren, lingered on the belted plaid, but said nothing. Raising her head, she gazed into his eyes. "Did you mean all you said to the priest today?"

Again Beth surprised him with her outspokenness.

"I meant most of it," he replied. "Some was said for effect only."

Her expression never changed, but the color of her eyes seemed to deepen. Last night's luster was replaced by dull disappointment.

"I'm sorry you overheard."

"Last night you let me think you cared for me. I thought you believed me. But today—" She shook her head and waved her hand. Words seemed to fail her.

"If you are indeed from the future, lady, from the world you described to me, you don't understand our ways. The less you know about what is happening the less affected you will be. You will be better off if you trust me."

"Yes, I heard how you were taking care of my well-being." She smiled bitterly. "I thought you were different from Bearnard, from other men of this time period, but you're not. In front of the priest, Adairs and Galloways, you ridiculed me and my feelings for you. You stripped away my integrity and exposed my vulnerability. You didn't allow me the stature of a pawn."

Her accusations made him feel uncomfortable, and he didn't like the feeling at all. "I did it to protect you as much as myself," he said, but knew she would not believe him. "Bearnard looks for weaknesses in people. When he finds it, he uses it as a weapon, destroying them. I cannot afford for Bearnard to find a weakness in me or you." He closed his hand into a fist. "He will exploit us, lady. We would become pawns in his hands."

"Whichever hand I'm in," Beth pointed out, "I'm a pawn. Are you telling me that one is better than the other?"

"Your brother is greedy and grasping. Where he is concerned, I can afford no conscience. I have to let him and the bishop know I am quite serious with my demands. I cannot let them know that you and I care for each other."

"Yet this greedy and grasping man is the one to whom I shall be released when the ransom arrives?"

"Never to Bearnard," Lawren vowed. "Only to the bishop."

She stared at him with soulful eyes that tugged at his heart and made him wish things could be different between them. Like a cormorant, guilt settled heavily on his shoulders; his conscience troubled him. But he could not give in to his softer and more intimate emotions. If he did, he would betray both of them. He was the protector of Clan Galloway, and it was his duty to protect them. He also had to protect her.

She was a strong, spirited woman, but the more he was around her, the more he realized that she was too soft for the harsh reality of life. Either she truly was from another time, or she had been unduly sheltered by both Alastair and the church.

"I wish I could keep you here so that I can guarantee your safety," he said, "but I can't."

"You mean you won't. It suits your purpose to receive the ransom of nightlaces rather than help me."

"Not my purpose," he replied, "but the needs of the people."

They stared at each other.

"If it were my purposes we were considering, things would be different. Always, lady, I must put the needs of the people over my wants and desires, over my own needs. I won't keep you because my people, nay, all Scotsmen, need the nightlace for now, for future generations."

"Once you get your plants," Beth said, her beautiful green eyes focused on him, "will your purpose in regards to me be different?"

"I can never offer you legitimacy, lady, never the sanctity of marriage."

"I'm not interested in the sanctity of marriage. I'm more interested in the sanctity of the heart. How do you feel about me?"

"No matter what my feelings are for you," Lawren said, "they can never come to fruition. I will not confess a lie to reenter the church, and I cannot take you to wife without bringing dishonor on you and on our children. If we do not think of ourselves, we must think of them."

"You told Shawe you would handfast me."

" 'Twas a spur of the moment thought. A threat only. No marriage between us is possible. You and our children would always be in danger. Bearnard would dedicate his life to killing them and you."

"If you wanted to marry," Beth said, "you could. You and your mother have been excommunicated from the church all these years and have safely hidden in the mountains. What would keep you from hiding with your wife?"

"If the woman were a Galloway, I would have no problem," he admitted, "but I have tender feelings for an Adair, lass, the chief's daughter." He clasped her hand in his and squeezed gently. "When my father was alive, Bearnard had no need to hunt my mother and me. We weren't a threat to either him or the church. We were excommunicated, but weren't declared heretics. Now we're becoming a threat, and you and our children surely would be."

"What if—the woman was willing to take the risk?"

"I couldn't let her." He rose from the chair and moved until he stood directly in front of her.

Beth stopped talking in third person. "It's my choice."

"Not really," he said quietly. "If what you have told me is true, madam, you come from another time and place. Our customs are foreign to you." He brushed a strand of hair from her cheek, and his eyes softened. "If you are truly from this world, you understand that neither of us has a choice, Beth. We never had one. Both of us are pawns of fate. Our paths are destined to pass but never to intertwine."

The inevitability of his words caused a deep sadness to settle over them. Beth hurt so deeply she couldn't speak. Even if she could, she had no argument left. The front door opened, and Sloane and the two headmen strode into the great hall. Lawren stepped away from her.

When they reached Beth and Lawren, Evan said, "I trust the lad is recovering well, madam?"

"Aye, headman, quite well. He's testy and demanding as only a ten-and-six year-old male can be who thinks he is now a man."

Evan, William, and Sloane laughed; Lawren smiled.

"If you'll excuse me," Beth said, "I'll prepare Lowrie's meal." As regally as she had entered the hall, Beth swept out.

Fate was indeed a two-faced god, Lawren thought grimly, both good and evil. Or perhaps fate was merely indifferent. Fate had brought Beth to him in his hour of greatest need, had saved his brother, had touched his heart. But this same fate would keep them apart.

Shawe had been right. No matter how much Lawren desired Beth, he would never allow her to be hurt because of him and his beliefs. Their being together, having children, all of that was nothing more than dreams . . . beautiful dreams with no substance. Whether Beth remained here or returned to her world, Lawren realized that he would never have her. She was lost to him through the ages.

Evan tossed several more pieces of wood onto the fire, the blaze sputtering and crackling. From afar Lawren heard his headman speak.

"You wanted to talk with me about the attack on the lads?"

"And the rescue," William added.

Lawren shifted his weight in the chair. Reluctantly he pushed thoughts of Beth aside and tried to concentrate on matters at hand. He looked at the parchment he still held, the letters dancing on the page before him. He carefully refolded the page.

"Sloane," he said, "tell the lads we're going to give Bearnard a chance to bring us the nightlace before we ride. William, bring

Jamie to me. Both he and Lowrie should be rested by now. 'Tis time they gave full account of their adventure."

Sloane and William strode out; Evan moved closer to the fireplace. A tray of food in her hands, Beth returned to the great hall as Lawren walked toward the stairs.

"Is Lowrie well enough for me to speak to him?" he asked. She nodded. "Don't upset him."

He and Evan followed her up the stairs. They had not climbed high when Beth spoke.

"Please find me a clean gown to wear until my belongings arrive."

"A gown?" he muttered, fighting his way through his troubled thoughts; Lowrie; the strangeness of the massacre; his conversation with Shawe; the subsequent one with Beth.

"Yes," she said. "This one is beyond repair. Quite dirty, torn, and bloodstained. I should like a bath and something clean to wear."

"Madam," he snapped, the events of the past month crushing in on him, "I have two men dead, two wounded, and God only knows how many Adairs crawling around in my territory, and you are fussing about a bath and clothes! Surely even you can understand we have more important matters to deal with."

She stopped walking. He bumped into her. Lawren stumbled back several steps, as did Evan. Beth turned. Her eyes sparkled with unshed tears, but she retained her composure.

"I notice that you took time to bathe and change clothes," she said softly. As thoroughly as she had looked at him when she first walked into the great hall, she looked at him now, making him acutely aware of the red tunic and kilted tartan that he wore.

He pushed his hand through his hair. "Aye, madam, I did."

"Rob and Damh are dead," she continued in that same soft tone. "I can do nothing to help them. I have saved Lowrie's life, and both he and Jamie are on their way to recovery. I need to be clean if I'm going to nurse the wounded. A bath and clean dress are quite important to me and require so little from you!

Neither are matters of the heart and will reveal no weakness in you that I can exploit."

Her gaze never wavered from his. "I may be your prisoner, but as long as I am Elspeth nea Adair I am a chief's daughter, and I refuse to dress like a beggar. Until my clothing arrives, I shall expect you to provide me with decent attire."

What did he know about women's clothing? He almost spoke the words aloud, but he saw the stirring of emotion deep within her green eyes. Outwardly she was poised, drawn to her full height, her head tilted arrogantly, but in her eyes was a vulnerability he had not observed before. Then he realized that neither of them was talking about clothing. Both of them were reeling beneath the stinging blow of fate. Each was searching for stability in the midst of these catastrophic events; the dress was Beth's symbol of this security.

Again he was inundated with the desire to take her into his arms and to hold her, to assure her that everything would be all right, that he would take care of her. But he couldn't make such a promise. Once the ransom was delivered, he would have to place her in custody of the bishop.

"Speak to Annie, she'll—"

"I did," Beth replied quietly. "She referred me to you."

Turning he said to Evan, "Get Annie for me."

With a nod, the headman clipped down the stairs, returning shortly with the old woman.

"See that Elspeth gets a bath and clean clothes," Lawren said.

"I'm busy." Annie gave Beth a spiteful look.

"You'll do what I say," Lawren snapped. Not only did he have to deal with matters of life and death, he had to settle petty quarrels between the women of the castle.

Annie jerked up.

"Draw her a bath." Staccato-voiced, he added, "Get her all the clothing she wants. And jewelry. And shoes."

"Where is she to bathe?"

"In my quarters."

Annie nodded.

"May I also have my own chambers?" Beth asked.

"Mayhap the dungeon would suit you," Annie threatened.

Shaking his head in frustration, Lawren waved his hand at the servant. "Madam," he said to Beth, "I'll give your request consideration."

"Thank you."

Beth turned and mounted the stairs, Lawren and Evan following her. No matter how irritated Lawren might become with her, he could only admire and respect her. Whether she came directly from the prioress or from Bearnard, whether she came from the future to the past, she had acted bravely since she had entered the castle. Many lasses would have succumbed to hysteria or to tears. Not Beth. She had stood up to him every step of the way and was still defying him. As she ascended the stairs, he followed her into his brother's chambers.

Sitting up in bed, flanked by pillows, Lowrie beamed at them as they walked in. "Evan," he called out, " 'tis good to see you. Elspeth said you were the one who saved me." He patted the side of the bed. "Sit down and tell me all about it. I don't remember anything after I was hit."

Beth set the tray on the chest as Evan and Lawren drew up chairs and sat to one side of the bed. While Lowrie ate, Evan recounted the story of the rescue.

When he finished, he said, "If you ever pull such a trick again, lad, I'll tan your backside."

Lowrie grinned. "You can't do that after I celebrate my birth date. I'll be a man, chief of the Galloways."

"Don't speak so hastily, lad," Evan said. "You'll not be a man until you have lifted the *clach cuid fir.*"

"The manhood stone," Lowrie scoffed with youthful arrogance. "I shall fly through the ceremony with colors."

"Only if I allow it," Beth said.

"You have nothing to do with it, woman," Lowrie snapped. "Don't overestimate your importance."

"Don't forget you owe her your life," Lawren said quietly.

"I shall repay—"

"You are freed of it only when she accepts your gift." Lawren turned to her. "Surely he will be recovered enough that he can lift the manhood stone on his sixteenth birthday."

"Don't consult with her," Lowrie snapped. "No Adair will tell me whether I can lift the *clach cuid fir*. The decision is mine to make."

From a corner of her mind, Beth salvaged a tidbit of information on the *clach cuid fir*. This was the coming-of-age ceremony that all Scotsmen underwent. They had to lift a stone that weighed from around a hundredweight to almost three hundred pounds and set it onto a nearby wall that must be at least waist high.

"I'm sure he'll be recovered enough to participate," Beth said, removing his tray from the bed and setting it on the chest.

"Lowrie!" a masculine voice called from the hallway.

"Jamie!" Lowrie looked up.

Jamie mac Galloway, followed by William, rushed into the room. His golden brown hair fell loosely around his face. His shoulder was bulky from bandages beneath his tunic, and his arm was in a sling.

"I thought sure you were dead." Jamie moved close to the bed and stared curiously at his friend's bandaged and shaved head. "Caledonia told my grandmother and me about your operation. A hole in your skull," he mused. He looked curiously at Elspeth, then at Lawren. "Is there any chance that his brains will spill out?"

"That would be a concern only if he had them." Evan snorted.

Beth laughed softly. "No, they're quite intact."

"Good day, William," Lowrie said. " 'Tis good to see you."

"Good to see you, laird." The headman shoved away from the door frame and entered the room.

"Annie is quite angry," Jamie said to Lowrie. "She is demanding to know how you slipped out of the castle without anyone's knowing."

"Aye, lad," Lawren said, "I've been wondering about that also."

" 'Twas quite simple," Lowrie bragged. "Knowing that Annie and the other kindred would be searching for me, we knew we could get out only if I were disguised. Leaving behind some of Rob's clothes for me to wear, Rob and Jamie left the castle together and rode a short distance. Jamie returned with Rob's helmet hidden in his satchel."

"When Lowrie and I left," Jamie picked up, "Lowrie put on Rob's clothing and his helmet. His face was hidden by the visor and the mail cheek-and-neck guard. You know he and Rob are . . . were the same built. Everyone thought he was Rob."

Lowrie laughed. "We wondered if we could get away with it, and we did! Rob said we would. Jamie and I didn't think so."

"Aye, he and I laid a wager," Jamie said. "If Lowrie escaped undetected, I would give Rob my gold torque."

"You were quite upset when he won the wager and demanded that you give it to him."

The lads laughed. For the time being, the memories of the wager wiped out the sorrow of his friend's death.

"Did you lads notice anything unusual about the attack?" Lawren asked. "Anything that will help us find the culprits?"

Jamie shook his head. "We had scattered in the canyon and were separated from each other. I heard a horse approaching, and thought it was either Lowrie or Rob. I looked up and saw the Adair warrior."

Eagerly Lawren said, "Would you recognize him again?"

"Nay, his face was completely hidden by a helmet. I couldn't believe Adairs were at the canyon. Before I realized what was happening, he loosed an arrow and it struck me in the shoulder. I fell off my horse and hit my head on a huge stone. I was dazed for a little while. I didn't see Rob anywhere. I called out to him. Then I looked around and saw the warrior kneeling over Lowrie. I don't remember anything else until Evan and the lads had arrived."

"I told you," Lowrie said. "I felt his tears on my face."

"Bah!" Evan and William scoffed at the same time.

"Warriors wouldn't be crying over you," William said. "Nay, he was stripping your torque from your neck."

"Aye," William agreed, "you lads were carrying expensive weaponry and jewelry. Any warrior would be proud to claim your possessions as his war booty."

"He was crying," Lowrie insisted. "I remember the tears."

"It can be as you say," Beth replied, "but it can also be Annie's tears that you are remembering. She cried over you when they brought you to the castle."

"That sounds more probable," William said.

Lowrie shrugged. "I know someone cried over me."

Beth walked over to the window, stepped into the alcove, and sat on the bench. Leaning back against the wall, clutching a pillow to her chest, she closed her eyes and enjoyed the morning breeze.

Last night she had clung to the hope that she was dreaming or hallucinating. This morning she faced the stark truth. She was in eleventh-century Scotland, and she had taken Elspeth nea Adair's place. The chances were great she would never return to her time.

She might not see the clinic again, her colleagues or her patients. What would happen to them? she wondered. Even if she could not return, she had to find a way to get some nightlace back to them. That was their only hope . . . and it was growing smaller with each passing moment. This was not a romantic movie set of the eleventh century; it was not an historical novel. This was reality, harsh, cold and cruel. She was a participant, not an actress, not an observer.

The conversation she had overheard between Lawren and the priest had unsettled her. Until that moment she had fully trusted him, had thought he cared for her. Then she realized that he, like Bearnard and the bishop, was a warrior intent on protecting what he considered to be the rights of the clan. And he would do it because honor was more important to these people than life itself, for a certainty more important than love.

On deeper thought, she realized that while she didn't accept

Lawren's motivations, she understood them. She could forgive him for that; he was fighting the only way he knew how. She was upset because he had openly flaunted her emotions for him, had belittled them and her in front of the priest, the Adair warriors, and the Galloways. She had thought Sam's jilting her at the altar had hurt. Compared to what she felt when she heard Lawren publicly mock her, it was nothing. Through it all, she still cared for Lawren, and she understood that he was protecting her the only way he knew how.

Coming to grips with that was difficult but not nearly as difficult as Beth's having to accept this primitive culture. She was going to have to become one of these people and give up her own personal standards to live by theirs. Most disconcerting of all was her being an Adair and not a Galloway. She would be stuck in the past loving a man whom she could never have.

A knock interrupted her thoughts.

"Come," Lawren called out.

Annie entered the room. She avoided looking at Beth, concentrating on Lawren instead. "Her bath is drawn."

"In the master suite?"

"Nay, in the mistress's wardrobe. The tub is already set up." He nodded. "That is good, Annie. I hadn't thought of it."

"Clothes, shoes, and jewelry are laid out. Is there anything else you want me to do?"

"Aye, appoint one of the kindred as her personal maid."

"Personal maid!" Annie exclaimed.

"Aye."

Beth couldn't help but laugh softly.

"What about the lass, Fenella?"

"Have you gone daft, Lawren mac Galloway! If you have no concern about your honor, consider your father's. Consider the clan," the old woman shouted and waved her hand toward Beth. "She is an Adair, our prisoner, not an honored guest."

"Good woman," Lawren said in a quiet voice that belied his anger, "my patience is at an end. Bridle your tongue. It has been loose since Elspeth arrived at the castle, and I have suffered much from you. Do not question my authority again."

"Aye."

Lawren waved to Beth. "Return to my chambers. Fenella will be along shortly to assist you in your bath."

Eleven

Not wanting to be alone, Beth would have much preferred to wait with the crowd in Lowrie's room, but she did not argue with Lawren. She had pushed as far as she dared. She returned to the master suite where she was served the morning meal. She quickly devoured the porridge, crusty bread lathered in cheese, and a glass of milk. Then she impatiently paced the floor and waited for Fenella. Two hours had passed before the child came bounding into the room, a large basket over each arm.

Her eyes glowed. "Annie said I was to be your personal maid."

"You are."

"I'll sleep in your room. And I won't have to work in the kitchen. And everyone will be jealous."

Beth laughed, immediately liking the child.

"If you'll follow me, my lady, I'll take you to your own apartment."

"My own apartment?"

"Aye, Lawren said you were to have your own rooms. Do you have possessions you wish me to carry for you?"

Grasping her watch, Beth shook her head.

"Come then." Fenella led the way out of the master suite. " 'Tis a grand apartment on the second floor. You'll have privacy. A separate bedroom. And a wardrobe, a huge wardrobe."

"Does this apartment belong to anyone?" Beth asked curiously, remembering Annie's reference to the mistress.

"It did belong to the lady of the castle," the child said over her shoulder, "but we haven't had a lady since Lowrie's mother died five years ago."

Beth followed Fenella down the stairs and into the bedroom. It wasn't nearly as large as the suite Lawren occupied, but it was quite comfortable and beautifully furnished. An ornately carved chest sat at the foot of the bed; another at the head. Tapestries hung on the plastered and painted wall and over the doors. A table and two trestle stools stood against one wall.

Much to Beth's surprise a desk sat in the large window alcove. The shutters were opened, and light spilled into the area. Walking closer, she ran her hands over the sheet of parchment that lay on top of the desk. Other sheets were rolled up, tied with ribbons and tucked into pigeonholes. Several bottles of ink set out. One by one she picked them up. Brown. Black. Red. Like the parchment sheets, quills pens were stored in the pigeonholes. She ran her fingers over the tips of the feathers.

Standing beside Beth, Fenella said, "This desk and the writing implements belong to Lawren."

Beth looked at her in surprise.

"After our lady died, Lawren used to come visit his father and stayed in these rooms. Since he moved into the castle, he said he was going to move it to the master solar, but he's been too busy." Running her fingers over the desk, she added proudly, "Lawren is educated. He can read and write and do numbers. He was Angus's clerk."

"Can you read and write?" Beth asked.

"I'm learning," Fenella said. "Lawren has some queer ideas. He believes that all people should be able to read and write. What I shall do with the learning, I don't know. I'm not destined to be a grand lady."

"Perhaps someday you'll be a clerk."

"A clerk!" Fenella laughed aloud. "I've never heard tell of a woman being a clerk."

Beth smiled. "You may be the first."

"I wouldn't mind," the child threw over her shoulder as she

crossed the sleeping chamber. She walked through an opened door into a much larger room where she set her baskets on the floor. "Here's your wardrobe."

Following her, Beth stepped through the door. She had been expecting a closet of sorts, but this huge room belied all her expectations. A fire burned in the fireplace; torches, in wall holders, and candles burned brightly throughout the room. Large tables and chests circled the room, and the walls were covered in clothing pegs.

In the center of the room and to the side of the fireplace stood a bathtub that was the size of a Jacuzzi and would easily accommodate five or six adults. It was filled with water, and the canopy drawn. Flagons of oil and dishes of soap sat on a small square table next to the tub. Towels and bathing cloths hung on a rack attached to the outside of the tub.

Fenella danced over to a smaller table and ran her hand over a silver basin and pitcher. "This is for washing your hair," she announced. "Isn't it grand? It belonged to our lady."

Again she twirled around. "You'll like the wardrobe, especially when you get all your clothing. We'll hang your furs over there." She pointed. "Tunics here." She clapped her hands together excitedly. "We'll hang them all over the room, and you can change clothes as many times a day as you wish."

"Aren't you forgetting that I'll soon be gone?"

"Nay, my lady." Fenella shook her head. "Annie says you'll not be rescued. Bearnard doesn't want you, just your inheritance. The bishop and prioress probably want to rescue you, but don't have the nightlaces."

Beth was startled at the matter-of-factness with which the child spoke. But she drew herself short. She shouldn't be surprised. This was Fenella's world; she understood its nuances. What was horrifying and startling to Beth was common occurrence to residents.

"Annie says the only way you'll be of any use to us Galloways is for Lawren to kill you and send your head to your brother."

Beth swallowed the bile in her throat. "Thank you, Fenella," she muttered. "Do you have any more good news for me?"

The child giggled. "Annie's angry because Lawren likes you."

Beth laughed with her and unashamedly listened as Fenella regaled her with castle gossip. She knew very few of the participants, but she enjoyed hearing their stories anyway. The next few hours were some of the most relaxing Beth had spent in a long time, certainly the most relaxing since her time displacement.

Yesterday and last night she had been exhausted; today she was feeling better. Still her body hadn't caught up, or hadn't slowed down, to her new time zone. She had a hint of a headache, and her joints seemed to be on the verge of aching. She luxuriated in the bath, only getting out when her skin was red and puckered.

After she dried off, Fenella helped her dress. Beth stepped into soft leggings; she slipped on delicate cloth shoes. Next came the undertunic, a chemise; then the brown overtunic.

Beth paraded in front of the looking glass attached to the wall, pirouetting this way, then that. This gown, simpler than the green one she had been wearing, reminded her of the long dresses women had worn in the sixties—the 1960s that was. She liked it; it fit well.

"Which girdle do you wish?" Fenella called out.

Beth moved over to the table laden with belts and sashes. She searched through them, pulling aside several. Finally she held up a yellow and brown diaphanous sash.

"This one."

Fenella quickly wove it through a gold chain-link belt and wrapped it about Beth's hips. She fastened it, so that the end of the sashes flowed down to Beth's feet. "Select your veils and wimple," the child said. "I'll arrange them for you."

"No veils. No wimple," Beth declared. "It's quite one thing to be garbed in a long skirt, quite another to have my head and shoulders trussed. I'll go without."

Seating Beth on one of the small benches, Fenella combed her hair dry. She oohed and aahed over it, brushing, stroking, running her hands through it. Finally she had pulled the sides up and clipped them in place with decorative combs. She plaited the back so that it hung in a single braid.

Standing back, Fenella asked, "I shall take the soiled clothing to the washroom. Is there anything you wish me to do before I leave?"

"No."

Fenella quietly collected the clothing in a basket and slipped out of the apartment, leaving Beth alone. She walked around the wardrobe, touching the tables, looking at the ironing implements—the board and the iron itself. Scissors, needles, thread. Braids and laces. Fabrics of all sorts. Beth touched a piece of silk; she ran her hand over a woolen tartan.

After she had explored each nook and cranny, she walked into the bedroom. It was more intimate than the master suite, much more comfortable for her. She sat on the bed, running her hand over the linen coverlet, richly colored in silk embroidery and appliqués. She admired the furniture, the intricate carvings inlaid with gold and silver. She finally stood in the alcove in front of the desk.

She brushed her palm over the parchment, traced her fingertip over the lines that had been ruled on it. Sitting down, she picked up the quill and ran it through her fingers. After touching the point, she dipped it into the inkwell, then started sketching. At first she found it awkward to use the quill, to get accustomed to its point, but she soon mastered it. Her hand flew over the page as she lost herself in her drawing.

She had no idea how long she had been working when she heard a knock on the door.

"Enter," she called. When the door opened, she said, "Fenella, I'm using some of Lawren's parchment. I shall need to replace it, the ink and quills. Where may I purchase some?"

"Since you haven't found your elusive manuscript," Lawren said, "have you decided to write one yourself?"

Startled, Beth dropped the pen, ink splattering on the parchment. Rising, she turned toward him. He still wore the tartan plaid and red tunic, but his face was beard-stubbed, his hair windblown. Beth's heart skipped a beat; she caught her breath.

He looked at her, his gaze slowly moving down the length of her body, as slowly moving back up. When his eyes locked with hers, she saw the fire of appreciation flickering in them; they warmed her . . . they set her on fire.

"Do you like your quarters?"

"Yes, thank you."

Beth heard a shuffle by the door. Looking beyond Lawren she saw Sloane standing in the corridor.

"I shall be leaving shortly," Lawren said.

"Leaving," she whispered.

"Lowrie is going to be all right?" he questioned.

"Yes." She searched his face. "I thought you were not going to ride against the Adairs."

"I'm not."

"How long are you going to be gone?"

He shrugged, then asked, "Are you happy with Fenella as your personal maid?"

"Yes."

"Good." He waved toward the doorway. "Sloane will be your protector."

Again she glanced at the Highlander in the corridor. "My protector or my guard?"

"Your protector. I trust him implicitly. Evan and William are my father's headmen, the two men whom he trusted most out of the clan. Sloane is mine. He will see that no one harms you. If you need anything, ask him or Fenella."

"Am I to be confined to this apartment while you're gone?"

"Nay, you'll have full run of the castle."

Pleased, Beth smiled to herself.

His next words cut short her pleasure. "At all times you will have Fenella and Sloane with you."

Beth looked over Lawren's shoulder at the warrior. "Is he

going to stay in my chambers with me, or am I to be locked in my room each evening?"

"Only Fenella will share your quarters with you, and you will not be locked in at night. You can go wherever you wish in the castle. Sloane is here only for your protection and will always be outside your door. If you need him, all you have to do is call."

Beth was finding herself to be one massive contradiction. One minute she liked Lawren; the next she didn't. She trusted him; she didn't. Earlier she had been disappointed in Lawren's behavior and misrepresentation of her to the priest. Now she was disappointed that he was leaving. Even though he was entrusting her to Sloane, Beth was frightened to be left behind. Annie was not the only Galloway who wanted her dead. Beth would wager that all of them did. Sloane was one man; he couldn't take on the entire clan and win.

Lawren had told her that he would protect her, and he had. In the short time she had been here, he had proved time and again that he was the only one who would, who could protect her. And if something happened to him, she didn't know what her fate would be. Ironically, this man who was holding her for ransom, was her lifeline.

"Where are you going?" she asked.

"To see if I can discover how the Adairs penetrated our lines of defense without our knowing about it. Also, I want to check to see if any more of the people are ill." He pulled his gloves from his girdle and started putting them on.

"Take me with you," Beth said.

He looked up.

"Let me help you."

"Another time. This journey will be too hard on you."

"Not nearly as hard as my remaining here without you."

"You will miss me?"

"I'll be frightened to be here by myself."

"I'm leaving Sloane with you. No one will hurt you."

"Not until we receive word from the bishop. And you have

said Bearnard is not going to honor the ransom demand. Annie also said it. The priest acted as if he thought it were impossible to find the plants. What if word comes while you are gone that the ransom isn't to be met? That you have been declared a heretic and an enemy of the people? What will my fate be?"

Lawren turned from her and walked across the room. Standing in the alcove in front of the grilled encasement, he stared out the window.

"Not even Sloane," she said, "if he were a mind to, could save me."

Lawren looked down at the desk top and touched the parchment.

"Even now," Beth said, "your leadership of the clan is tenuous. The kindred are not persuaded that keeping me alive is really exacting revenge on Bearnard."

Lawren picked up the page and held it closer to the light. Disregarding their previous conversation, he said, "You're an artist?"

Irritated, but determined not to lose her temper and perhaps a modicum of advantage that she might have, Beth answered, "I enjoy doing portraits. They relax me."

The nightlace," he murmured appreciatively. "You have captured its delicate beauty."

His compliment pleased her. She stepped closer and peered at her drawing, at the blossom in the bottom corner of the parchment.

Lawren stared at her thoughtfully. "I thought you said there were no more nightlaces, that people in your time considered them to be a legend."

She nodded.

"If what you say is true, and if you are Beth Balfour, how do you know what the flower looks like?"

"There is a fresco of you and of the nightlace on the wall of the master suite," Beth replied. "Remember, I told you about it."

"The painting of me?" he said. "Do you suppose, madam,

that you have traveled back in time to write both the manuscript and to paint my portrait?"

Although he teased her, chill bumps chased down Beth's spine. Remembering the author's signature at the bottom of the fresco, the cursive E, Beth glanced down at the parchment, now lying on the desk. With a start she realized that she was drawing Lawren. He was in the same pose as the one he had assumed for the fresco, as the one he had assumed last night when she had been telling him about her life.

"I have never seen a drawing like this, lady." Lawren slid onto the stool and studied the drawing more closely. "It's much too detailed and it looks real. It is quite eerie."

"My lady—" Fenella burst into the room. "I cut the laces from your green dress, washed and hung it up." She saw Lawren and hushed up. Moving to the desk, she peered curiously over his shoulder at the parchment. "My lady!" She gasped, her face white, her eyes huge circles in her little face. "You've drawn Lawren!"

"Not really," Beth said, wishing neither had seen the drawing since Lawren seemed displeased with it.

"Aye, 'tis," Fenella insisted. "I can tell from looking. His hair. His eyes. His nose."

" 'Tis unusual to draw such an exact replica of a person that one can easily recognize him," Lawren said.

"Aye," Fenella agreed. "Anyone who sees it will know it's Lawren."

Beth turned away from the man and child and gazed out the window.

"But I like it," Lawren added.

Beth spun around. "You do?"

"Aye. Perhaps you'll do a fresco of it in the master suite, one that has my symbol in it. The nightlace?"

"Perhaps," Beth mumbled, but her heart was racing.

Lawren's words jarred a memory. She had been touching the fresco plaster—not the plastered wall—when she tumbled back in time. In particular she had been touching the nightlace. All this time it had been niggling at the back of her mind, but she had been too preoccupied with other matters to give it thought. The flower on the painting, not the painting itself, must have been her gateway into time. If she painted the portrait, perhaps she would be creating her portal back to the future. Maybe she wouldn't need the brilliant scientist or his Dorian after all.

"I'm glad you were thinking about me," he murmured.

Trembling with excitement, Beth glanced down at the sketch. "It's difficult not to when my entire future lies in your hands."

"Can you ride a horse?"

Puzzled, she looked at him.

"You wanted to go with me. Can you ride a horse?"

She had only ridden twice and that was several years ago, but now was not a time for confessions. She nodded.

"Like you had performed surgery before."

"I can ride," she insisted, determined that her lack of experience would not keep her behind. "Let me go. I won't be a bother. I promise."

His grin softened into a smile. "You have been a bother since you appeared in my life. I doubt matters will change." He glanced down at the narrow skirt of her tunic, the delicate fabric shoes that tipped from beneath the hem. "You'll have to change your clothing. Fenella, get her a riding tunic. Leggings and boots."

"Aye," the child murmured.

"A heavy cloak and gloves," he added. "While you're dressing, I'll see to your mount." He strode toward the door. "Sloane, bring her to the courtyard when she is dressed."

The room was awhirl with excitement as Beth changed clothes. She hummed; she sang; she danced. She was going with Lawren, and she was going to paint the fresco. For the first time since she had traveled backward in time, she felt as if she were in control of her destiny, as if she were actually doing something rather than being victimized.

Fenella dashed here and there, returning with her arms laden with goodies. Soon Beth was attired in woolen trousers, fitted through the buttocks but loose in the legs. Alternatively, long fabric strips were wound closely from ankle to calf, like puttees, to protect the fabric from wear and tear and to provide protection from cold and dirt in bad weather. Fenella helped Beth into her tunic and belted it at the waist with a leather girdle so that the hem struck her knees. She slipped boots on her feet and tied them at the ankle.

Fenella scrambled through the wardrobe, filling a leather satchel with clothing, more clothing than Beth figured she would wear in a good while, but the child would not be dissuaded. She firmly believed in being ready for any likelihood. Chances were Lawren would be stopping at several of the hamlets, she said, and he and Beth would be visiting with important clan leaders. The satchel was so large and bulky, Beth expected Lawren to refuse to let her take it. She could hear Sam griping about it, or her father, or her brother-in-law.

When Lawren picked it up, he bounced it up and down in the air as if weighing it. He arched his brows. "We're only going to be gone a couple of days. You have enough clothing to last you for weeks."

" 'Twas my doing, Lawren." Fenella planted herself in front of him. "I'm her maid, and I want her to be proud of me. I must take good care of her. You'll never know when some of these clothing might be needed."

"Ah, lassie, you're right," he droned, slinging the bag over his shoulder and holding his hand out to Beth. "Are you ready, lady?"

She nodded. She had been ready for this all her life.

Astride a golden-red mare, William holding the reins, Beth waited in the courtyard as the Galloways assembled. The warriors made no secret of their irritation over Beth's riding with them. Thinking Evan had begun to like her, at least to accept her, Beth was taken aback when he as well as William voiced their disapproval. Lawren listened to his kinsmen's comments and complaints, but was not dissuaded from taking her.

Lawren mounted a huge back stallion. Evan, riding to the right of him, said something, and Lawren laughed, the deep, rusty sound washing pleasantly over Beth. In the afternoon sun, his black hair was burnished; the breeze blew it wildly from his face. It lifted his cloak from his shoulders and swirled it in the air, revealing his bright yellow tunic, black vest, and trousers. It emphasized his muscular physique.

As if he knew she were thinking about him, Lawren looked across the courtyard and smiled at her. He waved and beckoned her to join him. William, holding the reins to the mare, guided Beth to where Lawren was. They passed many of the kindred whom Beth recognized by face, having seen them in the great hall last night and this morning. When she rode past Jamie, she smiled. He nodded slightly, then quickly looked away. The others gazed at her scornfully.

But she was not as frightened of them today as she was last night. As long as Lawren was with the Galloways, she no longer feared they would lose control and do her bodily harm. Still, she had not grown accustomed to their open hatred of her, and probably would not.

Grunts of disapproval, frowns, and snide remarks followed her as she moved toward Lawren. Evan glared at her but moved so that she was to the right of Lawren. William handed her the reins, turned, and strode toward his horse.

"This is your first time to ride with Highlanders?" Lawren said.

Nodding, she smiled.

"It will be an experience you'll not soon forget. Nothing is as beautiful as the Scottish Highlands."

He caught her hands in his and examined her gloves, pushing them tightly on her fingers, making sure they were fastened around her wrist. Then he tucked the hood of her cloak more closely about her face, his gloved fingers lingering on her cheeks.

"The bite of the wind is sharp," he said, "and you're not accustomed to it. You need to protect your face."

The light strokes of his hands sent pleasure warmly through her. It curled around her heart, reminding her of the man whom she loved, of the man whom she could never claim as her own . . . whether she stayed here or returned to the twentieth century.

"Thank you for letting me ride with you." She glanced over her shoulder at Evan who scowled at her.

"You had better keep your gratitude until we have ridden up and down the mountains for several hours. You may be cursing, not thanking, me."

"Never." Beth laughed joyously. "Where is Sloane?" she asked. "Isn't he going with us?"

"Nay, you have me to protect you, so I'm leaving him to be with Lowrie."

Thinking about the broad-shouldered warrior with the bushy red hair and beard, Beth laughed. "I think the lad will find it quite difficult to escape him."

"Even I would find that difficult, if not impossible," Lawren confessed with a grin.

He raised his hand and brought it forward. The company began to move, he and Beth in the lead, Evan and William falling in behind them. Beth held her head high and sat a little straighter as she gazed at the banner man riding directly ahead of them, as she proudly noted the colors of the Galloways furling through the air.

Midafternoon they began their journey, traveling over a narrow trail that wound up and down one mountain after another. During their journey, other riders would periodically join them. Each of these men would ride beside Lawren and talk; then as unobtrusively as they had joined the column, they disappeared. By sunset, Lawren stopped the party at a brook.

"We'll camp here," he called out.

"It would be better for us to push on to the canyon," Evan said.

Surveying the sky, William said, "Aye, we can easily make it."

"That will take us about two more hours," Lawren said. "It will be dark by then. We won't be able to see anything when we arrive. Tomorrow will be soon enough to leave."

"Aye, but we know the terrain, and we shall have a full moon."

"The horses are tired. We shall rest them here."

"Rest the horses." Evan snorted as the kindred threaded farther down the brook to the largest pool of water. He glared at Beth. "Or rest for the woman? You shouldn't have brought her. She has slowed us down."

"Aye," William agreed.

"Set up camp," Lawren ordered, "and see to the evening meal. I shall set Elspeth up elsewhere, so she may have privacy."

William followed the order. Evan gave Lawren a long, hard stare before he rode off, leaving Lawren and Beth hidden in the copse of trees. Serenaded by the creak of leather, the low murmur of voices as the men talked to one another, and the whizzing of the horses as they drank, Beth gazed at the breathtaking sweep of the Highland glen. Ordinarily untamed and craggy, the hues of the setting sun colored it softly. Green-topped mountains dipped and rose around them. Wildflowers were dots of color: yellow, lavender, and red.

Large oak trees, reminding her of the power of the Highland warrior, jutted up here and there, but for the most part the glen was flat, covered with low growth. The delicate shades of bracken and heather on either side of the pathway were broken by the mountain stream. The rushing water was the deepest, the purest blue Beth had ever seen—the color of Lawren's eyes.

She looked over at Lawren. "It's beautiful."

"Aye, 'tis the Highlands."

Hearing a low moo, Beth turned to see several huge, red cattle with long hair and thick, stubby horns ambling through the brush.

"Ours," Lawren said. "This is where we bring them when we think they are in danger."

"Are these?"

"They were," he replied. "These were the sick ones that Evan treated the day Lowrie was attacked by Adairs. They're fine now. Our herdsmen watched them closely. One of them who rode with me today reported that the cattle had been given some poisoned berries."

"Deliberately?" Beth asked.

"Aye, someone evidently ground up and mixed berries in with the grain. The cattle wouldn't have eaten them otherwise. Once they tasted the berries, they probably stopped eating. That saved them."

"But who would have had access to the cattle's feed bags?"

"That's the question I've been pondering."

"It sounds as if your culprit could—"

"Be one of us," Lawren finished. " 'Tis a jarring thought, but it has crossed my mind. I hope I can prove otherwise."

He dismounted and led their horses close to the stream. After he had tethered them, he took off his gloves and shoved them beneath his belt. Then he unfastened Beth's gloves and slipped each of them off. After tucking them under her girdle, he caught her by the waist and swung her off the horse.

The minute her feet touched the ground, she knew she was in trouble. She wobbled and would have fallen, but he grabbed her. Until now she had not known exactly how stiff she was.

"Did you lie to me about knowing how to ride a horse?" he asked softly.

"No, I've ridden twice before," she replied. "A long time ago." She looked up at him, waning sunlight playing beautifully on her face. "But I couldn't be left behind. I wanted to be with you."

"Because you were afraid of what might happen to you?"

"I really wanted to be with you."

He searched her eyes, and Beth let him. She opened her soul so that he could read it, could know her feelings. She recognized that she and Lawren were star-crossed lovers, that she had loved him all her life . . . all her lives? She also knew that he and she would never be betrothed, never be married. All the things she had dreamed of, had wanted, would be denied her in this life as well as in her other one.

Again Lawren truly wished things could be different between them. The more he learned about her, the more he loved her, the more he truly wanted her. She titillated him, all his senses. She seemed to bring sunshine with her, laughter, the sheer joy of living. She filled him with an exhilaration he had not experienced before.

Pulling her into his arms, he temporarily pushed aside his concerns about the clan, about the massacre, the sick cattle, and a possible traitor in their midst. He would deal with these problems later. For the first time in his life, he allowed personal feelings to take precedence over the clan.

Tonight he was going to be selfish and take for himself. Although he could not fully possess Beth, he wanted as much of her as he could get. Her warmth. Her enticing femininity. Shawe had asked if he were going to imprison her indefinitely. Even then Lawren had known that forever would not be long enough for him to be with her.

She rested her face against his chest.

"I love you," she murmured, unable to keep the words secret.

It was a moment before he responded. "Love me?"

Releasing his hands from her waist, he raised his arms and caught her face between his hands. Strong, callused hands cherished her gently as if she were a fragile jewel.

"Do you understand what you have just said, madam?"

"Yes. I love you."

"Lawren the warlock?"

"Yes."

He threaded his lingers into her hair. Closing her eyes, Beth luxuriated in the sensations he aroused.

"No matter what happens to me," she confessed, "whether I

stay in your century, go to another one, or return to my own, I shall never love another man but you."

"Sometimes it's difficult to tell passion from love."

"I know the difference."

"You thought you loved Sam."

"I wanted to, but couldn't. I was already in love with you."

Through the ages, they stared at each other. Standards and beliefs, disagreements melted away, and they flowed into each other's heart and soul, never to be separated.

Tears sparkled in her eyes, glinted on the tip of her lashes. "Although we are not destined to be together, I shall love only you."

He gathered her into his arms once again. His grip was so tight she could hardly draw her breath, but she didn't care. She didn't want him to turn her loose. Pain assured her that she was alive, that this was real. Her happiness lay in his embrace, in his loving her as she loved him. She waited for his confession; none came.

Pushing back, she grabbed the material of his cloak in her hands. "We have to take the moment, Lawren. It's all we have. We have no promise of tomorrow. No guarantees, you said."

"None," he murmured.

Still he had not confessed to loving her or even to caring. Suddenly she was afraid of the answer, afraid that this had all been part of the diplomacy of revenge. Surely he had not used her. Surely not. She didn't think she could stand it if he had.

Tentatively she asked, "Do you—do you love me?"

She had been so sure of Sam, had pushed him into an engagement on her assumption that he felt the same as she did. Surely she had not made the same mistake with Lawren.

He drew back, again capturing her face in his hands. "Aye, lady, more than words can say."

"But you haven't even said the words."

"I have loved you for so long, lady, and always you are just out of my reach. Somehow my loving you and never being able to have you was easier to bear when the words were not spoken aloud. Now that both of us has confessed our feelings, I can't see it's being any different. I see even greater despair for us."

He kissed her softly, then brushed his lips up her cheeks to her temples. He stroked the pad of his thumb across her lips; then settled it in the corner of her mouth. She nibbled at it, and he quivered violently. He stared deeply into her eyes—green, lustrous eyes that made his insides weaken.

He lowered his head and captured her lips in a long, sweet kiss. When her lips parted beneath his, everything became a dim memory, the world an insignificant speck. He ran his tongue over her lips and then dipped it within.

He pressed his frame closer to hers, hardness revering softness, and felt her shudder. He brushed his tongue across the inner surface of her upper lip, lightly skimmed the smoothness of her teeth, and probed with delicate inquisition until her tongue met his and he drew her slowly into his mouth. Her low moan escaped in a breathy, feathery exhalation.

Beth raked her hands through his midnight hair and clutched at the thick length of it at the base of his neck. She was heady, but had long ago discarded caution and had no intention of trying to retrieve it now. If danger had a taste, Lawren was it and she was going to drink her fill. This might have to last her an entire lifetime.

Truly you are a warlock." She nipped playfully at his lower lip. "Dark. Delectable. Divine."

He growled and marched kisses down her throat, around her locket. She tilted her head back giving him plenty of room. He burrowed beneath her cloak and laid his face against her breast. Beneath the fabric of her tunic, he felt the flutter of her heartbeats.

"Warlock. Enchantress," he said. "We were created for each other."

He kissed her again and again, and his tongue mated with hers. Her past experiences paled in comparison to the heated sensations this man stirred in her. She had never been kissed so boldly, so passionately before. If this was primitive, so was she. She wanted the wild passion that he offered her; she craved and needed to be swept up in the fire of his desire, to be completely incinerated.

Sliding his hands beneath her cloak, he cupped her hips in his hand. He kneaded her buttocks and pressed his pelvis against hers. Hot and swollen, he fit wonderfully against her. His member throbbed painfully, and he wanted to bury it inside her. She sucked in her breath, then moaned softly.

He kissed her mouth again and again until her lips felt swollen and bruised. Then he slowly, gently pulled away. Sam's jilting her hadn't left her with the feeling of abandonment that Lawren's pulling away did.

She reached for him.

"I have to stop, or I'll make love to you." His voice was thick.

"I want you to."

"I have nothing to offer but myself and my love."

"That's enough."

"You say that now when you are caught in the throes of passion, but what of the morning when you realize you have been dishonored?"

"Is it dishonor to love?"

"Aye, for a bastard and a warlock to make love to a Christian and a chief's daughter."

"Since I'm not Elspeth, I don't share her religious beliefs," Beth said. "I don't fear the warlock and bastard. I don't believe loving either would bring me shame. Only deep joy and happiness.

"You could conceive a child. Our child."

"I would love to," Beth murmured.

"It is my greatest desire also," he confessed, "but it is also my greatest fear."

"I won't get pregnant," she promised.

"Is this another one of your little lies?" he asked gently.

"No, I'm sure."

"In your time can you even control nature?"

"In many ways we do. I understand my—my monthly flux. I know when I shall conceive."

The flames in his eyes burned hotter than the colors of the setting sun that splayed the sky.

"Are you sure?"

"About conceiving?"

"Nay, about making love with me."

"I have never been surer of anything in my life."

"Soon there may be no turning back."

"The moment I stepped back in time, there was no turning back," she said. "I'm haunted by a man with eyes of the warlock. I want to love him, want to be loved by him."

Twelve

Beth's confession of love hung beautifully between them. Lawren nodded. Stepping away, he strode to the horses where he quickly stripped them of saddles and blankets. He tossed the two clothing satchels and blankets over his shoulder and held out his hand to her. Side by side they walked until they reached the sheltered curve of the stream where he dropped the satchels and spread the blankets. After he gathered wood and had a fire going, he sat on the pallet.

Glad for the warmth of the blaze, Beth also sat down and ran her hands over the soft material, brushing out the wrinkles. Unlike the pallet she had slept on the night before, this one was not for a physician-and-patient vigil. This one belonged specifically to her and Lawren; it was theirs alone, an intimate emblem of a man's and a woman's coupling—their coupling. She was so excited, she was trembling; her breath was sporadic.

"I want to make love to you," Lawren said, not touching her with anything but his voice, "but I won't want you to awaken in the morning feeling shame and regret."

"I would never feel shame," she said. "I couldn't. I love you." She crawled closer to him; he didn't move. "My only regret would be our not making love."

The wind played with his hair, strands brushing against her cheeks. Beth realized Lawren would not initiate their lovemaking. He wanted to make love to her, but he wouldn't. All he held dear, his *enech* or honor, forbade his bringing shame on her. It didn't matter to him that her sense of honor was different from his. He was a product of the eleventh century and would always be bound by his cultural morays. They would always shape his decisions. She understood this.

She was a product of her age. If she remained here in this time period, she would always think like a woman of the twentieth century. She may not act like one, but she would think like one. Herein, would lie one of her conflicts. She would love Lawren and accept him for the man he was, and she would live and function in his century. But she would never truly be happy here.

"If you don't want to make love to me," she said, "tell me."

Flames leaped to life in his eyes.

"Otherwise, I shall take your clothing off piece by piece."

She touched the brooch on his shoulder.

"You are a spirited lass."

"Aye, and a lusty one."

He returned her smile.

"I want to, Beth, but—"

She leaned over and kissed him. Against his lips, she whispered, "Then we will."

She tried to unfasten the brooch, but the pin was securely fastened within the small lock. She twisted the material around, caught the brooch from another angle. Still she couldn't open it. Coming up on her knees, she turned it, looking at its backside, studying the pin and lock. She sighed and lowered her arms, her hands brushing against his weapons. Her fingers wrapped around the hilt of the dirk.

She drew it out of the sheath, exhilarated by the whisking of metal against worked leather. She held the dirk up, sunset colors reflected in its shining blade.

" 'Twould be much easier and quicker to cut your clothing off," she whispered. "And more exciting."

"Certainly more dangerous since I'm not sure you know how to use one of these." He chuckled with her, closing his hand over the weapon. He slipped it back into the scabbard, caught the brooch with one hand, and released the pin with a flip of his thumb.

Beth pulled a face when he drew it out of the fabric. He dropped the brooch as Beth eased the cloak from his shoulders and pushed it aside. She touched his chest, feeling his hard muscularity beneath the yellow tunic. She brushed her hands beneath his vest, pushing it off his shoulders. She fumbled with his weapon belts, muttering an expletive when she couldn't get them opened. She tried a second time, a third.

"If we intend to make love tonight," he whispered, "I shall have to undress myself."

He brushed her hands aside and removed his belts. Carefully he laid them next to the pallet, within easy reach. When he straightened, he caught the hem of his tunic. This time it was she who brushed his hands away.

"Let me." She pulled it over his head and tossed it aside.

She gazed at his chest. Lightly covered with crisp black hair, it was broad, beautifully sculpted muscles. He sat on the edge of the pallet and unlaced his cuarans. He took them off and laid them aside. He quickly removed her boots and unlaced her leggings. But he did not take them off.

She pushed back and gazed at him while he stood and unfastened his girdle. Slowly the leather fell apart to reveal his lower abdomen. Flat, taut muscle rippled in the waning light of day. He stepped out of his trousers. Beth was breathless with anticipation.

During her career as a doctor, she had seen many naked men. Sam had been a splendid specimen, but no one, not even Sam, had prepared her for the Highlander's beauty. The sun captured him in its glow. Contoured muscles, darkened with a light coating of body hair, ran from his chest to his feet. Visually Beth traced the hard line of his stomach to his erection. He was blatant masculinity, blatant desire, and he was hers.

Without speaking, he returned to the pallet and began undressing her. He removed the locket first and laid it beside his weapons. Her tunic followed. Then he slipped the chemise from her shoulders. He slid it down the length of her body. With his help, she squirmed out of the chemise and the leggings; then she was still, and he gazed at her.

"You're more beautiful than I had imagined."

He rubbed the tip of his fingers over the top of one breast, down to the areola, across the nipple. She trembled.

She touched his chest, his nipple with the tip of her fingers. She brushed the nest of black hair around it.

"You're more handsome than I imagined."

Their endearments were silly and wonderful; they were heartfelt. They laughed from sheer pleasure.

Lawren leaned over and kissed the creamy smoothness of her breasts; she shivered as the rasp touch of his beard followed the soft warmth of his mouth. As if the gentle abrasion were a fire, flames streaked from the tip of her breast to the juncture of her thighs. She sucked in her breath sharply and felt her stomach muscles tighten. Undiluted joy rushed through her veins, drummed in her heart.

She went into his embrace, primal need stirring in her as she felt the steady beat of his heart and the hardness of his chest. He pressed her back on the pallet, his mouth touching hers at the same time that he stretched his body along the length of hers.

"So muscular," she whispered, lightly running her fingers down the side of his thigh. "So hard."

"So feminine." His hand moved down her back. "So soft."

His hand glided to her waist, where his fingers splayed across her buttocks and kneaded her flesh. His touch added fuel to the fire that already burned in her.

His tongue swooped into her mouth, and he filled her with himself. Weakness permeated her body. Had she been standing, her legs would have buckled beneath her. He tugged her closer, closer so that she felt his hardness against her pelvis, and his hands ran down her body. Each stroke heightened her excitement; it whetted her yearning to know this man intimately. She pushed her hand through his hair, delighted by the soft strands between her fingers.

She knew how hard a man the Highlander was; she knew his purpose, his sworn duty. Although she didn't fully understand the nuances of the eleventh century, she did know that she wanted Lawren as she had not wanted another. She craved his touch. She wanted him with the same intensity, the same fervor he wanted her. She was willing to take—she would take—any risk necessary to have him.

As he claimed her lips in another hot drugging kiss, he moved his hand to her thighs. He teased; he tormented, coming closer and closer, but never reaching the nubbin that ached for his touch.

"Lawren," she begged.

His hand slipped over her thigh, through the hair and down to the secret place. Still he didn't quite touch her. So close. So far away. She moaned softly, twisted her buttocks, and pressed against him. His fingers slid down and touched the sensitive area, and she arched against him.

"Lawren." She moaned softly.

"Beth," he whispered.

He was thinking of her as Beth, not Elspeth. His concern was for her, not someone else.

She caught his face in her hands and brought it close to hers. They kissed long, hard, and desperately before he finally lifted his head and gazed at her with passion-laden eyes. He kissed down her throat, across the collarbone, back and forth in whisper-soft motions that teased and tormented.

His other hand brushed over her breasts and down her stomach. He traced his fingers around her navel; then they slipped lower into the soft triangle of hair. He kissed her mouth, her neck, her breasts as he slid his fingers into her secret place, moving them in and out. With each stroke she soared higher and higher.

Beth groaned and threw back her head against the cloak. She had never known such feelings, never. And though one part of her pleaded for fulfillment, another wanted this wonderful moment never to end.

Lawren removed his hand. He lifted himself over her, his knee spreading her legs farther apart. Gently, he pressed the tip of his arousal where his hand had been, and she felt the heat of it against her flesh. But he did not enter. Gently, he caressed her, rubbing her, murmuring endearments.

Although Beth was not inexperienced when it came to men, she felt virginal with Lawren. He made her feel special, and she appreciated his taking his time to build up her desire, to whet her passion for the ultimate coming together.

He continued to stroke with his hands; he kissed her; he whispered reassuringly to her. Gently his arousal probed between her thighs to make her ready; it massaged the opening of her femininity, hot flesh caressing hot flesh, asking for entry.

He touched and played with her body. The gentle forays reminded Beth of her emptiness, built up to the fevered pitch the fire of desire that burned within her. She gave herself to his kisses, taking his tongue fully into her mouth, taking him fully into her embrace, arching against him.

She wanted him fully inside her; he slid fully into her.

She welcomed him with breathless wonder. Her body trembled at the wonderful change she felt within herself on having received him. In the warm glow of the sunset, he was still dark, huge, and mysterious, but he cared for her. No matter what happened to them, she knew without doubt that her Highland warrior loved her. And she loved him.

He kissed her and moved inside her at the same time. A deep clenching thrill seized her, and Beth thought surely she would die from happiness. Closing her arms around him, she dug her fingers into his back. She held him tightly, and he began to slowly move in her. She clenched her hips and urged him on. He moved faster and deeper.

His hands, his lips spoke of his needs and desires. They told her of his pleasure in touching her. Hers did the same to him. He thrust; she arched and received. Their rhythm became one.

The friction between them built up a marvelous pressure that increased as their tempo increased.

Soaring as high as she could, her body trembling, Beth tore her lips from his and rolled her head to the side. She arched to receive his last thrust.

Together they cried out and held each other. When the spasms of their climaxes ended, he lifted himself from her and grabbed his cloak. When he had wrapped them in its folds, he lay on his back and held her in his arms. She buried her face against his shoulder, feeling the perspiration on his hot skin. In the firelight she saw the glistening sheen on his splendid body and rubbed her cheek against his damp chest.

The midnight-blue sky was covered with stars, their twinkling light casting the Highlands below in a mystical, beautiful haze. Clouds, like long, thin diaphanous veils, slithered across the moon, soon to disappear.

"I love you, Lawren mac Galloway." She threaded her fingers in the mat of hair across his chest. "I love the one called warlock."

"I love you. More than life itself."

"Yes," Beth murmured, tears flowing. "Yes."

She held him tightly, frightened that she was soon going to lose what she had so recently found. Their love was bittersweet. Both knew they must love enough to last a lifetime—a lifetime apart. The intimacy they had shared tonight, may possibly share again from time to time, was life held out to them.

She still had not told him about the death of the warlock as recorded in the manuscript. But it loomed over her, growing larger and darker with each passing moment. Even if they remained together, they would also be under a cloud, always wondering how much more time they had together, wondering when she may be taken from this century, wondering when he would be burned at the stake.

"What have I done to you?" Lawren murmured. "To us?"

"Made love to me. Made me the happiest woman alive. Don't think right now," she whispered. "Let's enjoy our moment."

A moment might be all they had.

Lying in each other's arms, they went to sleep.

Later Beth awakened and quietly sat up without disturbing Lawren. After she tossed several more pieces of wood on the fire, she unbraided her hair, then slipped to the brook. While she wanted to take a bath, she wasn't all that eager to get into the cool mountain water. But it was all that was available at the moment. She dipped in a toe, shivered, gasped, then took the plunge. After the gurgle of initial shock, she sank below the surface to wet her entire body.

As she rose, she tipped back her head, letting water rush down her face and over her shoulders. Night air touched her body, and she shivered, but the chill felt good.

She opened her eyes to see Lawren standing on the shore, gilded in moonlight. His calves, thighs, and flanks were richly hewn in hard, sleek lines.

Although Lawren and she had made love recently, Beth felt a hot throbbing in her lower body. Only Lawren had stirred this longing in her, had awakened her to desire. But the awakening was not enough; she must have more of him. He waded into the water.

When he stood in front of her, she said, "I'm glad we stopped here for the night."

"I am, too."

She laid her palm against one of his cheeks. He welcomed her touch; it was achingly sweet. He had battled with his conscience before taking her; now he would not stop. She reached with her other hand to cup his face and guide it to hers.

Her mouth claimed his, and she leisurely explored him with gentle strokes of her lips and tongue. She slipped her tongue between his lips; he received her. With the drugging kiss, she asked for an even hotter invasion. She brushed her palms down his chest; then she caught his shoulders in her hands and drew back to look at him.

Again wondering how long they would be together, knowing that no matter how long, it would not be enough time for them,

she studied him, memorized him. Memory might be all she had
of him. She would never forget how handsome he was, how
strong or vibrant.

But he was more than that. He was an herbalist, a warrior.
All sinew and uncompromising clan champion, he could be cold
and hard. He took with authority. Yet he was warm and soft and
caring. Now in his nakedness, all his glorious nakedness con-
fronting her, the warrior gave way to her lover. She felt a tremor
of vulnerability.

She caressed him, and he moaned against her mouth. The cry
incited a quivering response in her. She gave herself to the paradoxically ageless but newly aroused sensations that Lawren had
introduced to her.

Lawren kissed her again and again. As his mouth plundered,
his hands gentled and soothed. His hands slid down, over her
hips, the outside of her thighs. They trailed lightly over her
stomach. Her stomach quivered.

"I cannot get enough of you," he whispered. He nuzzled his
face between her breasts.

"Nor I of you."

He raised his head slightly to see the breeze swirling her
damp, unbound hair about her shoulders. Several strands tickled
him.

"Do you want me to braid it?"

He caught them with his hand. Last night they embodied the
fire; tonight they were silvery moonlight—soft and silky, as
elusive as night shadows.

"Nay." He shoved his hand through the thick length of it. "I
love to feel it." He buried his face in it. "I love to smell it."

She caught his face again and brought it to hers. They stared
at each other through passion-laden eyes before their lips met
in a fierce kiss.

She pulled her mouth slightly away, her lips brushing against
his as she said, "Make love to me."

Both fell back, cushioned by the lapping water. He kissed
her mouth, her cheeks, her neck. His lips moved persuasively,

and she parted to receive him. As he entered her slowly, pleasure rippled through his body from the soles of his feet to the top of his head. Although they had recently made love, she was tight and warm. She welcomed him, then closed around him, taking him captive.

He pulled back a little, then thrust in her all the way. Embracing him with her hips, she drew him to her, wrapping him in her warmth and softness. She trailed her fingers along his back, down his buttocks; she teased the indentation.

Overpowered with urgency, he shook. His rhythm increased; she moved with him. Gripped with the same urgency, Beth arched to meet him each time; she accepted him. She took; she gave.

He thrust one last time; she rose. Supreme bliss claimed them, consumed them, held them for several shattering moments before they surrendered to complete and utter satisfaction.

Shivering they dried off and quickly redressed. When they returned to the pallet, Lawren wrapped Beth's cloak around her. Then he built up the fire.

"I'll get us something to eat." He moved toward the main camp.

"Do you want me to come with you?" she asked.

Brushing strands of hair from her cheek, he kissed her forehead, then the tip of her nose. "Nay, stay here where you can be warm."

Soon after he was gone, Beth heard voices, raised in anger. They were too far away for her to tell what they were saying, but she figured they were arguing about her. At the moment she was too sated with love to be concerned about their argument.

Basking in the recent aftermath of her recent mating with Lawren, she drew her cloak more closely about herself. The wind, growing stronger, blew her clothes against her body. It brushed against her cheeks, whispered in her ears. It tossed tendrils of hair about her face; they teased her cheeks, the end of her nose.

"Here you are." Lawren stepped out of the dark shadows.

He set a large bowl of stew, a leather ale bag, and a loaf of bread in the center of the pallet. Squatting beside her, he tore off a piece of the bread and sopped it in the stew. When it was dripping with brown sauce, he held it up to Beth. She received it greedily into her mouth; as greedily she lapped the extra sauce from the corners of her mouth.

"I've never tasted anything this good before."

Lawren laughed. "Probably because you've never been this hungry before."

She broke off a piece of bread and chased a chunk of meat. When she captured it, she laughed and popped it into her mouth. Alternately they fed each other; they kissed; they murmured endearments. They drank ale from the leather bag.

By the time they had finished their meal, Beth noticed that the noise of the camp had subsided. In the distance she saw the dim glow of a campfire, but saw no silhouetted forms sitting around it.

"Has everyone gone to bed?" she asked.

"All except the guards," he said. "We shall be up and riding early in the morning."

Stretching, Beth said, "I guess it's time for us to sleep also."

"Later." He set the bowl aside and rose. "Let's go for a little walk first. I want you to see the beauty of the Highlands at night."

Single file, him leading the way and holding her hand, they walked up the trail to the head of the waterfall. Water finely sprayed on them, but Lawren led her onto another pathway, this one much more narrow, the bushes slapping against her clothes, making her glad that she wore long trousers and boots. Higher they climbed, the pathway becoming more and more perilous, the forest growing thicker and darker.

"Don't turn loose of my hand," Lawren instructed, "and don't be frightened. I'll take care of you."

"All right," she whispered, having utmost confidence that he would.

"Slump your shoulders," he ordered, "we're moving beneath a shelf overhang."

As they stepped onto the smooth rock formation, they were enveloped with the black velvet of night. Moonlight was blocked out altogether. Beth took a step; her boots slipped, and she yipped. Lawren caught her in his arms and held her.

"It's all right. Our walking surface is flat. You wouldn't fall over the side of the mountain."

"It's the dark," she murmured. "Makes it seem so sinister."

"Aye, but hides us from the others."

In the distance Beth heard the waterfall. Farther and farther they moved into the darkness.

"Wait here," he ordered.

"Let me go with you."

"Nay, stay here."

He moved away from her, and she heard the soft shuffle of his boots on the rock surface. He grunted; rock scraped against rock.

"Lawren?"

"I'm here." He was beside her again, touching her shoulder with his hand. "Move slowly, and don't turn loose of my hand."

Beth wouldn't have for the world. It seemed to her they had wound around for hours when he gave more instructions.

"On your knees," he directed. "We have to crawl for a ways."

They crawled.

Finally Lawren said, "We're here."

"Where?"

"Where I have planted a new garden of nightlace."

"The nightlace!" Beth said. Anticipation welled up. She scooted up closer to him, their shoulders brushing together.

"It will be pretty," he said, "but not as beautiful as it will be when they are fully flowered."

They crawled a little further. They stood, their shoulders bent, and took several steps. The farther they traveled, the straighter they were able to stand, and the faster they walked. As they stepped out of the cave, Beth gazed at the moon-drenched glen, at the small and intermittent silver-white patches. The entire meadow looked as if tiny lace doilies had been spread over the ground.

She gasped. "Oh, Lawren!"

"They only bloom at night, and they look like a coverlet of lace. That's why we've called them nightlace." He paused, then said, "When they're in full bloom, they will cover the entire area like one huge coverlet. They used to grow all over the Gleann nan Duir land."

"Isn't that the land that used to belong to the Adairs?" she asked.

"Aye."

"The destruction of the nightlace could be part of that earlier feud," Beth said.

"Probably."

"When will these be ready for harvesting?" she asked.

"They'll be fragile for several years, but we'll be able to pick a few of the blossoms in a couple of months."

"Not enough to curtail the illness."

"Nay."

Beth's disappointment grew. She was so close to the nightlace, so close to having what she had traveled back in time for, but she was also so far away from it. And the Highlanders were on the verge of an epidemic because most of the people were steeped in superstition and fear. What they didn't understand they tried to destroy. Others, selfish and greedy, took advantage of this fear.

His arm around her shoulder, Lawren led her further into the secret glen. Stepping carefully, they made their way to the edge of the nightlaces. They squatted and gazed at the flowers. He pinched one of the blossoms for her.

"Keep this for yourself," he said.

She held it reverently on her palm and gazed at it in the moon glow. "I'll cherish it always," she promised. "I'll put it between two sheets of parchment."

"Until then, we'll store it in the small pouch on my satchel."

She nodded but didn't relinquish the flower to him, not just yet.

"I have some medicinal nightlace powder at the castle," he said. "When we return, I'll give you some and I'll teach you how to prepare it for different potions."

As they walked back, Lawren talked with her about the night-lace. Again they discussed what he and his mother had been doing with it. He described all stages of the illness, recounted those cases where the patient recovered, those where they died. All too soon they had returned to camp.

Lying in each other's arms, they talked quietly until the wee hours of the morning. They made love again, and finally went to sleep.

Caledonia sat at the only table in the small cottage. In the dim flicker of candlelight and firelight, she dipped the quill pen into the inkwell and wrote on a sheet of parchment. Elsa, her friend and Jamie's grandmother, kneeled beside the fire where she stirred the porridge that bubbled in the huge cauldron. The door and the shutters on the small windows were closed.

Although the furnishings were meager, the room was comfortable. A bed. Several chests. The dining table and trestle stools. Several barrels of food. Smoked and dressed meat and herbs hung from the beamed ceiling.

"Lowrie and Jamie were brought home last night," the old woman said as she cut up culinary herbs into the cauldron, "and today Lawren and the lads have ridden out. I hope they learn how the Adairs slipped undetected into our territory."

"If it was Adairs," Caledonia replied.

"If not the Adairs, who would it have been?" Elsa asked. She laid aside her knife and looked up at her friend. "Who, Caledonia?"

Caledonia shook her head. "I only hope the bishop persuades Bearnard to send us the nightlaces."

Elsa snorted. "More cases of the illness?"

"Nay, we've been able to contain it so far, but we'll soon be out of the plant. Agnes sent a runner to the mountains last week to see if we had any she could have for the cloister."

"The prioress," Elsa said. "Did you send them to her?"

"Aye, what few I could spare." Caledonia laid her pen down and flexed her shoulders. " 'Tis a grave situation, Elsa, when the mother prioress sends to a witch for help. I need more of the plants so I can experiment with them, so that we know exactly what the curative is for the sleeping death."

After a few minutes of reflective silence, she started writing again, her column growing longer. Finally she sat back, yawned and rubbed her eyes.

"You are tired," Elsa said. "You should not work so hard. All day with your patients and all night with your writing."

"I have to complete the manuscript," Caledonia said.

She would never forget her start when Beth had told her about the manuscript. She had hardly heard another word the woman had uttered. Caledonia had always had a desire to write the book, but until the other night had not known that it was her destiny. She had no doubt that the manuscript of which Beth spoke was this one. And it would survive.

Laying her palm on the stack of parchment, she said, "I have the feeling that time is running out, Elsa, and I want people to benefit from my knowledge. What they have learned from me can be a foundation upon which they build. Think how wise we could be, how better able to care for the diseased if we pooled our knowledge, each generation learning from the preceding one."

If she could preserve the knowledge and the nightlace, Caledonia thought, she would possibly avert another epidemic in the future.

"I'm glad you're writing the manuscript and are collecting the knowledge," Elsa said, "but I doubt it will do any good,

Caledonia. I don't know that the masses shall ever have the need to learn to read, and the ones who are educated today are not interested in what other scholars have to say. They are in love with their own knowledge and want to save it for posterity."

"Aye." Caledonia sighed. "That is true."

Elsa continued to prepare the evening meal. Caledonia straightened several sheets of parchment, making sure that each was paginated correctly.

"Who will you get to bind it?" Elsa asked. "The church fathers surely won't."

Caledonia laughed softly. "One of the stationers will do it for me if I pay him handsomely enough. And I shall pay whatever price he asks. It is worth it to me." She carefully picked up the papers and tied them together with a red ribbon. "I have almost finished a lifetime of work."

Possibly a lifetime!

Rising, Elsa shuffled over to the table. " 'Tis beautifully done."

Caledonia ran her hand down the top sheet, stroking the letters she had meticulously formed. "A list of all the herbs that I know about," she said, "their properties, and a drawing of each. I've divided them into two groups. Kitchen and medicinal herbs."

"You have also written something about yourself," Elsa added.

"Nay," she said regretfully. "I wanted to, but didn't. Should the manuscript ever be discovered, mention of myself or the Galloways would ensure its immediate destruction. Without the personal history, without my name attached to it, it may be saved and used, possibly copied for future generations."

"Did you list the nightlace?"

"Aye, where would we be without it?" Caledonia replied. "It is our miracle plant. The leaves and roots facilitate the healing of wounds and keep them from becoming inflamed. The flowers, when used in a potion and taken internally, help the body grow stronger and keep people from coming down with diseases. And so far, it is the only herb that has helped people with the strange sleeping illness."

Caledonia rose and crossed the room. Cracking the door, she let the cool breeze play over her face.

"Since the church has outlawed the nightlace, no one is supposed to speak of it," Elsa said. "If anyone should discover that you have listed it in your manuscript, you would be punished."

Caledonia grinned. "They'll have to find the manuscript first and prove that the nightlace is listed. Then they shall have to prove that I've written it."

"With so few people able to write, they won't have a difficult time proving that," Elsa said. She slapped her hand on the lid of the meal barrel. "If only they knew what was hidden in here."

"Would you prefer that I move the manuscript from your house?" Caledonia asked. "If the bishop declares Lawren a heretic and orders him to be executed, he will do the same for me."

"Nay, if I felt like that I would not have insisted that you keep it in my cottage. I don't like the idea of the church or anyone telling a person what they can or cannot read or write, especially when that someone is a Saxon telling us Scots." Elsa laid the parchment on top of the barrel, then hobbled over to a shelf on the wall and picked up two wooden bowls. "Since I don't read or write, no one would even suspect me of having a book in my house. I like having it here."

"It puts your life in danger," Caledonia said. "You would be accused of being in league with the witch."

Elsa laughed softly. " 'Twould be a just accusation, Caledonia. I am in league with you, have been all your life." As the old woman dished up the porridge and set it on the table, she asked, "Do you think Lawren and the lads will find nightlace in the canyon?"

"Nay, there is only sorrow there," Caledonia said, "no nightlace."

"You have seen this?" Elsa referred to an ancient tradition

of divining through a cauldron of boiling water. She moved closer to Caledonia who nodded. "Is the water troubled?"

"Aye."

"Tell me what it says, Caledonia."

"I can read some of it, Elsa, but not all," Caledonia replied. "It's rather hazy. With the trouble comes comfort. Bearnard will meet his just reward. The plague will be stayed. Adairs and Galloways will be united, and Lowrie will assume the high seat of the Galloways." Sighing deeply, she leaned against the door frame. "The price paid for this will be Lawren's life. He will be burned at the stake as a warlock."

A grievous silence hovered in the room.

"Sometimes we misread the water," the old woman said.

"Aye, but not this time. 'Tis on the waters, in the wind, and in the trees. All have spoken to me."

"What will happen to Elspeth?"

"I'm not sure," Caledonia replied.

From the first moment Caledonia had walked into Lowrie's chamber, she had known that something was different about Elspeth. The woman had been completely encircled by the aura of fate. When Elspeth had told her she was a traveler from time, Caledonia had believed her. She had been reading about her in the water, so she wasn't surprised.

"My reading on Elspeth is hazy," Caledonia said. "It's as if she is here in person but not in spirit. Sometimes I see her with Lawren and know that the two of them are meant to be together. At other times I see her with Lowrie and have the same conviction that she and he belong together." She shrugged. "I don't have the sight on this, my friend."

"Have you told Lawren about your manuscript?" Elsa asked.

"Nay, only you."

"What shall I do with it if something happens to you?"

"If Lawren is alive, give it to him. If not, give it to Shawe."

"The priest?" Elsa said. "You don't think he'll destroy it?"

"Nay, he's the only one who has enough foresight not to destroy it. He's a Scotsman, steeped in our traditions, I trust him to do what is right. His allegiance is to God, not to the Saxons." She returned to the table, picked up her quill and a sheet of parchment. "I shall leave him a letter with the manuscript."

Thirteen

Lawren lay on the pallet, holding Beth. Normally his favorite pastime was watching dawn softly chase away night's shadows. Today he wished he could push back the first light and lie here with Beth forever.

She drew in a deep breath and snuggled closer to him. He held her tightly, kissing her forehead, brushing hair from her cheeks. Last night had been the most wonderful night he had ever known. Loving Beth . . . aye, he loved her and he accepted that she was a woman from the future . . . was the most wondrous thing that had ever happened to him. He had never been happier.

At the same time his heart had never been heavier. He had always known that his love for Elspeth could never come to fruition. Mating with her had always been a possibility; having a life with her had not been. He had not been able to conceive a future with them together. Even now as wonderful as the thought was, he couldn't envision him and Beth being together.

They didn't know what triggered her lunge through space; they didn't know what would send her back to her world . . . if she would ever return. And Lawren felt that time was running out for him. He would either be captured, tried and burned as a heretic, or he would spend the remainder of his life running.

Breathing deeply, he reached out, his hand brushing over his leather clothing satchel. He caught the buckle of the outside pocket and rubbed the metal between his fingers. In here was the last of his nightlace. The blossom he had given her was too young to be of any benefit to her, but what he had here in the pouch was ripe, ready to be used. Still he wanted to put off giving it to her as long as possible. At first, he hadn't trusted her. Now he was afraid that when she had some of the medicinal nightlace, she would disappear from the castle as mysteriously as she had appeared.

Lawren gently disentangled himself from Beth and pushed out from beneath the cloak. Bracing against the morning chill, he retucked the cloak around her, then quickly dressed. After he had shaved, he headed for the main encampment. The men were gathered around the fire, quietly eating their cold morning meal.

"I trust you slept well," Evan said, around a mouthful of cold beef and bread.

Lawren laughed softly. "That I did, headman. That I did."

Washing down his food with mead, Evan harumphed. "When will you be ready to ride?"

"By first light," Lawren replied.

Evan took another bit of meat and bread, chewed, and swallowed.

"Rain," he said.

"Aye, I smell it."

Evan pointed to a small cloth food bag. "I prepared the morning meal for you and the woman."

Lawren reached for it.

"Make haste and eat, laird. We've dawdled long enough. We need to be about our business. The woman's slowed us down, and so will the rain when it hits."

Grinning, Lawren nodded. Food bag in hand, he returned to Beth. Kneeling on the pallet, he stroked tendrils of hair from her cheeks and looked at the crescent of dark lashes on her smooth cheeks. He dreaded waking her up. He wanted to be with her, wanted to see her sparkling green eyes and radiant smile, but he also wanted to hold onto this magical moment as long as he could.

Beth stirred. "It's still dark," she murmured.

"Almost first light."

"Time for us to get up."

"Soon."

Smiling, she lifted the cloak. "Come back to bed."

He crawled beneath the cloak and snuggled up to her. Shivering from the chill of his clothing, she jerked awake and laughed.

"You did that on purpose."

Firelight played on his handsome face, softened by love. "Aye, I wanted to hold you one more time before we started for the canyon."

"Do we have time for more than a hug?" She pecked kisses along his brows, down the ridge of his nose, around his mouth.

"Nay. Evan would lay the whip to both of us."

"He's still angry," she murmured.

"Jealous. He wishes he were sleeping with a beautiful woman."

"You think I'm a beautiful woman?"

"Fishing for compliments so early."

"Any time I can get them."

"Aye, lady, you are." His lips captured hers in a fully satisfying kiss. Without lifting his mouth from hers, he said, "I brought you some bread, cheese, and beef. Eat hearty. We have a long ride today and won't stop for the evening meal until late."

She pushed up on her elbows. "The stars are gone."

"Aye, rain is in the air."

"I hope we get to the canyon before it starts," she said. "If we don't, it could wash away any evidence that might still be there."

"Aye." Reaching over, Lawren grabbed her clothes and stuffed them beneath the cloak.

"What are you looking for?" She quickly crawled into them.

"A clear picture of what happened," he said. "I'm hoping that I can track the Adairs and see how they so completely disappeared that none of my men found them."

Beth kicked out of the cloak, stood, and straightened her clothing. "Have you talked with Evan and William about your suspicions?"

"Nay, 'tis too soon."

She sat back down, and Lawren helped her with her leggings and boots.

"I need to learn more before I start accusing Galloways of being traitors."

"Why would a Galloway kill Lowrie?" Beth asked. "What would he have to gain?"

"It's quite possible Bearnard promised a Galloway the high seat if he helped with Lowrie's murder." Lawren opened the small food pouch and took out the contents of their morning meal. "Take care of your personal business. We need to eat and be on our way."

Drawing her cloak closely about her, she ran into a cluster of bushes, then on down to the brook where she finished her morning ablutions. When she returned, she sat on the pallet next to Lawren and wolfed down her breakfast and wished she had more. When she had taken a swallow of the mead, she closed off the bag and handed it to Lawren.

"I wish we didn't have to leave," she said.

"We'll come back another time. When the nightlace are blooming."

He lifted his clothing bag and unfastened the small outer pocket. From that he extracted several vials and some smaller pouches. Beth scooted closer and peered curiously.

"What is it?" she asked.

"The nightlace," he replied. He held up a vial. "We have already ground this into a powder, and it's ready to be used for a potion."

Beth took the vial and held it before the fire, looking at the opaque shadow the powdered nightlace made.

"If it's used for an ointment," Lawren said, "we have to add some other ingredients."

Beth recognized the herbs as he called them off. All of them had been listed in the manuscript.

"These are the roots," he said, untying a pouch. He caught her hand, turned it over, and dumped several brown nodules onto it.

Excitement skittered through Beth. Her hand trembled. At

last, she was seeing the miracle plant. She was holding it. She looked up at Lawren, knowing that anticipation glowed in her eyes and on her face.

"This is what I came for," she murmured.

Sadness flickered in his eyes. "I know."

"May I have this?"

"One of the nodules," he replied.

"I'm going to need more," she said, her mind leaping to the future, to the clinic. She was no longer a woman of the eleventh century. She was Dr. Beth Balfour. "We'll need to cultivate it."

"When the plants get large enough to transplant, I'll give you more," he told her. "And I'll teach you how to cultivate them."

Closing her hand over the root, guarding it as if it were the most precious jewel in the world, Beth looked at him through teary eyes.

"Thank you," she whispered and leaned over to kiss him.

Their lips touched in a beautiful soft kiss. He tasted her tears and touched her soul. Their heartbeat was one. They might be separated; Beth might return to the future; Lawren would remain here. She could not bring herself to think of his dying. But they would be together for all time.

"Forever," he murmured.

"Forever," she promised.

The ride last night had been idyllic, not so today. Lawren, Evan, and Jamie rode in front, immediately behind the banner man. Beth and William brought up the rear. She flexed her shoulders and squirmed on the saddle. Although it was padded, it was still hard and her buttocks were sore from having bounced on it all morning.

They had ridden the two or three hours to the canyon and Beth swore Lawren examined every inch of ground in it. She had stood beneath a tree as Lawren had Jamie narrate the incident over and over. They reenacted it time and again. Off their horses, they walked the terrain. On their horses, they rode it.

Jamie found the spot where they had been attacked. He lay on the ground next to the boulder. He leaped up and ran to another spot and flopped down. Rob fell here. He pointed. Lowrie had fallen there. Lawren said little.

The storm clouds hung heavier and blacker. Thunder rolled in the distance; lightning flickered in the sky. The wind had whipped up. Beth wished Lawren could find what he was looking for so they could be on their way.

At Lawren's command, they all mounted and rode out of the canyon. Beth wanted him to be able to get to the bottom of this massacre and to determine if one of the Galloways had betrayed him, but she was tired and hungry. She ached all over. Now they searched for tracks of the fleeing attackers.

From her vantage point, from the bits of conversations she overheard, Beth learned nothing substantial. Her stomach growled angrily, reminding her that it was lunchtime, but Lawren had warned her they would not be eating again until nightfall. She shoved hair out of her face and gazed at the sky.

The thunder and lightning were nearer; the wind had picked up.

Lawren halted the company at the base of a small, steep incline. He and Evan dismounted, and several other warriors joined them—the ones who had chased the attackers, Beth decided. Jamie remained on his mount a good ways back. As one of the men talked with Lawren, he waved his arms and pointed; Lawren nodded.

Unable to take the bodily abuse of the saddle any longer, Beth slid off the mare, quickly leaning against it when her legs almost folded. Gingerly she took several steps, pain tingling through her limbs. She hobbled over to a large rock and leaned against it. Lawren struck out, leaving Jamie, the two headmen, and the other men at the base of the incline. After a while, Jamie moved to his horse and slipped a leather water bag over his shoulder. He walked back to her.

"Would you care for a drink?" he asked.

She turned, her shoulder brushing the bag he held out.

"Oh yes!"

"I thought you might also like to have a bite to eat."

He held out a slice of brown bread thickly spread with cheese. This was not ordinarily one of Beth's favorite foods, but it looked better than any gourmet meal she had ever sat down to. Greedily she bit into the bread and the tangy cheese. Closing her eyes, she chewed and savored the taste. When she was finished, she circled her lips with her tongue. She licked her fingers. Every crumb had to be accounted for. Only when she had no more taste to savor did she take a swallow of water.

"Thank you," she murmured. "I was famished."

Grinning, he took the bag and looped it over his shoulder. "Do you think Lawren will find anything out there?" she asked.

Both of them gazed at the incline Lawren had disappeared behind.

"If anyone can, he will," Jamie replied.

An hour passed, and Beth paced back and forth. She divided her watch between Lawren and the quickly approaching storm. Finally Lawren appeared on the rise. He bounded toward them, his movements fluid grace and economy. After he talked with Evan and Jamie, he walked over to Beth. Jamie unhooked the water bag and silently handed it to Lawren. Then he edged back to where the headmen stood, giving Lawren and Beth their privacy.

"How are you doing?"

Grinning, she rubbed her bottom. "I'm a little sore."

"Aye, lady, 'tis a rough trip, and it's going to get rougher." A blast of wind sifted through his hair.

"Did you find something?" she asked.

He uncapped the bag and held it to his mouth, drinking deeply. When he lowered it, he said, "I think so, but I can't be sure. Whoever the attackers were they were smart. They wrapped cloth around their horses' hooves so they didn't leave a noticeable trail."

"But you found it?"

"Unusual markings that could be horses and riders and that do circle back to the village," he answered.

"Galloways rather than Adairs?" she asked.

"It's looking more and more like it could be." Walking away, he returned the water bag to Jamie. "Time to ride," he called out. "We'll head for the village. If we rush, we'll make it before the storm breaks."

Beth swung up on her mount and moved to William's side.

"Now that we've finished our business here at the canyon," Lawren said, "ride with me."

They had ridden for a few miles when they saw a boy, about seven years of age, running down the trail. Lawren held up his hand, and the column stopped.

"Help us! Help us!" The boy stumbled up to them, his hair wet with perspiration, his breathing heavy and ragged. "We have the sleeping-death. No medicine."

"We're on our way to the village now," Lawren said. "Not the village," the boy said. "The Kenna Galloways."

"Aye."

"You're the—the—"

"I'm Lawren mac Galloway, and we're going to help you. Who are you?"

"Wallace mac Kenna. My parents," he cried out. "My two brothers and sister."

"We'll take care of them," Lawren promised.

"More sick," the boy mumbled.

Lawren leaned over, caught Wallace in the crook of his arm and settled him on the horse in front of him. Without a word, he nudged the stallion and was soon in a gallop. Also without spoken command, William was by Beth's side. All raced behind Lawren.

As they rode, Lawren questioned the boy, learning that the illness had struck three days ago. His entire family was ill. Women in the village were nursing the sick, but one by one they were coming down with the illness. They had sent Wallace to get help.

By the time they arrived at the small cluster of houses, rain poured so heavily Beth couldn't see in front of herself. She hunched on the horse, sliding deeper into the folds of the cloak, trying to escape the pelting torrent. Wallace led them to the largest house in the hamlet, his parents' home. Lawren halted his mount, slid out of the saddle, and lifted the boy down.

"Evan," Lawren shouted, above the drum of the rain, "William, search for others who are sick. Bring them here. This is where we'll treat them. Jamie, you'll be helping Beth and me in the house."

Without waiting for a reply from his headman, Lawren slung his satchel over his shoulder and raced into the house. Evan began barking orders. William deposited Beth, and she followed Lawren inside.

As they took off their cloaks, they gazed around the small, dark room. A man and a woman lay side by side in a double bed. Three children—two boys and a girl—lay on a pallet of straw on the floor. Lawren knelt beside the adults, Beth beside the children.

"Fevered," she murmured, wishing she had a thermometer. Wishing conditions were more sanitary. "And delirious."

"But no rash," Lawren said.

Standing he moved across the room to the table. With the swipe of one arm, he cleared it of dishes and dragged it closer to the bed.

"Build up the fire," he ordered Jamie, "and get some more fuel. Fill a large cauldron with water and set it on the fire."

Wallace stumbled around the room. Lawren swept him into his arms and walked over to a corner, lying him on a pile of clothes. The boy struggled to his feet.

"Sleep," Lawren commanded. "When you wake up, you can help."

Sighing deeply, the lad fell over, asleep before his head touched the clothing.

Jamie stoked the fire, then set a cauldron of water on it to boil. By the time he walked out the door, Lawren had spread his vials and pouches on the table.

"I'll need some drinking water to mix with the nightlace," he said.

Beth walked over to a shelf on the wall next to the fireplace. She reached for the crockery pitcher and brought it back. As soon as Lawren had sifted some of the powder into two of the glasses, she poured the water. He stirred.

"Sometimes this is all it takes for them to start recovery."

Beth nodded. She wiped her hands down her trousers. She had been adamant in her belief that it was the cure for this illness. Now that it was time to test her theory, she was nervous. Her stomach was tied in knots. She prayed that the nightlace would work. While Lawren gave the adults some of the potion, Beth knelt on the pallet and gave it to the children. She talked quietly and soothingly to them.

Outside the rain continued to fall, pelting against the thatch roof and the stone sides of the house. Inside Lawren and Beth tended to the sick. Jamie kept the fire blazing and candles burning. By the time Evan brought the last patient in, their count had risen to ten. The few who had no symptoms, hovered fearfully in their houses at Lawren's orders.

"Can I help you?" Evan asked.

Wiping his hands on a cloth, Lawren shook his head. "We've done all for them that I know to do."

Exhausted, Beth sat in one of the straight-backed chairs and looked at the diminishing supply of nightlace. If anyone were to ask her what the elixir of the gods was, she would have to reply nightlace. It was so low, they couldn't treat many more. She felt the niggling of a headache and had ever since she arrived here. Closing her eyes, she leaned her head back and stretched her muscles and tendons. Time-travel didn't seem to agree with her.

Afternoon turned into evening and the rain continued to fall. Several more people became infected. Every four hours, Beth gave them a swallow of the draught. Evening turned into night, and when no more had succumbed to the illness, she breathed a sigh of relief. Perhaps they had stopped it. Ironically it was no longer raining.

Firelight burned dimly in the house as Lawren and Beth continued to nurse the Kenna Galloways. She sat on the floor next to Wallace's little sister, washing her face. She thought she saw the girl's lips move. She leaned closer, but heard nothing. She washed the boys' faces. Then she heard the croak.

"Mama."

The child had spoken.

"Lawren," Beth cried.

He threaded between pallets to kneel beside her.

The girl opened her eyes and stared at him. "Mama," she said. "She was sick."

"We're treating her," Lawren said. "How do you feel?"

She licked her dried and swollen lips. Then she turned her head and looked at her two brothers who lay beside her. Tears slid out of her eyes.

"We're all sick," she said. "All of us have the death-sleep?" She sat up and looked at her two brothers, at her parents. "Wallace," she cried out. "He's dead."

Hearing his sister call, Wallace shot up off the clothes and raced across the room. He gathered the little girl in his arms.

"I'm all right," he told her. "I was sick, but now I'm well."

"And the rest of you are getting well," Beth said. "We think the others will, too."

The girl shook her head. "No one gets well. 'Tis the curse of the warlock."

Lawren tensed, his face hardened. Without a word spoken between them, Beth understood his feelings—the hatred and hostility he must feel toward Bearnard and those who were ruining his reputation and corrupting his influence, his work . . . who would eventually take his life.

"It's not a curse," Beth said, "only an illness, and we think we have the cure."

"This man is getting worse," Jamie called from across the room. "He's swelling and turning red."

Beth and Lawren crawled to him. He was covered in a raw and angry rash. Lawren rushed to the table, returning with the nightlace draught. Holding the man's head up, they gave him a swallow.

Then they waited. He gasped for breath, and clawed at his throat. Then he moaned, tensed, and went limp. Blood gurgled out of his mouth. She felt no vital signs and sighed.

"He's dead," she said.

Lawren motioned for Jamie to come take care of the man's body, then he walked outside. Beth followed him. Without his cloak, Lawren leaned back against the house. Holding his head back, his eyes closed, he let the rain sluice down his face.

"Only one of the twelve has died," Beth said.

"One too many."

"I agree, but I think we're proving that it's the nightlace that is saving them."

"That and getting to them at the right time," Lawren said.

Beth peered quizzically at him

"I was so busy I didn't say anything when the man was brought in, but he had a light rash on his shoulder then. None of the others had it, and all of them seem to be improving."

"If we can get the medicine to them before they break out in the rash," Beth said. "Yes, that could be it. If the others come through the illness, we may have the breakthrough we've been looking for. The medicine and the time for treatment. We can prove there is no plague."

"I thought so, too," Lawren said wearily, "but I'm not so sure now. Even the children believe the sickness is the curse of the warlock."

Beth's heart went out to him. "You can't give up," she said. "We have to keep fighting. As my mother used to say, we'll just have to take it minute by minute."

She went into his arms and he rubbed her back. She laid her cheek against his chest and savored his warmth and strength. She didn't care that they were being peppered by the rain, chilled by the wind. Lawren's arms were her haven.

"We have enough nightlace to take care of these," Lawren said, "but what happens if we have another outbreak?"

"Everyone here thinks I'm Elspeth," Beth said. "Let me make an appeal to the prioress or to the bishop. Perhaps they will help us get the plant. Surely they are not so callous as to let innocent people die."

She felt his chest rise and fall as he inhaled.

"In the meantime," he said, "I must find more nightlace."

"Where?" Beth asked.

"Caledonia."

She leaned back, raindrops hitting her, clinging to her lashes, running down her chin. "Lawren, please let me make an appeal to the church."

He eased her away from him. "We'll talk about it later."

As soon as they entered the cottage, they examined each of the patients. To their satisfaction, all of them were breathing much easier. Their color was better, and their fever seemed to be going down. None had developed the rash yet. Although Beth wasn't sure, she took this as a positive sign.

They waited; they watched; they administered the next dose of nightlace at one in the morning. Beth prayed. Sitting in the chair, she leaned over the table, pillowing her head on her arms. She was so tired, she could hardly stay awake.

"Mary," came a raspy cry.

Lawren, standing in the doorway, raced to the bed, reaching it at the same time that Beth did.

"The sickness," the woman said. "I have—" She blinked and gazed at Lawren and Beth.

"You're going to be fine," Lawren told her. "We saved you."

"The curse," she murmured.

"It's no curse," Beth said. "You and your family are going to be fine. Your eldest son and daughter have already started their recovery."

"Who was the first one to take ill?" Lawren asked.

"Wallace. Then Mary. The other boys," she said. "My husband and me."

"They should be coming around shortly," Beth said.

As if her words were prophetic, her husband stirred.

Their hearts lighter, Beth and Lawren administered the last of the medicine in the early hours of morning. His entire supply of nightlace was gone, but one by one the people were recovering. The nightlace saved them. Beth thought of the small nodule she had in her clothing bag. She had not had to use it, and she was grateful. It would be enough to treat the people at the clinic, but what if others had succumbed? She had to have more for cultivation. Having a supply for the present danger was wonderful, but they must plan and prepare for the future.

After Lawren assured the others that they had the illness in check, he let the women of the hamlet come in and take over the nursing. He and Beth could rest. One of the Kenna Galloways offered their cottage to Lawren for the remainder of the night.

Glad for the privacy, Beth and Lawren quickly undressed, bathed and climbed into bed. Cuddled against each other, they lay there savoring their triumph. The only blight to their happiness was their having no more nightlace.

By the time the sun had risen next morning, Beth and Lawren had examined all their patients. Since there was no more nightlace, they were relieved that all were recovering. Lawren gave last-minute instructions to the Kenna Galloways. Then he helped Beth onto her mare, and he mounted his stallion.

They rode toward the village. Along the way he stopped at several of the hamlets and talked with clansmen, asking about signs of the illness and about the Mountain Cat massacre. The good news was that no more outbreaks of the illness were reported; the bad news was that no one could shed new light on Lowrie's attackers.

That night Lawren and his weary warriors returned to the stronghold. Quietly they led their horses to the stables. Turning his and Beth's horses over to William, Lawren guided her into the castle.

Warriors lounged in the hall, but it was noticeably absent of revelry. They straightened, their faces alight with curiosity as Lawren and Beth walked into the room. Sloane paced in front of the fireplace.

" 'Tis good you're home," the Highlander said. "Since Lowrie was attacked, we had begun to worry about you."

" 'Tis good to be home," Lawren said. Taking off his cloak, he hung it on a nearby wall peg. "Did the runner reach you with news of the Kenna Galloways?"

"Aye, all are doing fine. They want to know when you're going to send more nightlace."

"Aye, so do all the Galloways," Lawren muttered. He shed his gloves. "Where's Annie? She's always here to greet me."

"She hasn't been feeling well," Sloane replied. "She took to bed early this morning."

Lawren stopped.

"She assures me that it's nothing serious," Sloane said, "and has refused to let me in the room to check on her."

"I'll go see about her." Lawren strode in the direction of the servants' quarters. "She's an old woman and doesn't have the resistance to illnesses she once did."

Lundy grinned. "She thought you'd say that, sire, and she made me promise to tell you that she has springtime sniffles. You don't need to check on her. She'll be up and about on the morrow."

"Aye," Sloane said, "she was quite adamant about no one's disturbing her once she went to bed."

Reluctantly, Lawren stopped and returned to the great hall.

"Have you eaten?" Sloane asked.

"Nay."

Sloane turned to Rae. "Get Lowrie," he commanded. "Let him know that Lawren is home. Lundy, see that the meal is served." Both boys rushed from the room, each going in a different direction.

When Lawren and Beth reached the chairs that were grouped in front of the fireplace, Lawren took her cloak from her shoulders and hung it on the back of the chair. He unfastened her gloves and helped her slide them off. Settling her in one of the chairs, he dropped both pairs of gloves on the nearest small table. While he unfastened his weapon belts, Sloane gave orders for the tables to be set up.

When Lawren was sitting behind the head table, Beth beside him, Sloane asked, "Did you learn anything at the canyon?"

"Aye."

"Lawren," Lowrie exclaimed, moving into the room. " 'Tis good to see you, brother. We have heard from Bearnard."

Beth straightened as reality slapped her cruelly in the face. Perhaps she had purposefully pushed thoughts of the betrayal and of Bearnard aside. She hadn't wanted to think about anything outside her and Lawren.

"He is requesting that you and he meet at the border of Galloway and Adair territory under the white flag so you might talk. He also wants to speak with Elspeth to assure himself that she is unharmed."

By this time warriors filled the great hall. Evan and William strode from the entrance to the head table and took their places on the left side of Lawren. Jamie came rushing in through the entrance, waving when he saw Lowrie. He joined his friend and Sloane at the fireplace.

Servants quietly moved into the room with trays of food. Beth couldn't remember ever smelling anything so appetizing in all her life. Like the warriors who had traveled with Lawren, she was ravenous. Porridge. Duck. Leg of mutton. Fish. Beef. Beth didn't care what Lawren put on her plate. It looked good and tasted fantastic. She didn't care that she was eating with spoon and knife and fingers. And she really didn't care if she shoveled her food into her mouth. She was beyond hunger, verging on starvation.

When the meal was finished, Lawren shoved back in his chair, enjoying a glass of mead.

"Headmen," he said thoughtfully, "I believe we have a traitor among us."

"A traitor." The word hissed through the building.

Quietly Lawren shared his findings with the kindred. He related the poisoning of the cattle and the false alarm on the illness in the village that had drawn Evan, William, and Annie from the castle, leaving Lowrie alone and exposed. He finished with his discovery that the tracks of the attackers circled back and headed toward the village, not toward Adair territory. When he finished, no one spoke.

Lowrie, pacing back and forth in front of the fireplace, finally broke the silence. "Why would a Galloway want me dead?"

"So he could be appointed chief in your stead," Lawren replied.

"Someone working with Bearnard," Evan murmured.

"Do you know who it is?" William asked.

Evan and William looked at Jamie.

When the lad realized they were silently accusing him, his face blanched. "Nay, Lawren, I'm not a traitor."

" 'Tis true, Lawren," Lowrie said. "Jamie begged me not to leave the castle, but I insisted."

"Yet he is the only one who lived," William mused. "Escaped with only a scratch from an arrow."

"Aye," another said, "he is the one who saw the Adair colors and banner, the one who could tell us what happened to Lowrie."

"If we have a traitor in our midst," Evan said, "how are we going to protect Lowrie?"

"We could put him in hiding," William said.

"Aye," Lawren murmured.

"You will not!" Lowrie exclaimed. "I'm the future chief of the Galloways. I'm not a coward and won't spend the rest of my life in hiding."

"You won't have *a rest of your life* if something more isn't done to protect you," Lawren said. " 'Tis not a matter of being a coward, but one of common sense."

Lowrie opened his mouth to protest more.

"I'll think on the matter," Lawren said, "and let you know my decision."

Lowrie's eyes glittered angrily. "You're not going to tell me what I can or cannot do. I am the future chief of the Galloways, shall be so in two weeks, and I shall give the orders."

"Nay, Lowrie." Lawren spoke quietly, but his voice was undergirded with steel and brooked no argument. "I have authority over the clan until you have completed the coming-of-age ceremony. Then, and only then, will you be giving orders. Right now, you are my charge and you will do as I say. You will retire to your chambers now, and Sloane will guard the door."

Lowrie glared at his brother, then he looked at Evan and William. Neither of the headmen responded to his silent entreaty.

"Let me or William guard him," Evan said.

"Nay, headman, I need the two of you for other matters."

Both men acknowledged with a nod.

"If something happens to Lowrie during the night, Sloane," Lawren said, "your life shall be required of you."

"If something happens to him," the warrior declared, "I will already be dead, laird."

The kindred stirred, their comments rumbling through the room. They had been familiar with hostility and tension generated by their hatred and distrust of the Adairs, had almost reveled in it; they were accustomed to concentrating their hatred on an outsider. Now they had to wrestle with the idea that one of them was a traitor, in league with the Adairs.

"No more discussion tonight, lads, and no accusations," Lawren said. "We shall sleep on what we've learned and talk about it on the morrow." He rose and held out his hand to Beth. "William, send a runner to Bearnard and tell him if he wants to meet with me and to visit with Elspeth, he has to come to Galloway Castle. I shall expect him at high noon two days hence."

Fourteen

Lowrie sulked as he walked up the stairs. When he reached his chambers, Lawren pulled him and Sloane aside and talked to them in a low voice. Lowrie went into the room, and Sloane bolted the door from the outside and took his vigil in the corridor.

As Lawren and Beth turned away, Lawren said, "I know Annie doesn't want anyone worrying over her, but I'd like to look in on her."

Although Beth didn't like the woman, she agreed with Lawren. To tell the truth, she had missed the woman's scowls and whiplashing tongue. They trudged down the stairs, through a back hallway into the servants' quarters.

When Lawren received no answer to his knocking, he opened the door and walked into the small room that was well furnished. On one side of the bed was a large chest. It held several candles and a large basin and water pitcher. Grouped in front of the fireplace were two chairs, a blanket draped over the back of one, a small ottoman in front of the other.

Since this was on one of the lower floors, the window was much smaller than the ones higher up. The narrow rectangular slit allowed a sliver of starlight to slice into the room and fall across the bed that was flush against the wall opposite the fireplace. Embers glowed casting the room in a reddish-gold haze.

They could see the bulk of the woman curled beneath the covers on the bed.

"Annie," Lawren called. When she didn't respond, he stepped closer. "Annie?"

Beth picked up one of the candles on the chest at the head of the bed and moved to the fireplace. As soon as the wick sputtered to life, she rejoined Lawren. He shook Annie and called her name a third time. Handing him the candleholder, Beth pushed in closer.

"This is more than springtime sniffles." She touched Annie's forehead, and her greatest fear materialized. "She's burning up with fever."

The sleeping-death! both of them thought but didn't say.

Hurriedly Beth turned the old woman on her back. Her breathing was ragged, and she was delirious. She clawed at Lawren.

"Not Lowrie," she mumbled. "Not Lowrie."

Lawren looked at Beth. "The sleeping-death."

She nodded. "Bring the light closer." She pulled Annie's tunic aside and searched her shoulders and neck. "I don't see any sign of the rash." She pulled up both sleeves and examined the woman's arms. "We've caught it in time."

"We have no nightlace," Lawren said. "I've used all I have. She's going to die." Lawren thumped the candleholder on the chest and rose. He began to pace the small room. "All because of Bearnard and his greed. I shall kill him for this. He's responsible for killing my father, and I know he's involved with the attempt on Lowrie's life. Now Annie."

"We have some nightlace," Beth said quietly.

He stopped talking and stared at her.

"I have the root you gave me." She reached beyond the candle and picked up the pitcher, filling the basin with water.

The offer had been hard for Beth to make, the sacrifice difficult. She didn't like Annie, not one little bit, and she didn't understand Lawren's loyalty and devotion to her. Beth also knew that physicians didn't treat people based on their morality, but on their need for medical help. Annie was a human and deserved treatment. Beth also knew that whether she was a doctor or not, she would have made the same decision. She would have given up the root to save someone's life.

Lawren stopped pacing and stared at her, blankly, like he wasn't following her train of thought.

"I have the small nightlace nodule you gave me." Beth replaced the pitcher on the chest and rose, searching through the room for a washing cloth.

"That's all I have," Lawren said. "I don't know when I can give you another piece."

It was amazing, Beth thought, that uttering the words made reality ever starker.

"It's in my clothing satchel."

"What about you, Beth?"

"We shall worry about me when the time comes," she replied. "Right now, we have Annie to think about." She found a stack of folded cloths on the wall shelf near the fireplace. "Shall I go get it or will you?"

"You're sure?"

She nodded.

"I'll go."

After Lawren left, Beth threw more wood on the fire and lit more candles. She was sitting on the side of the bed, washing Annie's face when he returned. He had already pulverized the root and mixed the draught. Kneeling on one side of the bed, he gave Annie a swallow as Beth held her head and shoulders up.

Afterward, Beth walked over to the fireplace, and he followed. Standing behind her, he gently kneaded the tensed muscles of her shoulders and neck.

"I know how much this meant to you."

"We'll find some more," she whispered, fearing in the deepest recesses of her heart that they would not. She leaned back against him, resting against his chest. "We have to, Lawren."

"We will. I promise."

"I'll sit up with her tonight," Beth said.

"Nay, lady, you've been working day and night since you arrived at the castle. You have to have some rest."

"She needs me."

"We can get Fenella," Lawren said. "She survived the illness."

"That's right. She would have built up an immunity," Beth said. "But I need to be close by."

"You will be. You'll be in the master suite."

He led her to the chair with the ottoman.

"Wait here, and I'll go get Fenella."

After Lawren left, Beth settled her feet on the ottoman, pushed back in the chair, and gazed at the old woman. Before she had thought Annie was large and fearsome and had always imagined her with war clubs in both hands. Now Annie had shriveled up and looked like a defenseless old woman. She looked rather kindly.

Her breathing rattled in her chest, and she kept mumbling about Lowrie. His close encounter with death had hit the old woman hard. Even in her delirium she was worried and wanted to protect him.

The tapestry slid open and Lawren reentered the room, followed by Fenella. The child's face broke into a big smile when she saw Beth, but as Annie sucked in a painful gasp of air, it was wiped away. Fenella slowly walked to Annie's bed.

Looking back at Beth, Fenella said, " 'Tis the sleeping-death."

No question. A statement.

"Yes," Beth said.

"You've given her some nightlace?"

"Aye." Beth pointed to the chest where the half-filled draught glass set. "She needs to take a large swallow two more times tonight."

"She's not going to die, is she?" Fenella asked. She twisted her tunic skirt in her hand.

Beth shook her head. "She hasn't broken out with a rash, and that's a good sign."

"If she does, should I come get you?"

If she did, Beth didn't know what else to do, but she didn't admit this to the girl. "Yes."

Fenella sat on the edge of the bed. Fishing the cloth out of the basin, she wrung it out and tenderly wiped Annie's face. Tears ran down the child's cheeks.

"Annie seems gruff," she said, "but she's really a kind woman."

Not acquainted with that facet of the servant's personality, Beth made no response. She listened as Fenella talked about Annie's taking care of her family when they had the illness, of her taking them in when they were orphaned.

"We've got to save her, Lawren," Fenella cried. "We have to."

Kneeling, Lawren caught the child in his arms and held her. She cried against his chest.

"Tell me she's going to live, Lawren," Fenella begged.

"I can tell you that," he said, "but I don't know if she will or not. I think so, but I don't know so." He caught her by the shoulders and held her out from him. "But we're depending on you now. If Annie has broken out with the illness, others will, too. Beth and I need our rest so we can take care of them. We need you to help us."

"All right." She wiped her eyes with the back of her hands. "Shall I supervise the morning meal?"

"Nay, you take care of Annie. I'll let someone else handle that."

"Your clothing arrived today, Lady Elspeth," Fenella said dully. "I had them delivered to the wardrobe. I took care of unpacking for you."

"Thank you," Beth said.

Fenella spun around and gazed tearfully at Lawren. "What about Lady Elspeth? I'm her personal maid. Who will take care of her?"

"I will."

"Do her proud, Lawren."

"I'll try," he promised.

* * *

When Lawren and Beth stepped outside Annie's rooms, she caught her toe on one of the uneven floor stones and stumbled. Lawren swept her into his arms and carried her to his chambers.

"What are we going to do?" she asked as desperation overtook her. "We have no more nightlace and no possibility of finding any soon."

"I'll think of something," Lawren told her.

Beth had traveled back in time ostensibly to get the nightlace for those who were suffering from the illness in the future. But she was imprisoned here, and was worrying abut her patients here, about future casualties of the disease. And in order to fight this, she had to assume this other woman's identity.

"You must see I have to make that appeal to the prioress," she whispered. "To the bishop and to Bearnard himself if necessary."

The door to the master suite stood open, and Lawren walked through. The fire had already been banked, its bright flames lighting up the room. He kicked the door shut and set her on her feet. Before she knew what was happening, he had stripped her out of her clothes, tossing them heedlessly on the floor, and slid her beneath the covers. Sitting on the edge of the mattress, he tucked the blanket beneath her chin.

"Are you coming to bed?" Beth asked.

"Nay." He sighed. "I have other matters to attend to tonight."

"Matters more important than getting your rest?"

He sat on the side of the bed. "Much more."

Lifting her arm, she pressed her palm against his beard-stubbled cheek. "Lowrie?"

"I'm going to sneak him out of the castle and hide him."

"At the nightlace garden?"

"Aye, no one knows about it."

"What if Lowrie decides not to stay there?"

"He will. I'll leave Caledonia with him."

"You think she can watch him when a clan of Galloways couldn't?"

"Aye, she's resourceful. I'm leaving Sloane to watch over you."

"How long will you be gone?"

"The day after tomorrow," he replied. "I'm also going to look for more nightlace."

"Where?"

"The same places," he replied. "Where it has grown in the past. I'm hoping that some of it may have come up, that some was missed. I'm simply hoping, lady. I can't sit idly by and do nothing."

Beth understood his frustration. She suffered it also. Although she wanted to go with him, she knew she was needed here. He had to protect Lowrie, had to find some nightlace, and she had to tend the ill.

"Be careful," she murmured.

She cupped the back of his head and brought it down, his mouth covering hers. She slipped her tongue between his firm, full lips. His mouth moved urgently against hers. Intense love poured through her, and she wondered how she'd ever lived without him. She drove her fingers through the blue-black waves of his hair, cooled by the evening breeze. She sealed her lips to his. He tasted of the Highlands, clean and crisp, and his tongue was warm and questing in her mouth.

"Make love to me," she whispered.

"You've been through so much," he said gently.

"Aye, that's why I need this."

She pulled his tunic free of his trousers, slipped her hands up and under. His skin felt like hot silk.

"Don't leave without making love to me." She begged. "We may never see each other again."

He kissed her again, gentle forays turning into frenzied need. She moaned into his mouth, and her tongue danced wildly with his.

Abruptly he pulled away from her. Without a word, he stood and shed his clothing. When he was nude, she looked at his bronze, sinewy chest and finally to the dark pelt of hair below his navel. From that patch sprang his member.

She touched him, and he trembled. She smiled, realizing that her touch had caused his knees to buckle. He slid into the bed beside her, grabbed a handful of her hair and leaning over her, tipped her head back. His mouth descended, and he claimed her mouth in loving fury.

Wanting no foreplay, needing none, Beth pulled him atop her and wrapped her legs around him, locking them together. His body was warm and alive. He felt slick and erotic under her wandering hands. Her fingers found him again, warmly erect. He nipped at her shoulder.

"The nightlace in the portrait was my portal to this world," Beth murmured, "but you are my portal to happiness."

She guided his manhood to her secret place and he slid in. She cried out his name while her body shuddered around his pulsating shaft. He caught one of her nipples in his mouth and sucked, then moved to the other one. She dug her fingers into his shoulders and panted his name over and over, falling into the cadence of his thrust and parry.

Her whole being readied itself for the moment of tumultuous glory. She moved beneath him, with him, her breathing ragged. She gasped, tensed, and felt as if she had exploded into a million tiny stars. She whimpered contentedly.

He murmured her name and his hands cupped her buttocks, holding her against his grinding pelvis as his own pleasure rained over him. His release came in long, hard shudders, leaving him limp and panting. He pulled out of her slowly and fell to one side with a moan of utter satisfaction.

"I wish I could lie here beside you and hold you all night."

"Why can't you and Lowrie leave in the morning? After you get a good night's sleep."

"Are you really offering me a night's sleep?"

Beth flipped onto her side. Flinging a leg and arm over his brawny body, she kissed one of his nipples. "A good night."

He wrapped her hair around the fingers of one hand and pulled her mouth away from him. "Lady, you sorely tempt me. If I stayed here, it would be a good night, but I cannot. I need the cover of darkness." He brushed his hand through her hair.

"I don't want anyone to know that we're gone until the morrow. We'll have a good head start if anyone tries to follow."

Bringing his face to hers, Beth flirted with his mouth, nestling her tongue in the corners and biting gently on his lower lip. With a groan and a deep, hot kiss, he slid off the bed.

"I must leave now, lady, while I can."

Before he betrayed his honor, Beth thought, and she didn't argue further with him. She understood how important honor, or *enech*, was to the Highlanders.

She watched the pull of muscle in his buttocks and legs as he crossed the room; she reveled in his handsomeness, gilded by the glow of the firelight. He filled the basin with water, brought it over to the chest and set it down. Soon both he and Beth had cleaned themselves. She lay back down and watched as he changed clothes.

"Do you think anyone will suspect you're going to hide Lowrie?"

He tied his undergarments about his waist.

"Probably."

"How will you get him out without their knowing?"

He stepped into his trousers, then slipped the tunic over his head. "Through one of the sally-forth doors."

"A sally-forth door," Beth murmured. "Besides being a door, what is it?"

"Small doors around the bottom of the castle wall. There are several that my headmen know about, but this one is secret. Only Lowrie, Caledonia, and I are aware of it."

"Is that the way she would have sneaked me out of the castle?" Beth asked.

He nodded. "If we are under siege, we can send out spies through these doors. If we are overrun, we can use them to escape."

"Is anyone else going with you?"

"Nay, the fewer who know the safer Lowrie is."

"Please be careful," she urged, "and return to me."

"I will." He fastened his weapons about his waist. "Until I

return, Sloane will take care of you. I wish Annie were well," he muttered. "She would watch after you."

"She would be one of the first to kill me," Beth exclaimed.

"Nay, she hates you, and she would like to kill you, but she wouldn't, not unless I gave the order. If I told her to protect you with her life, she would. She has sworn fealty to the Galloways."

"Since Bearnard is coming here to talk with you, I'm probably not in any danger," Beth said.

"Let's not count on Bearnard's coming until we see him in the great hall of Galloway Castle," Lawren said.

"May I write Shawe, the prioress, and the bishop?" When he didn't answer, she said, "Like you, I have to do something."

"Aye, lady," he finally said, "write your letters."

"I shall wait to despatch them until you return."

"Nay, send them whenever you wish."

"You trust me?"

"Aye."

Pleasure flowed warmly through Beth. Fully clothed, he returned to the bed, leaned down, and gave her a last kiss. She blinked back her tears and watched as he strode to the door. He turned, lifted a hand to his mouth, and blew her a kiss. She caught it and tucked it against her heart.

"Keep it always," he said.

He walked out, the thud of the closing door resounding in the room.

"I will," she promised, tears running hotly down her cheeks.

She had never dreamed that loving would be so bittersweet.

The next morning Beth was sluggish. Her joints ached; her muscles were sore. Lawren had warned her about the horseback riding! Still, she didn't regret going. She quickly dressed, pulled the tapestry open, and walked into the corridor. She fully expected to find Sloane sleeping on his pallet, but he was up, twisting his tartan about his shoulders and waist.

"I tried to be quiet so I wouldn't awaken you," she said.

He grinned through his bushy red beard that was not braided today. "If I slept that heavily, I wouldn't be any use to you."

"I'm going to look in on Annie. You may stay here if you wish."

"Lawren told me to stay with you, and that's what I'm going to do."

Giving him a friendly smile and a nod of her head, Beth swept down the hallway to Annie's chamber. Sloane followed. They stopped by the kitchen, and Beth left orders for a cup of herbal tea. When they reached Annie's room, Beth entered and left the door opened. The Highlander leaned against the door frame with a view down the corridor.

The old woman was breathing much easier, and Fenella was asleep on a pallet in front of the fireplace. Beth bathed Annie's face and combed her white hair. She looked through both of the chests in the room and found a clean sleeping tunic. She laid it across the foot of the bed. Knowing that she and the old woman did not share an appreciation for each other, she had done no more. Fenella would help Annie change clothes.

One of the kitchen lads brought Beth her tea. Taking it, she walked over to the chair she had occupied last night, and sat down, resting her feet on the ottoman. A cool breeze wafted in through the opened window, and the room was pleasant. Closing her eyes, she sipped the beverage, letting its warmth seep through her aching joints and muscles.

Annie shuffled on the bed, drawing Beth's attention to her. Her fever had broken; her delirium ceased. No rash had broken out. Annie was going to be all right. Beth wasn't sure about herself.

She leaned forward and set the empty cup down. Again she stared at the glass on the chest; it contained enough draught for one more dose. No more nightlace! Unless Lawren could find some more. Until the garden would produce some new ones. What if she were transported back to the future before then?

Beth stayed with Annie. After she gave her the last dose of medicine, she held the empty glass for a long time. She stared at the tiny crystals that dotted the sides and layered the bottom. Gone! It was gone! She set the glass on the chest, but didn't leave until Fenella had awakened and taken care of her morning toiletries.

When Beth departed, she returned to the private apartment she had been given. She wandered through the wardrobe first, looking at all the fine clothing that had been delivered for Elspeth. She could see the care Fenella had given the garments. She had even matched veils and wimples and belts together. Beth thought of moving her clothing upstairs to Lawren's chambers, but decided to wait until she learned what her fate would be. There was always the possibility she would be ransomed.

Smiling, Beth returned to the sleeping chamber and moved directly to the desk. She retrieved her writing paraphernalia. Between her and Sloane, they carried it to the master suite. At first she thought about depositing it on the empty desk in the master solar, but she was going to do the painting in the bedroom. Wanting her materials close at hand, she spread them across the trestle table setting against the wall.

Although her head hurt slightly and her eyes ached, she started working on her sketch. Leaving the door open, Sloane stood watch in the corridor

Midmorning Fenella skipped up the stairs. A tray of food in her hands, she stopped first and served Sloane. When his large bowl was filled, she walked into the master suite.

Surveying the laden tray, Beth asked, "Is this the morning meal or morning feast?"

"I thought you and Lawren would be famished," the child replied.

"I am." Beth pushed her parchment aside and made room for the tray. "But Lawren won't be eating with me."

"Aye, he and Lowrie slipped out of the castle during the night," Fenella replied.

Beth cut her a surprised look.

Fenella laid the trencher, a thick slice of bread, in the bottom of the silver bowl. "He left a message for the headmen, telling

them that he has taken their advice and is hiding Lowrie."
Fenella beamed. "I was the one who read the letter to them."

"So you were a clerk?" Beth said.

Fenella shrugged, but the glow on her face didn't diminish.

"Is Annie still getting better?"

"Aye, she's fussing about everything. She doesn't like the
idea of the steward messing in her kitchen. He'll overcook the
fish. The beef will be too tough. He doesn't know a leg of
mutton from a boar roast. Too many spices in this, not enough
in that." Fenella grinned and shrugged. "She'll be up before the
day is over."

"There's so much food here," Beth said. "Would you and
Sloane share it with me?"

Fenella's eyes lit up. "Aye, I love baked fish."

"And you, Sloane," Beth said, "surely you could use more."

"Aye."

Using one of the eating knives, Fenella cut up several of the
fishes on the trencher and handed Beth the knife. She filled
another bowl with fish and carried it to Sloane.

As Fenella sat down at the table, Beth said, "I know it's good
manners to eat from your knife, but I think we can handle this
better with spoons. If we don't, I'm afraid my mouth will be
all cut up."

Fenella giggled. Using fingers and spoons, they ate.

When they were finished, Beth leaned back in her chair. "I
need some paint."

The child's eyes rounded. "The walls are painted."

"I'm going to do a different kind of painting, Fenella. I'm
also going to need some fresh plaster." She walked across the
room to the wall between the bed and fireplace. "I want it ap-
plied to the wall as soon as possible." She drew the imaginary
measurements with her hands. "Right here."

Sloane eased into the room, staring at the wall, then at Beth.

Clearly puzzled, Fenella said, "The walls are already plastered and freshly painted."

"I know. I'm going to paint Lawren's portrait here."

"Blessed Mary!"

Sloane and Fenella exchanged startled glances.

Beth returned to her desk. "I need brushes."

As if in a daze, Fenella stood there.

"Brushes," Beth said. "Where can I find some brushes?"

"We can make them," Fenella mumbled.

"All sizes?" Beth asked.

The child nodded.

"Here's a list of colors that I want, and the ingredients fo:
the mixing of each." She handed Fenella a small piece of parch
ment. "Can you see that I get them?"

Fenella read the colors aloud.

When she was through, Sloane looked at Beth. "Does Lawrer
know you're doing this?"

"Aye, he asked me to."

Fenella rolled her eyes. "People are going to be thinking he
a warlock for sure."

"Aye," Sloane droned.

Warlock! The word jarred Beth. It shouldn't have. By now
should be part of her everyday vocabulary. But it wasn't. Sh
had managed to push the thought from her mind. Because sh
and he had figured out how to use the nightlace, she had a:
sumed that others would realize he wasn't a warlock, that h
had brought nothing evil on them.

Her desire to paint diminished. She had to write her letter
She brushed her hand over her head, wishing she could get r
of the niggling hint of a headache. She would be glad when h
body adjusted to this time change.

The only way she was going to save Lawren, to prove th
he wasn't a warlock was to convince the bishop there was r
plague. As Elspeth she could do this, must do it. This was h
responsibility. Beth walked closer to the window, staring o
but seeing nothing. Even if she proved that the nightlace cou
heal the disease, she didn't know if she could save Lawren. I
was an unwanted piece in a game of political intrigue.

Beth remembered the manuscript. Lawren mac Galloway w

burned at the stake for a warlock. The church would continue to think this was a curse of God and Bearnard would use their beliefs to fatten his coffers, to enlarge his territory, and to build his own kingdom.

Paradoxically, her and Lawren's discovery that the nightlace administered prior to the breaking out of the rash had changed the complexion of the disease. But it had changed nothing. Despair wrapped itself around Beth, and she sighed.

"When do you want us to start?" Fenella asked.

Beth was so deep in thought, it took a little while for the words to penetrate. She turned.

"The brushes and the paint," Fenella said. "When do you want them?"

"As soon as possible," Beth replied.

"I don't know about this," Fenella said, with a shake of her head.

Jerking herself out of despondence, knowing she had work to do, Beth said, "I do."

Fenella slipped out with the tray, and Beth called Sloane. The two of them moved tables around so that the small round one set in front of the place where she was going to paint. While she waited for her paint to be mixed and her brushes to be made, she penned her letters to the three religious leaders of the community. When she was satisfied with them, she folded and sealed them. Then she gave them to Sloane to dispatch.

Several hours later, the table was filled with jars of paint and water and brushes of all sizes. Fenella and Sloane meticulously poured paint from the larger containers into the small individual oyster shells.

Beth put the large white tunic over her clothing and started to paint. As with the quill pen, it took her a little while to learn how to work with the brushes, but she soon had the hang of it. She worked quicker than she would have ordinarily, than she wished to work now. But she had to get the portrait done before the plaster dried. Although both Sloane and Fenella urged her to eat, she skipped the evening meal, wanting to take advantage of daylight hours.

For the most part Sloane stood in the corridor, but his curiosity would get the best of him, and from time to time he would walk into the room and survey Beth's work. Periodically Lundy and Rae would slip in and look at the painting. They mumbled to themselves, but said nothing to Beth. Sloane, however, voiced his surprise that the portrait looked so much like Lawren.

"It's a new painting technique," Beth explained.

"One you learned during your travels," he said.

Her travels! She stared blankly at Sloane. For a moment she was so truly Beth, she had forgotten that these people thought she was Elspeth. Then she remembered. Elspeth had traveled abroad with Alastair. Anything unusual Beth did would now be blamed on her travels.

"Yes," she said.

"Mayhap you would have been better off remaining at home and taking care of the castle." Evan's voice whipped across the room.

Beth turned to see both headmen standing in the door.

"The child said you were painting Lawren's chambers."

"I'm doing a portrait of him."

"This is the master suite," William said, running his hand down his scar. "Nothing should be done to it until Lowrie has settled in."

The two men strode into the room, pushed past Beth, and stared at the painting.

"This is a disgrace." Evan snorted.

"Aye," William agreed.

Both made comment on how much like Lawren it looked.

"Lawren gave me permission to do the fresco," Beth said. "Take the matter up with him when he returns."

"We shall," Evan promised.

Muttering between themselves, they crossed the room. At the door William stopped.

"Have you heard from Lawren?"

"No, have you?"

Shaking his head, he strode out. Sloane remained at his post, and she returned to her work.

Darkness settled gently over the glen. Although she didn't wish for heat and wished she could do without it, Beth needed light. She had Sloane build up the fire and light more beeswax candles. She was grateful for the evening breeze that wafted through the room.

She stepped back to survey her work. Although portraits were her specialty, she was stunned at how much she had accomplished in such a short period of time. She was also amazed at how complete it looked. It was almost as if she had only held the brush and daubed on the paint, as if some force greater than herself had done the painting.

Lawren looked alive. She had so truly captured his essence, she wanted to touch him. Never had she been so utterly consumed with creative force as she had been today and tonight.

By the wee hours of the next morning, she brushed on her last stroke. Lifting an arm, she wiped perspiration from her forehead. She then walked to the table and poured herself a glass of water. Drinking deeply, she turned and looked at the portrait.

"Are you finished?" Sloane softly called from the corridor.

She set the glass down and walked over to the small table that held her paints. Picking up the brush, she dipped it into the oyster shell of red paint. She quickly signed her E, her cursive E.

"Yes, it's finished."

Beth worried that when she looked at the painting in daylight, she would be displeased with it. But she wasn't. If anything she was more pleased. She felt as if she were staring at Lawren. She loved him so, missed and worried about him. She hadn't heard from him since night before last when he had left her.

Since Lawren had departed, Beth had left the wooden door

open. To give herself some privacy, she kept the tapestry curtain pulled. Opening it, she smiled at her guard.

"I'm going to visit with Annie," she said.

"I'm ready whenever you are," he replied.

At first, his dogging her heels had bothered her, had made her feel like a prisoner, but now she was quite accustomed to it. She truly liked the man. He had a warm sense of humor and didn't take exception to her—an Adair—being here.

When they reached Annie's chamber, Beth knocked on the door.

"Enter," the woman called weakly.

Wearing a plain sleeping tunic, Annie was sitting up in bed, pillows fluffed behind her back. Her hair had been combed into a coil on the top of her head. Sunlight slivered into the room and onto the bed.

"How are you feeling?" Beth asked.

"Weak but much better," the woman replied. She picked at the covers. "Fenella said you were the one who saved me."

"It was the nightlace," Beth said.

"Your nightlace." Annie wrung her hands.

"A small piece Lawren had given to me," Beth admitted. "Also at the Kenna Galloway hamlet, we learned that the disease is not fatal until the body is covered in a red rash. If we administer the draught before then, chances of survival are almost guaranteed."

"Fenella told me. Why did you save me? I know you hate me."

"I come as close to hating you as I do anyone," Beth said, "but I would never let my personal feelings stand in the way of my saving a patient."

"You should have let me die," Annie said. "I'm old."

"I'm a physician, not God. My duty is to heal not to determine who should or should not live."

"I don't know that I will ever like you, Elspeth," Annie said "but I'm beginning to admire you. I wouldn't have thought you had any honor, but you do."

"Thank you," Beth said. "Is there anything else I can do for you?"

"Nay, Fenella takes care of me."

"If you need me," Beth said, "I'm in the master suite." She paused, then said, "I guess you know Lawren is away."

"Aye, and so is Lowrie. Lawren has hidden him."

Beth nodded.

"Lawren thinks it is one of us," Annie said. "A Galloway."

"It could be," Beth said.

Annie inhaled deeply and closed her eyes.

"Someone who is working with Bearnard in hopes of being appointed the next clan chieftain," Beth went on.

Annie's eyes flew open. "Mayhap this isn't true, but you have convinced him of this."

"Will you always dislike and distrust me?" Beth asked.

"Aye," Annie said. "You're an Adair. You have wormed your way into his bed and into his heart. He's thinking with his heart now rather than his head. He'll be an easy man to convince."

"I had nothing to do with the attack on Lowrie," Beth said. "I'm not working with Bearnard to bring about the fall of the Galloways. All I want to do is heal this disease that is ravaging the land."

And return to my world with the nightlace so I can heal it.

"Without nightlace that will be impossible," the old woman said.

Despair closed heavily about Beth. Her chances did seem impossible.

By late afternoon Beth was sitting on a stone bench in the formal gardens. Any other time she would have been enjoying the beautiful spring sunshine, but she was too worried about Lawren. Hoping he would return soon, she had dressed especially for him and had not braided her hair. Straightening the blue tunic about herself, she leaned back against the stone fence and closed her eyes.

She smiled as she thought about him, remembering his impassioned touches, his tenderness, the sublime joy his lovemaking brought to her. She could not imagine their not being together.

"A rider!" the watchman shouted.

Beth straightened, holding her breast as she awaited the call that would identify the rider.

" 'Tis Lawren!"

She leaped to her feet and started running. Winding through the smaller inner yards, around pens and gardens, she forgot to be careful with her tunic and raced to the inner courtyard. She reached it as Lawren dismounted the huge black stallion. She paused, and across the way they stared at each other. Slowly he smiled and held open his arms. She flew into them, burrowing as close as she could, holding him.

"I was so worried," she said.

She shoved back and ran her fingers over his face, his shoulders, his chest. His jaws were covered in beard-stubble; exhaustion darkened the skin around his eyes.

"You're all right? Nothing happened to you?"

He smiled indulgently. "I'm weary and hungry, my lady. Otherwise, I'm quite content."

The wind blew, and a few strands of her hair wrapped around his arm. He caught it, gently disentangling it. Then he brushed his hands through the length of it.

" 'Tis beautiful," he murmured. "Like the fine silk thread. I'm glad you wore it hanging."

Beth glowed. "Come inside," she ordered. "I'll prepare you something to eat."

By this time the kindred had gathered around, but they were subdued and tense. For the most part, their countenances were dour, and they cast covert glances at one another. William and Evan waited at the entrance to the castle.

"Did you find any more nightlace?" Beth asked.

"Nay."

His arm around Beth's shoulder, Lawren guided her into the

great hall. As he passed his headmen, he asked, "Any word from Bearnard?"

"Aye," William clipped, falling in step with Lawren. "As you directed, he, Shawe, and a small escort of Adairs will be arriving here at high noon on the morrow."

"Any more cases of the sickness?"

"Not among the Galloways, and we have runners constantly riding and checking."

"But the cases outside Galloway territory are increasing," Evan said. "Shawe reported that the clan chieftains had appealed to the bishop for divine intervention."

"Divine intervention for what?" Lawren never slackened his gait. "For the illness or for me?"

"For you," Evan said. "Shawe said if you are tried for heresy and found guilty, you will be burned at the stake."

Beth shivered in Lawren's arm. Wishing he could spare her the pain, he drew her closer against him.

"And if they saw that—that painting on the wall in the master suite they would burn you without a trial."

Raising his brows, Lawren looked at Beth.

"I painted your portrait while you were gone."

"And wrote your letters?"

She nodded.

"You've been busy, lady."

"Shawe also reported that he had been searching for the nightlace but had found none," Evan added sharply.

"Bearnard has it," Lawren said. "But I don't know where. I've searched all the possible places where it could be grown."

"Good afternoon, Lawren," Annie said.

Lawren stopped walking and stared at his old nurse. Although she was pale, she waited for him in her regular place in front of the fireplace. Chairs had been grouped together and a small trestle table erected. Lawren walked to Annie and caught her in a hug.

"How are you feeling, good woman?"

"Weak but fine." She pushed out of his arms. "Is Lowrie safe?"

"As safe as I can make him." Lawren unfastened his weapons and hung the belts over one of the chairs.

"You're not going to tell any of us where he is hidden?"

"That would defeat my purpose, good woman."

She scowled her disapproval, and Beth wondered if this was the first time Lawren had kept a secret from her.

"What if something happens to you, and we need to get to Lowrie?"

"I have taken care of the matter."

His mother and Sloane, Beth thought. If something happened to Lawren, one or the other would know almost immediately. Both of them would protect Lowrie and bring him out for the coming-of-age ceremony, for the ascension to the high seat.

"The lads are bringing your meal," Annie said.

Lawren seated Beth in one of the chairs, and he sat in the other one. He shoved his hand through his hair. Beth wished she could whisk him up to the master suite where she could protect and take care of him. He needed rest.

"I'm told you suspect that one of us is in league with Bearnard and that we're responsible for Lowrie's accident," Annie said.

" 'Tis a thought," Lawren replied.

"None of the Galloways are in league with an Adair," Annie said. "The wench has beguiled you."

William and Evan's eyes sparked with interest.

"She saved your life," Lawren said.

"To ingratiate herself with you." Annie might be recovering from the illness, but her eyes had lost none of their spark or her voice its cutting edge. "She's after your soul, Lawren, and she'll do whatever is necessary to turn you against the Galloways, to point an accusing finger at them."

"Aye," William and Evan agreed at the same time.

Ayes rang out all around Lawren.

"You must avenge Clan Galloway of its dishonor," Annie said.

"How can I when I am the one accused of being its dishonor?" He picked up his glass of mead and drained it.

Lundy and Rae set the meal on the table in front of Lawren. Beth glanced at it, but at the moment food was the least of her concerns. She was worried about Lawren. The trap seemed to be closing around him, death coming closer and closer.

Although the Galloways went through the pretension of the meal, Lawren eating and reports being made, the anxiety level in the room was high. The Galloways hated her; they were suspicious of their kinsmen and of Lawren. Beth felt that at any moment one of them would leap to his feet, scream, and start hacking with his sword.

Lawren seemed oblivious to the tension. When he had finished eating, he drank another glass of mead. Then he rose.

"Annie see that a bath is drawn for me in the wardrobe. I don't wish to be disturbed for the remainder of the day or night. On the morrow we shall meet at break of day to discuss plans for receiving our illustrious guest." He held out his hand to Beth. "Now, kindred, I bid you good day."

Fifteen

"What are you going to be doing that is so important you don't wish to be disturbed this afternoon or tonight?" Beth asked as she and Lawren walked out of the great hall.

"Be with you." With an arm around her shoulder, he hugged her to him.

"And what are *we* going to do?" she asked breathlessly.

"First of all, I want to bathe."

"In that huge tub?" She shivered with excitement. "All by yourself?"

"In that huge tub"—his eyes twinkled as he glanced down at her—"but not by myself."

They chuckled softly, but their fantasy was short-lived, shattered when they heard angry rumbling coming from the great hall.

"Are you worried about the dissension among the clan?" she asked.

"Aye, but until I've discovered who is causing it, there is nothing I can do."

"You have learned nothing new?"

"Nay, but we shall see what the morrow brings. We can always hope that Bearnard has repented his sins and that the church will respond to your appeal. If we get the nightlace, we can stop the illness. Then I can concentrate on finding who tried to kill Lowrie."

"I hope so," Beth murmured.

"As long as he remains in the glen with Caledonia, he'll be safe."

"But Lowrie has a penchant for straying," Beth reminded him.

"Aye, the lad does, but this time it will take him longer to find his way out. By then I may have solved our mystery."

They were inside the room now, and Lawren kicked the door closed. Leaning back against it, he caught her in his arms.

"At the moment, lady, I want to enjoy you. It seems that I have been away from you for a lifetime."

"You have," she replied. "For many lifetimes."

He lowered his head, and Beth raised hers, their lips meeting in warm sweetness. But neither was satisfied with warmth or sweetness; they wanted fire and ardor. Desperation drove them. His clasp tightened; she wrapped her arms around him, pressing as close to him as she could, melding with him.

Her breasts swelled. They throbbed for the touch of his hand, of his mouth. She rubbed against his chest. His hands slid to her buttocks, and he nudged his growing hardness more fully against her.

The kiss deepened, their tongues entwined. They sparred in that age-old game of mating, that seemed to be new and freshly discovered each time they partook in it. Each took; each gave. Their frenzied need fed the flames of desire.

Lawren released her mouth, drew back, but still held her in his embrace. He gazed into her smiling face, into those glorious green eyes, heavy with passion, that aroused the same response in him.

He had always had a fondness for Elspeth, but he realized now that his feelings for Elspeth had not exceeded fondness and never would have. He could never love her as he loved Beth. Beth was part of his heart and soul; she complimented him, made him feel complete. She was one of the most giving persons he had ever met, one of the most honorable. Her saving Annie's life had endeared her to him, had confirmed his opinion of her.

"I love you, Elizabeth Balfour," he murmured.

"And I love you."

She leaned her head back. "You believe from the bottom of your heart that I'm not Elspeth and I'm not scheming with Bearnard?"

"Aye."

She sighed and laid her cheek against his chest.

"Annie is convinced that I'm an evil woman. And so are the other Galloways."

"Aye, and if you remain here you'll have to accept that you are Elspeth. You'll always be an Adair."

"Oh, Lawren!"

All the happiness in the world, not even Lawren's love could keep Beth's world from tumbling in on her. She felt as if she were suffocating.

"What am I going to do? I love you and want to stay here with you. But I need to return to the future with the nightlace so I can stop the same plague that you and I are battling. What am I going to do?"

Beth's heartrending plea cut deeply, painfully into Lawren's soul. "I don't know. I've also been giving the matter a great deal of thought."

She pulled out of his arms and walked to the window. Stepping into the alcove, she crossed her arms over her chest and gazed at the loch below.

"Have you thought about the possibility of returning to the future with me?"

"Aye, but I find myself facing the same dilemma as you." He walked up behind her, clasped her shoulders, and pulled her back against him.

"Your—your dilemma isn't the same as mine," she whispered. She turned and stared at him. "If you stay here, you're going to be burned at the stake. If you go with me, you'll have a choice of living."

"You said the—"

"I told you the truth," Beth cried. "The manuscript isn't complete, and I'm not sure exactly what happens to you. But there is an entry that states Lawren mac Galloway died and the plague was stayed."

A shadow flickered through his eyes, and the corners of his mouth ticked. She threw herself against him, holding him tightly.

"I'll give you all the information you'll need to find me," Beth said. "No matter where you may be, we'll find each other."

"If I knew for sure that I would be with you in your time period, I would take the risk. But we don't know what will happen. I could arrive farther back in time; I could go even farther in the future."

"We have to take the risk, Lawren," Beth said. "We must."

"Or, my love, I could be condemned to a life in the debilitated body of Callum Galloway." He caught her face and drew it up so they were looking at each other. "That would be more sorrow than you could bear."

She nodded, and laid her cheek back on his chest. He felt the moisture of her tears through his tunic and wished he could fight her demons for her, but he couldn't. He couldn't fight his own.

"Always there is this dark cloud hanging over us," she said, "shadowing our happiness, reminding us that we have crossed time's barrier, but are not meant to be together in any time." She burrowed into his strength.

There was a knock on the door.

"Lawren, may we enter?" Lundy called. "We have the water for your bath."

"Aye," Lawren called out.

"While they fill the tub," Beth said, pushing away from him and brushing the tears from her eyes, "let's return to the master suite. You'll need a change of clothes, and I want to show you the painting."

Holding hands, Lawren and Beth walked to the master suite. She led him directly to the fresco. Stunned, he gazed at it. This was the first time he had seen a portrait so perfectly captured on plaster. It looked so real he reached out to touch it. Beth grabbed his hand.

"Nay, love. You'll smear the paint."

He stepped back, his gaze sweeping from top to bottom, to the delicate blossoms strewn about his feet, the ones she had painted on his badge. He stood looking for a long time, saying nothing, but Beth read the admiration in his eyes, in his expression. He walked over to the trestle table next to the wall and poured two glasses of mead. One he gave to her.

"The nightlace," he murmured in salute.

"Forever immortalized." She held her glass up.

"Our love," he whispered, "forever immortalized."

They drained their glasses, and set them aside. As the foundations of their lives crumbled beneath them, they turned to each other and clung together. She was his reality; he was hers.

"As you leave the painting for me," he said, "you also leave yourself something of me. Something you will find when you return, and you will understand it now."

She stepped back and gazed at him, letting her love shine in her eyes, on her face. "I shall give you something more personal," she said and pulled off the locket chain. She slipped it over his head. "I'll give you my talisman."

He brushed his palm over it. "This is the grandest gift I have ever received."

"It comes from my heart."

She cupped his head in her hand and pulled his mouth against hers. She gave him a full, hot kiss, a kiss she wanted, one that he wanted also. It deepened, grew more desperate, hotter.

Not content with only their lips touching, with her holding his face, Lawren caught her in a full embrace. As he pulled her to him, Beth pressed against him. She could not get enough of him. His hands slid down to her hips, and he held her so that she felt his hotness, his bigness. Feeling it wasn't enough; she wanted his heat inside her.

When he raised his head, he was breathing heavily. So was Beth. His hand, big and callused, gently stroked curls from her face. He ran his hands through the length of it, letting the long tresses flow over his fingers. In the brilliant glow of afternoon sunlight her hair glistened rich and red. He stroked his fingertips over her cheeks, her lips.

"Come," he whispered, "let's return to the wardrobe. The afternoon is ours."

They strolled back to the mistress's quarters. The boys were gone, and the tub was filled with water. Lawren bolted the door and joined Beth at the tub. Sunlight pooled around them as he started to undress her. She caught his hand and brought it to her chest. She laid it over her heart.

"Let me undress for you."

Lawren gazed at the woman who stood before him. She stirred him more deeply than any other woman ever had. She was the dearest thing in his life. He couldn't bear to think of living without her. Without her he wouldn't be living; he would merely exist.

Excited, he nodded, and she danced away from him, the skirt of her tunic swirling through the air, revealing her smooth ankles and calves. Her gaze locked with his, she unfastened her girdle, held it for a moment, then let it fall to the floor. Gracefully she bent, caught the hem of her tunic and lifted it, the material slowly, seductively crawling up her body. Lawren's breath caught as the tunic glided up to reveal her thighs, her hips, the golden red curls at the juncture of her legs. The tunic caressed her inch by inch: stomach; abdomen; full and firm breasts; shoulders. Last, her beautifully flushed face with its red, pouting lips.

She had drawn the tunic over her head but had not dropped it. She still held it above her head with both hands. Lawren leaned toward her. Kissing along her collarbone, her shoulders, and up and down her neck, he murmured, "Every time I see you, my lady, you are more beautiful. More desirable."

Although she shuddered beneath his caresses and she wanted more, she danced away from him again. She tossed the tunic and it landed on his chest, slowly sliding down his body, catching on his manhood. Beth laughed; he smiled. He removed it. Laughing, flirting with him, she sat on the stool in front of the fire. She removed her shoes. Naked, she rose and moved to the bathtub.

Lawren saw the soft, delectable contours of her body. She caught the sides of the ladder with both hands, the movement thrusting her breasts forward. She climbed into the tub. Hard with desire, he gazed at her.

Her elbows propped on the side of the tub, she gazed seductively at him. "Are you going to join me?" she teased. "Or shall I bathe alone."

"Nay, lady, you'll not be alone."

She grabbed one of the washing cloths that draped over the side of the tub. Dipping it in the water, she brushed it across her shoulders, water sluicing between her breasts, droplets forming on her areolas. His eyes burned with desire.

"It's your time to undress."

Lawren began to take off his clothing. Never taking his eyes from Beth, he dropped his clothing piece by piece at his feet. Beth's eyes touched every feature of his face, his chest covered in the mat of crisp black hair, his lean, hard stomach. She dropped her gaze to his aroused manhood.

"You are so beautiful, Lawren."

"All of me?" His rich, husky laughter filled the room and chased away all other thoughts but them and their magical world. "Or just parts of me."

"All of you," she murmured, her gaze sweeping over him, then coming to rest on his manhood. "Although I have a great appreciation for certain parts over others."

Inhaling deeply, she raised her head, their gazes locking together. Her breath was liquid fire burning in her, settling in her lower body.

"Then you shall have as much or as little of me as you wish."

"All of you," she murmured. "Body, heart, and soul." She trembled with the force of the emotions he had unleashed in her.

He walked to the tub, stepped up and over into the water. They had bathed together in the stream, and while Beth had enjoyed it, it was not as exhilarating as this experience. The other seemed to be expedient. This one was downright erotic. He slowly kissed the soft curve of her throat. She arched, twisting to get closer.

His lips brushed hers warmly. She cupped the back of his head, holding him against her. She curled her hand through his hair.

He kissed her again and again, teasing and tormenting her with light brushing strokes before he fully claimed her mouth, before he possessed it with his tongue.

He kissed her with a deep thoroughness that left her breathless. His hand strayed between her thighs, moving gently against her. When she felt his finger slide slowly inside, she sighed.

He withdrew. She arched until she felt him flatten his body against her, his chest rubbing against her nipples. She played her fingers through his chest hair and found herself entranced by the hard, muscled contours of his body. He lifted his head and gazed down at her. They slid into the water.

Sitting with her back to the tub, she spread her legs. "Sit here," she said. "Let me bathe you."

She rubbed a handful of soft soap in her hands and lathered his hair. She cleaned it, massaging the scalp and kneading tension from his neck and shoulders. Sinking into beautiful oblivion, he let her fingers carry him further and further from reality.

Water gently lapped against his skin. Vaguely he was aware of her lifting up the silver pitcher and using it to rinse the suds from his hair. With spread fingers, she combed out the tangles.

"Lady, I think for sure that you and I shall be taking quite a few baths from now on."

Beth laughed. "I haven't even begun, my love."

She moved so that she sat in front of him. He stared into her eyes. She began to wash his face, careful to keep the suds out of his eyes. Lightly she touched his cheeks, his forehead, his bristled jaws and chin. She brushed her hands over his neck, cleaned his ears, feathering her fingers in every nook and around every curve.

Gradually fiery need replaced his warm lethargy, and all thoughts of a bath vanished.

She picked up the washing cloth.

"Let me show you how it is done, my lady."

He took the cloth from her and hung it over the side of the tub. He filled his hand with the same soap she had used, and he spread it over her breasts. He rolled her nipples, and his hands slid under and over her breasts.

Holding on to the side of the tub with one hand, he rose. She watched the water sluice down his body, through the patch of dark hair at his thighs. She caught her breath as he held out his hand, and she rose with him.

His hands still covered in soap, he brushed them over her shoulder, down her back and over her hips, around the gentle flare to her stomach. His hands slid lower to the russet triangle between her thighs. She swayed toward him. He retrieved the pitcher and filled it with water, rinsing her off. He stared into her passion-glazed eyes.

" 'Tis time to dry you."

He lapped the water droplets from her breasts; he licked along her abdomen, around her navel. Beth growled her pleasure. She shivered when she felt his fingers stroking her inner thighs. They went higher and higher, seeking her inner self. They whetted her hunger and reminded her of the passion they had shared two nights in a row. Weak with desire, she clutched his shoulders for support.

He pulled away and stepped out of the tub. Easily he lifted her out. He picked up a large cloth and began to dry her off. When he was finished, she took the cloth from him.

"I shall dry you. I want to touch you as you have touched me. To give you pleasure as you've given me."

Beth took the cloth in both hands and began to dry his arms. She rubbed the soft fabric over his body. Gently she patted the moisture off his shoulders and chest. His nipples hardened, and he caught and held her hands against him.

She lost herself in his fiery blue gaze, and she felt the rise and fall of his chest, the beating of his heart. She dried his back and buttocks. Then she brought her hands and the towel to the juncture of his thighs.

Gently, so gently, she dried him off, feeling a sense of wonder when he grew beneath her touch. She dropped the cloth and touched him with soft, gentle strokes, feeling again the wonder of the masculine body, the wonder of Lawren's body. She felt life pulsing strong and vibrant in him. Tenderly she cupped the swollen sacks that bore the seed of life.

The warrior trembled beneath her touch, and she experienced something new and exhilarating. She looked into those eyes that were exploding with passion.

He stooped, picked her up, and carried her into the sleeping chamber. "I'm ready for more, lady."

"So am I."

Lawren took her. He was in no hurry. Neither was she. Slowly they aroused. Fully they gave, each always thinking of the other first. In giving they received, and in receiving they gave. Together they climbed the path toward total fulfillment.

Their bodies grew taut. In that moment of explosive joy, when lovers become one, Beth tore her lips from his. Her gasp turned to a soft moan of pleasure, and she shuddered. Her arms tightened around him. She turned her face to his chest, her teeth softly biting his heated flesh, her fingers digging into his shoulders. She felt the moisture that formed on Lawren's skin, and she rubbed her cheek against his chest. She sighed and ran her palms over his chest.

"All my life I had heard about love, have wanted to love and to be loved," she said, "but I never knew it could exist as wonderfully as this."

"You once said that you would marry again only for love," Lawren said. "At the time I was doubtful. So few people really know love."

"We're blessed," Beth said. "We do."

"Aye, lady, we do."

He held her, rubbing his hands down her back, over her buttocks.

"Again we're looking into the two faces of fate," Lawren said. "We're blessed because we know true love. We're cursed never to have each other."

He rolled to his side, holding her tightly. He pushed the thick russet hair from her temples and covered her face with soft, quick kisses.

"You are wonderfully masculine." She ran her fingers lightly up his inner thigh to touch him, to feel him once more respond to her caresses. "And hard . . . again."

He chuckled. "Do you know what you're asking for?"

"Aye."

"Then, my lady, I shall not disappoint you."

Laughing softly, Lawren captured her lips in a kiss.

After they made love a second time, he fell into an exhausted sleep. Unable to sleep, Beth gazed at him. The glow of the waning sun illuminated his harsh features. His dark hair spilled across the bolster.

Rubbing her fingers over the silken strands, she gazed at the man to whom she had willingly given her body . . . her heart . . . and her soul. Annie had accused her of being a taker of souls, but she had given hers away before she took one.

Replete but tired, Beth lay down beside her love.

She was cuddled against him when he awoke. Sighing happily, he turned over and put his arm around her. She lay her face on his chest. He ran his fingers through her hair.

"The portrait is lovely, Beth. It and the locket."

She spread her fingers through the hair on his chest.

"Do you believe you'll be able to get back to your time through the painting?"

"Perhaps. I hope so. I was touching it when I traveled back here. I was touching the nightlace at your feet. The flower began to glow, and I was caught up in the radiance." She scored his nipple with her fingernail. "Lawren, if you were to travel back with me and if you were to inhabit Callum's body, you may not be debilitated. I'm here, but I'm still Beth. I look and think the same as I did in the twentieth century."

"I wish I could be sure of that," he said. "I suppose I'd have to do a lot of changing to live in the twentieth century."

"You would, but you'd get used to it. And you'd love it, Lawren," Beth said.

For a long time, they lay there talking about the future fantasizing about their being together. Later Lawren had Annie pack them a basket of food and they went horseback riding. In a secluded meadow close to the castle, they stopped, tethered the horses, and lay their blanket.

Pushing aside worries, they took their day. They frolicked through the glen, gathering herbs and berries. They chased each other; they made love; they bathed in the stream. They ate.

"What if something very important happened, and you were needed?" Beth asked as she lay on her back watching the colors of the setting sun splay across the sky.

"My order would promptly be disobeyed. The headmen would come get me."

She heard the smile in his voice.

"Do you think they know where we are?"

"Aye."

She bolted up. "You do?"

He cocked open one eye. "They're trained to be discreet, madam."

"Discreet!" she screeched.

Laughing, Lawren rolled over and caught her in his arms. He held her close and rocked back and forth with her. She traced her fingers around the locket and chain he wore, hers, now his, ultimately theirs.

"Oh, madam, I could become accustomed to a life with you."

"So could I," she murmured.

Their lips met in a soft kiss, warm and full. As always it was a promise of pleasure to come; more it was a seal of love. They kissed again and again, holding each other, touching, assuring, reassuring. Finally twilight crossed the skies, and stars started peeking out.

Both were quiet as they repacked the basket and headed for the castle. Although they had the evening, they could feel the encroachment of the real world.

Beth was nervous the next morning, and she was hungry. The morning meal had been delayed until high noon to coincide with Bearnard's arrival. She anticipated his arrival; she dreaded it. From all she had heard about him, he was a cruel man.

Most of the men of the eleventh century were hard, she conceded, but they had a basic level of humanity that softened their cruelty and meanness. So far only one, Shawe the priest, had imbued Bearnard with any redeeming qualities. Of course, that could be because she had heard mostly Galloways describe him.

Her long hair, brushed until it was shining, hung in deep waves about her shoulders. She walked back and forth in front of the wardrobe. She didn't like the fabric of this tunic. The color was too pale or too bright on the next one. Up and down she stalked, as if the tunics were the prey and she the predator. She had selected, discarded, and reselected every dress that was hanging out. Patiently Fenella had picked up each one, carrying it until Beth promptly changed her mind and made another selection.

Finally Fenella laid the latest dress on the nearby table. She rummaged through the discarded dresses, pulling out a beautiful green tunic with yellow and white trimming.

"My lady, wear this one."

"I don't know," Beth murmured. "The meeting today is so important. I must be dressed appropriately."

"Whatever you wear will be," Lawren said from the door.

Clad only in her long undertunic, Beth spun around. As usual he was inordinately handsome. Dressed in kilted tartan and red shirt, he wore his gold torque of leadership . . . and her small golden locket. Happiness swelled in Beth, and she smiled at him. Gold armbands gleamed on his forearms and his wrists. His black hair had been brushed back from his forehead in deep waves.

She held out her hands. "My Highland warrior."

"My Highland lass." His deep voice richly flowed over her.

Beth couldn't get enough of Lawren. Her love for him flowed so deep that he was now part of her, would always be, whether they were together or not. They had only been parted for a few hours, but she felt as if it had been days, weeks, months. She couldn't bear to think of her life without him.

"What do you think of this dress, Lawren?" Fenella asked, holding up her selection.

He nodded. "Anything my lady wears will be beautiful," he said, "but this one will capture the color of her eyes."

"Will it help me capture the sympathy of Bearnard?" Beth asked.

Lawren shrugged. "I don't know about Bearnard, but it will probably help with the bishop."

"Is he coming?"

"Aye, I received a note from him this morning. He has met with the clan chieftains and wishes to discuss the outcome of the meeting with me."

The outcome of the meeting. The words rang deadly through the room. Time, their worst enemy, was closing in on Lawren and Beth.

"What do you think?" she asked.

"There's no need to try to outguess him, my lady-love. Let's wait for his report." He took the tunic from Fenella and held it loosely against Beth's shoulders, the luxurious material draping to her ankles. "He's a Saxon, true, and his sentiments like with them, but he is also a man of the church. For the most part, he has rendered fair canonical judgment. Let us pray that he does so today."

Sorrow rested heavily on Beth's shoulders.

"He acknowledges your letter and is grateful that I allowed

you to write him and the prioress." Lawren returned the tunic to Fenella. "He has taken everything you said into account and hopes that it is reflected in what he has to say."

"Oh, Lawren," Beth murmured. "We must have hope. That inscription in the manuscript could mean anything. Perhaps you lived a full life, the nightlace grew back, and you were able to cure the people. It was no longer a threat. You died. The sickness disappeared."

"Aye, lady," he said indulgently.

She curled up in his arms and rested her cheek against his chest, brushed it against the smooth metal of the locket. She listened to the tick of the watch, marking time, juxtaposed against the steady rhythm of his heart, marking life.

"I'm sure Bearnard is relieved that the bishop is journeying with him," Lawren said. "He's not sure what we'll do to the Adairs, him especially, but he knows we won't kill the clergy." He chuckled. "At least, he hopes we won't."

Reluctantly Beth pulled away from the safety of Lawren's arms and started her dressing once more. He walked over to the table and pilfered through the girdles. Holding up a delicate gold one, he brought it to her. She went to take it, but he shook his head.

"Let me. I seem more adept with these fasteners than you do."

Holding out her arms, she allowed him to fasten it about her hips. She quavered beneath his gentle touches.

"I hope I always excite you like this," he murmured.

"I do, too."

When Beth was fully dressed, she stood in front of the bronze mirror on the wall.

"Bring the jewelry," Lawren ordered Fenella.

"The Adair jewelry that the priest delivered?" the young girl asked. "Or Galloway?"

"Get both," he said. "I'll let my lady make the decision which she will wear. Get the old necklace, Fenella."

"The one that—"

"Aye, lass, that one."

He stepped closer to Beth, standing immediately behind her, and they stared at each other through their reflections in the mirror.

"I want you to wear our jewelry," he said in a low voice, "because I love you."

"Then I shall wear it," she said.

"All others will interpret it differently," he said.

"As a mark of my belonging to you?" she asked. "Of being your possession?"

"Aye."

Fenella came running back, a gold necklace dangling from each hand. She held one up. "The Adair."

But Beth was looking at the Galloway jewelry. She caught the delicate chain between her fingers and caressed it. "I shall wear this one," she said.

Although Lawren smiled when he took it from Fenella, he hesitated to put it around Beth's neck.

"I'm sure," she said.

Fenella skipped across the room and returned the Adair jewelry to its coffer.

Lawren stared into Beth's eyes through her reflection in the mirror. "Please remember, Beth, that Bearnard and the bishop are astute men. They will be looking for any signs of weakness in either of us."

She smiled gently. "You've already warned me."

"I can't warn you enough," he said, still holding her gaze in the mirror. "Under no circumstances can we appear to be in love."

"I shall try," Beth promised.

"We have to do better than try." Returning her smile, he lowered the Galloways necklace over her head. "This belonged to my mother when she lived here at the castle with my father," he said.

Beth's eyes glowed.

"He wanted her to keep it, but she refused. She told him that it belonged to the lady of the house."

Lawren lifted her hair and pulled it through the chain. Then he straightened it on her chest. She brushed the tips of her fingers over the delicate gold.

"Lawren," she whispered.

He laid his hand over hers, and he mouthed for her to see, "I love you, Elizabeth Balfour, and forever you'll be the lady of my house."

Tears of joy washed her eyes. She, too, mouthed, "I love you, my darling Lawren mac Galloway, and it is with honor that I shall forever be the lady of your house."

"My wife," he said.

"My husband," she whispered.

"Here, Lawren," Fenella said, running back over, holding a garland of flowers and diaphanous veils across both her arms. "She won't wear a wimple and veils so I made her this."

Beth and Fenella laughed as Lawren took the delicate headpiece in his huge hands. In his effort to be careful, he appeared to be clumsy. Finally he held the circlet of flowers in both hands. Standing behind Beth, he set it on her forehead. The diaphanous train flowed down her back.

"What do you think of it, madam?" Fenella asked.

"Oh, Fenella, it is the most beautiful garment I have ever owned." Beth touched the flowing train.

Fenella's face lit up.

As Beth touched the necklace, her gaze moved to Lawren's reflection in the mirror, and their eyes caught again. She could see his appreciation, his love. Further in the deep blue recesses, she saw the shadow of sadness. She recognized it now because she, too, felt it. As surely as his joy and love flowed through her veins, so did his sorrow and sadness.

"You do me an honor by standing with me today, lady."

"I only hope you continue to think this as the day progresses," she said. She turned, the long tunic rustling about her ankles. "I'm frightened. I hardly know Bearnard, and he scares me."

"Aye, he frightens all of us." Lawren turned to Fenella. "Is my lady dressed and ready to meet her public?"

Fenella darted over to one of the far tables, and rummaged through a stack of folded garments. When she returned, she held out a kerchief, embroidered in green and yellow floss. She caught Beth's hand, pushed up the bell-shaped sleeve and tucked the kerchief beneath the tight sleeve of the undergarment. Releasing Beth's arm, she stepped back and nodded.

"Lawren is right, my lady. You are beautiful."

"Thank you, Fenella," Beth said.

"I wish you were a Galloway, not an Adair," the child said. "You would belong to us and not to them. Today I'll pretend that you are."

Yes, Beth thought, that's what she had been doing also. Pretending. Sometimes pretense was the only way she could cope with reality.

Beth smiled sadly. "Fenella, if you look on the bed in the adjoining room, you'll find a present."

"A present!" the child squeaked. "For me?"

"For you." Beth smiled.

Holding hands, she and Lawren followed Fenella into the bedroom.

"My lady!" Fenella gasped and rushed closer to the bed. She gazed at the fabric that was piled high. Then she spun around.

"That's for you," Beth said. "You may sew yourself some new dresses."

Fenella edged closer to the bed and touched the fabric. "New dresses. I may have several of them."

She picked up an armful and hugged it to her chest. She buried her face in it.

"Oh, lady, this is the grandest gift I have ever received." She lowered her arms. "Is it all right if I make some new clothes for Lundy and Rae?"

Beth nodded.

Fenella dropped the material on the bed and raced to Beth.

Throwing her arms around her, she hugged her tightly. "Thank you," she murmured.

"You're welcome," Beth said. "You have been a wonderful maid." She gave her a big hug. "Now run along. You may have the morning to yourself."

"Aye."

Lawren and Beth walked out of the room and up the spiral stairs. They exited at the walk atop the castle wall. The sun was quickly climbing the sky, but the day was pleasantly cool. A gentle breeze stirred. It lifted the material of the train and billowed it around Beth.

She felt like a princess in a fairy tale, but for the moment she didn't have to pretend. This was real; it was happening to her. Still exhilarated by the morning's activities, she touched her necklace. She glanced over at Lawren at her locket on his chest. Perhaps she and Lawren would never be formally married, but in their hearts they were and would be always.

Beth remembered the first time she had come to the castle. Its majesty and beauty had swept her away. The same was true today. A delicate mist settled over the isle. The mountains grasped for the morning sun. Each, a prism, turned the rays into a profusion of colored splendor.

When she had been in the twentieth century, Beth had imagined the mist, touched by the sunbeams, to be a delicate gold veil concealing a magical land of yesteryear. And it was.

Today colorful flags flew from the turrets and spires. Clansmen gathered. She heard the clank of metal as warriors rode into the castle courtyard, the clip-clop of horses' hooves over the flagstones. She saw the rush of villagers as they gathered.

Leisurely she and Lawren strolled the castlewalk. They greeted the guards who were posted intermittently. Later they were joined by Sloane. Today he was wearing his tartan plaid with a purple tunic. It clashed brilliantly with his red beard that hung in a single plait from the center of his chin.

"My lady." He bowed.

"Good morrow, Sloane."

"Any sign of Bearnard?" the warrior asked Lawren.

"Nay."

"You may want to come to the great hall," Sloane said.

"Evan, William, and I laid our plans earlier this morning," Lawren said. "They know what to do."

" 'Tis Annie. She's stirring up the kindred."

"She has a right to speak," Lawren said.

"Aye, but she's trying to work them into a lather. She claims that if Bearnard mac Adair does come, he should not be allowed to walk out of Castle Galloway."

Sighing, Lawren said, "We had better go to the great hall, lady. A certain amount of tension is good, but presently I'm more interested in getting the nightlaces than I am in a massacre."

As they retraced their steps to the door and stairwell, Beth glanced once more across the glen, across the loch that surrounded the castle. In the distance she saw riders moving from behind an outcropping of boulders. A dark green and brown plaid banner furled in the air.

She stopped walking and stared as a second banner man rode into the side. His standard belonged to the bishop and the church. Two riders traveled immediately behind the banner men. The colors of their clothing and of their horses' accoutrements obviously identifying them as Bearnard mac Adair and the bishop.

"I'm so frightened," Beth said. "I'm shaking."

Lawren's grip on her shoulders tightened. "This visit unsettles me also."

They stood a little longer and Beth strained to see Elspeth's brother . . . the man who would be considered her brother if she remained here. But his visage was hidden by his helmet with its long nose-guard and mail cheek-and-neck guard.

One of the Galloways sounded the lur horn.

"Come, lady," Lawren said. "Let us go to the great hall and await our visitors."

Sixteen

Her attention fixed on the entrance of the great hall, Beth sat in a seat of honor on the left side of Lawren. Outside she heard the noises of the approaching visitors. The clump of the horses' hooves; the rasping of leather; the clanging of metal. Finally the pounding of boots on the flagstones to the doors.

The bottom of the doors rasped across the stone floor as they were flung open. Galloways marched into the room. Behind them were the Adairs. Beth leaned forward slightly and gripped the armrests of the chair.

Lundy entered the room and, after a flourish from the musicians, shouted, "My lord Bishop Davies."

The bishop, an older man, strode into the great hall. He was portly, his round face framed with thick white hair that gleamed like pure limewash in the sun. Bushy brows, the same color as his hair, shelved piercing eyes. Blue and white robes swished about him as he walked.

Lundy's voice, loud and clear, continued with the introduction of the clergyman, but Beth didn't hear what the youth said. She stared beyond the bishop to the younger man who walked behind him. He removed his helmet and handed it to the nearest lad. Then he brushed his hand through reddish-brown hair.

"Bearnard," she whispered at the same time that Lundy shouted, "My lord Bearnard mac Adair, Chief of Clan Adair."

Shawe followed Bearnard and the bishop and was announced. Annie, her face drawn in disapproving lines, walked to the center of the building and waited for the three men to join her. She held herself so stiffly she emphasized her gaunt angularity.

After she sat Shawe at one of the tables of honor below the dais, she led Bearnard and Davies to the high table. As was customary, both men stopped in front of the high seat and paid homage to the acting chief and clan champion. Beth observed that Davies was much more sincere in paying his respects than Bearnard was. A slight smile was playing on her lips when Davies looked at her.

"My lady," he said.

Quickly she erased her smile. His brown eyes were keen, and he missed nothing about her. He gazed at the necklace.

"I trust you have been treated well during your incarceration."

"I have."

"Elspeth," Bearnard said, his dark green eyes searching her face, "I have been worried about you, lass. He hasn't—well—"

"Violated me?" she finished. "Nay, lord, and we are happy that he hasn't. Else I should hold you responsible and would exact revenge against you."

"I'm not the enemy, lady," Bearnard snarled. "The warlock is."

Beth received a certain amount of satisfaction as she baited the Adair chief. "Aye, but you have conveniently left me here in his clutches."

Bearnard's gaze dropped to her bodice, and he stared. "His necklace," he murmured, and jerked up his head. "You're wearing Galloway jewelry." Bearnard's face contorted in anger, and his eyes glittered. He glared at Lawren. "I'll have you for this, warlock. This will be the last time you publicly insult an Adair."

Lawren smiled and asked, "Have you brought me the night-lace?"

At a glance Lawren seemed to be leisurely lounging in the chair, but Beth felt the tension that emanated from him. His eyes, like those of every other warrior in the room, were sharp; he was assessing everything and everyone about him.

"Nay, they are to be found nowhere. That is one of the reasons why I agreed to meet with you. Here. At Castle Galloway. We must come to some sort of agreement over Elspeth's ransom."

"Nay, you must pay the ransom."

Davies followed Annie to the seat immediately on the right of Lawren, Bearnard to the left of Beth. Lawren waved his hand, and the musicians began to play. With laden trays, servants filed one by one into the great hall, serving the high table first, then the lower ones.

Glad that Fenella had given her the kerchief, Beth wiped the perspiration from her palms. She dotted it over her upper lip. Again she was on the verge of a headache. She closed her eyes and drew in a deep breath.

She felt a huge callused hand settle over hers. Bearnard's. It was strange and impersonal, holding no brotherly warmth or reassurance. She wanted to withdraw hers.

" 'Tis good to see you, Elspeth. I'm sorry you have been held captive by the warlock, but I have not been remiss in my duty. I have been planning how I could rescue you."

She slowly lifted her lids and gazed at Bearnard. Although he looked to be in his late thirties, he was weathered and old. Deep lines fanned out from his eyes and drooped at the corners of his mouth.

"Has he violated you?" Bearnard demanded.

"I told you he hadn't," she replied, "and he hasn't." She had freely given herself to Lawren and would do so again and again.

"I'm going to get you out of here." Bearnard curled his hand around hers, but his gaze rested on the necklace at her bodice. Hatred radiated from him, burning her. "It's a matter of finding what he's willing to exchange for you."

"I'm worth only nightlace," Beth replied. "Lawren believe you have some but are unwilling to give it up for me."

Bearnard looked around Beth, down the table at the headme on one side of Lawren, at Sloane.

Lowering his voice, he said, "I do have a little of it hidde away."

"You have gardens for cultivation?" Beth asked.

He brushed his knuckle over his lips. His eyes darted around. In an even lower voice, he said, "I have a garden, but we can't let this warlock know. We have to cleanse the land of him and his kind."

He gazed into her eyes, and he looked so sincere, Beth wanted to believe him. "Lawren is a warlock who uses this plant to cast his spells."

"No," Beth said. "He uses it to heal the sick."

"So you said in your letter," Bearnard murmured. "He is an intelligent man, Elspeth. He is showing you his good side only. He is not the kind herbalist you believe him to be. His soul is black and evil."

He laughed shortly. "Aye, I know he pretends to heal the people but it is only after he has cursed them with the sickness." His voice grew louder. When several looked curiously in his direction, he lowered it again. "He and his evilness must be destroyed."

"But we don't have to destroy the nightlace," Beth argued.

"Aye, 'tis his herb. His symbol. Without it, he has no power."

"What about the innocent people who are dying from the sickness?" Beth countered.

"Once the warlock is gone, sister, we shall be able to heal our land and our people."

"But we need the nightlace now, not later," Beth said. "It has always grown along the Gleann nan Duir lands."

"And it will once more," Bearnard said. His head tipped against hers as he whispered, "For a verity, I have a garden of nightlaces planted. After the warlock is gone, I shall bring them out, have Davies bless them, and they shall be used only for good." He paused, then added, "Whatever happens today, Elspeth, you must trust me."

She stared at him and studied his eyes. He was imploring her to believe him. While she didn't feel that he was a brother trying to reassure a beloved sister, she knew he was making a sincere request but she didn't know why or for whom.

"Do you understand? You have to trust me."

She nodded, then said, "Bearnard, we need the nightlaces now before more people die."

"We shall have them. Trust me," he promised. "Our holy bishop met with the clan chiefs, and they have appealed to him to declare Lawren mac Galloway a warlock."

Death's cold breath rattled through the room; chills racked Beth and she felt as if the chair had given way beneath her. She was dizzy; her breath caught in her chest. She grabbed the closest beaker of wine, not caring about the observance of protocol, and took several swallows of the potent brew.

"Of course, Davies, being a man of the cloth," Bearnard said, "shall offer Lawren an opportunity to repent and to return to the fold."

She set the glass down. "He won't."

"I hope not," Bearnard growled. "Shawe said he wouldn't, but Davies felt he had to extend forgiveness to him." Bearnard picked up his tankard and drained it of wine. "Soon, sister, you and I shall control the Highlands. Our land, Alastair's, and the Galloways."

Surprised, Beth asked, "How are we going to control the Galloways?"

Bearnard grinned. "I have encouraged Davies to press for marriage between you and Lowrie."

Startled, Beth stared at him. Remembering one of the first conversations she had with Lawren, she finally said, "I am my own woman now. I married once for convenience. I won't do it again."

"I know." Bearnard rubbed her hand and placated her. "I know you want to remain in the cloister, but first marry Lowrie. With Lawren gone, the lad is going to need an advisor. If you are married to him, I am the obvious choice. Both of you are yet young and fertile. As soon as you present him with a son, you may return to the cloister. Lowrie and I shall administer the kingdom."

"Don't you mean *you* shall administer the kingdom?"

"Aye, lady, I do, and I like the sound of it."

"The sound of what?" Lawren asked.

"Your music," Bearnard lied glibly. "I've never heard finer musicians."

Lawren glanced at Beth. Adept at reading his eyes, his expressions, his body language, she knew he had overheard that part of the conversation, if not all of it.

"The bishop was complaining that they were playing too loudly," Lawren said. He clapped his hands and lowered his hand, indicating that he wanted them to play softer.

"Where is Lowrie?" Bearnard asked. "I wanted to see the lad. I heard that he had recovered from his wound."

"Quite," Lawren said. "He's away now."

He leaned over and adjusted the necklace around Beth's neck. Obvious displeasure on his countenance, Bearnard clamped his mouth shut and tensed his jaws.

"Aye, when he knew that Davies and I would be here."

"When *we* knew you would be here," Lawren said. "Considering what happened to him, we're a little skittish for his life."

"Shawe told us about his remarkable recovery," the bishop said as he filled his mouth with baked pheasant. " 'Tis good for you that you held Elspeth captive."

"Aye," Bearnard drawled dryly.

Davies leaned around Lawren and looked at Beth. "Shawe also reported, Elspeth, that you had learned many medical skills during your travels abroad."

"Only a few, good father, not many," she said.

Annie, Lundy, and Rae moved back and forth along the high table, carving and serving food and refilling the glasses. Lawren ate little and so did Beth, which was surprising since she had been so hungry when she awakened. Bearnard and the bishop heartily imbibed of both food and wine.

Washing his mouthful down with wine, Davies waved his meat in the air, grease droplets landing on the tablecloth. "I met with the Highland chiefs, Lawren."

Lawren sipped his wine. As if on cue, the hall grew quiet.

"They are frightened of you." Davies's voice boomed through the room "Some even accuse you of being a warlock."

"I don't worship Satan," Lawren said, "and never have."

Beth caught the necklace in one hand and worried with it. She wanted to clasp his hand, to let him know that she believed in him, but he had warned her not to. He had cautioned her to appear totally uninvolved with him or the Galloways. Taking his own advice, he never looked at her.

"But you are not a member of the church," the bishop said.

"I didn't leave willingly," Lawren said. "The church excommunicated me because of who I am, of who my mother is."

Davies set his meat down, dipped his fingers into the small bowl of water, and wiped them on the tablecloth. "I don't need your arrogance. This is a serious matter. These chiefs have accused you of heresy. The majority believe you are guilty and are asking that you be punished."

The Galloways shuffled angrily at their tables; the Adairs gloated. All gazed from Lawren to the bishop, back to Lawren. Sloane and the Galloway headmen remained where they were seated, but they had ceased drinking and eating. They were ready for battle.

"What was your answer?" Lawren asked the bishop.

Beth glanced over at the door. Annie stood there, a battle hammer in one hand, a sword in the other. Although she had not fully regained her strength after having had the sickness, her face was animated, her eyes glinting. She was panting for a fight, Beth thought. The way the situation was progressing, she would probably get her wish.

"I would give you an opportunity to repent and to return to the church. You would have to confess openly that you are a warlock, a worshiper of the devil. You must turn your back on the ancient ways and on your mother, the witch."

"Thank you for your consideration, Davies," Lawren said "but my answer remains no. If I were to do what you ask, would be telling a lie. My mother and I are people of the land

Neither of us worships Satan. I am not a warlock and have never been one. I will die accused and innocent, but I will not live a lie."

Beth was proud of Lawren and recognized the courage it took for him to defy the church and the clan chiefs. Silently she cried. Openly Bearnard beamed. Davies looked disconcerted.

"You're speaking rather hastily," the bishop said. "I shall give you three days in which to reconsider your decision. If by that time you have not changed your mind, I shall declare you a heretic to be burned at the stake."

"So be it." Lawren finished off his wine, thumped his glass on the table, and waited for Annie to refill it. "What about Elspeth's ransom?"

"Bearnard has no nightlace," the bishop replied. "Shawe, the prioress, and I have collected what we could from the villagers. It's not a satchel full, but it's all we have."

Davies beckoned to Shawe, who picked up a leather satchel laying on the floor. Rising, he crossed the room and set it on the table in front of the bishop who shoved it over. Lawren unfastened and lifted the flap. The satchel was about one-third filled with fully grown roots, stems, and leaves.

Lawren and Beth exchanged a knowing look. This was enough to last for one or two more outbreaks of the sickness at most. Perhaps enough to sustain them until his secret garden was ready to be harvested.

"Will this be enough for you to release Elspeth?" Shawe asked.

Lawren reached into the satchel and brought out some of the nightlace. He held it on his hand, staring at it. Finally he looked over at Bearnard.

"You have plenty of nightlace, mac Adair. You could have easily filled the rest of the satchel."

"You're a warlock, mac Galloway," Bearnard accused, "and you use this plant for evil purposes. I will not donate anything to your cause. Be grateful that Shawe and Davies think differently from me."

Lawren carefully returned the plant pieces to the satchel. When he had tied off the flap, he looked at Davies. "I shall think on the matter, good father, and will give you my answer before you leave." Lawren clapped his hands. "Now, let's enjoy a contest between the Galloways and the Adairs."

For the next few hours, warriors competed in battle games: arm wrestling; knife and dart throwing; shooting the bow and arrow. The Galloways won every round, and Beth was pleased. Their prowess and skills were saluted with toast after toast.

Bearnard continued to drink, his face growing darker by the minute. After his examination of the nightlace, Lawren seemed to ignore the satchel. Not so Bearnard. Like a bird of prey, he watched it. Beth feared that at any moment he would swoop down and grab it.

"Bearnard, will you join me in a contest of skill?" Lawren asked.

Hands slapped on the tables; feet stamped the floor, and ayes rose all over the hall.

Blinking, Bearnard pulled his gaze from the leather pouch and glowered at Lawren. "Nay, I don't trust you, warlock. I fear a plot to kill or to maim me for life."

Lawren grinned and shrugged.

"Show us how you wield your whip, Lawren," Sloane called out.

"Aye," William shouted.

"No one is as skilled with it as you are," Evan added.

Leaning her weapons against the wall, Annie disappeared through the door. Shortly she returned, holding Lawren's whip in her hand. He rose, moved around the table and off the dais as she walked toward him. He took the weapon from her.

Beth tensed. She would never forget his demonstration the night she arrived at the castle. She could still hear the hiss as the whip sailed through the air; the snap as it curled around the wood. As if Lawren had unleashed the deadly beast, she shivered. With little imagination she could feel it biting into her flesh.

"Does anyone wish to help me?" Lawren invited.

All was quiet. Galloways looked at Bearnard. Highland custom declared that the chief, or the champion, of the visiting warriors should demonstrate his bravery by volunteering in competitive battle games. Bearnard did not. He and his warriors were afraid of Lawren. He was accused of being a warrior, and his reputation with the whip had preceded him. With one lash he could maim a man for life or kill him.

Sloane stood. "I'll do it."

"Custom demands that it be an Adair," Lawren said.

Sloane sat down; Beth rose.

"I will," she said.

Lawren stared at her for a long time before he said, " 'Tis your decision, lady."

She descended the dais and walked to stand before him. He positioned her, then stepped to the closest table where he deliberately hunted through a bowl of apples until he had found three of the smallest. He set one on each of her shoulders and one on top of her head.

"I shall knock each of these off without touching you," he said.

"Nay!" Davies shouted and rose. "Let someone else do it."

"Will the brother be as valiant as the sister?" Lawren asked.

His visage contorted in rage, Bearnard stared at Lawren.

"Aye," Davies said, "Bearnard will volunteer."

Snarling under his breath, the Adair chief pushed to his feet and lumbered off the dais to stand beside Beth. He curled his hands into fists as Lawren settled the apples on his head and shoulders. Against his robust physique, they looked even smaller and upped the value of the wagers. Chances of Lawren's getting them off without snipping the material or nipping Bearnard were slim.

Beth returned to the high seat, as Lawren took his place. Wagers were set, fresh drinks served, and the room quietened. Galloways and Adairs alike concentrated on the two warriors.

Lawren uncoiled the whip and snapped it through the air a couple of times. Holding his hand down, he drew his arm back, letting it slither along the floor. He popped and cracked it. Perspiration broke out on Bearnard's face, but he never moved or took his eyes off Lawren. He might be frightened that this was a trap to kill or maim him, but he was a Highland warrior. He would not dishonor himself or his clan; he stood erect and waited.

Lawren brought his arm back, then forward, leather slicing, whining through the air. Quickly and smoothly, he lashed an apple from Bearnard's right shoulder. Fluid movement brought his arm back, and the whip flicked through the air again; it bit into the second apple. As Lawren clipped the one from Bearnard's head, shouts sounded all around him.

Dazed, Bearnard stood there for a moment. Then he felt each shoulder and the top of his head, assuring himself that they were indeed gone, that he had not been touched by the leather. Bearnard beckoned to an Adair warrior to come examine him. When the man had assured his chief that his clothing was intact and he was unharmed, both returned to their seats.

Coiling the whip, Lawren held it out to Annie. She took it and walked out of the great hall into one of the stairwells. Lawren returned to the high seat. Evan and William led the Highlanders in a salute to their clan champion.

Davies rose and saluted Lawren. When he lowered his glass, he said, " 'Tis time for us to be returning to our homes, mac Galloway. Are you ready with your answer?"

"I am."

Tensely everyone waited. Seeming to be in no hurry to speak, he set his tankard down and ran his finger around the rim. He glanced over at Bearnard, at Davies, and finally at Shawe.

"I promised my dying father, Angus mac Galloway, that I would see that Lowrie ascended the high seat of the Galloways on his sixteenth birthday. That is less than two weeks from today, Davies."

He paused, then said, "I am agreeable to releasing Elspeth to the prioress in exchange for these nightlaces."

Davies breathed a sigh of relief.

"Under one condition. Let me honor my death-bed vow to my father."

Tension, like a bow string, was drawn tightly.

"Wait to have my trial for heresy until after Lowrie has ascended the high seat and become chief of Clan Galloway."

"Nay!" Bearnard leaped to his feet.

Davies worried with his beard.

"Do it, holy bishop," Shawe said. "Lowrie is next in line for the chieftainship by blood and choice of his father. A few more days will not matter."

But they would, Beth thought. Lawren would be able to personally protect Lowrie until he became chief, until the Galloways had their legitimate chief; it would give him more time to uncover the person, possibly a traitor, who had tried to kill Lowrie. A person who might try to assassinate him again after Lawren was gone.

Davies rose. "So be it!"

"Get your belongings, Elspeth," Bearnard ordered. " 'Tis time we left this den of devils."

"Nay," Lawren said quietly. "You'll not be taking her."

Shocked, Davies and Bearnard stared at him.

"You bargained with me," Davies said.

"Aye, lord bishop, with you, and I shall honor my word. We shall agree to entrust the nightlaces to Shawe. He can meet me at the cloister three days hence. At that time I shall turn Elspeth over to the prioress and Shawe will give me the nightlaces."

"So be it," Shawe shouted.

Bearnard growled angrily and waved in protest. "My lord bishop," he said, "this man is of the devil. We're giving him too much lenience. We can't afford to let him have both the nightlaces and Elspeth."

"I have only Elspeth," Lawren pointed out. "A man of the cloth will have the nightlaces."

"We can't guarantee that the warlock will not harm her," Bearnard continued. "That he will not fill her with his vile and evil seed."

"You can't guarantee that I have not already done that."

Adair and Galloway glared at each other, their anger and hostility clearly palpable in the room.

Davies sighed. "Why do you want three days?"

"You gave them to me," Lawren answered. "In case I should change my mind. At noon on the third day I shall either recant or deliver Elspeth to the cloister."

Davies nodded. "So be it, mac Galloway."

Bearnard pointed an accusatory finger at the bishop. "You shall live to regret this, Davies."

"I may be a Saxon," the bishop said, "but I am also a man of my word. I have spoken. So be it."

After the guests were gone, the servants began to break down the trestle tables. Even so the Galloways continued to mill in the great hall. Eventually they gathered around Evan and William. They talked in low, serious tones. Every so often one or the other of them would look at Lawren.

He didn't blame them. He understood their concern; it was his also. They still had Elspeth as a captive, whom they would have to feed and clothe. They had no nightlace and what they might be able to get was very little. Lawren was as good as declared a heretic. No matter what happened, battle among the clans seem inevitable. Things couldn't look grimmer.

Lawren guided Beth out of the castle, through a small door into the formal garden that was bright with greenery and colorful flowers. Although there were several stone benches scattered about, he led her to the one that rested in the shade of the flowered trellis. Sloane followed them, but remained at a distance to give them privacy.

" 'Tis a fact now," Beth murmured, playing with her kerchief. "You're to be executed."

Lawren caught her hands and held them tightly. He smiled dully. " 'Tis a fact that the bishop intends to declare me a heretic, but he has to catch me before he can execute me."

Beth looked at him with wide eyes.

"You don't think I'll give up without a fight, do you? Well, lady, I won't. They'll find that wanting me dead is a lot easier than having me dead. I'll give them the chase of their life."

"Lawren," Evan called.

Beth looked over to see the two headmen standing in the opened gate across the garden.

"May we join you?" Evan asked.

"Aye, headman," Lawren replied.

The two warriors crossed the garden. When they stood before Lawren, both seemed uncomfortable and nervous. William drew his finger along the length of his scar.

"I've said some harsh things to you, lad, about your being a warlock and bringing a curse on us Galloways."

"You have," Lawren agreed cheerfully.

William cleared his throat. "All of us know that you're not really a warlock, and we don't want you burned at the stake. We—well, all of us are glad you took the extra days to weigh your decision."

"We wanted you to know that we wouldn't think less of you if you recanted," Evan said.

"Evan, William," Lawren said, "thank you for your vote of confidence."

"If you don't recant," Evan said, "we shall see that Lowrie is safely ensconced on the high seat and that he has a successor appointed."

Lawren nodded.

"If you should ever ascend the high seat of the Galloways," William said, "I would be honored to swear fealty to you and to serve as your headman. If you ever need a friend, you can count on me."

"And I," Evan added.

"What if a man accused of being a warlock needed your help?" Lawren asked, looking from one to the other.

"He would have it," Evan said and held out his arm. "My hand on it, laird."

He and Lawren slapped their palms together.

Moving closer to Lawren, William said, "My hand and word also, laird."

Each man honored Lawren by addressing him as laird and by giving their promise of loyalty even should he become an outcast. Both turned and walked off.

"You're not going to change your mind," she said.

He shook his head.

"You wanted the three days so that you could find the person who tried to kill Lowrie?"

"Not really, my honor regrets to say," he replied. "All I was thinking about, my love, was you. I wanted us to have more time together."

He folded her in his arms.

"And it gives us a little more time to hunt for the nightlace."

"Nay, our search is over. If Shawe and the bishop could find no more, we can't."

"We can." She tilted her head back. "Like you, Bearnard has a secret garden of nightlaces."

Interest brightened his eyes.

"He wouldn't tell me where, but his are ready to be harvested. Now, Lawren. Right now."

The lur horn sounded. Visitors approached. Puzzled, Lawren looked over at Sloane who shook his head.

Lawren murmured, "Who could that be?"

Rising, he guided Beth out of the garden into the middle courtyard immediately outside the keep. Tending to their chores, people milled around. Some of them tended the domestic animals in the pens; others brought farming implements out of the sheds. Warriors trained horses in a nearby corral, and William and Evan stood outside the doors of the kennels. When the lur sounded a second time, people ceased their work and followed Lawren and Beth to the drawbridge. William, Evan, and Sloane stood immediately behind Lawren, their hands on their weapon hilts.

"Two riders," the watchman yelled from the opened gate.

Tension mounted. The headmen and Sloane moved more protectively around Lawren and Beth.

"From this distance it looks like a man and a woman," he reported.

"Do you see any colors?" Lawren asked.

The guard squinted in the distance. Finally he said, "Galloway."

Everyone visibly relaxed. Warriors stepped back, their hands falling to their sides. Most of the people returned to their chores. Others hung curiously about.

"The sickness?" Beth murmured.

Lawren shrugged. Evan and William murmured between themselves. Sloane glared into the distance.

"Surely not," Beth mumbled. "Hopefully not. We don't have any nightlace."

Anxiously, the five of them waited. Soon they heard the pounding of hooves on the stony pathway that led to the castle.

"Who goes?" the guard shouted.

The horses' hooves clopped over the drawbridge.

"Lawren mac Galloway," Lowrie called out. "And Caledonia."

"Lowrie and Caledonia," Lawren muttered irritably.

"What can they be doing here?" William demanded. "Will that boy never learn to stay put?"

"When I get my hands on him," Evan growled, "I'll—"

The riders pulled the horses to an abrupt stop. Lowrie slid off his mount, and Lawren rounded on him.

"Nay, Lawren." Caledonia rushed around her mare and caught him by the arm. "Our coming here was important. I'm the one who suggested it, not Lowrie. Come." Drawing her cloak tightly about her neck, she looked around. "Let us go somewhere private so we can talk."

"I want the headmen with us," Lowrie said. "And Jamie. And Annie."

Lawren stared at his brother.

" 'Tis a matter of vital importance, Lawren."

Lawren nodded and ordered Sloane to get Annie and Jamie. Turning, he led the way to the formal garden he and Beth had recently vacated. They cut across the yard and walked through the gate into the enclosed garden.

Soon Beth and Caledonia were sitting on the stone bench in front of the flower trellis. Lawren stood behind them, Evan and William to their right. Although Beth was eager to talk with Caledonia, to learn more about her and Lawren and to share knowledge of the sickness and the nightlaces, she sat quietly. The garden gate opened, and Sloane, Annie, and Jamie entered the enclosure. Both of them looked surprised when they saw Lowrie and Caledonia.

"Bolt the gate, Sloane," Lowrie ordered.

Sloane looked from the youth to Lawren who nodded his head. Annie shook herself free of Sloane's hand and walked proudly up the garden path. Sneering at Beth, she passed by the trellis bench, moving to a smaller one where she sat by herself.

Lowrie paced slowly in front of them. "I called you together," he said, "because I've remembered. All of it."

Beth tensed.

"You know who tried to kill you?" Lawren asked.

"I do."

"You saw the features," Beth said softly.

"Aye."

"What caused you to remember?" she asked.

"The helmet." His voice grew softer as he lost himself to memories. "This morning I was practicing with a dummy when the point of my sword caught beneath the chin-piece of the helmet. At first it glinted so brightly in the sunlight it blinded me. Then I remembered this had happened to me before when the Adairs attacked us. The helmet flew through the air, and I looked at the dummy. It had no features. No face."

"Of course it wouldn't," William said. "Dummies have no features."

Beth waved the headmen to silence.

"Some dummies do," Annie said. "Have you forgotten, William?"

" 'Tis right," Jamie said. "Rob, Jamie, and I used to play

dummy for one another, and as we grew older Angus was our dummy." The lad looked over at Annie. "And before that you were."

"Aye."

Jamie laughed. "Annie would wrap layers of cloth around her face, and pad her shoulders and chest. Even though our weapons were blunted, she didn't want us to bruise her any more than was necessary."

"I kept seeing the helmet fly off the dummy's head," Lowrie said. He played with the hilt of his sword.

"But you no longer see the dummy, do you?" Beth asked.

"Nay!" he exclaimed, his visage hardening. "I know who did it."

The men closed in around Lowrie.

"Who?" Evan demanded, his hand on his sword hilt. "I'll kill him."

"Not if I get to him first," William snarled.

"Who was it, Lowrie?" Lawren asked.

"Me." Annie rose, her back erect, her shoulders squared.

Aghast, all turned to stare at her.

"I'm not a traitor, and I'm not in league with an Adair." She displayed no evidence of remorse. "No Galloway is more loyal to the clan than I am. I have sworn my fealty to three clan chiefs and was prepared to do it for Lowrie."

"Loyalty! Fealty!" Lawren exclaimed. "You tried to kill Lowrie and Jamie and did kill Rob! What possessed you, woman?"

Very much in control of herself, she stared directly, defiantly into Lawren's face. "All of your life you have been different. It's as if you aren't a part of the Highlands and don't believe our laws. Time and again Bearnard mac Adair has insulted us, and you failed to seek retribution. Shame and dishonor piled up on us. All you could think of was that nightlace. Lowrie could do nothing. Evan and William did nothing. It was left up to me to take matters into hand."

"But you have brought an even greater shame on us," Lawren said. "You have turned against your own."

"Nay, I am a warrior. I fought a battle, wounded two and killed two. Sometimes you have to be willing to let warriors die for the good of the many." She rose and walked through the garden, trailing her fingers over the tops of the bushes. "We Galloways needed something to stir us up, something that would rally us together. What could it be? I wondered. Then the answer came. The Adairs striking deep within our territory and wounding two of our lads."

"You killed Rob and Damh and almost killed Lowrie," Lawren said.

"Damh was stupid," Annie replied. "Once he had seen me and Lundy, I couldn't allow him to live. No one else should have been killed. They shouldn't have been playing games. Lowrie should have stayed home like he promised he would, and he wouldn't have been hurt."

She stopped, pushed back some leaves, and picked up the scissors on the end of her chain. She snipped dead twigs from the plant.

"How did you do it, Annie?"

"It took planning and waiting, but it was quite simple."

Quietly she spoke, and they listened. As soon as Lawren and Sloane had left for the northern isles in search of nightlace, she put her plan into action. Using Lundy as her only assistant, she gave him pulverized berries and had him put them into the cattle's feed bags and to mix it in flour barrels in the village.

Because the berry was so poisonous, Annie knew the villagers and cattle would be sick within two days. Lundy was to return directly to the castle. Cry for help would soon come from both directions. When it came, she would be ready.

She told Rob she had found some nightlace in Mountain Cat Canyon, had even shown him a nightlace blossom as proof, and had insisted that he and Jamie ride into the canyon to find it. She kept instilling them with stories about how proud Angus would have been of them, how proud Lawren would be if they returned with the nightlace. She had never intended for Lowrie to go; he had sworn on his honor that he would not leave the castle.

"When Lundy returned from the village, I put out the word of the illness," she said, "and then volunteered to go for Caledonia myself."

"Aye," Lawren said, "you have to pass fairly close to the canyon. Who rode with you?"

"Lundy," Annie said. "I had some Adair plaid I had stripped from the cattle raiders a good while back. Lundy and I wrapped one around us. Because our lads were in Galloway territory, they never suspected they were going to be attacked. The three had separated and were searching for the nightlace."

She paused, then said, "I saw Jamie first. He didn't see me until it was too late. I picked him off easily. I wounded him in the shoulder as I had planned. He fell off his horse and hit his head on a boulder."

Annie walked a little further in the garden. Both Evan and William, keeping their distance, walked up either side of the fence.

"Then another lad rode over the rise," Annie said. "I thought it was Rob. I recognized his clothing, his helmet. He came at me with his sword. After fighting with him, I realized it was Lowrie. Only he could handle a sword like Angus. I tried to get away, but he wouldn't let me. He knocked me off my horse. In the struggle, I pulled him off his."

Her voice grew more animated the longer she talked. "He put up a fight, but I was stronger than he was, more seasoned. Then I fell, and he was going to kill me. I rolled over and used the hammer haft to knock him off his feet. He hit me with his sword, the point catching the bottom of my helmet. It flew off."

"You lay there on your back looking at me," Lowrie said. "It was as if you were training me to fight. Your face bound with the thick clothes. No features exposed. You tried to kill me, Annie."

"You were supposed to be home, not out at Mountain Cat

Canyon. We needed to avenge our shames. And we would have if you hadn't dishonored your word." Annie scowled at him. "Didn't I teach you better than that?"

"The hammer," Lowrie said, his voice growing thick.

"Aye, you were dazed. I leaped to my feet and gave you a merciful death blow. Then I turned and saw the third one charging over the hill."

" 'Twas Rob," Lowrie said.

"Aye, and he would have killed me if I hadn't pierced him through the heart with my spear. He died instantly. I returned to you."

"I don't remember fighting with you," Lowrie said, "but I remember you holding my head in your lap. Like you did when I was a little boy, and you cried. I remember your tears and your hand as you stroked my hair out of my face. But I couldn't see you. You were faceless like the dummy." He looked at Beth. "Why didn't I see her?"

"You didn't want to," Beth explained. "You couldn't accept that the woman who had nursed you as a baby and who managed your castle would want to kill you. You deliberately blocked her attack out."

"You left them there to die," Lawren said.

"Rob was already dead," Annie said. "And Jamie wouldn't have died from his little wound. I thought there was no hope for Lowrie."

"It was a miracle he survived," Beth murmured.

"Lundy told me riders were coming. We left, but not in time to keep Damh from chasing us. Lundy and I had our horses' hooves wrapped, and I led us through a back way. We rode on to the mountains and told Caledonia about the illness. I sent Lundy to the village with her, and I returned to the castle."

"All that time that you were talking to me," Lawren said, "telling me about Lowrie's leaving, you knew he and Rob and Jamie were either dead or dying in the canyon." He curled his hands into fists and glared at her.

"Neither of you is worthy to follow in your father's footsteps," Annie said, looking from Lawren to Lowrie. "Both of you have dishonored the Galloway name. Your brother received what would have ordinarily been a death blow, Lawren, and you were more interested in entertaining Elspeth nea Adair than you were avenging his death. You"—she pointed at Lawren—"you could not honor your word."

"This is your vengeance, Lowrie," Lawren said. "How do you wish to handle it?"

The two brothers, both men, stared at each other with mutual respect.

"Kill me," Annie said.

"All the way here, I thought I would," Lowrie said. "But dying would be so easy. You would be out of your misery. I want you to suffer. I shall bring you before the clan council and let them judge you."

"I shall go to a glorious death," Annie said, "holding my head high because I fought for honor."

"Nay, old woman," Lowrie said sadly, "I shall ask that you be cast out without name or kin or possession, that you roam the Highlands in shame the remainder of your life. Forever you will be faceless."

"Take my life," she cried out, "but not my *enech*."

"I shall give you your life," Lowrie said, "but you have given up your *enech*."

Beth marveled as the youth matured before her eyes. He didn't have to wait until his sixteenth birthday, he had become chief of the Galloways today.

"What about Lundy?" Lawren asked.

"I shall bring him before the council also and let them deal with him." He turned to William. "Take Annie and Lundy to the dungeon, headman."

Seventeen

Stunned, Beth sat on the bench in the garden. She watched William and Evan walk off with Annie, and Sloane went after Lundy. Beth worried about the boy. Annie was mature enough to have understood the full significance of her actions; she wasn't sure the boy did.

"What will happen to Lundy? Will he be ostracized also?"

"I'm not sure what judgment the council will render," Lowrie said. "He has committed a grave crime." He smiled and said kindly, "You are entirely too soft, Elspeth. Don't worry about the lad. The men who sit on the assembly are wise men. They shall know how to handle it with mercy and justice."

Beth drew back in surprise. Only several days ago she had been reassuring this boy that he was going to live to ascend the high seat of the Galloways. Now before her eyes this boy turned into a man, and he, the future chief of the Galloways, was reassuring her.

He turned to Jamie, "Come, my friend, let's go to the great hall and see if we can engage anyone in a game of chance."

Jamie's face brightened visibly, and the two friends walked out of the garden.

Only Beth, Caledonia, and Lawren remained in the garden. As if unable to believe his childhood nurse had done such a deed, Lawren strolled through the garden. Beth and Caledonia sat beside each other on the bench and talked. They discussed the sickness, more herbs and treatments, and lamented the exhaustible supply of nightlace.

Beth saw Lawren standing by himself. The breeze teased his hair and tunic. In a gesture she had grown familiar with, one she found endearing, he splayed his hand through his hair.

"I wrote letters to the bishop, the prioress, and Shawe," Beth said. "I told them Lawren was an herbalist, not a warlock, and I begged them to extend him mercy." She blinked back her tears of anger and frustration. "They did. They told him he had three days to accept their beliefs or he would be declared a heretic and burned at the stake."

Caledonia caught Beth's hands in hers. "You love my son?"

"With all my heart."

"I'm glad you found each other." Her eyes were awash with tears also. "I'm glad fate was kind enough to allow him to love before he continued his journey in the afterworld."

Lawren retraced his steps and soon stood in front of the women. "What are the two of you conspiring about?"

Caledonia laughed. "We were wishing we had the medicine and the knowledge to heal the world of all disease."

Beth stretched her shoulders. "This has been an eventful day. So much has happened, it's unbelievable."

"Aye," Caledonia agreed. Looking at Lawren, she said, "How was the meeting with Bearnard and the bishop?"

"The outcome was what I expected, but the tone was a little more pleasant," Lawren said. He smiled down at Beth. "I have a feeling that it was because of you and your letters."

"But they didn't persuade them to change their minds," Beth said.

"But they did extend leniency."

Lawren briefed his mother on what had happened.

When he finished, Caledonia rose. "Your death, my son, is too high a price to have to pay. Bearnard is the one who should be punished, not you."

She remembered her water divining in the cauldron—that Bearnard should be punished for his misdeed—but despaired of its coming to fruition. Once Lawren was dead, she knew it was only a matter of time before Bearnard would be calling for her life also; she didn't mind his taking hers. She had lived her life, had made her contribution to the people, but Lawren had not. He was young and knowledgeable. He had much to contribute, much to teach.

"Lawren," Fenella called out, racing directly from the courtyard. Following her was a young lad about her own age. "A messenger."

"I'm Fergus mac Adair, sire," he called, running past Fenella.

"Fergus mac Adair," Lawren said.

"Aye." The boy's eyes were wide with fear and his voice quavered slightly, but he stood quietly. "You're the one—the one—"

Lawren stared at him, giving him no encouragement.

The boy cleared his throat. "You're the one what's called the warlock."

"I am."

"I've come to beg for your help."

"What can I do for you, Fergus?"

"We need some nightlace, sire. Our entire hamlet is taken with the sickness. And we've heard that the nightlace is the only plant that will cure it. We want some of it, sire." He unfastened a purse from his belt and held it out. "We don't have much booty, sire, but what we have we're willing to pay you."

Lawren took the leather pouch, pulled the strings, and opened it. He thumped it into his palm.

"I know it's not much," the lad said.

A pittance. Dumping it back, Lawren closed the purse. "I'm sure you've heard that the nightlace is the devil's herb," Lawren said.

"Some says so," the boy said. "We don't hold with that."

"Take your goods," Lawren said, tossing the purse to him. "If I had the nightlace, I would give it to you, but I don't have any. Did you not go to Bearnard?"

"Aye," the lad replied. "He said that you had all there was in the kingdom. Said the bishop gathered it for you. Please let me have some, sire. You have the power to save my family."

"That bastard," Lawren swore. "Bearnard has a garden ready to be harvested, and he's not willing to let people know about it. He's willing to let his own clansmen die." He turned to the lad. "Are you head of this house?"

"Aye, sire. My father died yesterday. I'm the eldest son."

Rising, Beth moved to Lawren's side. "Gather all who are sick in your household, Fergus, put them in wagons and bring them here."

"To Castle Galloway?" the lad asked.

"Aye," Caledonia murmured, exchanging looks with Beth. "This way we'll have them in one central place, and the patients can be brought to us. We won't lose valuable time traveling from one to the other."

"Nay," Lawren said.

"You won't let me use Castle Galloway?" Beth asked.

"I won't let you do it, Beth."

She turned to him, her hands resting on her hips. "Many things in this century I haven't had a choice in," she said, "but this one I do. I'll turn myself over to the prioress, and you can get the nightlaces from Shawe. Remind him that you have two days for reconsidering your decision." She turned to the lad. "Bring your family here to Castle Galloway. I shall get the nightlace, and we'll treat them here."

The boy stared at her, his eyes finally showing recognition. "My lady Elspeth?"

"Yes."

"You're here with the Galloways?"

She smiled. "Make haste. Bring your sick here."

"What if others should want to come?"

"Bring them, but make no guarantees," Beth said. "We'll treat as many of them as we can before we run out of medicine."

When the boy disappeared through the gate, Beth rubbed her hand over her forehead. The day was cool, but she felt clammy. At times it was difficult for her to focus her attention on matters at hand. She had felt this way ever since she had traveled back in time, but today it seemed to be worse than usual, more long

lasting. She guessed she was feeling heavy because of the judgment hanging over Lawren. Before it had been somewhere out
there, would happen some day. Now it was looming big and
real in front of them.

"Are you all right?" Lawren asked.

"Tired," she replied, forcing herself to smile.

Within the hour, Lawren and Beth were on their way to the
cloister, and Caledonia was converting the great hall of Castle
Galloway into an infirmary. Escorted by Evan, William, and
Sloane, Lawren and Beth pushed the horses, making the trip in
two hours rather than the normal four. When they reached the
cloister, Lawren and Beth dismounted. The other three remained
on their horses. Agnes, the mother prioress, raced through the
opened gate.

"Elspeth," she cried, holding out her arms. "I thought we
would never see you again." She hugged Beth.

"I'm fine, Mother," she said softly. "Lawren mac Galloway
has treated me honorably."

The prioress stepped back and gazed curiously at Lawren.

"I didn't think you were bringing her for three more days."

"I wasn't," Lawren said, "but we've had an emergency."

"The sickness?"

"Aye."

"And you need the nightlace now," she said. "Shawe isn't
here, but he left the satchel in my keeping."

"Let Lawren have them, my lady prioress," Beth said.

"I don't know," the prioress said.

"Please. There is a large outbreak of the sickness among the
Adairs."

"The Adairs?" Clearly Agnes was surprised.

"Aye, they came to us seeking help and treatment."

"To the Galloways?"

Beth nodded. "Bearnard told them we were the only ones
who had any of the medicine."

The old woman turned, walked through the gate into the cloister. She returned shortly with the leather satchel. Handing it to

Lawren, she said, "I wish I had more to give you, but I don't. From now on, we shall be standing on prayer and faith alone for our healing. Please thank your mother for sending me some of the plants when I needed them."

"I will, Holy Mother," he said.

"My lady prioress," Beth said, "I know these nightlaces are to be exchanged for me. But I would like to ask for a special favor. Will you give me permission to return to the castle with Lawren? He and Caledonia are going to need help tending to the sick. I've been doing that for a long time, and know what to do without having to ask."

"And you're not afraid of coming down with the illness?"

"No, I'm not." And Beth wasn't. Nowhere in the manuscript did it say anything about Elspeth having the illness. Beth felt certain that she was immune to it.

"You have been freed from the devil's lair, my daughter," the old woman said. "You would willingly return?"

Beth nodded.

"What would you do if I should say no?" the old woman asked.

"I would remain with you because Lawren gave his word to the bishop, but I would worry and grieve because these people need me."

"Send word to Shawe, and he can come to the castle and get her," Lawren said.

The prioress nodded. "Go with God, my child."

The great hall was filled with people and commotion by the time Lawren and Beth returned. Sloane, William, and Evan brought people into the room and laid them on pallets. Fenella and Rae entered the room, their arms covered in bed linen. Jamie and Lowrie raced in the front door, their arms laden with straw. Pallets were being spread in any available space.

Relieved to see them, Caledonia took the satchel of nightlace and carried it to a large table erected in the center of the room.

Soon she had mortar and pestle in hand and was grinding it into a powder.

Immediately Beth and Lawren searched for the telltale rash, quickly separating those who had it from those who didn't. They also agreed that all would be treated in hopes that the disease had not advanced to the fatal stage yet.

Hours passed; afternoon turned into night; night into morning. Shawe slipped quietly in and began to work at their side. They gave medicine, washed fevered brows, spoke encouraging words until they were exhausted. Beth sat down on the floor and leaned back against the wall.

Lawren walked up and slid down beside her. "Go up to the master suite," he said, "and get some rest."

"I'm needed down here."

She glanced over at the door to see Lowrie and Sloane bringing in two more children. The two warriors were covered in perspiration, and by now they didn't know if it were from exertion or from the illness. Beth didn't know how much longer they were going to be able to help.

"More," she whispered. "What are we going to do? The nightlace is running out."

"And you, my lady-love, will be no good to yourself or to them if you don't rest." Lawren scooped her into his arms and carried her, protesting out of the great hall, up the stairs into the master suite. He gently deposited her on the bed.

"Stay here and rest," he ordered. "I'll send Fenella up with a cup of herb tea for you."

"I'm needed in the great hall." She tried to push up; he gently shoved her back down.

"Aye, that's why you need to rest."

He kissed her lightly and slipped out. She lay there for a long time, her arm over her eyes. She was so tired she couldn't think she couldn't relax; couldn't sleep. She flipped over on her side and stared at her painting, at Lawren's portrait. She reached out as if to touch it, but it was too far away from the bed unless she stretched. Right now she was too exhausted to make the effort.

She was numb, couldn't feel anything. She wished she could cry, that she could cleanse her soul of its grief and sorrow, of its exhaustion. But tears would not come. She heard the whoosh of the curtain, but didn't turn.

"My lady," Fenella said, "I've brought your tea."

"Thank you," Beth said. She sat up, taking the cup in both hands.

"I've also brought you some of the root, so you can use it later if you need to relax," Fenella said. Holding the golden-barked herb out, she measured a small piece between her fingers. "This much will make you sleep from morning meal to noon."

Fenella handed her a small leather pouch. "Put this purse on your girdle," she said, "and you can keep your herbs in here as we do."

Nodding, Beth took the root and pouch and laid them on the chest. She would slip the purse on her girdle later. Right now she wanted to enjoy her cup of tea.

"My lady," Fenella said, "what will happen to Annie and Lundy?"

Beth put her arm around the child and drew her closer to the bed. "I don't know what's going to happen," she replied. "Both of them are going to have to stand before the council."

"Lundy's scared," Fenella said. "He didn't know what she was going to do."

"He should have gone to Lawren and told him what happened," Beth said.

"He didn't want to betray Annie," Fenella whispered. "She saved us from the plague."

"I'll talk to Lawren about it," Beth promised. "I'm sure he and Lowrie will show mercy."

"You'll really talk to the laird for Lundy?" Fenella said.

Beth nodded.

"I better go help downstairs," Fenella said and walked to the door. She turned. "Don't forget your purse or the root. You may need it, and I won't be there to brew it for you."

After she drank the cup of tea, Beth lay back down, beginning to relax. Finally she fell asleep. She wasn't sure how long she slept, but she felt better when she awakened. Afternoon sunlight slanted through the window. She slid off the bed and slipped the purse over her belt. Lifting the flap, she dropped the herb in it; then she rushed out of the room, down the stairs into the great hall.

Lawren sat on the floor. His hair was tousled, and even now he ran his fingers through it. He looked up and saw her. Although exhaustion lined his brow and tightened his mouth, he smiled and waved. She zigzagged through the pallets, dropping to the floor beside him. She cupped his beard-stubbled cheek with her hand.

"You're the one who needs a cup of that tea and the bed," she said.

"Caledonia and Fenella are sleeping now," he told her. "I'll go in a little while. Right now, I'll stay here with you." He caught her hand in his and turned it palm up. He pressed a nodule of nightlace root in it. "This is for you. Keep it."

"I can't," she whispered. "No matter how much I wish to."

"You have to." He lifted the flap on her purse and dropped the root in there. "You must get this back to the present. We have to stop this disease, Beth. We can't let it ravage through the ages."

"We need it here."

"We need it there."

"Yes, we do." Glancing at the line of pallets, she asked, "Any more deaths?"

"Five so far. Lowrie, Sloane, and Jamie are taking care of them."

"Have any more been brought in?"

"No, but we're almost out of nightlace. A few more dose each. Shawe had gone out to see if he can find more." Lawre sighed. "If he doesn't, we'll have to choose who will get the draught and who won't."

More were brought in with the sickness. Beth was soon supervising the changing of the linen, helping Fenella and Rae with the washing and drying. They carried pails of water; they refilled pitchers and basins. They laid more pallets. They consoled grieving family members. Beth finally sent Lawren upstairs to rest. When she went to check on him later, he was sleeping.

They were running out of nightlace, Beth thought, and the list of patients was growing. She had one option: She had to appeal to Bearnard for help. Sitting down at the desk, she quickly penned a letter telling Bearnard of the outbreak of the sickness, its near epidemic proportions, and their need for nightlaces. She also informed him that they were nursing Adairs. She begged Bearnard to send her some nightlace so that she could take care of the dying. She had Sloane dispatch the letter with their fastest runner.

During the wee hours of the morning, the answer arrived. Bearnard was willing to entrust Shawe with as much nightlace as he might need to tend to the sick. His condition: Lawren would trade himself for the nightlace.

Tears scalded Beth's cheeks as she crumpled the parchment in her hand.

The next morning Beth and Lawren rode to Adair Castle. Shawe and Sloane followed behind. In the distance Lowrie, followed by William and Evan, led the Galloway warriors, a fearsome sight, Beth thought, but also a reassuring one. This time instead of calling for her death, they had sworn to protect her to their death.

When they arrived at the castle, Shawe and Beth rode ahead of the others. On this side of the moat, they reined in their horses. Bearnard walked across the bridge. He held four bulging satchels, one looped over each shoulder and two in his hands. He looked beyond Beth to Lawren and grinned.

"A small price to pay for you warlock."

"I'm sure our grieving clansmen would disagree with you," Lawren replied.

"Go into the castle," Bearnard ordered.

"Not until you hand over the nightlace."

Beth held out her hands. "Let me see."

Bearnard handed her one of the bags.

"All of them," she said.

One by one he handed them to her, and she laid them across the saddle in front of her. Lawren eased his stallion up until he was by Beth's side. She opened each satchel, and both she and Lawren examined the contents and determined they were night-laces.

"Are you satisfied?" Bearnard asked.

"Aye."

Bearnard caught the reins of Lawren's stallion. "If you want the nightlaces, warlock, surrender to me."

Beth looked at the brown leather bags, laying across her mare, and knew at this moment that her womanly instincts were much stronger than her medical ones. She wanted the nightlace, wanted to save the dying, but she wanted Lawren. She loved him and couldn't bear the thought of their being separated. She felt like a traitor knowing that she was going to leave him here.

She feared what was going to happen to him. She had learned that Bearnard was far worse than Lawren had described. He had no conscience or integrity, no soul, and she didn't trust him. She knew if it were possible he would capture Lawren and her— kill them both—and keep the nightlace. From the moment she received the letter and she and Lawren discussed the exchange, Beth had known this was their inherent risk.

Never looking at Beth, Lawren walked toward Bearnard. She reached up and clasped her locket. Bearnard stripped Lawren of his weapons and tossed them to the ground. His head high, Lawren strode across the drawbridge into Adair Castle.

Beth turned and started to remount. Bearnard caught her arm. "Nay, Elspeth. You're going to stay here."

"I'm needed at the castle." She tried to shake his hand off. "We're nursing Adairs."

"You won't be going back. You'll be staying here."

Shawe dismounted and moved to stand between them. "She's needed, Bearnard."

Adair chief and priest stared stonily at each other.

"I won't allow her to go back to that devil's den," Bearnard said.

"She is in the prioress's custody," Shawe said. "And the good mother gave her permission to tend the sick at Castle Galloway."

"She's safer here with me," Bearnard growled. "I'll see that she gets to the cloister."

"I'll send word to the bishop and the prioress that she's here with you."

Beth heard the threat that underlined Shawe's intent.

Eighteen

Beth didn't know where Bearnard had taken Lawren. H[e]
locked her in one of the upstairs bedrooms. After several hour[s]
she heard the outside bolt slide, and the door opened. Bearnar[d]
walked in. He glanced at the uneaten food on the small tabl[e]
by the cold fireplace.

"You weren't hungry?"

"Nay," she replied, trying not to antagonize him, hoping sh[e]
could find out where Lawren was and rescue him. She adde[d]
truthfully, "I'm rather tired. I haven't rested well recently."

"Nor have I," he admitted. He walked around the room, f[i]-
nally coming to a halt in front of the fireplace. "Have you giv[e]
any more thought to marrying Lowrie?"

Of course she hadn't!

"It does seem to be the practical thing to do," she said, "e[s]-
pecially if one is trying to mold a huge kingdom."

Bearnard smiled. He lightly scratched his shoulder and upp[er]
arm.

"Our kingdom, little sister. Yours and mine."

Although she wasn't his little sister, Beth figured it was m[ore]
his kingdom than hers.

"What are you going to do with Law—with the warlock[?]"
she asked, her hand closing over her locket.

"Burn him at the stake," he replied. "I've already sent [out]
proclamations of his confession."

"He confessed!"

Bearnard chuckled. "He will. By the time my men [

through with him, he'll confess anything. When he does, I want the people here to celebrate. I shall give a feast that people will talk about for years to come."

"He's in the dungeon?"

"Aye." Bearnard slumped in the chair next to hers.

His announcement, his certainty of its happening, drained the last bit of spirit from Beth. Exhausted from caring for the people and worried about the exhaustible supply of nightlace, she felt as if she were going to cave in. As long as she had Lawren with her, she felt as if she could bear anything. Now she wasn't so sure. She was torn in so many directions she didn't know what to do. Being here with Lawren was one matter. Being here without him was unthinkable. She wanted to return home to the United States; she wanted to rescue Lawren; she wanted to stop this epidemic.

Bearnard groaned, doubled over, and fell out of the chair.

"What's wrong?" Beth knelt beside him.

She rolled him onto his back and then she saw the red, angry fingers of the rash crawling along his neck. She ripped his tunic off. It was on his upper arms.

"You have the death sickness," she said.

He didn't respond.

"Where are some nightlaces?"

"I'm just tired." He grunted and pushed to his feet.

"Where is the nightlace?" Beth asked. "Surely you must have some here in the castle for medicinal purpose."

He staggered across the room but couldn't make it to the door. Beth ran behind him. She tugged and grunted, but he was a massive man. She barely inched him over the floor. Still she kept working. Finally, he roused enough to help her get him into the bed.

"You have the rash, Bearnard," she said. "I need to start the nightlace as soon as possible so I can save your life."

"I'm not going to tell you where it's planted," he said, his breathing ragged. "Nobody is going to know until the warlock dead. I'm going to protect it."

"If you don't tell me where it is," Beth said, "you'll die before the warlock."

His hand clamped around her wrist. He squeezed so tightly Beth thought surely he would break her bones.

"If you don't tell me where some nightlace is," she repeated, biting back her pain, "the warlock will outlive you."

Hatred as well as fevered delirium glazed his face. Like an animal, he thrashed on the bed, snarling and growling, but he didn't tell Beth where the plants were.

Searching through the castle, she finally located a sheet of parchment, a quill, and some ink. She wrote a note to Shawe telling him that Bearnard had come down with the illness; she asked him to come and to bring some nightlace. When it was folded and sealed, she called a servant and told them to deliver it to the priest at Castle Galloway and to wait for an answer.

Beth filled a basin with water and washed Bearnard's face trying to keep his fever down. When he regained consciousness she begged him to tell her where the nightlaces were. He wouldn't tell her. Hours passed. Shawe didn't come. She continued to beg Bearnard; he kept refusing. Finally he was listless and she feared he was about to lapse into the fatal coma. His skin turned brown; his eyes glazed over.

He clutched at her and gasped, "Save me. I'll not die before that warlock."

"I need the nightlace," she said. "Please tell me where it is."

"Head," he said, struggling to say more. His lips formed words, but no sounds came. "Wat—"

He gasped, coughed, and clawed at her. His face turned blue, the veins strutted. He tensed, sighed, then went unconscious. Knowing there wasn't anything she could do without the nightlace, Beth tucked the cover around his neck and hurried out of the room. She rushed down the spiral staircase into the great hall.

Glad it was empty, she pulled her hood over her head, remembering her words to Lawren so long ago that with her head covered, one woman very much looked like another. She raced to the other side of the building, peeking in doors until she found the stairwell that descended to the dungeon.

She patted her purse, glad that Fenella had insisted on giving her both the purse and the sleeping herb. All she needed was a few minutes. In the kitchen she filled two pitchers with mead, explaining to the servants that Bearnard wanted the dungeon guards rewarded for watching the warlock. The servants nodded their heads. They didn't begrudge the guards getting the mead. It was a small price to pay to be locked up with the devil himself. Beth slipped the powder into the mead and hoped that the pungent liquor would mask its taste and odor. She returned to the dungeon.

Both guards gratefully accepted the mead, gulping it down straight from the pitcher. Beth talked with them for a little while as she looked about the room, dank and darkened. Before they could grow suspicious, she returned to the top of the stairs and waited. Finally she heard their snores and sneaked back down.

The room was so dark, and she could hardly see. She felt as if the walls were closing in on her. The dampness was suffocating. She crept about until she saw the guards sprawled on the floor. She tiptoed around them.

"Look on the wall behind you," Lawren said.

"Lawren!" she cried out.

"Aye, love, 'tis me." Chains rattled.

"Get the keys," he ordered.

She rushed to the other side of the room, brushing her hands over the wall until she found the peg. With shaking hands, she removed it.

"Lawren," she called softly and peered through the darkness. "I can't see you."

"Over here." Again chains rattled. "Follow the sound."

She raced to the farthest corner of the cell. Squinting through the shadows, she saw him hanging from the wall. His arms were manacled together, as were his ankles. She saw a torch lying on the floor. Picking it up, she ran back to the elevated central fire and stuck it into the blaze. When it was burning, she held it up and looked at Lawren.

She held her breath, afraid they had already begun to torture him. "You haven't—"

"Nay, lass, they haven't touched me yet. Bearnard is too smart for that. Shawe warned him that the bishop would be coming and would have him skinned alive if premature harm came to me. Where's Bearnard? Why did he allow you to come here?"

"He didn't," she replied. "He's sick."

She tried to reach the ankle manacles, but Lawren was too high. Settling the torch in a corbel, she dragged up a chair, stood on it, unlocking the chain.

"He's covered with the rash, and he's unconscious."

She unlocked the wrist manacles.

"No telling how many more will break out with the sickness," Lawren said.

"He told me where the garden was."

"Where?" Lawren grabbed the key and undid his feet.

"Something about head and waters, I think. Do you know what he could mean?"

They embraced and held each other. They kissed; they ran their hands over their faces, their shoulders until each was assured the other was all right. They kissed again, long, thoroughly.

"The—the garden," Beth whispered.

"Aye." Holding her close, he pressed his cheek to the top of her head. After a moment, he said, "The only place I can think of, and it's a remote possibility, is the headwaters of the Gleann nan Duir Loch, an old fountain where offerings were left for the Ancient Ones."

"Yes," Beth exclaimed, "that has to be it."

"The Christians filled it in many hundreds of years ago so it's going to be difficult to find."

"We'll do it," Beth promised.

They slipped out of the castle through one of the sally-fort doors. Beth didn't know how long they walked, but she was getting so tired she didn't know if she could put one foot ahead of the other. Lawren slackened his pace so she could keep up with him.

"It's just a little farther," he told her.

Finally they reached a gully. At the bottom and in the moonlight she saw the altar of stones and figured that must be the place. The embankment was so steep, she slid down. It was dry and rocky. If water had ever flowed from here, it certainly did not at the present time. Hadn't for millions of years, Beth guessed irritably. She and Lawren searched for what seemed like hours; she fell down exhausted, and he continued to search.

"Beth!"

She leaped to her feet and looked around. She couldn't see him.

"Beth, come here."

"Where?"

Lawren seemed to materialize from some nearby rocks; they were tall and sentinel. He held out his hand.

"Here." He pushed back a bush and said, "Turn sideways."

Doing as he directed, Beth sucked in her breath and pushed through the rocks.

"Around this one. Behind this one."

Rocks pressing against her on both sides, she felt herself getting claustrophobic. But she kept inching sideways, moving, ever moving. She was breathing heavy, her heart pounding.

"Look!" Lawren shouted.

Suddenly she was free, and she looked around. The ground looked like a delicate lace cloth. Thick and solid. Beth had never seen such beauty in all her life. She felt as if she were becoming one with the silver radiance.

"Nightlace," she murmured.

Lawren draped an arm around her shoulder and drew her to him. "This is ready for immediate harvesting."

"Oh, Lawren," she murmured. "We've done it."

She held her head up, and he lowered his. Their lips met in deep kiss.

"I wish I could make love to you here," he whispered.

"We'll come back," she promised.

They worked for several hours gathering nightlaces. The plants were delicate, and they had to move cautiously through them. As soon as they had enough to work with, they returned to Castle Adair and rushed upstairs to see about Bearnard. Shawe was sitting with him. A lone candle flickered in the room, shadows dancing on the wall.

"He was dead when I arrived," he said.

Beth walked to the side of the bed and looked down at Elspeth's brother. She didn't like or respect him, but she was sorry that he had died like this.

"Surrounded by nightlace," she said, "yet he died. He wouldn't tell me where it was until it was too late for him."

"It's not your fault," Shawe said. "You did everything you could to save him."

"Come on," Lawren said, his hands gentling her shoulders. "Let's get more of this ground and tell the servants how to administer it. Then we can go home."

"I'll take it down," Shawe said.

Lawren cocked a brow.

"Your mother taught me how."

After Shawe was gone, Beth pulled the cover over Bearnard's head and said, "I can't return to Castle Galloway with you, Lawren." She turned. "This is my home. As long as I live here in the eleventh century, I'm Elspeth nea Adair. This is my home and I am now the immediate heir to the high seat of the clan. Since Bearnard is dead, this is where I belong at present. I must tend to my kindred."

Lawren slowly, regretfully nodded his head. "Aye, 'tis true. Mayhap now, lady, our clans can live in peace."

An hour later, Lawren reluctantly left Beth; he promised that he would return as soon as he could. He also promised that he would see that the nightlace would be distributed among the Highlanders. Shawe, taking several satchels of the nightlace traveled to the cloister with the promise that they would also distribute the nightlaces. More and more patients were brought into Adair Castle, and Beth worked through the night. Eventually her exhaustion caught up with her, but no more were dying. She had contained the sickness.

Leaving instructions with her servants, she mounted her mare and rode to Galloway Castle. She had been trained to be a doctor, but since she had come to the eleventh century, she was so involved with being a woman, she had forgotten much of her medical training. But woman or physician, she knew that in order to take care of others, she must first take care of herself. But she hadn't. Now she was worried . . . about herself. About Lawren.

She was so tired she didn't know if she could make the journey or not. All she wanted was to sleep. When she almost slipped off the mare a couple of times, she stopped, took off her girdle, and used it to tie herself to the steed. If only she had a bed and could sleep.

Nay, if only she had Lawren. She wanted to feel his arms around her, to hear the steady cadence of his heart, to have him promise her that everything would be all right. All right. The words became her litany as she rode. She reached the drawbridge.

"Lady Elspeth," the watchman called out, "is that you?"

She tried to answer, but she wasn't sure if he heard her or not. Her heart screamed for Lawren; surely he would hear her. Surely he would come. She couldn't bear it if he didn't. The mare clipped over the moat. The girdle had worked itself loose, and Beth slid out of the saddle into Lawren's arms.

"My love," she whispered. "My husband."

"Aye, my lady-wife."

"I fear I was so busy taking care of others, that I didn't take care of myself," she whispered. "I was so cavalier. I didn't think." She licked her dried lips. "I didn't think I could catch it."

"Dear God, no!" Lawren shouted, his cry reverberating

through the castle yards. Holding her close, he strode across the courtyard and through the great hall.

"Bring me some medicine," he shouted.

Long, determined steps carried him up the stairs into the master suite.

"I'm so sleepy," Beth murmured.

"Don't go to sleep, Beth," he begged. "Stay with me."

He laid her on the bed, and Fenella brought him a basin with water.

"I'll take care of her," the child said.

"Nay," he answered gently, lightly brushing auburn curls from her face, "I will." Sitting on the side of the bed, he wrung out the cloth and wiped Beth's face. He pulled her tunic aside.

Fenella peered over his shoulder. "Mayhap we got to it soon enough—"

She stopped. Beth's neck and shoulders were covered in the ugly, red rash. Tears ran down Fenella's cheeks.

"Oh, my lady," she cried.

Lawren ripped Beth's sleeves off. Her arms were raw.

Caledonia entered the room with the medicine. Fenella rushed over and took it from her. She brought it to Lawren.

"Keep it," Beth murmured.

"Nay!" He held it to her mouth and insisted that she drink it. "We've been doubling the amount for those who have a slight rash, and it has helped some. We'll give you even more."

He cradled her in his arms, and she felt the moisture of his tears on her face. "You can't die on me, lady."

"I don't know why this is happening," she said. "The manuscript said nothing about Elspeth's illness."

So tired that nothing seemed to matter, Beth looked at Lawren's portrait. The portrait she had painted of him, the one that would endure the ages and be classified as a superb forgery. This was the man she loved, would love forever. Slowly her gaze moved from the top of the painting down to the toe of his boot where she had painted the delicate nightlace blossom, where she had sighed her cursive E.

She felt for the pouch Fenella had given her. It was gone. She must have lost it when she tied herself onto the mare with her girdle. "My purse," she mumbled.

"I have it, my lady," Fenella said. "The guard found it at the drawbridge." She edged over and laid it on the chest.

"Give it to me," Beth said. "I want to hold it."

"Come, Fenella," Caledonia said, holding out her hand to the child. "You and I will mix some medicine."

Taking the purse, Beth ran her fingers over the leather and felt the lump of nightlace. She still had it, and they had found even more of it, but she didn't have hopes of ever returning to the future.

The colors on the painting blurred together. She stiffened.

"Lawren," she cried.

"I have you, my darling. I have you. I'm not going to let anything happen to you. I promise."

"Don't turn me loose," she begged.

His voice was thick. "I won't."

"I can't see."

He kissed her forehead, her eyes, her cheeks.

"I'll see for you."

"Lawren"—she weakly pushed away from his chest—"what's going to happen to you? Don't let them burn you at the stake."

"Nothing will happen," he assured her. "Now that Bearnard is dead, I have no accuser. I'll have Lowrie and Shawe appeal to the bishop."

"Yes," she mumbled. "Yes, they'll do it. I wish I wasn't leaving you like this."

"You're not, my love." Tears flowed down his cheeks, but the Highland warrior didn't try to stop or to hide them. He loved this woman more than life itself, and there was nothing he could do to save her. "We will always be together. Love will find a way."

She brushed her hand up her chest and felt the locket. She struggled out of his arms. "Yours," she whispered. "I gave it to you. When we were—were married." She slipped it off and put it over his head. "Always we'll be bound together by time."

He kissed her lips very gently, and it was the sweetest, the most wonderful kiss Beth had ever had. Although she knew this was her good-bye kiss, she also knew that everything would be all right. He was telling her so.

"Let me see the portrait one more time," she said. She was growing weaker and had noticed the progression of the skin rash. She could feel it covering her body. "Move me so that I'm in front of it."

He swept her off the bed and knelt in front of the portrait with her. She gazed at it. "You're so handsome, my husband."

"Not really. You just saw me through love's eyes."

"Yes," she whispered, "I did."

She reached out and touched the painting. She brushed her fingers over the toe of his boot, over the nightlace blossom. A silver radiance filled the room, taking her and Lawren into its essence.

"Beth!" Lawren shouted.

"We're together," she called out. "We're going together, Lawren."

"Nay," he cried from afar, "you're leaving me. Beth, come back."

She tried to answer, but couldn't. She spun through space. She reached for him; she hunted him.

"Don't leave me, Beth."

I'm not.

Then she saw him. He was far away, and he was crying. She lunged for him again but couldn't reach him.

"Lawren!" she screamed from the bottom of her heart, pain searing through her body. He had heard her heart-scream before and answered. Maybe he would now.

She screamed louder and louder. She flailed her arms and legs. She tried to move to him, but the closer she came to him the farther he seemed to get from her. Then he was gone. Lawren was gone! Tears scalded her heart, her soul, her cheeks.

* * *

The spinning stopped.

"Lawren," she murmured.

She opened her eyes but didn't move. She was lying on the floor of the master suite at Galloway Castle. She was sure of the place but not of the time period. She looked around. Electric candles in the corbels. Her suitcase. She pushed up on an elbow and looked down at her clothes. Her cotton pajamas. She looked at the portrait, at Lawren's portrait, and wondered if she had ever been gone.

Shakily she pushed to her feet and touched her cheeks. They were wet, burning, almost raw, and she realized she was crying. She reached for her locket. It was gone. She had left it with Lawren.

She had not only left the locket with him. She had left her heart, her soul, her entire reason for living. Again she looked at his portrait and knew that she would never be the same again. Her life, such as it would be, would be dedicated to her work.

Wondering how long she had been gone, she stood and walked over to the desk. She looked at the calendar, then at the clock. She had been gone only a few hours. She searched for some sign of Elspeth but found nothing. Had they really changed places in time? she wondered.

She hit something with the tip of her foot. It slithered across the floor. Moving closer, she bent and saw the small leather purse that Fenella had given her. Her hands shaking, her heart beating so fast, she thought she would pass out, she reached out and touched it with her fingertips. Then she cried aloud and caught it fully in her hands. She opened it and pulled out the nightlace. She held it to her heart.

"Thank you, God," she murmured, over and over.

This was her proof that she had traveled back in time, had met and loved Lawren mac Galloway, the warlock. This little purse would be her most treasured possession.

But she still did not have enough nightlace. She needed more.

She had to find the place where Bearnard's garden had been. Driven to find it now, she changed into her jeans and shirt and rushed down the stairs. She knocked at Minerva's suite. Minnie, wearing her slacks, shirt, and sweater, opened the door. She didn't seem to be surprised to see Beth.

"What can I do for you?" she asked.

"I apologize for coming down so late," Beth said, "but I ran across some information about a place where the nightlace could have been planted without anyone's knowing about it. I was so excited about the possibility of our finding it, I couldn't wait until morning."

"Come on in." Minnie swept the door open.

A tall, thin man, sitting in one of the recliner chairs in front of the television, rose as Beth entered. Like Shawe, the priest, he was gaunt and angular, but his eyes were friendly, his smile warm.

"Beth," Minnie said, "this is my husband Clyde Graham."

After the formalities of introduction were observed, Beth asked them if they knew anything about an artesian fountain in the mountains that had been used in ancient days as an altar for offerings to the gods. Beth pretended that all of her information came from her research rather than trying to convince them she traveled back in time. There would be plenty of time for that later if it were necessary. As she described the landmarks she remembered, Clyde kept shaking his head.

Discouraged, Beth finally said, "The rocks are like sentinels, Clyde. They're tall and skinny but close together, and they're hidden. You have to turn on your side and slowly edge through them."

Clyde rubbed his hand down the crease that lined his jaw. Finally he said, "During the past century we've used so much rock for construction I doubt they would still be standing. But I do know about a place up in the mountains. It's got a mound of stones that could possibly have been an altar hundreds, and I mean hundreds, of years ago. I'll take you in the morning."

"I know this is an imposition, Mr. Graham," Beth said, no

understanding the force that compelled her to immediate action, "but can you take me tonight? Right now?"

Beth had to go there now. This minute. She was more sure of this than she was of anything else in her life. Holding her breath, she awaited his answer.

"It's late," he murmured, and looked over at his wife, "and it's going to be hard to find in the dark."

"We have torches," Minnie said softly.

"All right, lass," Clyde said, "we'll go."

"I'll let the nurse know that we're leaving," Minnie said.

"May I come with you?" Beth asked.

"Yes." Minnie beamed. "I think Callum would enjoy your saying good night to him."

A few minutes later as Minnie talked in low tones to the nurse, Beth stood over Callum's bed. She held his hand and rubbed it. She was surprised at how much better he looked tonight than he had earlier. He was still gaunt, but she saw traces of the vibrant and muscular man he must have been before he took ill. In sleep his face was relaxed. For a moment she thought he would smile.

His covers were tucked around his waist, revealing his upper body. Even beneath the pajama top he wore, evidence still remained of once highly developed muscles. He reminded her so much of Lawren, that she felt as if she were staring at her love.

Closing her eyes, she forced herself back to the present, reminded herself that she was Elizabeth Balfour, and the man in the bed was Callum Galloway, laird to the Galloway Keep.

"We're going into the mountains," she whispered, "to find the nightlace." A tear slipped out and splattered on his hand. She rubbed it with the pad of her thumb. "We're going to find it. I know we will." She leaned over and kissed him lightly on the forehead. "Sweet dreams. I'll be back to visit with you in the morning."

He opened his lids and stared at her. Startled, Beth gazed back into lucid eyes, into eyes that were exactly like Lawren's. He smiled, lowered his lids, and sighed, going back to sleep.

Hours later after winding up several mountains, Beth and the Grahams arrived at a clearing. Flashlights in hand, they started searching the area. Slowly they climbed up; they eased down. Up again. Down. Around. Thousands of circles later, they found the pile of rocks, but it looked nothing like the one Beth had seen in the past. This didn't even look like the same place . . . period. She was so disappointed, she flopped down.

Flashing his light up the incline, Clyde said, "We've never had an occasion to have this analyzed, but I'm almost sure this is where the headwaters for the loch were once. Probably they've gone underground during the years."

Beth and the Grahams continued to search but found no brook, no fountain, and no nightlaces. Finally they sat down to catch their breath. This had to be it, Beth thought. This had to be where Bearnard had planted his garden of nightlaces. If this were the spot, dormant seeds might be in the rocks and soil. She decided she would have her team search for them. If they found nothing, they had lost only a little time.

Clyde flashed the light on the disheveled pile of rocks, on what he had thought might be an altar. "When Callum was a child, he and I used to come up here. One time we found the remains of a gold ring. Callum always played like it was one of the high places."

"The altar to the gods," Minnie said.

Beth shrugged. She was too tired for the roller-coaster of emotion. One moment she was soaring with hope, the next plunging to the deepest depth of disappointment.

"Could be," she said. "Also could be somebody lived up here through the years and lost it."

Clyde and Minnie went off on their own to search. Beth returned to the spot Clyde thought was the headwaters. As he had pointed out, if the sentinel rocks had been here, they were long since gone. She sat down on one of the small boulders.

Clouds covered the moon, and the glen was shadowed darkly. A beautiful mist had hovered all evening and now settled over them. Out here she felt close to Lawren. She knew she wouldn' be returning to the States. Her home was here in the land where her beloved was . . . strangely she could not think of him as being in the past. Although she would never be able to see him again, she planned to stay here in Gleann nan Duir where she could be close to him, where she could occasionally visit with Callum and Micheil and with Minnie and Clyde. But she would never see Lawren again, never talk to him, never hear his deep laughter.

"Beth," she heard someone whisper. A man? Lawren?

She tensed when a Highlander materialized from the silvered shadows. At first she thought it was Lawren. He was tall and broad-shouldered, his black hair flying about his face as he walked. But he was not dressed like her Highlander. He was wearing one of Callum's suits. Callum?

"Beth."

He looked like Lawren, sounded like him. She didn't know what to think. Startled, she stumbled back.

"I told you we would be together," he said.

Beth continued to step backward.

"Don't be frightened." He stopped walking toward her. "I'm Lawren."

"You can't be."

He held out her locket and smiled. "Ah, lady, we've changed roles. 'Tis my turn to convince you of my true identity."

She heard him talk to her; she watched the watch spin as the chain dangled from his outstretched fingers.

"I am Lawren mac Galloway, and you Elizabeth Balfour are my lady-love, my lady-wife."

She looked up at him. She flashed the light on his face. It was him. She saw his happiness; she heard the rich sound of his laughter. He held out his arms. Dropping the flashlight, she rushed into them.

They touched each other's faces, their arms, their hands. They proved to themselves that each was real, that they were together.

"You do look like Elspeth," he said.

"And you look like Callum," she said. "You're heavier than

he is." She stopped short. "Callum? Where is he? How did you get here?"

Lawren chuckled softly. "One question at a time."

He led her to a boulder, and they sat down beside each other. He took her hands in his.

"When you returned to your time period, Elspeth returned to ours. Like you, she had the illness, and it was several days before I learned that Beth Balfour was gone and that Elspeth nea Adair had returned. She had evidently contracted the illness before you and she changed places in time. When she entered your world, she was too fevered and delirious to know what was happening."

"The time change saved her life," Beth said. "Only a few hours passed here, so her disease didn't progress as quickly as it would have otherwise. No one even knew I had been gone or she had been here."

"Elspeth thinks her time journey was thought induced by the illness and fever," Lawren said. "I had no trouble convincing her she had been so ill she had forgotten all that happened since she arrived at Galloway Castle from the cloister. She was grieved by her brother's death. While she was recovering at Galloway Castle, she fell in love with the young chief."

"Lowrie!" Beth exclaimed. "He's the chief."

"Aye, and he and Elspeth are married with my blessing."

"Galloways and Adairs are united."

"Aye."

"What happened to you?"

"I was to be burned at the stake."

"They didn't pardon you? Lowrie and Shawe didn't speak for you?"

"Lowrie and Shawe spoke for me," he said, "but the church did not pardon me. Or Caledonia."

"Caledonia," she murmured.

"Aye."

"Oh, my darling." She held him.

"They took your watch away from me and said I couldn't have it back. They claimed it was of the devil. The morning w were to be executed, the last person we could talk to was a priest. Both Caledonia and I asked for Shawe. I asked him to get your locket so I could have it. He promised he would try."

Pensively he said, "I'm not sure what he and Caledonia talked about, but the next morning he came to see us again. He was carrying a manuscript satchel. After he slipped me the locket, he spoke with Caledonia."

"The manuscript?" Beth asked.

Lawren shrugged. "I don't know. Neither Shawe nor Caledonia ever mentioned one to me. I'll have to look at it in the museum. Perhaps I can tell if it's my mother's handwriting."

After a long thoughtful pause, he said, "Then they came and led us into the courtyard. They tied us to the stake and stacked the wood around us. Caledonia told me not to worry. She had divined with the water, and she now understood that I would be all right. She was going to the afterworld. I was going to another one. I wasn't paying much attention at the time, and her words didn't penetrate until I awakened here."

Again he paused, swallowed, then said, "Once they torched it, the flames leaped into the air. Soon I couldn't see my mother for the fire. Holding onto your locket, I called your name aloud and I started spinning through space. Then I saw myself tumbling toward me from the other direction. We passed each other. Then I blacked out."

"You and Callum were changing places," Beth said. "He died here, and took your place back there."

"Fate has given us another chance to be together," he said, "to love each other."

After many long and fully satisfying kisses, Beth drew back and looked at him. She traced her finger around his mouth.

"How did you know to find me here?"

He kissed along her mouth, nibbled at first one corner, then the next. "When I came to, I was lying on the floor to Lowrie's suite and a woman was sleeping in one of the chairs. Things were similar, but not quite the same."

As he described it—the wheelchair, the medicine, the railing around the bed—Beth knew he had been in Callum's room.

"Because of your experience," Lawren said, "I knew what had happened to me. Without awakening the woman, I searched through the wardrobes, little things that they are, and found some clothes that fit me. I changed, then walked through the castle. I found only a few of the servants and a young lad asleep."

"Micheil," she said. "Did you look at him?"

"Aye, I remembered your telling me about him."

"Don't you think he looks like Lowrie?"

"Aye. After I left him, I went to the master suite and saw my portrait. It's aged a little, but looks basically the same."

She snuggled against him, glad that she had more than memories; she had his warmth and strength.

"I also found your belongings there and knew you were still at the castle."

"But you couldn't have known that I was up here searching for the nightlace."

"I read the notes you left on your desk."

Contented, Beth relaxed in his arms. When she had traveled back in time, she had known that she did not belong in the eleventh century. Deep within she had known no sense of peace about remaining there. Now she had deep peace.

Both she and Lawren knew he was in her world to stay. They would spend their lifetimes together.

Suddenly the moon glow seemed brighter, and they looked around the small mountain pasture. But it wasn't the moon or starlight that caught Beth's attention. The entire meadow was covered with shimmering white lace. The nightlace, and it was ready for harvesting. She gasped with surprise and wonder. Once more she saw the Highland magic.

Promising not to share their secret until they had time to cultivate the nightlaces and to save them, Beth and Lawren returned to where she had left Minnie and Clyde.

"Oh, Beth," Minnie cried, "we were so worried."

"Aye," Clyde said, "we thought something had happened to you."

"It did," Beth said, her arms draped through Lawren's.

Clyde saw Lawren and flashed his light on him.

"Callum!" Minnie whispered. "Callum Lawren Galloway, is that you?"

"Aye, 'tis me."

"How? What? When?" she said, her words garbled.

"I really don't know what happened," he said, "but I awakened in my room and knew who I was, knew where I was."

"I knew it," Minnie cried, for the moment accepting her miracle by faith alone. She rushed to Lawren and embraced him. "I knew you would recover, and I knew it would be a complete recovery. Micheil needs you so much." She pulled back and looked at him. "Oh, Callum, I'm so glad you'll be well for his sixteenth birthday."

Perhaps a time would come when explanations would have to be made, Beth thought, but maybe not . . . certainly not tonight.

Clyde extended his hand and clasped Lawren's. "Good to have you home, lad."

"Good to be home."

"How did you know we'd be here?" Clyde asked, then said, 'This used to be your favorite place to come when you were a youngster. Did you remember it?"

"I remembered it," he admitted, "but I also read the notes that Beth left on her desk."

"Are you ready to go home, son?" Clyde asked.

"Aye," Lawren replied, "I'm ready."

He looked at Beth and smiled. Both knew they were home at last.

JANE KIDDER'S EXCITING
WELLESLEY BROTHERS SERIES

MAIL ORDER TEMPTRESS   (3863, $4.25)
Kirsten Lundgren traveled all the way to Minnesota to be a
mail order bride, but when Eric Wellesley wrapped her in his
virile embrace, her hopes for security soon turned to dreams
of passion!

PASSION'S SONG   (4174, $4.25)
When beautiful opera singer Elizabeth Ashford agreed to care
for widower Adam Wellesley's four children, she never
dreamed she'd fall in love with the little devils—and with their
handsome father as well!

PASSION'S CAPTIVE   (4341, $4.50)
To prevent her from hanging, Union captain Stuart Wellesley
offered to marry feisty Confederate spy Claire Boudreau. Little
did he realize he was in for a different kind of war after the
wedding!

PASSION'S BARGAIN   (4539, $4.50)
When she was sold into an unwanted marriage by her father,
Megan Taylor took matters into her own hands and black-
mailed Geoffrey Wellesley into becoming her husband instead.
But Meg soon found that marriage to the handsome, wealthy
timber baron was far more than she had bargained for!

*Available wherever paperbacks are sold, or order direct from the
publisher. Send cover price plus 50¢ per copy for mailing and
handling to Penguin USA, P.O. Box 999, c/o Dept. 17109,
Bergenfield, NJ 07621. Residents of New York and Tennessee
must include sales tax. DO NOT SEND CASH.*

Taylor-made Romance from Zebra Books